THE LURE OF OIL
THE CRY FOR WATER

THE LURE OF OIL
THE CRY FOR WATER

A Dowser's Dream Diverted by Drought

A NOVEL BY
don carlson

TATE PUBLISHING & *Enterprises*

The Lure of Oil, The Cry for Water
Copyright © 2008 by don carlson. All rights reserved.

This title is also available as a Tate Out Loud product. Visit www.tatepublishing.com for more information.

No part of this publication may be reproduced, stored in a retrieval system or transmitted in any way by any means, electronic, mechanical, photocopy, recording or otherwise without the prior permission of the author except as provided by USA copyright law.

Scripture quotations are taken from the Holy Bible, King James Version, Cambridge, 1769. Used by permission. All rights reserved.

This novel is a work of fiction. Names, descriptions, entities, and incidents included in the story are products of the author's imagination. Any resemblance to actual persons, events, and entities is entirely coincidental.

Published by Tate Publishing & Enterprises, LLC
127 E. Trade Center Terrace | Mustang, Oklahoma 73064 USA
1.888.361.9473 | www.tatepublishing.com

Tate Publishing is committed to excellence in the publishing industry. The company reflects the philosophy established by the founders, based on Psalm 68:11,
"The Lord gave the word and great was the company of those who published it."

Book design copyright © 2008 by Tate Publishing, LLC. All rights reserved.
Editor Amanda R. Webb
Cover design by Janae J. Glass
Interior design by Kandi Evans
Published in the United States of America

ISBN: 978-1-60462-285-0

1. History: United States: 19th Century   2. Fiction: Religious: Historical

08.02.15

DEDICATION

To Anne–Marie,
whose intuition and insights never cease to amaze

CHAPTER I

The cork bobbed up and down in the muddy stream several times, but Seth was too busy watching the approaching stranger to realize a fish had taken his bait. It was the biggest man he had ever seen. "Better tend to your fishin' before it gets away," the man shouted, fully aware that his sudden appearance had distracted the young boy. "Looks like a big one!"

As Seth looked down at the fishing pole he had made from a small sapling, it jerked free from the stone that anchored its stubby end to the ground. He dove and caught it just as the tip of the pole and the last visible bit of line sank into the water. With the pole now in hand, Seth felt a surge of raw power tugging him toward the water's edge. And just as quickly, he felt himself drawn backward by a huge hand that had grabbed his shirttails.

There was a silvery splash midstream, and the tip of the pole sprung from the water. The line had snapped. His fish had gotten away.

"That's a real shame," consoled the stranger as he loosened his grip. "Fish that big are most often in the ocean."

Intrigued more than before, Seth stepped back to look again

at the huge stranger who had emerged only minutes before from the edge of the woods. The man also stepped back, then bent down to retrieve a birch branch he had dropped in the grass. Less than two feet in length, its main limb divided into two smaller, perfectly matched branches. Grasping a branch in each hand, he pointed the main limb upward. "This is Drake," he murmured softly. "Someday it's gonna make me rich."

Only one thing mattered to Seth. "Who are you, mister?"

"My name's Jonah," the man replied. "Who are you, young fella?"

Ignoring the stranger's question, Seth continued his own interrogation. "Why were you in our woods?" he demanded.

Jonah smiled and stooped down on his right knee. Now at eye level with Seth, he explained. "Just passin' through on my way west, and it looked to me like those woods cut a mile or two off the road."

The stranger was right. The woods offered a potential shortcut to anyone on foot. Used by Seth himself when he went to a nearby field for wild strawberries, the shortcut had become a visible path.

Satisfied with the reply, Seth could no longer ignore the branch that Jonah had called Drake. "What's that stick for?" he asked.

Amused by the boy's curiosity, Jonah laughed and repeated his earlier question. "What's your name, young fella?"

"Seth," the boy answered.

Extending a large, callused hand, Jonah said simply, "It's good to meet you, lad."

The two shook hands and, with formalities over, Jonah handed the Y-shaped branch to Seth. "Sticks like this are called divining rods," he began. "In the right hands, they can find water. They can tell whether it's a spring or an underground reservoir. The rods can even tell how far down the water is. But not many people have the gift or the patience to develop the gift. It takes lots of practice to become a real dowser."

"How come you call it Drake?" demanded the youngster.

"Named for the first fella to strike oil by drillin' for it," replied Jonah patiently. "Man named Edwin Drake, but lotsa folks call him Colonel. He started the oil boom west of here—little place called Titusville, Pennsylvania—back in the summer of Fifty-nine."

Seth toyed with the rod, holding it by the stump and waving the two branches toward the creek. "Look," he exclaimed, "I found water. And I didn't even have to practice."

Jonah laughed again. The boy's apprehension had not only disappeared, but had been replaced by youthful innocence. Seth, he guessed, was no more than eleven or twelve. His dull, blue shirt bore lots of black thread from repeated mending, and his pant legs were rolled up because they were at least a size too large.

"That you did, young fella," Jonah hollered back. "'Course, anyone could have done that. If you really want to know whether you've got the gift, you gotta begin by holding the rod proper." Jonah rose slowly, gently recovered the rod, and, with unmistakable reverence, seized each of the two diverging branches in the palms of his hands. He then pointed the outstretched rod upward at a forty-five degree angle.

Seth watched Jonah carefully. Reaching out, he asked Jonah for another chance to hold the divining rod. But Jonah hesitated. Regarding the rod as somewhat sacred, he now realized that the youngster might damage it. "Maybe another time," he said as he separated his belt from the back of his worn, faded pants and slipped the rod into the gap. "It's time for a little nourishment."

Jonah kneeled down again on his right knee, reached into his other rear pocket and withdrew a large slice of dark bread. He offered to share it with Seth, but the boy rejected the offer. Instead, he found his curiosity returning, and he began to question Jonah further.

"Where you from, Jonah?" Seth asked.

Jonah was busy chewing and, for the next few minutes, sat silently on the bank of the stream until he had finished his late day meal. "Come from a little town in Massachusetts," he finally answered. "Don't much care for the place," he added. "Folks there are just too nosy."

Seth failed to realize that the aspersion was cast to encompass him. Almost immediately, Jonah felt a pang of guilt. Knowing the boy meant no harm, he looked up at the setting sun and muttered to himself softly, "It's time to be gettin' on."

But Seth persisted with his questions. "Where ya gonna stay, Jonah? It'll be dark soon, and it might even rain."

Apart from the clothes on his back, his divining rod, a few small coins, and one more slice of bread, Jonah had nothing else. And after spending the last three nights sleeping in the woods along his way west, he was not looking for another night on pine needles and hard ground.

"Can't say for sure, young fella," Jonah shrugged, "but the woods by the stone wall look pretty invitin'. It'll be easy to hit the road again from there first thing in the mornin'."

Getting to his feet, Jonah scanned the valley in which they stood. Woods covered the hills that rose up from the small plain straddling the creek. Much of the valley was covered with grass, soon to be cut for hay or opened for pasture. It was lush and green, picturesque and trim. Here and there were small fields of corn and the occasional island of dense brush. Less than a half mile away was a house and barn, weathered but neat, a small vegetable garden, and a couple of aging apple trees.

"That your place?" Jonah asked.

"Yeah," the boy replied.

"That barn of yers looks even more invitin'," Jonah probed. "Any chance yer folks would let me bed down there tonight? Won't bother no one."

"I can ask," Seth answered, "but you'll hafta wait here."

As Jonah nodded in agreement, Seth wound the broken line around the end of his fishing pole, picked up his little packet of extra hooks, and headed toward the barn. Looking back, he saw Jonah stretch out by the bank of the creek to watch the setting sun. Only then did Seth realize it was almost suppertime. *Why,* he wondered, *hasn't Mother called?*

Seth started to run, partly out of curiosity and partly out of hope that the stranger could stay and, with the new dawn, show Seth that Drake really could find water below the ground.

Once he reached the barn, he leaned his fishing pole against one of the open doors, turned toward the house, and nearly tripped and fell as he watched the kitchen door open and another stranger emerge.

Seth's mother Betsy followed the man onto the small porch, shook his hand, murmured something Seth could not hear, and started back into the house. Spotting her son, she stopped and called to him.

"Seth, come meet our new preacher."

It was not unusual for strangers to stop by the farm from time to time. But two, so utterly different in their appearance and manner, gave Seth pause. His gait slowed.

The preacher was thin and tall. He had long, dark sideburns

that evolved into a full, closely trimmed beard. Spectacles rested part way down the man's nose. He wore a tall, stovepipe hat and the finest suit Seth had ever seen. He stood erect and, as he turned toward Seth, he lowered the small satchel in his right hand to the floor.

His mother, who had always seemed tall to Seth, appeared quite small alongside the preacher. Her light brown hair, which fell to her shoulders, and her ever-present smile gleamed in the late day sun. Her simple, cotton apron, though plain, seemed to sparkle as well.

By now, Seth was almost up to the porch steps. He hesitated as further inspection revealed an unsmiling and somber figure.

Betsy sensed her son's unease. "Isn't it wonderful?" she exclaimed. "We finally have a preacher. Reverend Small has come all the way from Philadelphia, and he's looking for a place to stay. Ruth Black sent him over to see us."

"I really wish you would reconsider, madam," the minister entreated. "Once I begin my ministry, I'll be able to pay you a small sum from whatever offerings people can see fit to give. As you can see, it's almost sundown, and I have nowhere to go."

Repeating the rejection she had offered inside, Betsy reminded the clergyman. "It's not the money. Even though my husband has been dead for nearly three years, people will surely talk if I take in a male boarder."

It was a difficult decision for Betsy. The few dollars she earned from selling milk and eggs in the village would hardly be enough to cover feed for the animals in the winter ahead. She had hoped that the school would attract a woman teacher to replace the man who had rushed to the oil fields in the western part of the state. But the position remained empty, and the likelihood of a woman boarder seemed increasingly remote.

"But madam," the minister argued, "no one will engage in such talk if you give me room and board. I am a man of the cloth whom your townsfolk have called. If anyone is at risk, it is probably me. Those who gossip will be quicker to condemn a minister residing in the home of a young widow than they will to condemn you."

"True enough," exclaimed a voice familiar only to Seth. Startled, the two adults followed the voice to a large figure looming beside one of the apple trees. "Folks who gossip would just as soon pick on a preacher as anyone else," the voice continued.

"Who are you?" demanded Betsy, more stunned than fearful.

"Name's Jonah," the man answered in a slow, measured reply. "Just passin' through on my way west. Spotted this young fella fishin' and decided to stop and chat and rest a spell. Be needin' a place to bed down before long."

"He wants to stay in our barn tonight," added Seth, "and I told him I'd ask."

"Perhaps you should accommodate us both," suggested the preacher, smiling broadly for the first time. "With this gentleman nearby, the people who start rumors won't know whether to talk about him or me!"

Amused by the illogic and disarmed by her son's appeal, Betsy threw up her hands in mock despair. "This will surely give them something to talk about," she laughed, assuming that she could send off both men in the morning.

"Reverend Small, meet Jonah," she implored with a sweeping wave, an exaggerated curtsy and another laugh. "Jonah, meet the Reverend S.E. Small."

"Seth, take Reverend Small's satchel up to grandpa's old room and get a quilt and a towel out of the hall closet for Jonah. Then bring in some water so Reverent Small can wash up before dinner," she instructed. "Reverend, you can follow Seth up to your room and, Jonah, you can wash up at the well as soon as Seth brings down a towel for you. You're welcome to join us for dinner."

With that, she headed back into the house, letting the screen door slam shut, something she rarely did. Unlike any other door in the township, it had been crafted by her late husband from something he had read or seen.

A simple wooden frame covered with muslin, it was somewhat effective in keeping the kitchen bearable on the hottest summer days. To help keep out flies each time the door was opened, it had a strong spiral spring that pulled it shut rapidly with a loud, sharp whack.

While she admired the door, she had little patience with the noise it produced. Within hours after the door was up, Betsy had developed a technique or two to keep the door from slamming shut and had insisted that her husband and son use them.

Seizing the preacher's satchel, Seth followed quickly, carefully slowing the screen door with his foot as he often did whenever he remembered.

Moments later, Seth emerged from the house carrying the quilt, the towel, and a small metal pail for water. Clearly excited that his new friend would remain over night, Seth forgot to slow the door, and it slammed shut with a louder than usual thud.

"Seth," his mother cried from the kitchen, "come back here and close that door the way you've been taught!"

He obeyed without argument and headed again for the pump.

Jonah, who had already rolled up his sleeves, waited beside the pump, ready to wash his deeply tanned face, arms, and hands. As he raised and lowered the pump handle, he spoke softly. "Thanks, young fella. Ain't slept indoors in a while. It'll sure be nice to wake up warm and dry in the mornin'."

Seth replied simply. "I'm glad you can stay, Jonah."

At that point, the preacher emerged from the house and called to Jonah, "Come, join me on the porch. I'd like to thank you."

Having left his suit coat, hat, and spectacles in his upstairs room, Reverend Small now appeared far less grim and austere. Though still party covered by his open vest, his white shirt reflected the setting sun in such a way that it created an aura that intrigued both Jonah and Seth.

Jonah swung the pump handle up and down a time or two as Seth slid his water pail beneath the pump's dripping spout. The bucket filled so quickly it overflowed. After Jonah finished washing his face, arms, and hands from the water in the pail, Seth handed him the towel. After throwing the quilt onto a bench outside the barn, Seth followed his Bunyan-like friend to the porch. But Jonah stopped at the steps, resting one foot on the second step and the other on the ground.

"I'm here to tell people about the one true God," the preacher volunteered, reaching down and extending his hand to Jonah in friendship. "What brings you to these parts?"

Jonah grasped the outstretched hand and shook it gently. As he started up the steps, his divining rod slid out from beneath his belt and fell to the ground. Seth, who watched it fall, cried out in alarm, "Jonah, watch out for Drake. It's by your foot!"

Warned in time, Jonah retrieved the divining rod unharmed. He inspected it carefully. Satisfied that it was unscathed, he eased it back under his belt.

Reverend Small immediately recognized the small branch from something he had seen in a magazine or newspaper months before and resumed his effort at conversation. "Isn't that something called a water witch?" he asked pleasantly. "Are you a dowser?"

"Kinda," replied Jonah, chuckling at his unintended vagueness.

"That rod's pretty good at findin' underground water. In the right hands, it should be just as good for findin' oil."

"Is that why you named it Drake?" asked the preacher.

"Yup," answered Jonah.

"Dinner," called Betsy from the kitchen.

The two men rose and strode side-by-side toward the kitchen but, as they neared the door, Jonah paused to allow the preacher to enter first. Spellbound by the powerful aromas of a cooked meal, Jonah let the screen door slam behind him. He recovered quickly, however, and went back outside. Reentering, he used his foot as Seth had done to counter the force of the door's strong spring. The door closed silently behind him.

Betsy watched in obvious amusement. "That's better," she remarked approvingly.

The preacher positioned himself behind the chair at the head of the table, missing the fact that it was not one of the four places set. "That's my husband's chair," Betsy exclaimed. "I've set your place across from me, Reverend. And Jonah you can sit across from Seth."

It was a simple meal, composed entirely of greens and other vegetables from the small garden behind the house. But for someone who had been living on a few mouthfuls of bread and an occasional drink from a creek or a spring, it was heaven sent. In fact, Jonah was about to praise the cook and her cooking when Betsy spoke again, this time to ask the preacher to offer grace.

Reverend Small lost little time launching into prayer.

"Almighty God, we give thanks for this food," he began. "We pray that it will nourish and strengthen us. May it gird us against the sins of sloth and avarice. May it fortify us against envy and pride. May it renew us for our battles with Satan. And may the hands that prepared this food be blessed."

Jonah felt uncomfortable, but he wasn't entirely sure why.

Betsy picked up a platter containing peppers, onions, and zucchini and, without comment, passed it to the clergyman. One by one, the platter and the other bowls made their way around the table until everyone had helped themselves.

Seth broke the silence. "What's sloth?" he asked.

"It's one of the devices of the devil," answered the preacher. "It's a word we use for folks with idle hands."

"And what's avarice?" asked Seth.

"That's another tool of the devil," Reverend Small continued with undisguised glee. "It's a word we use for folks who have an unhealthy desire for wealth and riches."

Jonah's discomfort began to turn to anger. But he remained uncertain whether those words were intended for him. He chose instead to praise the meal before him.

"It's a fine dinner, ma'am," he muttered softly. "Be happy to help with any chores before leavin' in the mornin'."

Betsy too had been uncomfortable with the prayer and, although she had largely ignored Jonah until now, she looked closely at the large man across the table. Her first thought was how much easier life could be with someone like Jonah to work the farm. But just as quickly, she began to wonder who this man was and why he had made such an impression on her son.

Betsy lit two lamps, one in the center of the table and another near the sink. The soft light offered little help. Jonah appeared tired but alert, powerful yet kind. He was unshaven, and his full head of hair was somewhat unkempt.

"Where are you going?" she asked.

"Goin' to Oil City," Jonah replied.

"Why?" countered Betsy.

"Findin' underground water is gettin' pretty easy," answered the stranger. "Now it's time to use the gift to find oil too."

"Are you not like all the others drawn to the oil fields?" challenged Reverend Small. "Is it not the promise of easy riches that set you upon your present path?"

"Sure is," answered Jonah without hesitation. "But what's wrong with a little money? Seems to me it's how ya spend it that really matters."

"That's the seed that Satan plants in the minds of everyone driven by greed," responded the clergyman. "But we all know that easy riches are always wasted on sinful excesses or used to satisfy the drives of greater greed."

The zeal with which the preacher attacked Jonah left Betsy so uneasy that she rose from the table, asking Seth to take the plates and silverware to the sink. As she hastily washed the dishes, Betsy suggested it was time for all of them to retire.

Reverend Small pressed on, however, declaring, "Money is the root of all evil!"

"Then let me get a good grip on that root," retorted Jonah, his patience exhausted. "Can't imagine doin' anything wrong. Especially when there's folks like you around."

Turning to Betsy, he repeated his offer to help. "Couldn't help but notice, ma'am, that there's hay to be cut and there's a barn door off the track."

Betsy could no longer turn away help that she clearly needed. "That door is much too heavy for me," she replied. "If you could put it back on the track, I'd be grateful. As for the hay, Seth and I can handle that with our sickles."

"A good scythe can take that field down in no time," Jonah

replied. "Waitin' for it to dry means stayin' on a few days if that's all right with you."

"There's a scythe and a stone to keep it sharp," agreed Betsy, "and, as long as you're willing to mow the field and pitch the hay into the loft, you're more than welcome to stay. I can't afford to pay you, but you can join us for breakfast and dinner, and Seth can bring water and a sandwich to you in the field."

"That'll take less than a week," said Jonah, "providin' there's no rain."

Recognizing Jonah's genuine willingness to help and his own failure to volunteer in any way, Reverend Small also offered to help hay. "I'm certainly ready to join you in the field," he announced. "I've never handled a scythe before, but I'm not afraid to learn. If you can find one for me and Jonah is willing to teach me, I'll try to earn my keep too."

"Okay, Reverend," said Jonah, "but you'd best leave your coat and hat in the house."

"Don't worry about that," insisted Betsy. "My husband's shirts and pants may be a little small, but I'm sure they'll be fine."

Betsy was elated. The dread of haying with no one other than Seth had been troubling her ever since the grass had reached ample stage for cutting. Once she brought the cows into the barn for winter, they would need plenty of hay in the mow above.

"If the good reverend can learn to swing a scythe, Seth can too," said Jonah with a wink. "With all this work to be done, the lad can't spend all his time fishin'."

For the first time since his father had left for the war with the South, Seth felt genuinely happy. The burdens that his mother had accepted and endured were about to be shared. And not only would he learn to master the scythe, he would learn to master Drake.

"Thank you both," declared Betsy, reaching for a lantern from the kitchen cupboard. When she tried to hand it to Jonah, he rejected it. "Thanks, ma'am, but the notion of takin' any kinda fire into a barn never struck me as a very good idea."

The men rose from the table. After a simple, "Good Night," Jonah headed for the barn and the quilt Seth had left there. Midway, he paused to enjoy the evening stars and the good feeling within.

Jonah awoke to the call of a rooster. For the first time in weeks, he felt rested. There were no hunger pangs or chill from sleeping on the ground. As the rooster beckoned again, Jonah rose and, after a brief visit to the outhouse, washed beside the outdoor pump. Back in the barn, he dried with the towel that Betsy had provided.

Minutes later he rounded up the family's two cows, drove them into their stalls in the barn, found a milk pail, and began to milk the larger of the two animals, a Guernsey that seemed more hungry and thirsty than curious.

"That's my job," objected a small voice from the half-open doorway. "Leave my chores be," demanded Seth as he headed toward Jonah and the Guernsey.

"You can take the pail inside," Jonah replied. "No one will know you didn't do the milking."

As the last teat gave away its final stream of milk, Jonah pushed back the little stool on which he had been sitting. "Haven't done that in a long time," he confided. "Had a small farm once but gave it up after learnin' the gift of findin' water."

Seth took the pail and headed for the house where his mother transferred the milk into a small, covered pail. Later, after she skimmed off some of the cream for butter, she took the pail out to a small, covered spring-fed reservoir behind the house to keep it cold.

When Seth returned to the barn, he milked the smaller cow

while Jonah struggled with the door that had slipped off its track. The two finished their tasks simultaneously, and they walked toward the house together but silent.

Inside, they found Betsy at the stove. The preacher was sitting in a chair trying to put on shoes that were clearly too small. Already dressed in clothes that Betsy had brought down from the attic, Reverend Small was nearly ready for his first day in the field. Sensing the futility of his present efforts, he cast the small shoes aside and reached for his own.

Eggs that Betsy had planned to sell in town now graced the table, some boiled, some fried. Fresh bread, butter and honey, jams and jellies, and a large pot of coffee left little room for anything else. As the two men beheld the spread before them, they shook their heads in disbelief when Betsy apologized because there was no bacon, sausage, or meat of any kind.

"We have much for which to be grateful," corrected the preacher. Asking that each head be bowed, he offered a brief but simple prayer. "O Lord, hear our thanks for this bounty. Bless the hands that prepared it, and may our labors this day be worthy of this great feast."

There was little conversation. Jonah allowed himself three fried eggs, two slices of bread smothered with honey, and two cups of coffee. Betsy encouraged him to take the last two eggs and more bread, noting that he had not only fixed the barn door but had probably helped with the milking as well.

Seth, who had enjoyed a bigger breakfast than usual, looked pained. Jonah rose, placed a hand on Seth's shoulder, and praised the lad with a laugh. "This young fella was so noisy doing his morning chores that he woke me up," fibbed Jonah. "Time we got to work or we'll have nothin' to show for the rest of the day."

Seth darted out the door ahead of the men and, in his excitement, let the screen door slam shut. Betsy started to call Seth back but, sensing his new spirit, swallowed her words.

After the three reached the barn, Jonah handed the preacher a scythe and then handed Seth a large sickle. His earlier search of the barn had also produced another scythe as well as a fine stone for keeping the cutting edges of the blades sharp. All three blades glistened in the sun, a sure sign to Seth and the Reverend Small that Jonah had been busy before breakfast.

The dowser swung his scythe over his shoulder, moving it forward until he could balance it easily with his right hand. Reverend Small quietly took note and duplicated the same motions until his scythe was resting comfortably on his shoulder.

Seth needed no instruction. As soon as he was handed the sickle, he let it hang straight down beside his leg with the tip of the blade pointed behind him. Thus armed, the three headed for the field. Jonah was the first to break the silence.

"You learn quickly," he told the preacher. "When we get to the field you can watch me until you're ready to try your hand at it. With Seth, we'll take down this field in no time."

It wasn't long before they reached the nearest edge of the field. Jonah slid the scythe off his shoulder. With the obvious ease of experience, he swung the scythe gracefully in a counter clockwise swath. Tall, green stalks of alfalfa and clover fell behind the blade, covering much of the short, grassy stubble that remained above ground. The scythe had barely stopped before Jonah swung it back to the right and then forward once more into the standing grass.

Back and forth in seemingly effortless motion, Jonah cut several large swaths of grass before pausing to engage Seth and Reverend Small.

Emboldened by the ease with which Jonah swung his scythe, the minister attacked a nearby stand of grass, swinging the tip of the scythe into ground with such force that he nearly fell. He recovered quickly, however, and tried again. This time the blade was much too high, and only the very tops of the stalks fell to the ground. Again he tried. Though breathing hard from the unfamiliar exertion, he managed to slice through the grass cleanly, leaving a swath as neat as Jonah's.

The morning passed quietly and, as the sun raced toward its zenith, the two men made pass after pass through the knee-high grass. Though he mastered the fundamentals of the cutting height and the broad swing of his scythe quickly, Reverend Small soon noticed that he was cutting far fewer swaths than Jonah. Competitive by nature, Reverend Small began to increase the frequency of his swings and was soon perspiring freely and breathing more and more heavily.

From time to time, Jonah would look over and, without missing a stroke, inspect the minister's progress. Secretly pleased, he would glance back at the mown grass at his feet and inhale its pleasant scent. Jonah also watched Seth's performance from time to time and, although disappointed at the lad's frequent and lengthy breaks, chose to say nothing.

Jonah took note of the stubble that remained after each swing of his scythe. When the grass appeared torn rather than cut, he would stop to sharpen his blade. Only once did he pause long enough to pass the stone over the blades borne by Reverend Small and Seth. But as they reached mid-morning, Jonah put down his scythe and summoned his fellow workers to a small stream that bordered the field and led ultimately to the creek that Seth liked to fish.

The preacher watched as Jonah and Seth knelt at the edge

of the stream and sipped its cool, refreshing water from cupped hands. Dropping down beside them, he knelt on one knee, lowered a cupped hand into the stream, and drank heartily. As he rose, he exclaimed that even though the stream was hardly wide or deep enough for a baptism by immersion, its water was as blessed as that of the River Jordan. Jonah muttered an amen, and the three resumed their work without another word spoken. Each soon escaped into his own reverie.

Jolted from their task by the rhythmic clang of a wooden spoon beating against a metal pail, they looked up to see Betsy standing nearby in the shade of a sugar maple. Her rosy cheeks bore an angelic smile and her left arm bore a small basket, covered with a gingham cloth, which contained several sandwiches of bread, freshly picked tomatoes, and cheese.

Her brightly colored apron camouflaged the drab dress beneath it and, in the midday sun, Betsy was as radiant as her smile. Her hair fell gracefully around her shoulders, and her slim but ample figure cast a delicate shadow on the ground.

"It's time to eat," shouted the boy as he ran to his mother.

Betsy set a pail of water on the ground, reached beneath the gingham cloth for a sandwich, and handed it to Seth. With youthful impatience, the boy began to nibble away at the bread as he squatted beside her.

After accepting the sandwiches that Betsy handed each of them, the two men joined Seth on the ground, forming a semi–circle around the pail, the basket, and Betsy. She took nothing for herself, explaining that she had had her lunch while preparing the meal for her laborers. In the midst of their chitchat, she encouraged the men to help themselves to the remaining sandwiches and water, and one by one the sandwiches disappeared. After being passed around several times by Seth and the two men, so too did the water.

Reverend Small was the first to rise. Trying hard to balance his professional bearing with his ill–fitting, makeshift clothing, still soaked from his morning toil, he raised his water cup in a toast to Betsy. "Without a doubt, this is the best lunch I've ever had," he declared. "Had I known that manual labor could be so richly rewarded, I might have chosen farming with its rich biblical ties as my profession."

"Don't get too carried away, Reverend," cautioned Jonah. "If Miss Betsy cooks up another feast like she's likely to, ya won't have anything left to say after dinner."

All four, including Reverend Small, laughed heartily, and Betsy began her trek home.

Returning to the tools they had laid aside, the three males began to work once more. It took the clergyman a few swaths to recover the rhythm that he had perfected before lunch. The smooth swing of the scythe quickly returned, but as he advanced through row after row of newly mown grass, he suddenly felt his right foot sink into a small pool of water, fed by a tiny, gurgling stream. Only by leaning against the long arm of the scythe was he able to keep from falling.

"What in heaven's name is this?" he yelled, looking at the whitish mound where the water erupted from the earth. Seth, who reached Reverend Small first, answered without hesitation. "It's just an old salt spring. There's another one by the woods."

Jonah helped the minister pull his foot from the now murky water and then turned to Seth. "Maybe ya can show me the other one after we finish mowin'," he suggested.

"Sure," replied the boy, "it's easy to find."

Ignoring the mud and water that had oozed into his only shoes, Reverend Small once again grasped the handles of his scythe and, stepping carefully over the pool, resumed mowing the grass he had left untouched.

Jonah smiled, not only in respect of the man who had tormented him the night before but in the realization that he could now test a theory that had bewitched him for months. Were salt springs a clue to underground oil? Was his dream as close as the other spring?

Renewed by this unexpected prospect and the extra strength of a second wind, Jonah began swinging his scythe in wider and more frequent swaths. His quickened pace was soon noticed and then matched by both Seth and Reverend Small.

CHAPTER 2

Returning to the field in mid-afternoon with cool water and some wild strawberries from Seth's favorite patch near the woods, Betsy was surprised and delighted to find more than half the field mowed. *If the weather remains dry for the next few days,* she mused, *the haymow in the barn will soon be filled.*

Her visit was announced by Seth, who was clearly tired. Both men were also beginning to show signs of fatigue but, refreshed by the water and a handful of berries each received, they lost little time getting back to work. Less than an hour later, however, Jonah called a halt. "It's time to quit," he declared. "If we don't stop now, we won't get to do any fishin' today."

And with that declaration, all three started toward the house.

As they neared the barn, they found Betsy heading toward the small shed housing the reservoir from which she drew her water for drinking and cooking. No more than four foot square and less than a foot deep, the pool was cold and clear. Lined with stone and caulked with clay, it also offered safe storage for the milk that Betsy drew each day from her cows. Some of the milk was delivered to folks in town, and some of it was used to make butter and cheese.

What she was unable to sell or use was given to her two sows and the litters they produced.

Having just finished the afternoon milking, Betsy offered a simple greeting along with a promise that dinner would be ready within the hour.

"Let's go fishin' and wash up later," Jonah suggested, hoping that Reverend Small would excuse himself and take advantage of the time to rest. "Should be a good time to catch that one that got away. The big ones usually come up from the bottom about now to feed."

Seth needed no encouragement. "I'll get my pole," he answered. Breaking into a run, he soon disappeared into the barn—only to emerge seconds later with his pole, its broken line, and missing hook.

"Looks like you've thought of everything except the bait," chuckled Jonah.

"I did not forget," responded Seth. "I keep my night crawlers down by the creek."

"Sorry, young fella," said Jonah. "Shoulda knowed ya kept 'em there." Then, after pausing long enough to reflect on his statement, Jonah added, "Matter of fact, it strikes me that you deserve to be called 'Mister Fisherman.'"

Although he remained silent, Seth clearly liked the idea.

As the two began walking toward the creek, Betsy emerged from the shed. Greeted by the sight of Jonah and her son walking side-by-side surprised but delighted her. It had been much too long since Seth had had such companionship and, even though she knew little about Jonah, she couldn't help but regard that view as a blessing.

Jonah planned to remind the youngster of his promise to lead the dowser to the other salt spring. But looking down at Seth, he observed a lad who was no longer suspicious or cautious but one who was happy, enthusiastic, and innocent. *Maybe I can find the other salt spring by myself,* thought Jonah, *even if it means searching by moonlight.*

"What do ya suppose that big one was?" asked Jonah, now focused on fishing.

"Probably a pickerel," Seth reckoned.

Not far from the bank where they had first met, Seth paused beside a cluster of shrubs and a badly cracked clay crock half-buried in the ground. Reaching inside, Seth pushed away some withered grass to pick up one of the large worms lying on top of a thin layer of soil. Then, realizing there was no longer a hook on his line, he put it back and sat down to unwind the line from his makeshift pole.

Seth moved swiftly, retrieving his packet of fishhooks from his pocket. After withdrawing a medium-sized hook, he tied it to the end of the line and moved the cork a little further away. "Looks like I was lucky," Seth declared. "I still have my cork and most of my old line."

"That you were, young fella," replied Jonah.

Moments later, Seth cast the hook and its wiggling nightwalker into the muddy water and watched as the current began to pull the cork and line downstream. Nothing happened for several minutes. But when Seth started to set the pole beneath a rock he had long ago lugged to the bank, the cork disappeared from the water's surface so suddenly that Seth nearly lost the pole.

"Must be the same one," shouted Jonah. "Let 'em run so he won't break the line again."

Seth raced along the bank of the creek, allowing the fish some freedom. Once he saw the cork reemerge, he drew the pole back to keep the line taut.

Jonah, who was nearby, started to reach for the pole but immediately reconsidered and stepped back. It was important that the outcome be decided without his intervention.

Seth soon laid the pole down on the ground, dragged the rock on top of the pole, and began pulling the line in as he stepped into the muddy water. The line danced crazily, but the fish remained completely out of sight. Seth tugged in some of the line, wrapping it around his left hand. Confident the fish had little energy left, he gave the line a strong, swift jerk. A small, odd-looking creature flew out of the water and landed on the ground directly behind him.

"What's that?" cried Seth. It was nothing he had ever seen before. It flipped and flopped with such vigor that the boy could hardly make out its features. Jonah grasped the line between the cork and the hook, and held aloft a short, rotund fish with a large head beset with little bumps on each side.

"That's a white-horned dace," proclaimed the adult. "I haven't seen one of these in a few years. Trouble is, they're not good eatin'. You might as well throw it back."

It took little effort to detect Seth's disappointment. He had clearly hoped to impress Jonah with his fishing. But confident that his new friend was knowledgeable and correct, Seth seized the fish, removed the hook from its lower lip, and tossed it back into the water.

"Let's try again," suggested Jonah. "That big one is still out there waitin' for ya."

"No," answered the boy, shaking his head as he twirled the pole in the air, winding the line around its slender stem. "Let's get back to the house."

They were almost back to the outdoor pump when Seth remembered Jonah's interest in the other salt spring. Although it meant retracing some of their recent footsteps, Seth proposed that they head toward the woods and the spring that so intrigued his companion.

"But we better hurry if we're gonna be back before dinner," he added.

Surprised and delighted, Jonah quickly followed.

"How far is it?" asked Jonah, hoping that his interest was neither suspicious nor urgent.

"Less than a quarter mile," responded Seth. "See that clump of brush by the edge of the woods? It's over there."

Within minutes, they reached another small pool of shimmering water. It was ringed by muddy ground, peppered with the tracks of birds, small game, and deer. Jonah reached down, scooped up a handful of the water, and tasted it. A puzzled look followed, and he reached down for another sample. "Can't make out any salt," said the bewildered dowser.

"I never tasted any either," Seth answered, "but my folks and everyone else around here have always said it's fed by a salt spring."

"Well, until we see some bullheads and bass in there, it'll never have much to offer ol' fishermen like us," joked Jonah. "Time we headed back."

Neither spoke as they ambled toward the house. Seth was clearly preoccupied by the appellation of "Mister Fisherman" that Jonah had bestowed upon him. Jonah himself was starting to wonder how quickly he could resume his journey west.

Betsy and Reverend Small waved greetings from rocking chairs on the porch as Jonah and Seth approached. "Dinner's ready," shouted Betsy. "We've been waiting for you two."

As she rose from the chair, Betsy turned her head toward the kitchen door. Her long, auburn hair drifted gently past her left shoulder, revealing a facial silhouette that amplified her delicate beauty. The sight was one Jonah could not ignore and, despite his inclination to avoid women in general, he found himself not only admiring the young widow but, for the first time in a very long time, experiencing a tinge of jealousy.

Jonah shifted his gaze toward the well and its cast iron pump and discovered that Seth too was headed there. Rather than wash up inside, the lad had decided to mimic his new friend by cleaning up at the well. Jonah stripped to his waist, baring a strong muscular frame still wet with perspiration from his day in the field and the brisk walk to the salt spring. He then grabbed the pump handle and, with a few quick strokes, generated a mini waterfall into a bucket from which to wash.

Amused when Seth removed his shirt, Jonah gave the pump a few extra strokes so the boy could wash up as well. Likewise, when he rolled up his shirtsleeves to hide some of the signs of perspiration, he soon found Seth busy doing the same thing. Jonah's emergence as a role model left him uneasy and, to interrupt the cycle of imitation, he ordered the lad to hurry up so they would not be late for dinner.

Betsy too was giving orders. Upon leaving the porch, she informed Reverend Small that he was to allow no one to enter the kitchen until she summoned them. Although unaccustomed to taking orders, particularly from a woman, he managed a smile while assuring her that no one would be permitted past him or his chair.

"Gentlemen," Reverend Small thundered in a deliberately theatrical style, "it's not yet time to sample the gourmet meal that the mistress of the house is preparing. Come join me, and tell me why you're empty-handed. I was looking for a pail full of fish!"

"I only caught one," lamented Seth, "and it wasn't a good eatin' fish so I threw it back."

"Might better fish after dinner," suggested the clergyman. "You can almost always count on bullheads after dark. At least that's been I've been told."

Both Jonah and Seth registered surprise at the minister's apparent familiarity with fishing, but neither responded directly to his suggestion. Instead, Seth turned the conversation to the trek that he and Jonah had just completed.

"We've been out to the other salt spring," he revealed.

"Why?" asked Reverend Small.

Concerned that the discussion might involve Drake and ignite a new assault on wealth, Jonah intervened. "Been studyin' salt springs for years," he explained. "Still tryin' to figure out how they get so far inland from the ocean."

The minister was about to probe more deeply but, at that moment, Betsy's voice rang out from the kitchen, inviting them inside for dinner.

Jonah reached the door first and, after allowing the others to enter, stepped inside and eased the screen door shut. No one, save Betsy, noticed his attentiveness, and she was quick to declare, "That entitles you to at least two pieces of pie, Jonah."

By now, both men were spellbound by the sight and smells before them. The vision of a table groaning under the weight of many dishes was especially delightful to Jonah. There were platters of fried chicken and pork chops, a ceramic boat filled to its brim with flour gravy, newly picked peas and lettuce and boiled potatoes. The aroma of bread fresh from the oven was especially overwhelming. And, in the midst of it all, Jonah spied a large pitcher of water, which had begun to sweat in the warm air of the kitchen.

Once again, Betsy asked the minister to offer grace.

"O Lord, great are the rewards to those who labor in your fields," he intoned. "Whether we harvest grass for the animals or lost souls for your Kingdom, we give thanks for each and every opportunity you set before us." And, with a grin unseen by the others, he added, "Hear our thanks for this bounty, O Lord. May we enjoy it before it gets cold. Amen."

Awestruck by his lightheartedness, neither Betsy nor Jonah knew how to react until they opened their eyes and saw the gentle smile that remained on Reverend Small's face. And then they laughed, faintly at first but gradually deeper as they realized that Reverend Small was far more complex than they first assumed.

"Eat up," ordered Betsy. "You sure earned your keep and then some."

It was a meal that Betsy could ill-afford. She had bartered not only the eggs on hand but eggs yet to be laid for the pork chops. As the day had worn on and the teamwork she had witnessed produced more hay than she could have wished, she was overcome by a desire to feed the men well. Now, as the laughter turned to pleasant and interesting conversation, Betsy took comfort in that decision.

Though normally a light eater, even she ate heartily. And, when it finally seemed there was nothing left to consume, Betsy made enough room on the table for coffee and a blackberry pie. Both Betsy and Reverend Small reminded Jonah that he was due an extra slice.

"That was the best meal ever," declared the dowser. "Ya shouldn't have gone to such trouble, Miss Betsy, but since ya did ya better find some more things that need doin', 'specially if ya expect me to finish off two pieces of pie!"

Once the pie and coffee were finished, Jonah inched back from the table, announcing that it was time for him to retire to the barn.

Scanning the table, Betsy could see that, although happy and clearly content, everyone including Seth was visibly weary.

Despite his fatigue and full stomach, Jonah was unable to sleep. Something about the spring troubled him. Having already decided that it held no promise, he was completely baffled by its reappearance in the forefront of his thoughts. Tired muscles eventually drew him into a sound and restful sleep but, as he dozed off, the spring remained foremost in his mind.

Jonah awakened well before daybreak. Peering out through the open doors of the barn, he could see a star–studded sky and a brilliant moon approaching its full phase. But the image of the spring reappeared in his thoughts, and once again it lingered, refusing to be dismissed. Only then did Jonah appreciate the need to return to the spring with Drake.

He sat up, brushing aside the hay that had found its way onto the muslin sheet he had been given. He had made his bed inside a stall, which he had since learned was meant for a horse that Betsy's husband had hoped they could one day afford. The stall was quite narrow, and there was a wooden trough in front that ran from wall to wall. Built for hay and grain, it now provided shelter and security for the divining rod that Jonah affectionately called Drake.

The night air bore a light chill, forcing Jonah to roll down his shirtsleeves. Doing so brought on a smile as he recalled Seth's eagerness to imitate his habits. With Drake in hand, Jonah retraced the steps he had taken to the spring. Once there, he lost little time engaging Drake. The divining rod sprang to life almost immediately, displaying energy far greater than any he had ever experienced. The stub of the divining rod was being drawn toward the earth with such force that Jonah's calloused hands nearly lost their hold.

Moving in a northerly direction, he found that the energy

subsided after just a few steps. But then, while trying each of the three remaining compass points, he watched in disbelief as the rod responded to an even greater force along a westerly path. It was not only the strongest he had ever felt but constant, lasting well beyond the point where he expected it to fall off.

Suddenly aware that each hand was clenched like a vise and his heart was pounding as it never had before, Jonah was jubilant. *If this ain't oil,* he concluded, *it's gotta be an artesian well.*

Over and over, he repeated his search, slowly defining the perimeters of that unseen energy that sent Drake into the oddest behavior he had ever seen. Spellbound, he missed the first gentle rays of the rising sun and with them, the first frantic calls by Seth.

"Jonah," shouted Seth at the top of his lungs. "Where are you?"

By the time Jonah traced the cries to the barn, he was no longer the only one awake.

Betsy too followed the cries toward the barn and raced out of the house barefoot, wrapped in a blanket she had hastily pulled from her bed. Standing just inside the open barn door was Seth. His expression was pained, and his cheeks bore the moist streams of tears.

"Seth, come here," commanded his mother sharply. "What's wrong?"

"Jonah's gone," explained the boy. "Both he and Drake are gone."

Startled by Seth's cries, Jonah gave up his activity at the spring and raced back silently toward the house, baffled and alarmed.

Betsy drew her son to her side and, after making eye contact, suggested that Jonah was probably no farther away than the creek, perhaps even fishing. Yet in her heart, she too was troubled by his absence. His quiet ways, his willing labor in the fields, and his influence on Seth had deeply impressed her and, for the first time since she had learned of her husband's death on the battlefield, she sensed a level of hope that had frequently eluded her.

When Jonah finally rounded the front of the house, Drake in hand, he was met with Seth's tear-stained cheeks and Betsy's obvious distress. "I'm here, young fella," yelled Jonah, who was nearly out of breath from running as far and as fast as he had.

Face to face with mother and son, Jonah tried to explain his intrigue with the spring. "Didn't think a little time by myself at the spring could cause a commotion," he continued in an effort to reassure them.

"All that noise scared off the deer drinkin' at the spring," he added jokingly. "Not only that, they ran away so fast they left their white tails behind." When neither Betsy nor Seth laughed or smiled, Jonah tried a different tact. "Fishermen never cry," he said sternly as he headed back to his bed in the stall.

Peering down from the window of the second floor bedroom where he had remained during the early morning crisis was Reverend Small. Also awakened by Seth, his initial impulse was to race outside. But, as he hurriedly dressed, he began to struggle with the realization that he hoped Jonah was really gone.

On the one hand, he endorsed the bond that had developed between Seth and Jonah. On the other, he found it hard to balance all the good that Jonah was achieving in the field against what he perceived as evil—Jonah's desire for easy riches. And then it struck him. *There is something more. I'm competing with Jonah not only for Betsy's attention, but also for her admiration and affection.*

Reverend Small reached the kitchen just as the screen door slammed shut behind Seth. Betsy, who had already entered, said

37

nothing and advanced toward the wood stove to begin breakfast. Seth took a seat at the table, looked at the clergyman, and turned away, wiping away the last of his tears.

Breakfast was modest. Betsy brought milk and coffee, bread and jams to the table. She smiled at the minister and instructed Seth to call Jonah. Once they were all seated, she reached for the bread she had sliced so carefully and began to nibble, preoccupied with the events and the exchanges that had shattered her morning.

"May I offer grace?" asked Reverend Small. "It seems especially proper now that the lost has been found. Don't you agree, young man?"

As Seth nodded yes, Betsy offered a flustered apology. "I'm sorry, Reverend," she explained. "I forgot we hadn't done that. Guess I'm too busy thinking about too many other things."

"Oh, Lord, we give thanks for this food and for the opportunity to work this day in the fields you have nurtured. And if it be your will, may we complete these tasks in a timely fashion so that we may continue to pursue our dreams and renew our journeys. Amen."

Silence fell over the kitchen, and except for Jonah, no one seemed interested in eating.

"Better get out to the field before it gets much hotter," suggested Jonah after a second slice of bread and jam. "The more we can cut this mornin', the less there'll be when it gets real hot this afternoon."

He rose and left the kitchen, discovering as he carefully closed the screen door that no one was behind him. Undeterred, he picked up his scythe from the barn, accelerated his pace as he headed for the field, and began to whistle a song he had loved as a child. Although he remembered most of the tune, the words were long forgotten. It was a truly joyful moment, and it made Jonah smile.

Though faint, the whistled tune reached the kitchen, and Betsy too began to smile. It had a bouncy, uplifting melody, and each note paid special tribute to the whistler. Jonah's talents took on a new measure. Even Reverend Small, coffee cup in hand, began to smile. "What a beautiful tune," he murmured.

With the silence now broken, Betsy began to remove dishes from the table. The break in conversation had given her time to think, and her first words were to her son.

"Seth, I want you to go apologize to Jonah. He did you no harm, and he has tried very hard to treat you kindly. He also needs help. Get out of that chair, get your sickle out of the barn, and get down to the field now." Her voice was stern, well beyond the level she reserved for his occasional misbehavior or his infrequent antics.

Reverend Small, somewhat daunted by this newly revealed side of Betsy, got up from the table and offered an apology of his own. "Sorry to delay your cleanup," he volunteered. "I should have left with Jonah. Guess I was too busy thinking about everything but work."

Hurt by the tone of his mother's words, Seth ran to the door and, unintentionally, let it slam shut. He lost little time following her orders, however, and he was soon on his way to the field with an unsharpened sickle in hand. Though still a good distance away, Seth could hear Jonah still whistling the same song. As he listened, he could feel his pain disappear.

"Jonah," he shouted as he got closer, "how about sharpening my sickle? It's not sharp enough to cut through soft butter."

"Bring it here, young fella" answered Jonah. "And ya better watch me closely so ya can do it yerself next time. Won't be here forever, ya know."

"I'm sorry I cried," Seth apologized. "I lost my dad a while back, and I figured I lost you too. He promised to come back, but he never did. Why do you have to go? Why can't you stay for a while at least? Can't you and Drake hunt for oil around here?"

The torrent of questions and the longing they reflected left Jonah uncomfortable. Although still uneasy with the distress that Seth had displayed earlier, Jonah reached for the stone in his pocket, seized the sickle from Seth's hand, and began to swipe the stone along the cutting edge of the blade, changing from one side to the other after each stroke.

"See how simple that is?" he asked. "Now it's yer turn."

After handing Seth both the sickle and the sharpening stone, Jonah placed his large hands over Seth's, gripping them lightly. He tilted the stone slightly so that it would follow the bevel of the cutting edge, and then he began to slide it back and forth along the blade until Seth picked up the unmistakable rhythm of the skill.

Jonah eased his grip little by little, and Seth soon realized he was entirely on his own. With each stroke of the stone across one side of the blade and then the other, his confidence grew until it produced a smile that stretched from ear to ear. It was so contagious that Jonah began to smile too.

Looking up, Jonah spotted Reverend Small a hundred yards away, bearing a scythe across his shoulder. "Guess he'll need help sharpenin' his blade too," lamented Jonah loudly but only half seriously. "Looks like there won't be much hay cut this mornin'."

Hearing Jonah's lament, Reverend Small took a deep breath and tried to express the feelings that had welled up inside. "Jonah," he confessed, "I have been wrong about you."

"How's that?" responded the dowser, somewhat baffled.

"Your desire for easy wealth has blinded me to your readiness to help this family without any promise of reward," the minister explained. "I think it's now clear to all of us just how much you're desperately needed and wanted."

"Better let me sharpen your scythe," suggested Jonah, uncertain how else to respond.

"Jonah, your calling is here on this farm not in the oil fields. Are you really ready to give in to greed and lose your soul?" Reverend Small continued. "Need I remind you once more that 'money is the root of all evil'?"

"That root still looks good to me," laughed Jonah.

It was more than the clergyman could handle. Unaccustomed to such disregard of his counsel, he was about to chastise the burly laborer once more. But wisdom prevailed, and he said simply, "Maybe you better sharpen my scythe."

Jonah ran the whetstone across the blade with such skill and speed that the sharpened edge soon began to glisten in the sun.

"Let's get to work," he directed as he handed back the scythe.

More alfalfa and clover fell that morning than the day before. Spurred by silence, each of the three cut swath after swath with a determination that defied fatigue and thirst. Only when they saw Betsy approach with her water pail did they break stride, and only then did they pause to look at one another.

It was a welcome break, sweetened further when Betsy announced she had a surprise.

"After breakfast I walked over to Blake's store and sold my latest quilt for some nice, cold ale," said Betsy proudly as she removed the cover of the pail. "You gentlemen have really earned something more than water. I hope you enjoy it."

"Except you," she added hastily to her son. "I have a jar of water here for you."

As she started to hand the uncovered pail to Reverend Small, she was startled to see him raise his hand upright in refusal. "Water's fine for me too," he declared. "I vowed long ago that I would never touch alcohol."

"There's no harm in a little ale," cajoled Jonah. "If memory serves correct, the Bible tells us the good Lord changed water into wine. Heck, a whole lot of folks seem to get drunk quicker on wine than they do on ale."

But the clergyman shook his head and, without engaging in debate, headed off to the small spring–fed stream, which bordered the field.

"I'm sorry, Reverend," apologized Betsy while he was still within earshot. "I surely meant no harm. All the farmers here like ale while they're haying."

"Sure was nice of ya, ma'am," said Jonah as he reached for the pail.

Then, looking down at Seth, he added, "If this young fella keeps workin' like he has this mornin', he'll be deservin' a little swig too."

Seth beamed. But Betsy frowned, unhappy that her gesture had drawn a quiet rebuke from the man she had especially tried to reward. Then, without fully recognizing Jonah's intent, she handed Seth the water jar she had brought and set out after the clergyman.

As Jonah took a drink from the pail, he realized that Seth was watching him closely. "Ready for yer first taste of ale?" he asked, certain that Betsy was too preoccupied to notice.

Seizing the pail from Jonah's outstretched hand, Seth took a big gulp and coughed it up.

"Let that be a lesson to ya, young fella," admonished Jonah with a grin. "Never drink too much or too quick when you're hot and tired, even if it's only water. It's not good for ya." At the same time, he also reached for the pail, concerned that Seth, who was still coughing, might spill its precious contents.

Betsy was midway between Jonah and Reverend Small when she began to reconsider. *Why am I running after the preacher?* she asked herself. *I haven't done anything wrong. A little ale never hurt anyone.*

She then rejoined Seth and Jonah and quickly discovered there was little left of the ale. Unaware that Seth had drunk twice from pail, she teasingly chided Jonah. "That ale was meant for three days work, not one," she declared with a half-hearted scowl.

"Sorry, ma'am," responded Jonah. "Been a long time."

As Betsy peered at Jonah, her focus began to fix on Jonah's facial features. *If he was scrubbed, shaved, and combed, he would be a fairly handsome man,* she thought. But, as she tried to conjure up that image in her mind, the voice of Reverend Small broke the silence. Refreshed from his visit to the stream, he solemnly announced it was time to get back to work.

"Yeah, enough of this palaver," agreed Jonah, now conscious of, and uncomfortable with, Betsy's penetrating gaze.

Scythes and sickle were hastily sharpened and the tall stalks of alfalfa, timothy, and clover began to fall once again.

CHAPTER 3

After some initial small talk, dinner that night was strangely quiet. Both men praised the large chunks of ham that Betsy put in front of them, and Jonah made a special point to reiterate his thanks for the ale. The meal was nearly over when the Reverend Small finally resumed speaking.

"Seems hard to believe that three days have passed since I arrived," he began. "I'm enjoying my labor in the field, but I can't lose sight of my purpose. I came to preach to the folks here in answer to their request and, apart from you and Ruth Black, I've neither seen nor spoken to anyone."

"Lots of folks know you're here," interrupted Betsy. "Both Ruth and I have telling folks all about you, and the Blakes have put up a little sign in their store. It says that there will soon be a revival by the Reverend S. E. Small from Philadelphia. We haven't got a meeting place yet, but Ruth is trying to get the schoolhouse. It's not big, but it's never used on Sundays."

"It sounds like a good place to start," replied the preacher with a hint of enthusiasm. "And, if we get the crowds I hope and pray for, we can move outside and have services every Sunday morning as long as we have such good weather."

Looking at Jonah, he continued. "I'll keep up with the haying as best I can. I just hope you will stay on as long as it takes to fill the hayloft."

Jonah had been peering out the window, deep in thought. The mention of his name brought him back to the discussion almost instantly, but he was uncertain how to respond, if at all. As Betsy and even Seth looked to Jonah for some reply, he overcame his reticence and began to share his innermost thoughts.

"Stayin' till the hay's in the barn might just cover all that ale," he assured them, "but stayin' beyond that comes down to oil. What do ya think about sinkin' a well by the salt spring? There's probably nothin' there, but Drake acted real funny down there this mornin'. My hands and arms were real sore afterwards, and the whole thing's got my curiosity up."

"Just can't get your mind off oil and easy money, can you?" asked Reverend Small brusquely. "Jonah, hard work and trust in Almighty God is what really matters—not riches. I still don't know you as well as I'd like, but down deep, I'm sure you're a good man. Don't let Satan lead you astray with the temptation of earthly treasure."

"Seems to me you're puttin' the wagon before the horse," drawled Jonah, convinced it was time to take on his tormentor. "How do ya know what strikin' oil will do to me? How do you know what'll happen to any money that might come my way? How can ya be so sure money will corrupt me? And who says it's easy money? Sinkin' wells ain't no fun if they come up dry!"

The words tumbled out so quickly that Jonah seemed as surprised as everyone at the table. The expressions that met his glances left little doubt he had struck a blow. Betsy wore a smile suggesting support. Seth sat on the edge of his chair, clearly waiting for the clergyman to respond. And Reverend Small sat silent, moving his hand to his chin in a thoughtful pose.

After a moment or two of reflection, he replied softly. "It isn't that simple, Jonah. You may have good intentions. You may be planning to give it all away to people who really need it. But those are simply intentions, intentions that are easy to hold before all that wealth comes your way. What happens after you actually see those riches? Will you still want to give it away, or will you rather keep a little for yourself? How long will it be before you want to keep it all for your own pleasure? How long will it be before those pleasures become sinful?" And without waiting for an answer, Reverend Small added, "You know what they say about good intentions. The road to hell is paved with them."

Jonah folded his arms across his chest and looked down, eager to hurtle back a new salvo with the same explosive charge that carried his initial retort. He quickly realized, however, that the exchange was beginning to intrigue Betsy and that his standing with both Betsy and Seth might be at stake.

"Ya could be right," he finally conceded. "No way a knowin' till them riches are all mine."

Betsy, somewhat more intrigued by the possibility of oil on her farm, turned her glance to Jonah and decided to test his commitment. "How can you drill without money? Neither you nor I have money for all the equipment it would take."

"It won't be all that expensive, ma'am," answered Jonah. "All ya need is a couple good trees, some heavy rope or chain and some iron to make a drill bit. Promise the blacksmith a small cut, and we might not need any money at all."

Then, looking straight at the minister, he added, "The only

other thing I'll need is some help settin' up the drilling rig, somethin' called a springpole. One man can't do it alone."

Without knowing what it was he was being asked to do, but very much aware of Betsy's growing interest in such a venture, Reverend Small took them all by surprise, including himself, by announcing his reluctant readiness to help.

"On one condition, Jonah. In return for my help," he insisted, "you'll come to every one of my worship services."

"That's too high a price," replied Jonah, half in jest and half in earnest. "But if ya agree to settle for every other Sunday, ya got a deal."

"Say yes," demanded Betsy with a smile that absolutely no one could refuse.

"So be it," surrendered the minister. "Hopefully, we will all learn to spurn the false paradises of this life and devote ourselves instead to the true paradise of the hereafter."

The suddenness with which they had arrived at an agreement amazed them all. And before the implications could dampen the moment, Seth rose from the table and moved beside Jonah, asking aloud, "What's a springpole?"

"Can't get into that right now," chuckled Jonah, "but when the preacher learns what he's got into, it might make even him swear!"

There was momentary silence, broken with a nervous giggle from Betsy. And then they all laughed, happy that the two men were no longer at odds even if they were not yet friends.

"Guess us men better call it a night," counseled Jonah, winking at Seth. "We've got a lot more hayin' to do before we can even begin thinkin' about drillin' for oil."

With that, he headed for the kitchen door and, engrossed by all that had happened, forgot to ease the screen door behind him. It had hardly slammed shut when he heard a chorus inside commanding him to return to close the door properly. He did amid a new round of laughter.

Outside, Jonah found a darkened sky. The moon and stars helped him find his way back to the barn, illuminating the path with such brilliance that each little stone was clearly visible. Midway between the house and barn, he paused to enjoy their light and the prospect of sinking his first well for oil.

Inside, Reverend Small had now moved to the kitchen door and, seeing Jonah looking up at the heavens, he found his curiosity unleashed. *Who is this man called Jonah?*

Betsy, meanwhile, had moved most of the dishes to the basin she used for most kitchen chores. As she went about her tasks, her thoughts drifted to the man at the door. *His laughter revealed facial features I haven't seen before. For the first time I see a man my own age who, when he smiles and laughs, is as handsome as my late husband. Becoming the wife of a preacher might be worth considering.*

Her wandering thoughts, however, raised the specter of a less pleasant consideration. *When all is said and done, I know no more about this man of the cloth than I do about the man who might someday make me rich.*

"Reverend Small," she asked as he turned away from the door, "is there a Mrs. Small?"

"Only my mother," he replied matter-of-factly. "Very few ministers like myself can afford the luxury of a wife and family. As a newly ordained clergyman, I have many fields to harvest. Whenever I crave the comforts of home, I remind myself of the words of our Lord: 'The harvest is plentiful, but the laborers are few.'"

"I understand," responded Betsy. "My husband was also committed to a great cause, abolition, and it cost us his life on the battlefield."

"My condolence, madam," said Reverend Small stiffly, as he turned to retire to his room, afraid that the conversation might lead in uncomfortable directions.

But Betsy was not about to allow their talk to end on that note. "When I was at Blakes today, one of my neighbors asked 'What does the S. E. stand for?' and I told him I didn't know."

"Samuel Ebenezer," revealed the preacher as he marched away from the kitchen.

Jonah rose shortly before dawn, and although it was still dark, he found his way to the pump with first light. The water he drew was cold, but he enjoyed the bracing effect it had on his hands and face. Invigorated, he dried quickly with a fresh towel that Betsy had set aside for him and then headed back to the barn to sharpen the scythes and sickle.

Each stroke of his whetstone left the cutting edge of the blades visibly sharper until, in no time at all, they were ready for the day ahead.

Wide-awake and growing restless, he headed for the woods, trying to remember where he had seen some of the tall, straight hemlock that he would soon need for his drilling rig. He stayed close to the edge of the woods, within sight of the salt spring, assuming he might have to drag the felled trees to the drilling site by himself.

The search was over quickly. Within a radius of no more than fifty yards, he found both a hemlock and an oak that matched his need. The trunk of the hemlock was roughly fifteen inches across at the ground, and it was tall and needle-shaped. It was also the closest of the hemlocks to the spring. The oak was farther away, but it too was nearly ideal. There were two major limbs jutting off from the trunk of the oak forming the strong, solid fork that he needed.

Pleased with his discoveries, he set off toward the spring, pausing only once to look back. With the location of the trees now etched in his mind, he resumed his walk. And, even without Drake, he seemed to feel a gentle tug from the earth as he neared the small salt spring. The beauty of its clear, sparkling water and the runoff it produced were hard to ignore, and he paused for a moment to watch its runoff meander toward the creek in a narrow, shallow ditch.

But Jonah decided not to stop and linger. Instead he ambled back toward the barn, just in time to hear the first notes of the rooster announcing the new day. The rough–hewn bench beside the barn door awaited him. As he was about to sit, he heard the kitchen door slam shut and peering in that direction watched Seth approach, milk pail in hand.

Jonah spoke first. "Good mornin', Mister Fisherman," he declared with a smile.

"Mornin'," responded Seth with a yawn. He set the pail down near the bench, and after waiting briefly for a reply that never came, he ambled over to a wooden fence that encircled a small field and attached it to the barn. Free to roam about the enclosure, the family's two cows watched as Seth climbed over the fence.

"C'mon, Betty, c'mon Bertha," called Seth. "It's milkin' time."

By then, the cows were already waiting to enter the barn. Seth herded them inside and as soon as they inched their heads through the wooden stanchions in their stalls, he pulled the open bars shut.

Grabbing two empty pails in front of the stanchions, he headed for the pump outside where he filled each with water. Once he had watered the animals, he threw down some hay from the loft above and then began milking.

Jonah, still outdoors, was deep in thought. *Finding the timber for my drilling rig has been easy and, as long as I can get some help from Reverend Small or other able-bodied men, I can raise the drilling rig without difficulty. The real challenge is the drill bit.*

Recalling the various shapes of bits he had seen, he reckoned it would have to be at least six inches in diameter and upwards of sixteen inches or more in length. Its bottom would have to be cone-shaped or chisel-like to cut through hardpan and any rock beneath it. And there would have to be a loop on top to attach a rope or chain. Any good smith could produce it, provided Jonah could come up with funds.

"Breakfast," invited Seth after finishing his chores. Jonah nodded in agreement, and the two set off for the house.

Reverend Small was already seated at the kitchen table, gingerly nursing a cup of hot coffee. Steam was still rising from its surface as he lowered it to the table. Only then did Jonah realize that the shirt the minister was wearing was the one he wore the first time they had met.

"That's hardly fit for hayin'," suggested Jonah.

"It's time for me to be about the work of the Lord," the minister replied. "If I don't get out and meet folks soon, they'll be looking for someone else. Miss Betsy promised the Blakes that I'd visit the store today. I'll spend the day there, talking to the folks who come by."

"Suspect we can get along without ya," observed Jonah. "What do ya think, Seth?"

The youngster pondered for a moment and then suggested thoughtfully, "Most of the hay that we cut the first day is probably dry enough to turn over. Guess we can get along without help for that."

"He's right," thundered Jonah, grinning at both the forethought and the confidence with which the lad spoke. "Been hotter than blazes, and that hay's been dryin' fast. The sooner we can turn it over, the sooner we can get it in before it gets wet."

Reverend Small remained silent, uncertain whether he should cut short his day to return to the field in the afternoon.

"It will be good to see some of that hay turned," said Betsy as she finished washing the pans she used to cook breakfast. "After that, you can stack it, and I'll ask one of our neighbors for a team and wagon to bring it up to the barn. That's when we'll need extra help."

Jonah was on his feet before Betsy had finished speaking. "Let's go, Mister Fisherman," he commanded. "Ya can show me where to look for the pitchforks."

Reverend Small rose too. "I should be able to get back early this afternoon," he volunteered.

Shortly thereafter, Jonah and Seth headed toward the field, each with a rake, a pitchfork, and a small lunch put together hurriedly by Betsy. Then she and Reverend Small, now formally attired, headed off to Blake's store.

The store was nearly two miles away. Although it was warm, it was not uncomfortable. Large maples and other species dotted the road to the village, offering some welcome shade. Some of the adjacent fields were fenced with slender rails from locust and other trees. Here and there, cows and sheep munched leisurely on grass that was slowly turning straw–like from the lack of rain and what was becoming a merciless heat wave.

"Why is there no church?" asked the preacher as he and Betsy walked along the dry, hardened road. Only once had he been in town, and that was a brief excursion in search of Ruth Black, the woman who had asked his denomination to send someone to minister to the small population and its neighboring farmers.

"There was until a couple years ago," explained Betsy, surprised that he seemed unfamiliar with the history of the church, "but it caught fire and burned to the ground. Then we lost our preacher," she continued. "A few weeks after the fire, the good Lord called him home. With his passing, no one gave much thought to rebuilding the church. No one, that is, until Ruth. When her husband died last fall and there was no one to give him a proper burial, she wrote to the bishop, asking him to send someone. It seems the bishop or someone down there in Philadelphia was waiting for us to rebuild the church first."

"Getting people back to church won't be easy," Betsy added. "After working hard all week, the men like to rest up on Sunday. Besides, they would much rather get a new teacher for the school, and most of the women would too."

"I might be able to help at the school until a new teacher can be found," Reverend Small volunteered. "Indeed, maybe that's the way to get these folks back to church."

Betsy smiled but hesitated to voice her approval. The thought of reopening the school was urgent but, she wondered, how would Seth and the other youngsters take to the preacher.

Rounding a bend, they could see the few buildings that made up the village. From a half mile away, only two stood out. One was clearly the schoolhouse, somewhat isolated from the other buildings by a large field that surrounded it. Another, which Betsy pointed to with her finger, was their destination—Blake's general store.

What they saw was actually the back of the store. The two-story structure was built into an embankment. The bottom floor was level with a nearby creek, the same one that Seth loved to fish, and the second floor was level with the street in front of the building.

Closer but harder to see were the remnants of a large, stone foundation which, Betsy now hastened to point out, was all that remained of the old church.

"How did the fire start?" asked Reverend Small, returning to the subject of the church.

"No one really knows," answered Betsy. "The door was never locked. So there were always lots of rumors. Some folks blamed a neighbor of mine, claiming he and a woman he was courting at the time went inside to get out of the rain. According to that story, he dropped his pipe when they started to snuggle up and some of the hot ashes fell between the boards in the floor. Of course, nothing happened until long after they had left. It's not too hard to imagine but, I for one, don't believe it."

With his curiosity now engaged, Reverend Small accelerated his questions. "And what other theories were there?" he asked.

"I should never have told that story," protested Betsy. "It was pure rumor and, as I said, I've never believed it."

"You're right that no one should spread rumors for they are the devil's delight," agreed the preacher. "I can certainly live with the mystery, but I would like to know about all the other theories."

"Well, there is another theory that still makes the rounds," teased Betsy with a smile.

"Oh," replied Reverend Small with undisguised interest.

"It involves a man who used to work at the bank," began Betsy. "It's probably untrue, but a lot of folks swear to it because the fire happened right after a sermon by the minister who later died."

Their pace had brought them into town, and when Betsy spotted townspeople nearby she quickly decided to change the subject.

"This is our town," she announced. "I can't believe we got here so quickly."

Despite the mounting suspense, Reverend Small realized it

would do little good to press Betsy to finish the story until they were headed home. She was now focused on the purpose of their visit.

"It was a fine walk," he responded enthusiastically, tipping his stovepipe hat to two passing women.

"Those two gossip terribly," Betsy muttered softly once she was sure she could not be overheard. "It's because of folks like them that I didn't dare to let you board at my place. God only knows what they are saying about me boarding both you and Jonah."

That said, she opened the door to Blake's store, and they stepped inside.

Art Blake looked up from his ledger, summoned his wife, and strode toward the door. "Reverend Small, welcome! And a good day to you too, Betsy," he added with a huge smile. "We've already had a few folks come by just to see you, Reverend, but they said they'd come back later. Everyone's delighted that you're here."

"It's good to know that folks here are ready to return to Sunday services again," replied the minister, stretching out his hand in greeting. "Seems it's been a long time since they were able to worship together as a congregation."

"Well, yes and no," chuckled Art. "Over the last couple years, we've had a few fellas come for a week or two and preach fire and brimstone. They didn't go over very well so they'd hit the road again—lookin' for greener pastures."

"Does that mean the people here don't believe in hell and eternal punishment?" asked Reverend Small.

"Most do," answered the businessman, turning serious long before he intended. "But they want to hear something beside that all the time. There's a lot more to the Bible than damnation."

There was a moment of hesitation on the part of the minister.

He had hardly expected a discourse on good and evil with a man he had just met. Yet fire and brimstone was sometimes part of his own sermons and the prospect of rejection gave him pause. *Isn't this what the sinner must hear?* he pondered.

Just as he was about to uphold the notion, he felt Betsy's hand touch his arm. "You're absolutely right," she said, looking directly at Art Blake. "And no one offers more from the Good Book than Reverend Small. Just wait till you hear him preach!"

The minister brought an unclenched hand to his face, extended his index finger over this mouth in obvious contemplation. Uncharacteristically silent for yet another moment, he began to grin and then laugh.

"It's not every day than I have such a powerful advocate," he said, shaking his head in undisguised amusement.

"It's good to meet you, Mr. Blake," he added, "and it's very kind of you to let me meet people here in your store. I am indebted to you, sir."

Art acknowledged the comments with a nod and moved with dispatch to reposition two chairs from the front of a dormant pot-bellied stove to a place closer to the front door. "Please come and sit a spell," he said. "There will be plenty of time to stand once folks start coming."

Within an hour, the store was crowded, almost entirely of townspeople. Betsy introduced them one by one, often with a word or two about each woman's expertise in the kitchen or each man's specialty or achievements as a farmer or craftsman.

Mrs. Blake, known to them all as Esther, set out tea and homemade shortbread, and the atmosphere soon became more relaxed and less formal. Seizing the moment, Reverend Small moved to the center of the gathering and, raising his hand, managed to draw the attention and silence of most of the crowd.

"Getting to know each one of you personally will take a little time," he began, "but the prospect of your friendship is all the incentive I need to do so as quickly as I can. In the same light, I hope you're eager to get to know me and the message that I bring.

"My message is simple. There is eternal life, and therein lies a choice you can neither avoid nor escape. It is a choice between sin and salvation, a choice between Satan and God. Who can deny the daily temptations of Evil? And who can claim that they are sinless?

"By the same token, who can deny the countless mercies and blessings of a loving God who's there for all to see, not just in our own lives but in the lives of your neighbors? And who can claim they are worthy of such mercies and blessings?

"I have many more things to tell you, but I would like to leave you with this assurance: It is never too late to choose the salvation that God offers us through His son Jesus."

A hush prevailed for a moment or two while the crowd waited to see if Reverend Small would continue speaking. When it was clear he would not, Ruth Black, who joined the crowd just as he started speaking, began to applaud.

Betsy began clapping too, and the others soon followed suit.

Ruth then wove her way through the crowd, making her way to the minister.

"We have permission to use the school for worship," she announced. "It's not very large, but it should hold all the folks that used to go to church plus a few more." Well known for being direct and terse, she lost no time in demonstrating both attributes. "Can you begin preaching this Sunday?" she asked in a manner that bordered on demand. "I realize it's already Thursday, but I'm sure we can notify just about everyone in a day or two. Most folks are aware that you arrived nearly a week ago."

Having met Ruth the day he arrived, the minister was not entirely surprised by her manner. "Of course, Ruth," he replied.

Addressing her as Ruth was a bit of a gamble. Although he suspected she preferred to be addressed as Mrs. Black, at least initially, he chose to be equally direct, hoping to win her approval and friendship.

He was right. Ruth smiled broadly. "That's good," she said, moving confidently to the middle of the store to announce in a loud and forceful voice that Reverend Small would preach his first sermon at ten o'clock Sunday morning at the schoolhouse. With that, she strode to the door and departed as quietly as she had arrived.

And just as suddenly, Reverend Small found himself facing a man he had not yet met. "Sounds like you might be different from most of the other preachers I've heard," the man declared without introducing himself. "I might just come by to hear you." When his remarks failed to produce any hint of reaction, the man thrust out his hand in greeting. "Meet another sinner," he said harshly, "damned like all the rest of these people."

Although he continued to withhold a reply, Reverend Small found it hard to hide his curiosity. A quizzical expression emerged on his face, and he gripped the outstretched hand unhesitatingly as he examined the man from head to toe.

"You'll learn about me soon enough," the man added as he inched through the crowd toward the door. Several in the store halted their conversations after recognizing the man, but they resumed talking almost as soon as he took his leave.

Reverend Small was about to call the man back but, once again, he was interrupted by Betsy. "It's been a busy day," she said softly, "but there's still time to get home to help with the haying." She steered him to the door with such determination that he had to resist briefly, both to thank everyone for coming and to express the hope he would see them all again on Sunday.

Reverend Small exercised patience until at last they were well out of town, alone on the road back to the farm. On the one hand, he enjoyed the attention and company of this attractive young woman named Betsy, but he was also becoming annoyed at her interference, which at times tended to undermine the formality he often required.

Intruding into his conversation with Art Blake was bad enough, but arbitrarily terminating his opportunity to meet people was simply too much. He was, after all, a man of the cloth who deserved and expected proper respect. And just as he was about to admonish Betsy with carefully chosen words, she asked coyly, "Did you notice how quickly the store filled up?"

"It was those two women we passed on our way to the store," she declared. "They must have gone door–to–door. It seemed like the whole town knew you were there before you even got to sit down. And they didn't lose much time getting there themselves."

"What really surprised me though," she continued more seriously, "was the way Lucas Bennett snuck into the store and then marched right up to you like he belonged there."

"Who is the man?" questioned Reverend Small, fully aware that he had once again been manipulated by Betsy, innocently or otherwise. The man had captured the minister's interest and, even if it meant putting off his admonishment to another day, he chose to hear Betsy out.

"Why he's the one most folks think set fire to the church," she explained, "and he may well have had good enough reason."

Betsy paused, turned her head toward the minister, and coolly waited for his reaction. But there was none. Despite his fascination, Reverend Small looked ahead indifferently, carefully avoiding Betsy's glance. Her silence did not last long.

"I thought you were interested," she teased.

"Only up to a point," he replied. "Unless there's proof of some kind, I'd rather regard the man as innocent. Regrettably, too many men—and women for that matter—are permanently harmed by speculation and unfounded rumors."

"Well then, you might as well hear the gossip from me," sniffed Betsy half seriously. "Sooner or later, someone is going to tell you all about these things. At least I can try to share the details with you without stretching the truth."

"If you must," said Reverend Small in his deepest, exasperated tone.

"Lucas Bennett is a real scoundrel," she began. "As far as we know, he has never put in an honest day's work. Instead, he's gotten rich cheating people."

Try as he might, the minister could no longer contain his curiosity. "Doing what?"

"It's all very simple," Betsy explained. "Sometimes when the farmers need loans and the bank turns them down, Lucas finds out. He waits until they're desperate and then offers them small personal loans at high interest."

"And how can you be so sure?" asked Reverend Small skeptically.

"Because he tried to cheat me that way!" she shouted angrily.

Betsy quickly recovered her composure, but it was clear from the minister's startled expression that he was unsure what to say or ask next. Rather than wait for comment or query, she resumed her story more softly.

"Lots of folks have told me about his wily ways," she continued. "In fact, I might have fallen into his trap if I hadn't been warned by some of my neighbors."

"When did this happen?" the clergyman asked.

"Just a few months after I learned my husband had been killed in the war," she answered. "We have never had very much, and I sold the few things we had to keep the farm. If it hadn't been for the Blakes, I might have lost the place."

"What you've told me can hardly be called gossip," Reverend Small consoled. "But what does Lucas have to do with the fire?"

"He used to go to church every Sunday," Betsy responded, "probably to find out who needed loans. Someone finally told the preacher how Lucas managed to get the big offerings he put in the collection plate. When he was asked about his schemes, Lucas denied them. As time went on, more and more people told the minister the same story. Eventually, he decided to preach about greed and, even though he didn't mention Lucas by name, everyone knew who he was preaching about."

Betsy paused once more.

"The fire," she revealed slowly, "was the following week."

CHAPTER 4

As they drew near the farm, Betsy was the first to notice the long, neat windrows of hay that Jonah and Seth had produced while she and Reverend Small had been at Blake's. As she glanced from one side of the field to the other, she discovered the two creating small haystacks from the windrows that were fully dry.

"Look at all they've done," exclaimed Betsy, slowing her pace so that she could admire the agility and confidence with which Seth handled his pitchfork. It was increasingly clear that Jonah was fulfilling a critical role in Seth's development and maturation.

Reverend Small, who had said little after Betsy's revelations about the church fire, also acknowledged the progress in the field with admiration and enthusiasm.

"It's hard to believe they've done all that in the short time we've been gone," he replied. "If I don't get out there soon, there'll be nothing left for me to do!"

With that, he removed his coat, tie, and hat and headed toward the field with the clothing over his arm. He had barely left the edge of the road, however, when Betsy reminded him that he had neither rake nor pitchfork.

"If you're going to the field to work," she counseled, "you better go to the barn first and find some tools."

"You are right, of course," replied the minister. "If I seemed impulsive it is only because I promised to help. And, believe it or not, I have come to enjoy my time in the field."

"After you find the tools, you better come to the kitchen for some lunch," Betsy added. "We're back early enough that you can probably eat with Jonah and Seth. Judging by all the work they've done, I doubt that they've taken time to stop to eat."

"Then I might as well change into my work clothes too," said Reverend Small.

Moving with dispatch, he quickly changed, scoured the barn until he found a pitchfork, took the pail of water and the small lunch sack that Betsy handed him, and set off for the field. Jonah watched him approach but continued working until he was within earshot.

"Looks like we've got company," he announced loud enough for both Seth and the minister to hear. "Might even be someone ready to do a little work."

Jonah drove his pitchfork into the ground, removed a damp bandana from his hip pocket, and began to wipe his forehead, face, and neck. "It's good to see ya, parson," he chuckled. "Yer just in time for lunch!"

Reverend Small, now just steps away, laughed at the ribbing and quickly concurred when Seth cried, "Let's eat."

With that, the two men eased into kneeling positions on the ground and then sat on their upturned heels. Seth was quick to follow, and each of the three opened the small sacks of food packed by Betsy. It was well past noon and, although the sun was at its height, the men had made an unconscious decision to stay where there was no shade.

"Once this hay is in the barn, it'll be time to start setting up the springpole," said Jonah, reaching for the pail of cool water that Betsy had sent with the minister.

"I'll do what I can," replied Reverend Small, "even though I'm not all that keen about it."

"Why not?" challenged the man who still remained a stranger.

"Well, to begin with, you already know how I feel about easy riches," answered the minister. "But there is also the trouble that an oil strike will most likely bring. It's sure to attract some of the worst of society, not to mention the end of this farm. I've heard about the boomtowns, the lawlessness, the farmland covered with derricks. Is this what you want for Seth and his mother?"

"Why not look at the bright side?" demanded Jonah. "If we hit oil, she'll have a much easier life. If she doesn't want to stay on the farm, she can go anywhere she wants. And she can give this young man the best of everything!"

"Maybe, but maybe not," retorted Reverend Small, trying hard not to become unpleasant or loud. "Oil no longer commands the high prices it once did. Just go to the store in town if you doubt me. Too much oil isn't going to bode well for the picture you're painting."

"Ya argue well," sighed Jonah. "But this is eastern Pennsylvania, close to big cities like Philadelphia and New York. If we can get oil to them faster and cheaper than the western part of the state, it should mean pretty decent profits for folks here."

"I won't break my promise," lamented the clergyman, "but I can certainly hope and pray that it all comes to naught."

The Lure Of Oil, The Cry For Water

"Who knows," said Jonah with a grin, "maybe it'll be my prayers that get answered."

"What's that?" asked Reverend Small. "Did I hear you say you pray?"

"Oh, from time to time," Jonah admitted, "but it usually takes a spell of trouble that won't go away or somethin' like a dream of strikin' oil."

"You sound like most folks," the minister smiled. "Maybe there's hope for you yet!"

Seth, who had listened closely to the exchange, rose to his feet. "I used to pray that my dad would come home, but now I know he won't," he said softly. "Why bother saying prayers?"

The two men exchanged glances. While Reverend Small paused to make a thoughtful reply, Jonah spoke out sharply. "'Cause it's the right thing to do, Mister Fisherman."

Satisfied that that was sufficient for the moment, the clergyman got up too. "Getting this hay stacked is also the right thing to do," he suggested, "and we better get back to it now."

By late afternoon, they had raked and stacked all but the hay that still needed more time to dry. "Well done, men," Jonah announced, and they all began to laugh, especially Seth. Like the men, the lad threw his rake and pitchfork over his shoulder as they headed for the barn. Sweaty and tired, each lapsed into private thought.

At dinner, Betsy marveled at all the work the three had accomplished. She also spent a good part of the meal telling Jonah and Seth about the warm welcome the people in town had given Reverend Small. And to celebrate all the events that day, she produced a huge strawberry and rhubarb pie that was quickly devoured.

Long after they had cleaned their plates and emptied their cups and glasses, they remained at the table. In the midst of all the small talk and occasional banter, Jonah reminded them of his determination to erect the drilling rig in pursuit of his quest for oil.

"Won't be easy," he warned. "But after lookin' around the farm, it looks like there's just about everything we need to get started. Let's just hope we hit oil early on. Could be we'll need to buy some things if the drillin' starts runnin' deep."

"When you reach that point," Betsy interrupted, "you'll have to stop. There's no money for such risk, and I have no intention of taking a loan."

The swiftness and finality of her remarks caught Jonah by surprise. "Let's hope we're lucky," he countered. "If not, there's lots more territory west of here." With that, Jonah rose, bid everyone goodnight and headed for the barn.

Reverend Small, Betsy, and Seth sat speechless, each stunned at the way the meal had turned from a happy, joyful event into a sad, disturbing one.

The minister was first to speak. "How do you really feel about Jonah's plan?" he asked Betsy. "I know you can't afford to buy the things he may want or eventually need, but is money the only obstacle in your mind?"

Left visibly downcast by the prospect that Jonah might resume his trek west, Betsy remained silent. But Reverend Small persisted, unwilling to let her avoid his query. "Are you not uneasy about all the evil that an oil strike might unleash?"

"What do you mean by evil?" Betsy asked half-heartedly.

"After the first discovery of oil by Colonel Drake," the minister replied, "Titusville and the surrounding area were soon overrun by men whose only aim was wealth and whose only guide was greed. Within months, they defiled the land and the streams and, when their recklessness led to fires, even the air. Surely, you have heard of their contempt for the land and nature."

"It's not that simple," answered Betsy. "I have been asking myself over and over what my husband would have done. I can only guess that he would be as uncertain as I am. But what I know for sure is that he loved this farm. He worked very hard, and nature rewarded his hard work. For him, oil might be another reward of nature. On the other hand, I also know he tried to live by the Good Book. If he knew what happened after they struck oil out west, he would probably be uncertain too.

"But what difference does it really make? He's not here, and the situation is not the same as if he was. Even though I love this farm as much as he did, I love my son even more. I want to keep the farm, but how long is that possible with the few things I can sell or trade?

"When I think about how you and Jonah appeared out of nowhere, I know in my heart that you are both godsends. And then I think, 'Maybe oil is too!'"

"Satan always makes evil look inviting," the minister responded. "Had it not been for my own uncertainty, I would not have agreed to help Jonah put up this rig of his. Even now, at the risk of breaking my promise, I would love to back out. The trouble is that might hurt my ministry. So I'll do what I tell everyone else to do—pray for guidance."

"I hope I haven't hurt Jonah's feelings," Betsy lamented. "I don't know what I would do without his help. Striking oil is obviously very important to him, and I'm sure he's ready to move on if I continue to discourage him."

"No doubt," nodded Reverend Small, "and that would be a tragedy. Perhaps we can both support him. But we can also hope and pray that if he does strike oil, we can avoid some of the sins that are sure to entangle us all."

"Oh, goodness," cried Betsy, changing the subject completely, "I forgot to tell you and Jonah that one of my neighbors is willing to let us borrow his team and wagon to bring in the hay tomorrow. I meant to tell everyone the good news during dinner, but it slipped my mind. Please go to the barn and tell Jonah so that he'll be ready in the morning."

"Of course," said the minister, rising from the table and starting toward the door.

"And please tell him that even though I can't take a loan, I will try to help him get what ever else he needs for his drilling," Betsy added.

Outside, as his eyes adjusted to the moonlight, the clergyman discovered Jonah sitting on the bench beside the barn. The dowser was clearly deep in thought. Even the sound of the approaching minister failed to divert his attention.

"It's too nice a night to be troubled," suggested Reverend Small. "Besides, I've got some good news. There'll be a team and a wagon here in the morning. With a little luck and more hard work, we'll have that hay inside before the rain finally comes. Are you ready to put up with me again tomorrow?"

Jonah nodded in agreement but remained largely preoccupied.

"Betsy also wants you to know that even though she can't take a loan," the clergyman added, "she will try to help you get what you need from her friends and neighbors."

"And how about you, Reverend?" Jonah challenged.

"Look, Jonah, you already know I am opposed to the whole idea," Reverend Small responded. "But I made a promise, and I'll do my best to keep it. I just pray that the good Lord sorts it all out according to His will. And remember, you made a promise too. My first church service is very close at hand."

Jonah's solemn expression vanished. "Can't keep my promise till ya keep yers," he laughed. "Once ya help set up the drillin' rig, ya can count on me bein' in back of everyone that shows up for yer sermon."

"Fair enough," the minister replied as he headed toward the house and the light shining through the screen door.

—

The sound of the approaching horses brought Jonah from the barn with three pitchforks slung over his shoulder. Betsy, Seth, and Reverend Small emerged from the kitchen, and the three waved in unison as the neighbor, Stephen Barnes, better known as ol' Barnes, pulled the team to a halt with a gentle tug on the reins.

Barnes, now in his seventies, still handled the team like a man half his age.

"You must be the new preacher," he shouted, looking directly at the lanky, oddly dressed male on the porch. "Sorry I didn't get over to Blake's yesterday," he added hurriedly, "but I had to tend to some hayin' myself."

Turning his gaze toward the imposing figure with the three pitchforks, he queried, "Can you handle the team?"

"Most likely," answered Jonah with measured assurance, "but it'd be kinda nice if this young fella here could take the reins once we're in the field. Ya needn't worry about the team and the wagon. He learns real quick."

Barnes jumped to the ground, nodding approval. He handed the reins to Jonah and, with a slight limp, walked to the porch. "I'd help if I could," he told Betsy, "but I've got more hay of my own to cut. Looks to me like you've got about as much help as you need."

"The team is a really big help," Betsy replied. "We'll see that the horses are fed and watered before we bring them back."

The aging farmer, well known for his brevity, simply said, "Good," and started home.

After throwing the pitchforks into the back of the wagon and climbing up to the seat, Jonah called to Seth. "Come on up here, Mister Fisherman, it's time you learned to drive a team." And as Seth scrambled toward the wagon, Jonah added, "You too, Parson!"

It was quickly apparent that Jonah was as skillful with the team as Barnes. He headed toward the most distance stack and, once they reached the field, handed the reins to Seth. The lad seized them without hesitation, gripping them carefully in just the same way that Jonah had held them. By the time they reached the stack, Seth had mastered several of the basics.

Jonah quickly established a routine. After he and Reverend Small finished pitching each stack of hay onto the wagon, Seth drove the team to the next closest stack. Once the wagon was full, the two men climbed up with Seth and rode to the barn. There, the clergyman remained on the wagon, pitching hay to Jonah, who had climbed into the loft.

They labored throughout the morning, passing by the creek from time to time to water the horses. As the kitchen clock struck twelve, Betsy met them at the barn with bread, cheese, and water, still cold from the spring–fed reservoir from which it was drawn.

There was little conversation. Each of the men had withdrawn into their personal worlds. Though eager for adult approval, Seth began to realize that his success in handling the horses was no longer praiseworthy but now taken for granted. With time to think, Seth began to appreciate his new skill and with it a keen sense of pride.

The horses meanwhile nibbled on the few stalks of grass that had managed to grow under the canopy of the maple where Jonah had tied them. It was a handsome team, well kept, well mannered, and well trained. And eager to work. When Jonah rose to his feet, the team snorted approval and turned their heads toward the field, signaling their readiness.

Without a word being spoken, Reverend Small and Seth stood up as well. Seth was the first to reach the wagon. After untying the team and climbing aboard, he took the reins without asking and, mimicking Jonah, shouted out, "Let's get back to work!"

The men exchanged smiles and promptly obeyed. Reverend Small swung his lanky frame onto the back of the wagon while Jonah joined Seth up front. And the haying resumed.

By mid-afternoon, Jonah threw the last haystack onto the wagon. The minister, who was standing atop the largest and highest of the day's loads, caught it in midair and steered it to a low spot. He then sank his pitchfork into the huge stack and sat down beside it.

Jonah elected to walk beside the wagon with the long handle of his pitchfork resting on his right shoulder. He kept pace with the plodding team until they neared the weathered barn. As they crossed the road, he quickened his pace and, by the time Seth pulled the team to a halt below the doors to the loft, Jonah was inside waiting for the first fork of hay.

Reverend Small was on his feet, steadying himself with his pitchfork which was still anchored in the hay. As Seth shouted, "Whoa!" and pulled back on the reins, both men were ready to move in unison. Each fork-full of hay thrown into the loft by the minister was stabbed by Jonah and thrust wherever it would best maintain the shape of the mound he had begun creating that morning.

Done at last, Jonah emerged from the barn covered with sweat and hayseed. Outside in the still air, he began to sneeze. And when Reverend Small and Seth started to laugh at the dowser, they suddenly found themselves sneezing as well.

Betsy waited in the kitchen until she saw the empty wagon. Smiling in gratitude, she marched to the barn with a pail of cold water and a cup of cold ale. "This should help," she announced, handing the pail to the minister and the cup to Jonah. "I'm in your debt," she continued. "There's more hay in that barn than I can ever remember. The almanac says we'll need plenty this winter. It's a big relief to know it's there."

Seth took a single gulp from the pail after Reverend Small. Instead of drinking further, he waited in the futile hope that his mother would return to the house and Jonah would offer him a fresh taste of ale. She remained close by, however, and the ale soon disappeared.

The two men had lost little time in quenching their thirst. After savoring the final drop, Jonah turned the cup upside down. "Must be a hole in this thing," he cried.

Eager to get back to the barn for some grain for the horses, he handed the cup back to Betsy.

"Pump some water for the team," he shouted, his voice trailing off as he disappeared inside. Instinctively Seth knew the task was his. Although his day had been limited to driving the team, he was more tired than he could remember. Nevertheless, he obeyed immediately.

It took a few buckets of water to satisfy the horses' thirst despite the fact they had drunk from the creek not long before.

Jonah, meanwhile, brought out two pails of grain. He held one, then the other, at chest level, giving each horse a chance to enjoy a well-earned reward. And it wasn't long before both pails were empty.

While Jonah fed the horses, Betsy and Reverend Small retired to the kitchen. Only Jonah and Seth remained outside.

"Can you take this team over to Barnes' place?" asked Jonah. "Sure," the boy replied, heading for the wagon and the reins. "Are you going with me?"

The question gave Jonah pause. He found Seth's growing self-confidence pleasing. "Guess it depends whether or not ya want some company," he answered.

"It ain't far," Seth replied, "but sure could use the company."

"Okay," agreed Jonah.

Seth maneuvered the team back to the road, turning in the direction of the Barnes' farm. It was a short ride, and when he got there, the old farmer was waiting for them beside his barn. "Done already?" inquired the old farmer.

"Every last blade," Seth shouted, recalling a phrase he had heard his father once use.

Barnes was surprised to see the boy handling the team, but did his best not to show it. His apparent qualms were not lost on Jonah, however, and the dowser hastened to put Barnes at ease. "If it hadn't been for this young fella, we'd still be pitchin' hay. He and your team get along just fine. Whenever Miss Betsy can spare him, you might want to hire him."

"Back that wagon over to the outhouse," barked Barnes, winking at Jonah.

It was a command Seth had learned early in the day and, with a flip of the reins, he ordered the team back. The performance surprised and delighted the normally taciturn neighbor. When the lad wrapped the reins around the brake handle and jumped to the ground as he had done throughout the day, Barnes applauded.

"Looks like I could use both of you," he said, shifting his glance toward Jonah.

"Not today," replied the dowser. "But we will give ya a hand getting the harnesses off and the team back to pasture."

Working together, the two men finished the task with dispatch. Seth watched closely and even though he was not yet big enough to bridle and harness the team, it seemed certain that he would know what to do when that moment came.

Supper was at least an hour away when they got back. As the two began washing away the sweat and the hay from their faces and arms at the pump, Jonah stopped abruptly.

"Makes no sense washin' up here when there's a creek nearby," he observed. "Water might be a little muddy, but it's bound to be deep enough for a quick swim."

And off he went, leaving Seth at the pump.

At supper, the conversation focused primarily on the day's accomplishments. For Betsy, it meant she could most likely survive another winter, and for Reverend Small, it was the certainty that his future was in rural America, an environment in which he now felt very much at home. For Seth, it was the knowledge that he had grown a little taller, physically and figuratively. And for Jonah, it was the reality that his dream might soon be realized.

CHAPTER 5

At breakfast the next morning, there was fresh excitement as talk shifted to Jonah's dream of finding oil. Since Drake had already found a promising drill site, Jonah explained that he was now ready to build his drilling rig, something he called a springpole.

"Springpoles have been around for centuries," explained Jonah. "Some say they were invented by the Chinese. There's nothin' cheaper. Long as a man can find some good trees, some rope, and a chunk of iron for a bit, there's not much more he needs.

"Already picked out the trees, and there's plenty of rope in the barn. 'Bout the only thing missin' is a drill bit. A good blacksmith can make it, but it's gonna take a few dollars."

"There's a smith on the edge of town," interrupted Betsy. "He's a little cranky sometimes, but he won't cheat you. Chances are you'll have to help him figure it out, but if anyone can make your bit, I'm sure he can."

"When you're ready to go talk to him," she added, "Seth can take you there."

"Don't plan to say much," Jonah continued, "'cause that'll just set folks ta buzzin.'"

"I hadn't thought about that," exclaimed Betsy, wrinkling her brow and peering down in distress. "Do you have to tell him you're going to be drilling for oil?"

"Rather say it's for water," replied Jonah, "providin' the good reverend here won't get mad at me for tellin' a little fib."

Reverend Small, who had listened intently but had said little, rose from the table, shaking his finger at the dowser, half in jest but half in earnest. "Don't you see, it's all wrong," he insisted. "You haven't even started, and you're already knee-deep in lies."

"Now don't go and lecture me again," sighed Jonah. "Can't see no harm in tryin' to keep folks from gossipin'. Sayin' yer well is low and ya need to drill for more water can't hurt no one."

"Then what?" demanded the preacher. "What do you say when they ask where? Perhaps you've never read the words of Sir Walter Scott, 'Oh, what a tangled web we weave, when first we practice to deceive!'"

"Won't much matter if we hit oil," stormed Jonah in rebuttal.

"Probably not," mimicked Reverend Small, "providin' the good Lord doesn't get mad at me for lettin' you follow Satan's call."

"Please stop," pleaded Betsy. "We agreed to support Jonah. There's no sense getting everyone excited about oil unless it happens. I don't see any harm if he tells the blacksmith that he needs something to drill for water."

"Well, come to think of it," observed the minister, in a sudden thought, "Jonah might just make the money he needs for his bit by offering to find water on some of the other farms around here."

"Not a bad idea," responded Jonah, "as long as someone else does the diggin'."

"Why don't we go see the blacksmith now?" asked Seth, eager to get out of the kitchen.

"Makes sense," answered Jonah, "and if it looks promisin', we'll take down trees for the springpole after we get back. That'll keep us goin' till it's time for ya to do some fishin'."

Reverend Small, who was also relieved by the break in bickering, seized the moment to announce he would spend the day getting ready for his first service.

"It's almost here, and I have a lot to do," he declared. "I can't let folks down. They're expecting something more than an ordinary sermon. And I suspect you are too."

"It better be good if you expect me to stay for the whole thing," challenged the dowser with a mischievous grin. "Promisin' to come don't mean promisin' to stay."

By now, Jonah and Seth had made it to the kitchen door. "Let's go, Mister Fisherman!" commanded the dowser. And off they went.

As they walked toward the blacksmith shop, Seth launched a cascade of questions. "Do you really think there's oil by the salt spring? Why do you need a bit? Why can't we just dig for the oil? And what if we don't find any? Does that mean you'll go?"

Jolted by the inevitable question that he had evaded since his decision to stay, Jonah was forced to weigh his reply.

"Well, first off, it seems pretty likely there's somethin' besides water around that spring. Drake's never pulled so hard. Can't say for certain it's oil, but the only way to find out is to drill, and that's where the bit comes in.

"If it's oil, it's most likely down deep. Too deep to dig. What the bit does is cut a hole through the dirt and rock till it either hits water or oil or it don't. Anyway, kickin' down a well ain't easy. Hard to say what'll happen if nothin' comes of it."

"Can't you stay even if you don't find oil?" Seth rejoined.

"Don't really know for sure, young fella," Jonah answered in genuine honesty. "Let's just hope we hit oil early on."

Seth said nothing but, after spotting a stone on the road, he took careful aim and kicked it off into the brush.

Jonah rued his candor. He had no wish to hurt the boy yet he had no desire to make a promise he might never keep. As he grappled for something to say, he too spotted a stone and sent it flying deep into the roadside brush. The act startled Seth. Uncertain whether Jonah was angry or simply challenging him to a kicking contest, the lad picked up another stone and hurled it aimlessly into the woods.

"Yer never gonna hit a rabbit or a squirrel tossin' stones like that," Jonah grumbled deliberately. "Watch this."

The dowser reached down, snatched up three good-sized stones and, in rapid succession, threw them at a fence post several feet away. All three hit the post with a staccato of loud thumps.

Distracted from his disappointment, Seth picked up a single stone and tried hitting the same post. He missed.

"That's somethin' else ya can learn," said Jonah, stuffing his hands into his front pockets. "If ya get good enough, ya can bring down a squirrel sittin' in a tree. 'Course, it'll take three or four of 'em to make a decent meal."

Then, for the first time that Seth could remember, Jonah laughed. "Just joshin', young fella," he chuckled. "Did hit a squirrel once, but never could again. Must'a been an accident."

"You had me fooled," the boy laughed.

With the edge of town now within sight, Seth pointed to a house and shed just off the road. The shed had two large, open doors. Nearby were an outdoor forge and a small pile of charcoal. "That's where we're going," the lad announced.

"Not a word about oil," ordered Jonah.

The blacksmith saw them coming and wandered outside to get a better look at the approaching large, barrel-chested stranger.

"This ain't the new preacher I've been hearin' about, is it?" asked the blacksmith.

"No sir," Seth replied. "This is my friend Jonah. He came by the same day as the preacher and stayed on to help with haying and some of the other chores."

"What brings ya here?" the smith inquired.

"Find water for a livin'," answered Jonah. "The well on this young fella's place is lower than it ought to be. Already got a pretty good idea where to drill for a new well, but the springpole is gonna need a good drill bit."

"Ya want me to make the bit?" queried the blacksmith.

"Ever made one?" the dowser asked.

"Can't say that I have, but I make most things that folks draw up for me."

Jonah bent down, took a small broken branch from the ground, and began to draw the outline of the bit he wanted.

"That shouldn't be hard," proclaimed the smith, "but it's gonna take more iron than I've got. Could take a while. You ready to put some money down for it?"

"Not yet," hedged Jonah. "How much ya lookin' for?"

"At least five dollars to get started," he was told.

"Been travelin' west. Ain't got near that kinda money," revealed the dowser. "Neither does this young fella's mother. Know anyone lookin' for help?"

"Not off hand," said the smith, "but I've got to get some iron anyway. I'll do your bit for ten dollars. Come back when ya can pay me the five dollars to start."

"Should be back before long," declared Jonah confidently.

On their way home, Seth began pummeling Jonah with a new round of questions.

"Where are you gonna get all that money, Jonah? Can't you start without the bit? What makes you so sure you won't hit oil if you dig? Can't Drake tell you how deep to go? If no one offers you money to work, will you give up and leave?"

"Ya sure ask a lot of questions," bemoaned the dowser.

"Could start puttin' up the springpole now," he continued, trying to answer Seth's questions, "but that's a little like puttin' the wagon before the horse. It don't make much sense to do all that work without the ten dollars for the smith."

"And diggin' for oil don't make sense neither," he added. "Even the colonel went down seventy feet. And most other folks have been goin' down a lot farther. Fact is, Drake's a little hard to read sometimes. But one thing seems sure—whatever it is, it's big!"

"Why don't you ask ol' Barnes if he needs help," offered Seth. "He said it looked like he could use both of us. If you worked for him, you wouldn't have to move on."

"Been thinkin' about that," agreed Jonah. "Maybe we oughta head over there. Could be ol' Barnes is willin' and able to pay for some help. Findin' out now will save doin' it tomorrow. If he don't need help, we can start lookin' elsewhere in the mornin'."

It was nearly noon when they reached the neighboring farm. As they approached, they saw Barnes working alone, scythe in hand, mowing in a field that had barely been touched. After every few swaths, he'd pause, rest for a moment, and resume cutting. Looking up during a break, he saw Seth and Jonah approaching and put down his scythe. He headed toward them, meeting them on the road.

"What brings you two back so soon?" he asked wearily.

"Well," began Jonah, "seems this young fella and his mother are beginnin' to run a little low on water. Figured we could kick down a new well with a springpole if we could find a few dollars to cover a drill bit from the blacksmith. Ya said you might be able to use the two of us," the dowser added, "so we figured we'd see if ya needed help now."

"How much are you asking?" Barnes inquired.

"The bit's gonna run us ten dollars," Jonah replied, "and we'd kinda like to start while the weather's half decent. The quicker we can make the ten dollars, the quicker we can start."

"Come up to the house," invited the farmer. "My wife Bessie should have some lunch ready about now. She can't come to the field with food or water anymore, but she's still does a mean job in the kitchen. I'm sure she'll find something for all of us."

Jonah and Seth settled on the porch while Barnes went inside. When he returned, he was laden with bread, cheese, and a large pitcher of water. As he sliced enough bread for the three of them, he looked at Jonah and asked, "Are you ready to do some more haying?"

"Could be if the money's good," the dowser answered.

"If you help me finish cutting that field, turn it over in when it's ready and bring the hay in as soon as it's dry, I'll give you five dollars," Barnes declared.

"That's shy of what we need," bargained Jonah.

"If you can find me a good well, I'll give you the other five."

"Done," said Jonah, with a smile and a nod, clearly delighted that his search was over so quickly. "Just remember that once the site is marked, yer gonna hafta get someone else to do the diggin' or the drillin'."

Barnes too was pleased. Too proud to go hunting for help, he was determined to go it alone as long as he could. The fact that help had come to him was almost too good to be true. If the money would help Seth and his mother, that was even better.

After a brief lull, Jonah asked, "Where do ya keep your tools?"

"Scythes are hanging up in the barn. So are a couple sickles," he answered, "assuming the boy is part of the bargain."

"Yup," Seth intervened, eager to show his mettle.

For the rest of that afternoon, the three cut swath after swath of tall grass, letting it fall in orderly windrows across the field.

When they reached and mowed the last corner of the field, Barnes was jubilant. "It's so dry we can probably turn some of this over in a day or two," he declared. "And the rest we can probably do a day or two later." Jonah agreed.

When they got back to the road, the old farmer stuck his hand into a pocket, pulled out a five-dollar bill, handed it to Jonah and said, "Go tell the smith to start on your bit."

The gesture took Jonah completely by surprise, but his only display of emotion was a small smile and a muted thanks. "Seein' there's still time before dinner, might as well get it done now," he announced. "Care to go along, young fella?"

Seth nodded enthusiastically, even though he was tired, and the two started down the road toward town. Halfway there, the lad spotted and kicked a stone into the bush, but the dowser ignored the challenge. Seth tried again and, when his attempt to engage Jonah was disregarded a second time, he decided to indulge in youthful curiosity.

"How long's the blacksmith gonna take?" he asked.

"Never did discuss that," Jonah replied. "Guess it depends on how quick he gets the iron. Doesn't matter much, 'cause we still got a lot of hayin' left to do. After that's done, we've gotta take down a couple trees, trim off the branches and set up the springpole. Not likely we'll finish all that in a day or so."

"Ya sure ya want to walk all the way to the blacksmith?" Jonah probed, sensing Seth's fatigue. "Not a bad time to work in some fishin' even if it's still a little hot."

"Rather see what the smith says when you give him the money," said Seth, declining the suggestion. "Bet he'll be surprised."

Jonah laughed. "Ya know, this strikes me as a pretty good omen. Who'd a thought we'd get the five so quick? Just wait till your mother and the preacher hear what's happened!"

"What an omen?" asked the boy.

"Well, it's a sign," the dowser explained. "There's all kinds of signs, good ones and bad ones. Like when your mother called the preacher and me godsends. Seems to me the chance of hittin' oil is gettin' better everyday. But remember, young fella, we gotta keep it to ourselves."

It wasn't long before the blacksmith's house and shed came into sight as they rounded the last bend outside of town. Jonah quickened his pace and, despite his fatigue, Seth managed to keep up. The smith, who was outside scavenging through a pile of discarded scrap iron and steel, caught sight of them approaching but kept to the task at hand.

As Jonah and Seth left the road, the smith looked up and asked, "Still lookin' for work?"

"Got half the money," replied Jonah holding the bill in his outstretched hand. "Figured ya needed it more than me."

"Truth is, I was expectin' ya," drawled the blacksmith. "I saw ya workin' for ol' Barnes when I went by his place this afternoon.

He's a good man. Never keeps ya waitin' for your pay. I know 'cause I shoe his horses."

"Any idea when ya can start on the bit?" the dowser asked.

"About the time you finish hayin'," he was told as the smith headed toward the house.

"Good," proclaimed Jonah.

At supper, talk focused on Reverend Small and the worship service he would lead Sunday morning. After assuring both Betsy and Reverend Small that he would attend as promised, Jonah retired to the barn, never mentioning the money or the visit to the blacksmith. That he left for Seth to reveal.

—

The crowd began to build outside the schoolhouse long before Reverend Small had even left the farm. By the time he arrived with the Blakes, who had come by to pick him up in their buggy, the grounds were covered by scores of people, young and old, dressed in their Sunday best. Most were busy, engaging in conversations with neighbors and friends.

It was a sunny morning, still pleasant from the cooler temperatures that lingered after sunrise. The sky was almost cloudless, a sign of the scorching heat to come. In anticipation, several families took shelter beneath two large shade trees.

Revered Small got his first glimpse of the crowd from the road, long before Art turned the horse onto the school grounds. "Praise the Lord," murmured the minister, deeply touched by the turnout. Even the Blakes seemed surprised by the size of the crowd.

"Looks like half the county is here," said Art. "Guess we did a better job getting the word out than we thought."

As he pulled the horse to a halt beside the school, the buggy was quickly surrounded. The new minister was warmly welcomed and, as he alighted and moved among those greeting him, he recognized several faces from his visit to Blake's store. After chatting briefly with several families, he pulled a watch from his vest pocket, checked the time, and strove toward a table and chair someone had placed near the schoolhouse door. He removed his hat, placed it on the chair and, Bible in hand, turned toward the still-growing assembly.

"Come closer," he invited the crowd, "and listen to the word of our Lord!"

The people closest to him began to take places on the grass. Men who were chatting with their peers rejoined their families, and many of the women produced family Bibles they had brought with them. The chatter subsided, and the entire field became silent. Nearly everyone focused on the man standing beside the table, each waiting for his first words.

"Many of you here this morning may be expecting a sermon on fire and brimstone," he began. "And I won't disappoint you. Such sermons are all about man's rebellion and God's wrath."

Reverend Small paused briefly to turn the pages of his Bible to the passage he sought. "It's here in the nineteenth chapter of Genesis, beginning at the twenty-fourth verse," he told the crowd. "'Then the Lord rained upon Sodom and upon Gomorrah brimstone and fire from the Lord out of heaven; and he overthrew those cities, and all the plain, and all the inhabitants of the cities, and that which grew upon the ground.'"

He paused again, building anticipation among the women and men alike, even those who had heard such sermons before.

"But we can't stop there," he declared. "The message is not only about God's anger and wrath, it's also about His love and mercy. Let's not forget the conversation between God and Abraham that we find in the preceding chapter, beginning with the twenty-third verse. 'And Abraham drew near, and said, "Wilt thou also destroy the righteous with the wicked? Peradventure there be fifty righteous within the city; wilt thou also destroy and not spare the place for the fifty righteous that are therein? That be far from thee to do after this manner, to slay the righteous with the wicked: and that the righteous should be as the wicked, that be far from thee: Shall not the Judge of all the earth do right?"'"

Once more, he paused. "Let's not ignore the fact that God offered to spare the city if He could find as few as ten righteous people within its walls.

"What, then, does it mean to be righteous?" he asked, gazing across the assembly like a schoolteacher waiting for someone to raise a hand. "Is it simply living in an upright manner? Is it nothing more than doing what you believe is right? Let's see what Scripture says!" he cried.

"We can find countless clues to righteousness throughout the Bible," he continued, "but for today, let's see if we can find some of the characteristics in the writing of Saint Paul. Turn with me, if you will, to the Book of Romans, chapter twelve, starting with the ninth verse."

Reverend Small paused again, waiting and watching as many in the crowd, particularly women and some older children, searched through their Bibles hurriedly, sometimes in cheerful competition with their neighbors. When their eyes shifted from the Scripture back to their new minister, he resumed.

"'Let love be without dissimulation. Abhor that which is evil; cleave to that which is good. Be kindly affectioned one to another with brotherly love; in honour preferring one another; Not slothful in business; fervent in spirit; serving the Lord; Rejoicing in hope;

patient in tribulation; continuing instant in prayer; Distributing to the necessity of saints; given to hospitality.'

"Sounds easy enough, does it not?" he asked. "Who among us does not hate evil or does not hold fast to that which is good? Don't we all try to love one another? Don't we all try hard to be patient in tribulation?

"Perhaps we should go on," he suggested, raising his Bible.

"'Bless them which persecute you: bless, and curse not. Rejoice with them that do rejoice, weep with them that weep. Be of the same mind one toward another. Mind not high things, but condescend to men of low estate. Be not wise in your own conceits.

"'Recompense to no man evil for evil. Provide things honest in the sight of all men. If it be possible, as much as lieth in you, live peaceably with all men. Dearly beloved, avenge not yourselves, but rather give place unto wrath: for it is written, Vengeance is mine, I will repay, saith the Lord. Therefore, if thine enemy hunger, feed him; if he thirst, give him drink: for in so doing thou shalt heap coals of fire on his head. Be not overcome of evil, but overcome evil with good.'"

His voice rose as he uttered the final phrase of the passage and, with a flourish, he closed the Bible in his outstretched hand. He placed the book reverently on the table and then sat carefully on the table's edge.

"Who among us can declare themselves righteous?" Reverend Small asked the assembly. "Who can say they live day-in and day-out by even these simple standards? I doubt anyone. Let's not forget the sixth verse in the fifty-third chapter of Isaiah: 'All we like sheep have gone astray.' Friends, to truly understand our Creator we must first recognize that He is not simply a God of fire and brimstone, but more emphatically, a God of love.

"What better example is there than the sixteenth verse of the third chapter of John, a verse that I'm sure most of you know, 'For God so loved the world, that he gave his only begotten Son, that whosoever believeth in Him should not perish, but have everlasting life.'

"This is where we must start," he concluded with a broad smile. It was certainly one of the shortest sermons he had ever delivered, yet deep inside he was confident it achieved what he hoped to achieve. Even now, he had their rapt attention. Every eye and ear was his.

Reverend Small then lowered his head, closed his eyes, and began to pray.

"Almighty God, rest your hand upon every individual here today, blessing them and helping them and their families according to their most personal and most pressing needs, physically, mentally, emotionally and, above all, spiritually. May they never hesitate to turn to Thee, O Lord; for this we pray in Jesus name. Amen."

Although surprised and pleased by the brevity of the service, the crowd remained silent and immobile. Would he not continue in some way? Even though there were no piano or other musical instruments, would he not lead them in a favorite hymn or two?

It took only a moment or two for the minister to recognize their bewilderment. "Ah, I can see you're all looking for more," he exclaimed. "Let's take a vote. If you'd like me to resume with my entire three-hour sermon, remain seated. But if you'd like to visit with me for a little bit and come back for more next Sunday, please rise."

Bewilderment quickly turned to amusement, and the crowd bounded to its feet. Those closest to Reverend Small engaged him in conversation while those further away tended to coalesce into small groups. And, as the adults chatted, the kids broke away from their families in search of friends.

The minister moved deftly through the crowd, eager to show his respects to those he had met at Blakes and, at the same time, greet those he had not yet met. Given the size of the crowd, it was a hopeless task. Supporters, like Ruth Black and the Blakes, were largely ignored while others, like the blacksmith and his family, warranted brief but good, old–fashioned handshakes and small talk.

Betsy, Seth, and Jonah, who had arrived just moments before the service began and had begun chatting with Stephen Barnes, were rewarded with a smile and a wave. The smile began to fade, however, when Reverend Small suddenly spotted Lucas Bennett within a few feet of Jonah.

"You must be the dowser I've been hearing about," declared Lucas as he extended his hand. "Could be," replied Jonah as he grasped the hand and shook it gently.

"My name's Lucas," the man continued. "Allow me to welcome you to our neck of the woods. Are you here to stay a spell or just passing through?"

"Too early to tell," replied Jonah. Intrigued by the open, friendly manner of this short, balding intruder, he added, "Sure seems like a nice enough town."

"If you can really bring in wells with your divining rod, it's a perfect place to open business," said Lucas. "Let me know if you decide to stay. I'd be happy to help get you started."

By now, Betsy had maneuvered herself alongside Lucas so that she could reveal her irritation to Jonah without Lucas's knowledge. But when neither her frown nor her finger over her lips caught Jonah's attention, she spoke out forcefully.

"It's time for us to go, Jonah!"

"And for me as well," said Lucas. "Good meeting you, Jonah."

"Never speak to that scoundrel again," admonished Betsy as soon as Lucas was out of earshot.

"Why not?" challenged Jonah. "Seems like a decent sort. Who knows, he might even be a big help someday."

"Take my word for it," sighed Betsy. "He's no good."

The young widow moved swiftly toward the road, leaving Seth and Jonah to ponder her last words. But just as Jonah was about to follow, he felt a hand on his shoulder.

"Thanks for keeping your promise," declared Reverend Small. "It meant a lot to see you here when I know you could have been using the Lord's Day for some well-deserved rest. I hope you found some good in my message."

"Well, maybe, a little," allowed Jonah, "but if being good ain't good enough, ya got a long way to go."

"That I do, Jonah. That I do," agreed Reverend Small.

"And remember yer promise," said Jonah as he set off with Seth.

"That I do, Jonah. That I do," repeated the minister, now encircled by the family whose invitation to their home for Sunday dinner he had accepted.

To keep pace with Jonah's long strides, Seth found himself running then walking, then running again. But, far sooner than Seth expected, they overtook Betsy, walking past her and others on the road with neither greeting nor comment.

Perhaps it's just as well, thought Betsy as she watched Jonah and her son forge ahead in their unpretentious race. *Rather than give folks something to talk about, it's better that I walk back to the farm alone.*

She was still deep in contemplation when Barnes and his wife pulled alongside with a small wagon they used whenever they visited town. He pulled the team to a halt, reached down to help Betsy board and, with a smile, suggested that they wave as they passed Jonah and Seth who were well ahead but still in sight.

"I can't see where that would hurt," giggled Betsy.

Barnes chuckled as he gave the team a light touch of his whip. By the time they caught up to Jonah and Seth, the team was kicking up just enough dust to send the two scurrying off the road. Both Betsy and the Barnes laughed and waved vigorously as they drove by.

The trip was over in no time and, after letting herself down from the wagon, she made a point of asking Barnes what he thought of Jonah.

"One thing's for sure," the old timer responded, "he's not afraid of work."

"I was hoping for more than that!" lamented Betsy.

"Well," Barnes reflected, "I like to summer and winter with folks before I make any judgments. Truth is I like Jonah, and I have no cause to find fault with the man up to now."

"Thanks," replied Betsy. "That helps."

Back in her kitchen, she began putting together a midday meal, much of which came from her small garden. She was still at work when she spied Jonah and Seth through the kitchen window. They paused at the pump long enough to wash off the dust on their hands, arms, and faces before parading into the house.

"I was ready to give you up as lost," teased Betsy.

"We'd have been here long ago," muttered Jonah, "but some crazy folks in a wagon kicked up a storm and covered us with dust. And since we swallowed most of it, we don't need much to eat."

"Try anyway," instructed Betsy as she steered them to the table. "There's not much nourishment in a dust storm."

Once seated, the three hesitated until each realized that in the absence of Reverend Small, there was no one to offer thanks for the food before them. It had become a ritual they had learned to accept, appreciate, and now, it seemed, require.

"What we need is a little prayer," suggested Betsy.

"How about a prayer from way back?" asked Jonah, delighting Betsy and Seth.

"Lord, please bless this food and the hands that prepared it," he prayed softly with his head bowed and his eyes closed. "Amen," intoned the three in unison.

"No need for the preacher to know it was me," ordered Jonah.

"Agreed," said Betsy.

CHAPTER 6

Supper that evening was a happy affair as Reverend Small shared details of his day. The response to his first sermon exceeded his fondest hopes and dreams. Many of those with whom he spoke praised his brevity while others admired the note of anticipation on which he closed. As he mentioned the names of individuals and families who had captured his attention and interest, he sometimes paused in the hope that Betsy might offer some personal commentary about them. But she refrained, content to let the minister reach his own opinions.

Jonah and Seth listened politely, alternately intrigued and amused by the conversations and experiences that Reverend Small related. They especially enjoyed his accounts of the invitations to Sunday dinner that he received since, in many instances, the woman of the house promised him blue ribbon meals and desserts.

Saved until breakfast the next morning was a glowing account of the invitation he accepted, the meal he enjoyed, and the time spent getting to know the family whose hospitality included a tour of their huge farm, the largest in the county.

"These are real God–fearing folks. They are far more concerned about discovering the will of God than they are about success and prosperity," the minister remarked casually, hoping that his not-so-subtle intent would not be lost on the adults present, especially Jonah.

"Time for me to get over to Barnes," announced Jonah, rising from his chair. "If we're ever gonna get to know what prosperity is, Seth and I better earn our first five dollars!"

"Far be it from me to impede your enterprise," lamented Reverend Small as he crossed his arms, threw his head back, and slowly nodded in half-hearted despair.

The week slipped past quickly. With Jonah and Seth assisting Barnes and Reverend Small visiting families throughout the township, Betsy devoted her daytime to chores she was accustomed to doing herself. Having already begun to harvest a variety of vegetables from her garden, she set aside two days to clean and expand her root cellar, a small room her husband had dug out beneath the house to store crops like beets, carrots, and potatoes.

It was also a retreat from the midday sun and heat. Even with the door open, the room was nearly dark; but it was comfortably cool. Once her eyes adjusted to the dim light, she dug away at one of the dirt walls, enlarging a waist-high cavity for additional storage. She removed the dirt in buckets, often waiting until they were almost too full and too heavy to carry.

But it was also a time for Betsy to struggle with the tension created by Jonah's pursuit of oil. *Is it wrong to wish for wealth?* she wondered. *Is it any less acceptable to prosper from oil than to prosper from successful farming? Having lost my husband to the moral issue of slavery, must I again be deprived by another moral issue? Is that not terribly unfair?*

At other times her thoughts shifted to the men responsible for her dilemma.

Jonah is clearly a good man. To be sure, he is often quiet and reserved, but he is also practical and wise. He can be humble or combative but, when he chooses the latter, it is usually with wit. His bond with Seth and his help with the farm are truly godsends.

Yet, in many ways, Jonah remains a stranger. Where is he from, and why did he leave? Is he driven simply by a need to prove he can discover oil as easily as water with the help of Drake? Or is wealth his only true ambition? If he does strike oil on the farm, will he stay or will he hit the road? Is he just another drifter unable to ever settle down?

And what of Reverend Small? He too is obviously a good man. He is no longer stiff and formal but relaxed and genuinely at ease with those around him. Nor is he still as prone to rush to judgment. His ministry is winning over many, though only time will tell how lasting the appeal.

He is thoughtful and kind, not only helping in the field but sometimes in the kitchen as well. In the case of Seth, he clearly defers to Jonah, but it seems certain that he will befriend the lad whenever appropriate.

If only he would stop criticizing Jonah's pursuit of oil and the wealth it might bring. His pledge to help raise the springpole is untested. And as his relationships with the community grow, will he move to another home where larger, more comfortable quarters and better food are certain?

Despite a brief urge to dismiss both men as opportunists, Betsy chose to think of them as potential rivals for her hand.

By Saturday, Jonah had secured the other five dollars he had been promised by Barnes in return for dowsing for water. After an extensive search, Jonah and Drake had found a highly promising site, which Barnes was content to mark and leave until he was ready to dig or drill. And, to the delight of everyone, Barnes had presented Seth with a fine ham for all the work Seth had done.

With the help of Art Blake and his buggy, Reverend Small had managed to visit many of the families who had previously been bulwarks of the church. He had been cheerfully welcomed by all and assured of their support. Once they learned he was unmarried, wives with unwed sisters often prevailed on him to remain for leisurely meals.

When Art Blake returned with his buggy Sunday morning, he was pleasantly surprised to find Reverend Small joined by Betsy, Seth, and Jonah. Art summoned Betsy to the front seat and assigned the two men and Seth to the rear. As they pulled into the field beside the school, they discovered they were the first to arrive.

While Betsy and Seth sought the early morning shade on the western side of the schoolhouse, Art and Jonah moved the teacher's desk outside. Reverend Small followed with a chair and was soon engrossed in last minute Bible study and prayer.

Art and Jonah meandered over to the buggy where Art broke their silence. "I don't mean to talk out of school," he began without recognizing the pun, "but neither Betsy nor Reverend Small really expected you to join them here this morning." When Jonah just nodded in response, Art continued. "Make no mistake, we're all really glad you came."

"Well, just between the two of us," Jonah replied, "it ain't quite like it appears. The good preacher and me have a deal. In return for listenin' to his sermons, he promised to help me raise my springpole."

"I heard you plan to drill for more water out there," Art acknowledged. "Frankly, the whole thing strikes me as a little strange since

I've never heard of Betsy's well going dry. Is it really worth the trouble?"

Reaching down for a stalk of grass, Jonah stifled an impulse to reveal his real intentions. "Maybe not," he finally said, "but I'm hopin' to hit an artesian so she'll never hafta worry."

The answer seemed to satisfy Art. After noting the arrival of several families, he set off in search of Esther, who had chosen to walk from their home above the store. Jonah, realizing that others might be as curious, if not suspicious, about his springpole made a mental note to tell Betsy, Seth, and Reverend Small so they could explain his plans as he had just done with Art.

Jonah retreated from the gathering crowd until he found a grassy spot far enough away to be alone yet close enough to hear the sermon. While he waited for Reverend Small to begin, his mind began to wander back to the springpole, the five dollars in his pocket, and his dream of striking oil. Thus engaged, he was caught off guard when a voice from behind sounded a greeting.

Turning, he found himself face to face with Lucas Bennett.

"It seems like too nice a morning to be sitting in church, even if it is outdoors," Lucas began. "But, who knows, maybe the sermon will be worth our time. Mind if I join you?"

Jonah nodded reluctantly and then scanned the grounds to see if Betsy was likely to see them. She was and she did. As Lucas dropped down beside him, Jonah could feel Betsy scowl even though she was too far away for any visible confirmation.

"You know, Jonah, I've been thinking about you a lot," said Lucas. "You've got a great future here if you decide to stay. Once you hit water, the word will spread quickly, and there will be more work than you can handle. I like to invest in success. Tell me what you need, and it's yours."

"Already got more than enough," said Jonah, flattered by the unsolicited offer. "But thanks just the same."

Both men watched as Reverend Small lifted his Bible over his head as a means of quieting the crowd. It didn't take long. With a loud, solemn call to prayer, heads bowed down. The second Sunday service had begun.

"Heavenly Father, you know each and every heart. You know our ups and our downs, our joys and our sorrows, our hopes and our fears. Only you, O Lord, know why each of us is here today. Whether we're here because we want to be or because we have to be, abide with us and lead us, O Lord. Help each one of us find a meaningful relationship with Thee."

He then closed with a simple "Amen."

"For those of you who might have felt short–changed last Sunday, I have good news," the minister proclaimed with a broad smile. "Today's message is the three–hour sermon that most of you postponed by getting to your feet."

"Oh, no!" cried someone to the delight of the crowd.

"Such insubordination will not be tolerated," said Reverend Small, trying especially hard to look stern, "unless you make amends by promising to bring someone new next Sunday."

"So be it," sighed the same voice.

The banter was rewarded by laughter from the crowd. Charmed by his good nature and his humor, young and old alike smiled approvingly. And as he experienced their warmth, he could sense their longing for spiritual insight. Thus emboldened, he picked up his focus from the previous Sunday with a challenge:

"My friends, when all is said and done, aren't we deceiving ourselves when we think we can live completely righteous lives? Haven't we all fallen short? Aren't we all weary and heavy–laden? Aren't we all searching for peace of mind and true happiness? Of course we are. We're no different than anyone else, present or past."

"It began in the Garden of Eden," Reverend Small continued, "and men and women have struggled ever since to put themselves right with God. Do you really think we're different? Just ask Saint Paul. In the third chapter of Romans, the twenty-third verse, he declares '... all have sinned and come short of the glory of God.'

"Isn't it time we all acknowledge our sinful nature and turn to God for forgiveness? When we do, we find something truly incredible. We find that God is waiting to forgive us, again and again and again, if only we ask.

"Yet as simple as this seems, it's here that we inevitably come face-to-face with the hurdles of faith and reason. Good people, it's not enough for me to declare that there is a God. Nor is it enough for me to declare that He loves each and every one of us. Only you can decide whether God is real and, if so, whether you want a personal and lasting relationship with Him and with His son, Jesus Christ.

"Should you conclude, as I have, that there is a God and that He is a loving God, these words of Jesus, recorded by Saint Matthew in the eleventh chapter, will assume significant meaning and promise: 'Come unto me, all ye that labour and are heavy laden, and I will give you rest. Take my yoke upon you, and learn of me; for I am meek and lowly in heart: and ye shall find rest unto your souls. For my yoke is easy, and my burden is light.'"

By now, the morning sun had slid behind darkening clouds, and the first few scattered raindrops began to multiply. Prodded by his wife, Art Blake rose to his feet, strode quickly to the school building, and reopened its door. Reverend Small hesitated briefly but, as people scrambled to their feet, he encouraged women and children to take shelter. Most of the men and boys headed for the large shade trees that surrounded the field and the umbrella–like protection they offered. Two, however, remained on the grassy expanse, seemingly indifferent to the light, intermittent rain.

"Guess the Lord didn't care too much for that sermon," laughed Lucas, holding up his outstretched hand and watching a few tiny drops collect in his palm. "Just goes to show there are better ways to spend Sunday morning. But then, if I hadn't come by I probably wouldn't have had a chance to palaver with you."

"Can't rightly agree," replied Jonah, sitting upright with his arms wrapped around his knees. "This ain't no ordinary preacher. He ain't afraid to work up a sweat in the field. And, fact is, he's gettin' pretty good with a scythe."

"What's that got to do with his sermons?" challenged Lucas.

"Well, he's pretty good with words too," drawled Jonah. "Gotta admit he makes me think about God Almighty. Kinda wonder what else he might say this mornin' when this little shower lets up."

Moments later, the rain did stop. Having barely dampened the ground, it proved disappointing to the farmers who had started to pray for a good, soaking rain. Reverend Small, meanwhile, returned to his open–air pulpit, urged everyone to bring a neighbor or friend to the next service and then lifted his arms and pronounced a brief benediction. Almost immediately, he was once again surrounded by families anxious to invite him home for a visit over Sunday dinner.

By now, Jonah had managed to break away from Lucas, only to find himself under the burning gaze of Betsy as she and Seth left the field and headed toward the road home. Eager to assure Betsy that he had done nothing wrong, he lengthened his stride just enough to join mother and son at the edge of the road.

"Hope ya haven't jumped to any conclusions," teased Jonah.

"About what?" retorted Betsy with a lingering stare.

"Lucas," muttered Jonah defensively. "Trust ya noticed he came up behind me and did most of the talkin'."

"About what?" she repeated.

"Says he wants me to stay around and work up a business findin' water for folks who don't have enough for themselves and their stock," Jonah answered. "He even offered to lend me money to get started."

"I'll bet he's already figured out what you're up to," said Betsy, more clearly annoyed.

"Don't see how," Jonah responded, shaking his head in disbelief. "Except for Seth and the preacher and yerself, no one knows we're lookin' for oil. Not even the smith."

Then, after pausing to search his pockets, he added, "Come to think of it, the smith needs the rest of the money for the drill."

"Wait until tomorrow for that," Betsy commanded. "It's a sin to do business on Sunday. That's what I expect from heathen, and I'll not have anyone like that around Seth and me. Today is for worship and rest."

Coming from Betsy, the words stung more than earlier rebukes from Reverend Small.

Why is she so mad? he wondered. *Didn't I refuse Lucas's offer? Didn't I defend Sunday worship in general and the preacher in particular? Isn't she being terribly unreasonable?*

As these thoughts took hold, Jonah fell back, leaving Betsy and Seth to walk alone. Soon aware of their separation, Betsy quickly realized she had been too harsh. Taking Seth's arm, she stopped and turned to look back.

"Don't dawdle," she commanded with a widening smile. "Seth and I are hungry enough to finish dinner all by ourselves."

"Yes, ma'am," replied the bewitched and bewildered Jonah.

—

After helping Seth with morning chores and a hasty breakfast, Jonah headed toward town alone, anxious to make his final payment for the bit. As he walked, his mind wandered between the events of the previous day and the expectation that he could begin drilling before the week had passed.

Without the boy to slow his pace, he arrived at the blacksmith shop even before the smith had a chance to begin his daily routine. "Should have your bit ready sometime tomorrow," volunteered the smith as he stoked smoldering embers that had been banked overnight. "Probably ain't necessary," added the smith. "But I'd kinda like to get the eye on top centered a little better. The bit's not balanced as good as it could be. Once it's true, it should drill straight down with a little more impact from each strike."

"Appreciate it," said Jonah, digging in his pocket for the five dollars he still owed. "Here's the rest of yer money."

"How's your springpole comin'?" asked the smith.

"Still hafta cut down the trees and trim 'em, but they're all picked out," Jonah responded. "Should have all the timber cut by suppertime."

"Got enough rope?" the smith inquired.

"Enough to get started, but, to be honest, it wouldn't hurt to have a bit more," the dowser answered. "Settin' up the springpole is gonna use up a lotta rope, but it's gotta be sturdy. Can't risk it comin' down. Chances are we could run out if we hafta go down very deep."

Concerned that that the questions might be leading toward

revelations he could ill afford to make, Jonah bid the smith a good day, promising to be back before dark the next day.

His walk back to the farm took even less time that the journey to the blacksmith's shop and, as he approached the farm, Seth ran to meet him.

"How come you didn't wait for me?" the lad demanded.

"Couldn't afford to let ya get all tired out, young fella. We got a lotta work to do today. There's trees to drop and trim. After that, we need to drag the poles over to the salt spring."

The prospect of cutting down trees ended Seth's brief assault. "I'll go get the axes from the barn," the youngster offered. With nothing more than a nod of approval from Jonah, Seth disappeared into the barn and, moments later, emerged with two axes and a small hatchet.

Jonah set the sharpest ax aside and sent Seth back into the barn for the stone he used to sharpen the scythes and sickle.

"This ain't the best way to sharpen an ax," he lamented, "but it'll hafta do. Coulda taken these with me to the blacksmith this mornin'. He's got a wheel that woulda dressed these up in no time."

Once Jonah produced an edge on the blade that he was happy with, he started to put the stone in his back pocket. Seth, however, reached for it, explaining, "Maybe I better sharpen up my hatchet too."

Jonah watched silently as Seth ran the stone back and forth across the cutting edge of the hatchet, trying hard to duplicate the strokes he had witnessed. "Bear down a little harder," the dowser instructed, "that blade's really dull."

Yet rather than wait for the boy to tire from the almost impossible task of sharpening the hatchet with the small stone, Jonah grabbed the two axes in one hand, turned toward the spring, and beckoned Seth to follow.

The tall slender hemlock that Jonah had chosen looked even more perfect as they neared the spring and the edge of the woods.

"That's the tree we'll use for the springpole," Jonah said, pointing the two axes at it with the enormous might of his right hand and arm. "We'll start with that one. After it's trimmed and sized, we'll take down that oak over there to cradle it." Upon reaching the hemlock, Jonah circled it slowly, looking first at its trunk and then at its upper branches.

"Let's see how good we can drop it," he suggested, heading toward a nearby sapling with a trunk slightly larger than the handles of the two axes. With a few swings of the sharper ax, he quickly felled, trimmed, and cut the sapling until he had a four-foot long stake that he hammered into the ground several feet in front of the hemlock. "This is where it should fall," he told Seth. "Haven't dropped a tree this high in a long while, but with a little luck that trunk should fall dead center on top of that stake."

"What if it don't?" asked the boy quizzically.

"Sounds like ya want a wager," laughed Jonah. "Tell ya what—if the hemlock drops on that stake, ya gotta give me yer slice of cake or pie next time we get dessert. If it misses, ya get mine."

Seth folded his arms across his chest as he had seen Jonah do whenever he pondered a question or thought. "Done!" declared the lad, recalling the give-and-take between Jonah and Barnes before they agreed on the compensation for haying Barnes fields.

"Shake on it," Jonah ordered with a massive grin and an outstretched hand. Seth responded without hesitation and then followed Jonah to the oak. "Stay here till it's safe," the dowser said, "and say goodbye to yer dessert."

The dowser circled the hemlock once more, examining both the trunk and the shape and size of the needled branches above. After reflecting briefly, he began cutting a notch on the face of the trunk opposite the stake. Within minutes, Jonah stood back and took note of a clean, v-shaped notch that ran parallel to the ground. He then moved to the opposite side of the tree, cutting just above the notch. He swung the axe with fervor. Each blow shook the upper reaches of the tree with a resounding thud that fascinated Seth. Even the ground near the oak shuddered from the force of the axe as it bit into the hemlock.

As chips began to shower exposed roots of the tree, Jonah chopped with increasing vigor. Suddenly, there was a loud crack. He stood back and carefully examined the wounded tree. With two more well placed blows, the hemlock fell. As its upper reaches hit the ground, it sprung slightly to the right, a reaction set in motion by a large, unyielding limb.

"Let's take a look, young fella," Jonah shouted.

Jonah approached from the right side, Seth from the left. Yet even from a distance, both could see that the fallen tree was resting tightly against the stake and not on top.

"Shucks," declared the dowser. "Guess ya get to double up on dessert tonight. If it wasn't for that limb, ya never woulda seen that stake; it woulda been drove right outta sight."

Seth could barely hide his glee. "I've been thinkin' about that," he responded, hands in his back pockets, mimicking some of Jonah's slow, deliberate mannerisms and speech. "If ya promise to go fishin' with me after dinner, I'll let ya keep yer pie."

"How'd ya know it's pie?" demanded the adult.

"Is it a deal?" Seth insisted, without answering the question.

"Better think about it for a while," bargained Jonah, "it sounds like a high price to pay for a little piece of pie. By the time all the trees are dropped and trimmed, the time will be better spent restin' up instead of fishin'."

"You can always rest up by the creek," the boy countered.

"Suppose so," sighed Jonah, encouraging the lad's developing skills in negotiation and persistence. "Would ya be willin' to trade a half hour of fishin' for that slice of pie?"

"Make it an hour," Seth implored.

"Done, but not a minute more," surrendered the dowser as he returned to the stump, which protruded from the ground like a newly erected gravestone. While removing the axe he had buried in the top of the stump, Jonah directed Seth to clear away smaller branches with his hatchet, well away from the larger limbs that the dowser planned to trim working upwards from the base of the trunk.

As the morning sun grew hotter, they paused occasionally to enjoy the spring's clear, cool water. And once they reached a point about three-quarters of the way to the treetop, Jonah chopped off the smaller, remaining part of the tree.

What remained was a giant toothpick, somewhere between thirty feet and thirty-five feet long, neatly sheared of its limbs, large and small. Next on Jonah's agenda was the severed branches.

"How about haulin' those limbs over there," directed Jonah, pointing to a site where they would be out of the way.

Seth concurred with a silent nod, his hope of getting back to the house for an early lunch now dashed. Branch by branch, he created a pile several feet away from the fallen hemlock and, in doing so, surprised both himself and Jonah by the size of the limbs he was able to drag and throw onto the pile.

Shortly thereafter, Jonah felled the oak. Only then did he suggest that they break for their midday meal. Tired and hungry, the two headed toward the house for the bread and cheese that Betsy had promised. Seeing them approach, Betsy moved quickly to the porch to welcome them back for the late lunch.

"Anyone hungry?" she teased with a slight wink.

"Little bread and cheese would be good," answered Jonah seriously, failing to recognize Betsy's lighthearted flirting.

"I'm not hungry, I'm starved!" shouted Seth.

"Well, go wash up, and I'll bring the food to the porch. There's no need to eat in the house. I've been baking, and the kitchen is hotter than Hades," Betsy responded.

Jonah reached the pump first, gave the handle a few rapid strokes, splashed his face and arms just enough to get wet, and then ignored the well-worn towel Betsy had left. By the time Seth finished at the pump, Betsy had delivered their meal.

Seth did most of the talking over lunch, amusing Betsy with his slightly exaggerated account of the bet he had won. "I figured he'd drop that hemlock close to the stake," gloated the youngster, "but I was pretty sure he'd miss!"

"Sure hope you are better at drilling than you are at cutting down trees," said Betsy, aiming a big smile and another, longer wink at Jonah. "I can't be baking pies for men who can't hit stakes or oil wells."

The wink was unmistakable, and Jonah was flustered by it. "Always do my best," he eventually responded, "but there ain't much in the way of guarantees when it comes ta droppin' trees or strikin' oil."

"Well, there might just be an extra helping of pie for you tonight if you keep at it and quit early enough to take Seth fishing," she promised. "It's blueberry."

Jonah, already on his feet for the hike back to the woods, smiled cautiously. "Guess that means doin' a whole lot better," he pledged. "That's my favorite pie."

With that, he started back toward the woods with Seth trying desperately to keep up.

Work on the fallen oak went quickly and smoothly. Jonah soon created a Y-shaped post more than eight feet long to serve as a fulcrum, one that would hold the narrower end of the hemlock aloft. While he shaped the post, Seth kept busy cutting branches in fireplace lengths as Jonah had ordered.

Eventually, Jonah signaled an end to their workday, noting that their next task would be to collect rock and stone to anchor the largest end of the springpole.

Homeward bound with axes and hatchet, they talked about fishing and Seth's dream of catching the one that got away. And, in no time at all, they found themselves sitting by the creek. More than an hour passed without a nibble even though Seth frequently dangled the line in and out of the water, trying to rouse any fish that might be in the neighborhood.

Like all good fishermen, he took the experience in good humor. But, on the way home, Seth extracted a number of fishing stories from Jonah, and the dream of catching a pike, a big brother of the pickerel, was born.

Long before they reached the house, they could see Betsy and Reverend Small on the porch, deeply engaged in conversation. The late afternoon sun reflected softly off Betsy's cheeks and forehead, revealing a beauty that Jonah could hardly ignore. Unable to look away, he experienced a tinge of rivalry with Reverend Small, heightened by Betsy's angelic smile and her obvious enjoyment in their conversation.

If he succeeded in striking oil, thought Jonah, maybe he could then compete for this wonderful creature who could captivate him one moment and admonish him the next. On the other hand, if the well produced only water—or, heaven forbid, came up dry—it might be best to resume his journey.

"Time to get dinner on the table," announced Betsy as the fishermen drew near.

Reverend Small rose to his feet as Betsy disappeared into the kitchen and, after waving to Jonah and Seth, began to tease, "Where's the fish? No sunnies or perch or bullheads?"

"Probably time to try a lake or a pond," the dowser answered in genuine seriousness. "We know there's somethin' big in the creek but chances of catchin' somethin' worth writin' home about is bound to be a whole lot better in still water."

"I know right where to go!" exclaimed Seth. "There's a lake just beyond Barnes' place. Some of the men in town go out there to fish. They say the fishing there is really good."

"Well, Mister Fisherman," said Jonah, "if we ever get my springpole up, we might find some time to traipse over there and do some serious fishin'." Turning to the clergyman, he added, "And, speakin' of the springpole, Parson, ya better be ready to start workin' in the mornin'."

"Can't say that I am, but I will be," answered Reverend Small, beginning to indulge in Jonah's syntax. "Can we get the springpole up in a day or it this going to take a few days?"

"Hard to say," the dowser replied. "Guess it'll depend on how hard ya work, but it sure would be nice to see it up tomorrow."

The call to dinner brought a swift end to their exchange.

CHAPTER 7

By the time they reached the salt spring, Reverend Small was silent; pondering where in the Bible he might find an answer to his growing anxiety. It was no longer a matter of not wanting to help the man he had come to respect. Nor was it a matter of wanting to deprive Betsy and Seth of a potential source of income that could improve their lot.

Rather, he was troubled by the prospect of striking oil and the likely, if not inevitable, chaos he was certain it would bring. The stories he had heard and read about concerning the discovery of oil in western Pennsylvania rushed back into his consciousness. What he remembered most were the tales of the countryside quickly overrun by hundreds of strangers whose sole objective was wealth and whose primary motivation was greed.

But what troubled him most was his own growing involvement. Opposed from the outset, he now found himself helping to erect the machinery. Even worse, he concluded, was his participation in the deception concerning the true purpose of the springpole.

If Jonah succeeded and his worst fears were realized, would not his role be recalled, his personal integrity tarnished, and his ministry weakened or repudiated?

"There it is," proclaimed Jonah proudly, pointing to the long, trimmed hemlock. "All we're missin' now is some good-sized rock to hold down the lower end."

Reverend Small focused on the hemlock and the neatly cut oak post beside it. Having seen drawings of Drake's drilling rig, he was stumped by the sight of nothing more than two logs. "How can you possibly drill with these?" he asked.

"It's real simple," answered the dowser, drawing the letter Y on the ground with the handle of the shovel he had brought with him.

"It's just like settin' a fishin' pole on the bank so ya don't hafta hold it all the time. Ya cut a little branch so's it's like this Y, and then ya push the stubby end into the bank, set the pole in the notch, and put a stone over the fat end of the pole."

It took the minister a moment to visualize the image that Jonah described but, as it emerged in his mind, the minister was taken by its simplicity. "So the drill hangs from the springpole just like a hook hangs from the fishing pole?" he surmised aloud, waiting for confirmation.

"That's it," confirmed Jonah, "but we're talkin' a pretty big pole, some pretty heavy rope, and a stirrup for yer foot!"

"I can see how you set up the springpole, but I still can't see how you can drill with it," Reverend Small responded, clearly intrigued by the mechanics.

"That's where rope comes in," explained the dowser. "Ya tie a couple ropes near the small end of the pole. Ya put a loop at the other end of one of 'em so that it hangs three feet or so off the ground. That's the stirrup. Ya tie the drill bit to the end of the other rope so's it hangs a little bit above ground. When ya put yer foot in the stirrup and jump up and fall back to the ground, the tip of the pole comes down and the bit falls straight down and drives itself into the ground. The trick is to jump on the stirrup with all yer weight so that the bit drops fast and hits hard. As the bit drills deeper and deeper into the ground, ya need more rope so ya hafta add extra as ya go along."

Pleased by the interest shown by the minister, Jonah added, "It's nothin' new. They say the springpole was invented by the Chinese long before yer friend Jesus was born. Some say it's good enough to drill all the way to China if yer so inclined."

Reverend Small smiled, momentarily distracted from his moral and spiritual struggle. He could sense the challenge and the adventure that drove Jonah in his quest of such an uncertain and elusive prize.

But, having already concluded that he could not keep his promise, the distraction, however welcome, was brief. His search for a rationale or compromise that he could defend in his own heart and mind had raged for days. Yet the more he struggled, the more he realized he could not in good conscience support Jonah's quest. Slowly, but inexorably, he had come to see it as the simple pursuit of mammon. What made the issue so difficult was that he had also come to respect Jonah's more admirable virtues.

Disappointed that his quip drew nothing more than a smile, the dowser turned toward the woods and a large ledge of rock that jutted out from the rising terrain. As conspicuous as the rock itself was a series of horizontal seams created over the years by the relentless forces of nature.

"Looks like there's enough rock there to hold down a dozen springpoles," he said, looking at his two companions. "All we gotta do is break away a few good-sized slabs and drag 'em from the woods to the springpole. And that's where ya can help the most."

"I can't do it, Jonah," the minister declared faintly. "I know I promised to help but, now that the time has come, neither my faith nor my conscience will let me."

Jonah started to curse but caught the words before they left his open mouth. He turned away from Reverend Small and looked instead at the woods and the rock. "Can't say this is much of a surprise," he eventually responded. "Fact is, a man's only as good as his word. It don't matter much whether he's a farmer, a fisherman, or even a preacher."

The words cut like a lash, and Reverend Small felt a surge of anguish. Like Jonah, he stifled an instinctive but unpleasant retort. "I know you've kept your word, Jonah," he responded. "You've been a faithful friend who's gone well beyond your side of the bargain."

"Well, no need to fret about it," Jonah replied.

"But that's what makes this so painful," the minister answered. "You're the salt of the earth, Jonah, and I hope and pray that you won't judge me by this one situation alone."

Then, almost as an afterthought, he added, "There is one thing I can do. While I can not help, neither will I hinder."

"Hope ya don't expect thanks for that," the dowser retorted.

Sensing hurt rather than hostility, Reverend Small decided to press on in the hope of salvaging their growing friendship.

"Jonah, I was wrong to promise something I knew I should not do, and I'm deeply sorry. What you must understand is the fact that it's not so much what you are doing, it's why you're doing it. Many may admire those who discover gold and silver and other quick and easy wealth, but I am not sure God does.

"Jesus tells us, 'Lay not up for yourselves treasures upon earth, where moth and rust doth corrupt, and where thieves break through and steal: But lay up for yourselves treasures in heaven, where neither moth nor rust doth corrupt, and where thieves do not break through nor steal: For where your treasure is, there will your heart be also.'"

The dowser remained silent, offering neither rebuttal nor comment of any kind. After a few moments passed, the minister resumed his defense, counting once more on the words he had memorized from the sixth chapter of Matthew.

"'No man can serve two masters; for either he will hate the one, and love the other; or else he will hold to the one, and despise the other. Ye cannot serve God and mammon.'"

And again, there was no reply.

"There is one more thing, Jonah," Reverend Small added with obvious conviction. "I am now more certain than ever that our paths have crossed for His purpose."

Jonah took a deep breath, sighed, and shook his head in continued disbelief that the help he had counted on was being withdrawn. The reasons didn't matter. All he could see were the components of a springpole he could not erect alone.

"Just go and take the boy with ya," he finally remarked with unconcealed exasperation.

Seth, however, was not about to be dispatched so easily. "I can help just like I did yesterday," he argued.

But Jonah chose to ignore both Seth and Reverend Small, wandering off into the woods alone toward the rock ledge. Once there, he began to inspect the seams more closely, running his finger along those closest to the top. With a wedge, a sledgehammer, and a little luck, he thought, he could break off what he needed and slide them into place with a horse, maybe one of ol' Barnes' horses. Now deep in contemplation, he realized there was no sense in trying to get a horse until he had broken free a few large pieces of stone first. That too posed a problem since he had no wedge and no sledgehammer. All he had were the two axes he had brought from the barn. Somehow, they would have to do.

His train of thought was soon broken, however, when he realized that Reverend Small had followed him to ledge. So too had Seth. But it was the minister who spoke first.

"Jonah," he persisted, "you can't serve God and mammon. Easy riches are an idol, a false god."

"Well," said Jonah, "servin' God is your business, not mine."

"That's only partly true," the minister answered. "God hopes that each of us will come to know and serve Him. Whether we do or not is a choice he leaves up to us. Once we recognize the huge depth and breadth of His love, we quickly realize we have no choice but to return that love. And that's when we discover, deep within, a desire to serve Him."

"Good grief," Jonah exploded, "ya can't even keep your latest promise. Ya just said ya won't hinder. What else do ya call all this jabberin'? Let me be. There's work to get done."

"As you wish," replied the minister. "Come on, Seth, let's give Jonah some time to think."

Seeing Jonah's mood, Seth complied. As the two departed, the dowser swung the head end of the dull axe at the rock.

"Blast it!" he thundered.

Try as he might, Jonah found it impossible to concentrate on the challenges that now loomed large. He had no help, no tools, no money. *This isn't worth it,* he decided. *It is time to move on, time to continue west where I know there is oil.*

As tempting as it was to go back to the house to disgrace the preacher in front of Betsy, he ruled against it. Doing so would only leave him vulnerable to the inevitable pleas of Betsy and Seth to stay. Yet something more held him back. His leaden feet refused to move.

Is it because I cannot leave without offering them an explanation? Or is it because there might be oil under my feet? It's neither, he realized. *It's simply the thought of running away, and I've never run away from anything.*

As he came to that realization, he began to hear the crunch of footsteps inside the woods. It was unmistakably human and unquestionably near. His eyes and ears converged on a small gully, partly hidden by underbrush. From it, seconds later, emerged a familiar face. It was Lucas.

"What are ya doin' here?" demanded Jonah.

"That's simple enough," replied Lucas. "I just came by to see how you're getting along. How come I don't see any springpole or any water bubbling out of the ground? Or, for that matter," Lucas added slowly, "any sign of help?"

The intrusion annoyed Jonah, and he ignored Lucas's question. But as Lucas spied the neatly cut and trimmed trees that Jonah had ready for the springpole, he quickly expressed his approval and began to commend the dowser.

"Guess I only had one eye open," he laughed. "Looks like you're pretty good with an axe. That post and pole should serve you well. You're a whole lot further along than I thought."

"There's still a mite more to do," Jonah countered in the face of Lucas's praise. "Still gotta break free a few slabs of rock to anchor the one end of the springpole."

"Big as you are, I don't see you raising that pole alone," Lucas challenged tactfully.

"Ya volunteerin'?" countered Jonah.

"Wish I could, but I've got spindly legs and weak back," parried Lucas. "What I can do is line up some help for you if it's worth anything to you."

"Ain't got a cent, and ya know it," the dowser responded disgustedly. "If ya can't help, it's time for ya to get outta here and let me get back to work. Besides, it looks to me like ya just came by to poke around and snoop."

"That's no way to treat someone who tried to get you to settle here and set up a business," Lucas retorted with a hint of indignation. "Have you forgotten my offer already?"

"Don't need help from the likes of you," Jonah answered in growing frustration.

"Guess I better go," said Lucas, turning back toward the gully. "But, for what it's worth, Jonah, don't believe everything you hear."

As Lucas's footsteps through the twigs and leaves of the woods began to fade, Jonah released the axe he had been holding in his right hand. There was a small thud as the head hit the ground and a second, lighter sound as the handle struck a dead branch a few inches away.

Then he lowered himself beside a large beech and sat with his back against its trunk. His hands fell into his lap, his head drooped, and his eyes peered at the only pants he owned and a knee patch that Betsy had sewn on. While she mended the tear, he had worn an old pair belonging to her late husband. Although they were big enough to suffice, he felt awkward in them, a memory that continued to disturb him even now.

Wrestling with the events of the day, Jonah closed his eyes and, minutes later, nodded off. Yet even in sleep, he seemed to struggle with the temptation to return to the open road. Awakened by noisy squirrels, he remained faced with the same persistent thought: *Why stay?*

The more he pondered the question, the more he became certain that peace of mind, if not oil, awaited him beyond the hills of central Pennsylvania. He rose decisively, ready to resume the long trek to the known oil fields in the west. Only then did he remember that Drake, his bark–clad guarantee to the fortunes of oil, was back in the barn, safely hidden from view.

After uttering "blast it" once more, Jonah knew instinctively that he could not leave without his divining rod. The question was whether to go back in daylight or darkness. Seth—and in all likelihood Reverend Small himself—had certainly shared with Betsy the minister's decision and Jonah's angry reaction. Going now, he reasoned, would surely risk an encounter with Betsy, a likelihood he viewed uneasily.

The sun was virtually at its apex, and the midday meal was close at hand. Jonah had hardly begun to grapple with the latest issue when he began to sense the approach of Betsy and Seth, well before they came into view.

"We're here to help," announced Betsy, "but not until we've all had a bite to eat."

"Ain't very hungry," said Jonah, somewhat lying to Betsy and to himself. Despite the fact that he had not quarried stone as he had planned nor dug the hole for the yoke that would support the springpole, he could feel a pang or two of hunger.

Betsy would have none of it. She knelt down, uncovered the small basket she had brought, and handed Jonah bread that she had sliced back in the kitchen. Trapped by her gesture and his own appetite, the dowser reached for the food without hesitation. "Guess a bite or two can't hurt," he conceded.

Seth, meanwhile, removed the lid from the pail of spring water he had brought, and all three were soon eating silently.

Betsy broke the silence. "Reverend Small told us he backed out of his promise to help you," she began. "And he also told us why. At first, it sounded like a poor excuse to get out of work even though we know he's not afraid of work. It took a while, but I finally realized that his conscience simply wouldn't let him do it."

"It don't matter," Jonah lied again, wiping away a breadcrumb that had stuck to the corner of his mouth.

"He really feels bad about it, Jonah," Betsy persisted. "He went up to his room after he told me about it, and he wouldn't come down for lunch. I'm afraid he's thinking about leaving and going back to Philadelphia."

"Horse feathers," interrupted Jonah.

"I'm serious, Jonah," Betsy rejoined. "When he and Seth came back to the house this morning, he told me he had just hurt his best friend. Then he told me what happened. You may not believe this, but he tried very hard to put aside his qualms and help you anyway."

"He's got enough friends here in the valley to last till doomsday," Jonah argued. "He can surely do without me."

"It's time to get to work," Betsy declared. Jonah's apparent unwillingness to at least try to understand the dilemma that Reverend Small faced troubled her. Yet equally perplexed by the prospect of an argument that might leave them all losers, she summoned the most cheerful voice and smile she could muster. "Show me what we need to do."

"This ain't women's work," Jonah protested. "Besides, nothin's gonna get done without a sledgehammer and a wedge. Looked high and low, but couldn't find either."

"Look by the woodpile," instructed Betsy. "Seth and I often use them when we split firewood. And before you go, tell us what we can do while you're gone."

Her plucky nature had escaped Jonah in the past, and now, face to face with the determined widow, he was awestruck. "Well, ma'am," he began hesitantly, "it might be better if you and the boy go fetch 'em since ya know right where they are."

Betsy did not immediately respond. The pause made Jonah uneasy. "'Course, if ya prefer, we can all go back together and hunt 'em down," he proposed. "Might not be a bad idea to pick up a shovel or two while we're at it."

Again, there was no response, so Jonah started toward the house and barn by himself, eager for relief. He had barely gone more than a few steps when Betsy called him back.

"Jonah," she began, "I'll go find the sledge, the wedge, and the shovels since I know exactly where they are. Then I'm going to get Reverend Small to bring them out here, and when he does, I expect you to accept his apology. You will, will you not?" she demanded in the authoritarian voice and bearing that she had mastered during the early days of marriage and motherhood. Too flustered to argue, Jonah agreed.

Reverend Small was still in his room when Betsy and Seth returned from their lunch by the salt spring. After instructing her son to call the minister, Betsy searched for the tools she had promised Jonah. Within minutes, she had dumped a sledge, a wedge, and two shovels beside the porch steps. Looking up, she found Reverend Small watching her admiringly.

"Those can only be for Jonah," he surmised aloud.

"Yes," she confirmed, "and you are the only one who can take them out to the woods. He's expecting you to bring them."

"After all that happened this morning," the minister replied, "he's probably ready to drive me into the ground with that sledgehammer. I've never seen him so mad."

"That was this morning," Betsy explained. "I'm sure he's ready to hear you out and accept your apology. But there's no time to dawdle. Seth can take the shovels. You take the rest and get out there now before he changes his mind."

Unaccustomed to commands, least of all from a woman, he remained frozen, mentally searching for an appropriate reply.

"Don't you understand," she finally pleaded, "you and Jonah cannot let this destroy your friendship. You shouldn't have waited until the last minute to tell him you couldn't help. It took him completely by surprise. He's probably forgotten almost everything else you said. Go back and talk to him again."

"That's easier said than done," he argued. But after further reflection, he grabbed the tools and added, "But I'll try."

As the clergyman raised the sledge to his shoulder, Seth duplicated his movements, raising the two long-handled shovels until they rested beside his neck. The two then set out for the salt spring, ambling along slowly at first. Once Jonah was in view, Seth began to quicken his pace, and Reverend Small let the youth race ahead. If he was greeted with hostility, or even indifference, he thought, he would simply leave the tools without comment and return to the house.

Much to his amazement, he was greeted with a disarming yet genuine smile. "Like it or not," joked Jonah, "yer helpin'."

"Guess I am," conceded the minister with a reciprocal smile as he dumped the tools on the ground. "This wasn't exactly my idea," he continued somewhat defensively, "but I'm glad I did it."

"Well, let's not get too serious," counseled Jonah. "Don't want ya blamin' me for doin' anything ya ain't comfortable doin.'"

"I've never been torn apart like this, Jonah," Reverend Small explained, "and I'm not sure you understand why this is such a predicament for me."

"Probably not," the dowser admitted, "but there's no denyin' that yer hurtin' and, after a while, that gives me pause."

"That makes two of us. When I got back to the house and began thinking about the pain and anger I've caused, I was ready to pack up and leave," the minister revealed.

"Quittin' crossed my mind too," confessed Jonah.

"Let's try starting out fresh instead," Reverend Small suggested. "Let's see if there isn't some way I can help without compromising my integrity and my beliefs."

"That's easy," replied the dowser as he picked up the sledgehammer and wedge. "As long as folks think we're drillin' for water, no one can fault ya if we hit oil instead."

"But that's the whole point, Jonah," lamented the man of the cloth. "I can't ignore what I already know. Your real goal is oil not water."

"Well, what about doin' some of the other work, like mowin'?" Jonah asked. "Once we get some rain, that field we mowed will be ready for a second cuttin' before ya know it."

"That I can do," declared Reverend Small enthusiastically, extending his hand. "Let's shake on it."

Jonah took the hand without reservation, pumping it vigorously before relaxing his grip. That's a handshake, thought the minister, trying hard not to wince.

"Maybe I can help both of you," proposed Seth.

"Maybe ya can," answered the men in unintentional unison.

With that, Jonah picked up the sledgehammer and the wedge and headed for the rock ledge. Knowing exactly where he planned to position the wedge, he lost little time finding it. With a few light blows of the sledge, he lodged the wedge firmly in the seam. He then stepped back, eyed the head of the wedge carefully, and hit it dead center with a resounding blow.

It was hard to tell what was louder—the distinctive, unmistakable sound of metal striking metal or the explosive sound of rupturing stone. With a single swing, the wedge had completed what water had begun centuries before.

It was a display of power that left Seth and Reverend Small momentarily awed. Jonah, however, almost immediately scrambled to the top of the rock ledge after grabbing one of the shovels. To his delight, he observed two large, thick slabs of stone, each well suited for the intended role of anchoring his springpole.

He carefully steered the blade of his shovel under the upper slab and, slowly but confidently, inched the slab forward until it fell to the ground below.

Minutes later, the second slab crashed to the ground.

With his spectators still somewhat in awe, Jonah repeated the process until there was a pile of stone at the foot of the ledge. Only then did he pause to wipe away the large beads of sweat that ran freely down both sides of his face.

"Probably a good time to stop," he told the pair. "Movin' this stone to the salt spring can wait till tomorrow."

On the way back to the house and barn, Jonah explained that he planned to return to the spring with Drake so he could pinpoint the precise location for the springpole. Recalling the force that had nearly wrested Drake from his hands earlier, he smiled in anticipation. "Should be worth watchin'," he hinted.

"Tempting as that may be," the minister responded, "I think I'll forego the privilege. But one of these days, I would like to see you use Drake to find water instead of oil."

"Gotta say one thing for ya," Jonah replied, "ya sure are stubborn!"

Both men laughed, reflecting both the restoration of their earlier rapport and a new, deeper sense of mutual respect. Even Seth, who remained quiet, couldn't help but smile.

At supper, Betsy probed for details of the rapprochement. Her efforts were largely fruitless, however, except for the revelation that the minister and Seth would return to the hay field alone when it was time for the second cutting. Jonah, she learned, would concentrate entirely on drilling for oil.

The good-natured banter between the two men resumed the next morning over breakfast and continued until Jonah and Seth headed for the salt spring with Drake and Reverend Small headed for town.

"I hope you hit that artesian well before the day is over," said the minister, only half in jest, as they parted outside the house.

"Could happen," nodded Jonah with a grin, "and, if it does, we know who to blame."

Reverend Small walked with a comfortable gait, taking time to enjoy the morning sun, the songbirds that seemed to sing only for him, and the occasional rabbit or squirrel that fed nearby in the fields or scampered across the road ahead.

Although he had begun the day in bedside prayer long before breakfast, he soon found himself in meditation, thinking back over the events of the day before. As his thoughts skipped from the agony of breaking his promise to the handshake that offered absolution, he was quickly lost in wonder with the realization that his prayers had been answered.

Looking back, he recalled his fervent prayers in search of a spiritual answer to his dilemma. Largely obscured by the urgency and frequency of his prayers was his progress from hesitation to resolve to the ultimate declaration that he could not in good conscience help Jonah erect the springpole. Then, in the euphoria that followed Jonah's willingness to forgive, if not forget, he now realized he had failed to see the hand of God. And, as that recognition burst into his consciousness, he looked up into a cloudless sky and uttered a simple but heartfelt thanks.

Minutes later, he found himself opening the door at Blakes' store where a warm and hearty welcome awaited him.

"How's that for coincidence?" asked Esther, looking at Art with a degree of satisfaction. "I told you Reverend Small was feeling enough at home in the country to begin talking about the way summer disappears before you know it."

Rising from her chair to fetch a cup, she turned toward the minister and, with a laugh and a smile big enough to light the whole store, continued, "We were planning to get out to the farm to see you this afternoon. With all we've been hearing about your hard work in Betsy's hay field, we figured it was time to get out there before she changed you into a farmer!"

Art, who was sitting in front of a small handsome desk that he and his wife used for the daily routines of business, winked and then feigned a grimace. Esther, meanwhile, poured their guest a cup of coffee, drew up another chair and, with a flourishing wave, beckoned Reverend Small to take a seat nearby.

"Before you start bending his ear," suggested Art, "maybe we should find out what brought the good preacher into town today."

"Nothing urgent," said Reverend Small. "I had a little time on my hands this morning, and I thought we might talk about the future, if you're not too busy."

"You must have been reading my mind," declared Esther. "I told Art just this morning that it was time to start thinking about putting up a new church. We can't have folks sitting on the ground forever, especially when the winds start up and the snow starts falling."

"We know folks like what they've been hearing," interjected Art, "and we're pretty sure they're ready to rebuild the church."

"We also know it's about time we started passing around an offering plate," Esther added, cutting off any elaboration by her husband. "The folks here are not rich, but they know you deserve compensation for your ministry. Even those who have little or no money will find something to share with you."

Reverend Small was momentarily stunned, the very issues he planned to raise were being addressed by the Blakes. While the thought of rebuilding on the ashes of the old church was as challenging as it was appealing, the apparent consensus that it was time to start helped assure him that his place was here in this rural community.

"What we had in mind was to ask everyone to stay after you finish the service on Sunday," Art explained. "Ruth Black has offered to have you over for dinner, and she can tell everyone that her chicken and dumplings won't wait. That way, you two can leave so folks can say whatever they want."

"We don't expect any real resistance or opposition," interjected Esther, "but after all these years here in the store, we know that some folks just like to be contrary. Once they get a chance to speak their minds, though, they usually follow along with everyone else."

"It sounds as though you and Ruth have thought through everything," said Reverend Small, shaking his head in admiration at the initiatives about to be taken.

"Of course, you can stay if you wish and ruin everything," joked Art.

The minister laughed with the couple but, after a moment or two of reflection, grew uneasy with the plan. "I'm sure you're right about giving people the freedom to speak their minds by arranging for me to leave," he began, "but I certainly don't want anyone to think I'm afraid to stay. Some of them may have some honest criticism. Wouldn't it be better for me to stay or come back before everyone goes home?"

Art and his wife exchanged glances, laughed again, and tried to reassure Reverend Small that their plan had been carefully conceived. "We've already discussed that and ruled it out," answered Esther. "There's bound to be a crank or two who won't say a word if you're not there. But as sure as there's little green apples, they'll have plenty to say if you are."

"They're the kind of folks who just like to talk," explained Art. "They're not about to say anything nasty or unkind, but if they think they've got your attention, they'll just go on and on till suppertime."

"Or till the cows come home," laughed Esther.

"Well, I'll do as you suggest," mused the clergyman, "provided you send someone for me if my sermons or my honor is suddenly at stake."

"Not even then," proclaimed Art, still in a light-hearted mood. "We'll defend you better than you can defend yourself."

"I hope I'll never regret this," grinned Reverend Small.

CHAPTER 8

Monday had all the earmarks of another scorcher when Jonah took to the field with Drake. As planned, he started well away from the site where his divining rod had first been drawn toward the ground with the most wrenching force Jonah had ever experienced. Seth trailed alongside the dowser, watching as Jonah kept Drake suspended in a spoke-like pattern to and from the salt spring. From time to time, the divining rod would bend toward the ground but never with an arc big enough to halt Jonah's slow, methodical gait. Seth eventually tired of keeping up, broke off a stalk of grass to chew on, and plopped down near the spring.

Nearly a half hour passed before Jonah reached the westerly arc on his compass-like search around the spring. Once he started the new series of paths, Drake began its downward pitch with growing intensity, so much so that even Seth began to take notice. Then, at almost the identical spot where the dowser had first suspected oil, Drake nearly flew out of Jonah's hands, drawn inexplicably to the earth beneath it. "Get me a rock," ordered Jonah.

Seth, unable to fathom the phenomenon he had just witnessed,

The Lure Of Oil, The Cry For Water

sat motionless. Rather than wait, Jonah grabbed a large nearby stone and placed it on the spot where he had left Drake.

"Bet ya never seen anything like that," Jonah bellowed.

"How'd you do that?" demanded the boy, rising slowly.

"Wasn't me," Jonah replied. "Whatever's down there is real powerful. Can't guarantee it's oil, but it sure don't act like water."

With the spot safely marked and Seth back on his feet, Jonah handed Drake to the lad and strode toward the long, trimmed hemlock and the oak post he had cut a few days before. He grabbed the hemlock about a third of the way from its smallest end and began to drag it toward the marker. Even though the distance was not that great, it was more than Jonah could do alone without pausing midway. As he dropped the springpole to the ground, he realized he was breathing hard. *Is it the exertion or the excitement or both,* he wondered.

Seth, meanwhile, approached with the divining rod in his hands. "What do you want me to do with Drake?" he asked, somewhat uneasily.

"Maybe ya better keep holdin' it till this hemlock is in place," replied Jonah.

Seth smiled, clearly pleased that he had been entrusted with the dowser's most valuable possession. When Jonah resumed his struggle with the springpole, Seth grasped the rod as he had seen Jonah do. Walking back toward the stone marker, he waited for Drake to perform its magic once more. When nothing happened, he ran to a different spot, trying to repeat the experience he had seen. And again, nothing happened. In youthful frustration, he began to run in a new direction. This time, however, his path took him across the small stream produced by the spring and, as his feet began to sink in the soft earth, he fell, landing squarely on the outstretched rod.

129

Jonah, who was trying to position the small end of the springpole over the stone, saw Seth fall. As he watched Seth rise, he began to stare in disbelief. Drake had snapped in two. Jonah consciously trapped an oath in his throat and dropped the springpole involuntarily. It bounced as it hit the earth, coming down hard on his right foot. Yet even as his face revealed intense pain, he remained silent.

Seth looked first at the irreparable damage and then at Jonah. Somehow, he managed to stifle both the impulse to run and the impulse to cry. Instead, he continued to look at Jonah, waiting for the dowser to break his silence. It seemed like an eternity, and when Jonah finally did react, it was a familiar expletive. "Blast it!" he exploded.

"This whole thing is jinxed," lamented Jonah. "Shoulda realized that the first night at supper. It's gotta be that preacher prayin' extra long and hard. It'll take forever to find a new rod like Drake."

The words pierced Seth's mind and heart like a dull arrow, leaving him ever more crestfallen. "I'm sorry, Jonah," he cried. "I didn't mean to break it. I was just trying to get it to work like it did for you. I figured I could be a dowser too."

"Maybe it was meant to be," reckoned Jonah, touched by the lad's genuine distress. "If it ain't the preacher, maybe it's God himself tryin' to tell me somethin'."

As Seth tried to hand Jonah the remains of Drake, Jonah suddenly realized that although the boy was visibly scared of the possible consequences, he had neither run nor made feeble excuses. To Jonah, these were admirable signs of early manhood.

"It's time to be gettin' back to the house," suggested Jonah, "before there's any more trouble."

"But it's still early," argued Seth.

"It's time for me to figure out what to do next," said Jonah, placing a hand on the boy's shoulder. "And it's time for ya to keep growin' up like a man, just like ya did now when ya broke Drake. Ya stood yer ground. Ya didn't run. Yer dad would be real proud, young fella."

"If I didn't run, how can you?" asked Seth. Exhibiting a maturity well beyond his age, he actively challenged his mentor. "Just because the preacher doesn't like what you're doing is no reason to quit."

Jonah was truly struck by the simplicity and the logic with which he had just been challenged. As he tried to sort through his own thoughts and emotions, he recognized the wisdom that underlay Seth's question. But the lad's words still smarted.

"Ya make it more simple than it is," he responded weakly, trying hard not to rebuke the youngster. "Movin' west was always my plan. Even though Drake was onto somethin', it could just as easy be water as oil. It'd be nice findin' oil on yer place, but the most likely guarantees are further west."

"Guess we'll never know unless you stay or someone else comes along," Seth persisted.

Given his size, Jonah was unaccustomed to such testing, least of all by a child. There was a flash of exasperation, then, just as quickly, a sense of surrender. But rather than let the lad off too lightly, Jonah seized the last word, "Maybe so, Mister Fisherman, but as long as it's just you and me, ya better remember to respect yer elders."

Seth realized it was a time to be silent. However, instead of heading toward the house, he headed toward the other shovel that had not yet been used. Without a word, he picked it up and brought it to his mentor and friend.

"Well, maybe it's a bit early to be going back," grunted Jonah as he took the shovel. "But this ain't a very good time to be askin' for promises. All this bad luck is kinda hard ta take."

His equivocating brought on a smile that he hastily dashed.

Returning to the fallen hemlock, he began to walk alongside it looking for the ideal pivot. At a point dictated as much by luck as by experience, he began to dig a hole for the post. It was easy at first but, as he dug deeper, the ground became rocky and hard.

"Fisherman," he called out, "fetch me a pick."

Seth scrambled toward the remaining tools. Even before he reached them, however, he realized the only pick was back in the barn. Turning sharply, he headed in that direction and shifted from a walk to a sprint.

"I'll be right back," he shouted over his shoulder.

Jonah kept on shoveling, pounding the point of the shovel into the hardened ground until it loosened up enough rock and earth to be scooped up and thrown aside. With his back to the house and barn, he failed to see Seth return. He was, therefore, somewhat surprised when the lad was suddenly by his side, pick in hand.

"Shoulda told ya to get a crowbar and whatever rope there is," said Jonah apologetically.

"Okay," acknowledged Seth, turning once more toward the barn after handing Jonah the pick. This time he walked, pausing only long enough to swipe a blade of grass from the ground to chew on while he undertook his unwelcome but willing journey. Upon his return, he found that Jonah had not only deepened but also enlarged the hole.

"That's a good way down," Seth observed, as he dropped the crowbar and a fairly large coil of heavy rope.

"Yeah, but it's not far enough," Jonah replied. "The post has gotta bear a lot a weight and a lot a stress. That means goin' down a good bit more. It also means gettin' plenty of rock around it. After ya rest up, ya can start bringin' over some of them stones."

By noon, Jonah had completed the hole, using all the tools that had been brought to the site, and Seth had created a good-sized pile of stones beside it. After inspecting it carefully and pronouncing it ready, Jonah strolled over to the post. Rather than carry it, he raised one end and dragged it toward the hole just as he spotted Betsy approach with a basket and pail.

She arrived just as Jonah slid the largest end of the post into the opening he had spent most of the morning creating.

"Come and eat," instructed Betsy as she uncovered the basket to reveal bread, cheese, and fresh berries. Tired and thirsty, Jonah reached first for the pail still hanging from her arm. As he slipped the handle of the pail past her hand, he found himself captivated once again by her poise, her easy smile, and her natural beauty.

But, having sworn to himself a long time ago that he would never allow himself to be rejected again, he turned away to drink freely from the pail. Only then did he discover it was filled with ale. Betsy had again bartered away milk and eggs for the ale she knew he enjoyed.

"Save some for tomorrow," she teased, exhibiting the charm that Jonah was determined to resist. Handing the pail back to her, he took the basket, joined Seth who was already sitting on the ground, and offered it to the youngster.

Once Seth had begun to eat, Jonah broke away a large handful of bread and a small piece of cheese.

Seth spoke first. Pointing to the remains of Drake, he informed his mother that he had accidentally broken the device that had seemed destined to lead Jonah to oil.

"Jonah thinks it's bad luck," the boy continued, "and he's thinking about leaving."

"Oh, no," bemoaned Betsy. "I thought you were happy here, Jonah. No one is standing in the way of your dream anymore. We are all trying, one way or another, to help you sink your well."

"Ain't left yet," replied the dowser defensively, sorry that he had revealed his inclination to Seth. "But this whole thing does seem jinxed. If it ain't one thing, it's another."

"I can see you managed to get a lot done this morning," said Betsy enthusiastically as she tried to change the subject. "At this rate, you should have your springpole up in another day or two, and then all you'll need is your drill bit."

Jonah simply nodded in agreement.

"Will a little more ale help?" she asked, unable to suppress an urge to wink.

"That might help," confessed Jonah, eager to resume work. He took the pail once more, finished its contents, and then called to Seth. "Time to anchor the post, young fella. All ya need to do is throw some rocks around it once it's lined up."

Sensing it was time to leave, Betsy swept up the pail and the basket, both of which were now empty. After offering a word or two of encouragement, she started back to the house.

As Jonah held the post upright, Seth worked with speed and deliberation to fill the hole from his pile of stones. From time to time, Jonah moved the post from side to side to jiggle the stones until they anchored it securely. Once free to let go of the post, Jonah headed for the rock ledge for larger pieces of stone as insurance against the stresses that the post was certain to sustain. With the addition of a few large stone slabs against the post, he stepped back.

"We're gettin' there," announced Jonah, confident it could withstand the rigors to come.

Refreshed by the progress, he moved swiftly to the upper reaches of the long pole that now rested over the spot Drake had chosen. Jonah lifted the tapered end of the pole and, moving forward, wound some of the rope around it a couple feet from the end. He secured the rope with a knot, added and secured a second length of rope next to the first one and then raised the pole higher and higher until he maneuvered it into the Y-shaped saddle at the top of the post. As he balanced the pole so that the heaviest end rested tentatively on the ground, the two lengths of rope tied to the tip fell to the ground and landed close to the drilling site Jonah had marked with a stone.

"It'll stay if you sit on it," Jonah commanded. Seth moved quickly and straddled the other end of the pole, using his weight to prevent it from moving upward. Jonah, meanwhile, grabbed the shovel. Digging furiously just beyond Seth, he dug a deep trench, directed the lad to move aside, slid the butt end of the pole into the depression, and covered it with the dirt he had removed.

Despite all his exertion, he kept at work, carrying larger and larger slabs of rock from the foot of the ledge to the pole, securing the end under the mound of dirt. When satisfied at last, he returned to the ledge to find the largest and heaviest slab left. Too big to carry, he flipped it end over end until it finally rested on top of all the other stones and the wooden trunk beneath.

"That, young fella, is a springpole," he proclaimed proudly, now out of breath from the accelerated pace of his labor. "And that," he added, as he pointed to the two coils of rope which sat almost directly on top of the marker, "is where we're gonna drill."

"It looks good," declared Seth. "It's hard to believe you did this all by yourself."

"Tain't so," insisted Jonah. "Ya helped a lot!"

The dowser knew there was still a great deal of work to do, but they had already accomplished far more than he had anticipated. So, as he scooped up some of the tools, he announced with a huge smile, "It's time to go fishin'."

Though he said nothing, Seth was delighted.

During their walk back to the barn, each was caught up in his own reverie. For Seth, it was the simple pleasure of fishing, a distraction from Drake and the torment that would not go completely away. For Jonah, it was the logistics of getting the drill bit from the blacksmith to the springpole.

The silence continued at the barn where Seth went in search of his fishing pole, uncertain where he had left it last. Jonah, meanwhile, put the tools back where they belonged. That done, he headed for the pump and the refreshment it promised.

Seth appeared moments later with his pole firmly in hand. He had replaced the hook, hoping to better his odds.

Once they reached the creek, Seth promptly baited the new hook and tossed it into the middle of the slowly moving current. It had barely struck the water when there was a silvery splash, and the line grew taut.

Seth reacted with all the skills of an experienced fisherman, yanking the pole to set the hook. He then watched as the line tore in one direction and then another. Seth chose to play the fish, glistening just beneath the surface as it tried desperately to free itself. With each turn upstream or down, the lad moved along the bank with the fish, trying hard to keep it from the weeds that might offer escape.

Even Jonah was fascinated. He watched with admiration as the boy and the fish tested one another. As the contest raged, there was little he could do but offer encouragement, first in whispers, then in shouts. When the fish broke out of its domain into the air above, it confirmed what seemed certain. It was the largest pickerel either had ever seen, so large it seemed more like its cousin, the freshwater pike.

"Don't lose him," cried Jonah, more excited than Seth had ever seen him. "Keep him away from the weeds!"

The pole bent one way, then another. And, just when it seemed Seth's prize was at hand, the pickerel lunged for the weeds. Seconds later the line relaxed. The prize was gone. There was little Seth could do but draw the line in. Though clean and unbent, the new hook was still at the end of the line.

"Blast it!" cursed Jonah for the second time that day. "Coulda swore ya had him."

"Me too," groaned Seth, turning the pole so that the line wound in a spiral until he was able to press the hook into the bark. Having lost the fight, he was in no mood for more fishing, a fact that Jonah recognized immediately.

With the pole flung over his shoulder, Seth turned toward home, and Jonah fell in step beside him.

"Don't take it too hard," consoled the dowser. "Pickerel ain't that good eatin'. Wouldn't have been much good for anything except, maybe, showin' him off to your mother and the preacher. Besides, he'll still be there next time."

"Do you think it was the same one that got away last time?" asked Seth.

"Could be, but not likely," replied Jonah. "Seen some pretty good-sized pickerel over the years, but that was surely the biggest.

Looks like ya can count on at least two good ones waitin' for you next time."

"Wash up, dinner's almost ready," shouted Betsy from the kitchen door as she saw the two approach.

Most of the dinner talk was commandeered initially by Seth's fishing and then by the accident that destroyed Drake. After listening sympathetically, Reverend Small expressed genuine sadness that the dowser's indispensable tool had been irreparably broken.

"Like many things," the clergyman observed, "Drake had the power for good and bad. Instead of grieving, let's rejoice over all the good Drake did by finding water."

Jonah took a deep breath and chose not respond immediately. But, after a moment or two, he observed, "It strikes me that the same good and bad can be said about drillin' for oil."

Betsy, who couldn't help but burst into a huge smile, nodded in quiet agreement.

However, rather than engage in debate, Reverend Small shifted the discussion to his visit with the Blakes and the likelihood that he would soon be able to provide Betsy a small stipend for his bed and board. Still uneasy about leaving the upcoming service so his parishioners could freely discuss the questions of a new church, weekly offerings, and anything else that might strike their fancy, he probed for reactions from his dinner companions.

"It makes perfect sense to me," said Betsy. "Once Art Blake gets them to look at such things, I'm sure they'll come together like they always do when it's time to work side-by-side. The folks here may not have much, but they're proud and they'll do whatever it takes to hear the Word and learn more about their Maker."

"Wish findin' oil was as sure as gettin' your new church," added

Jonah disappointedly. "Chances are we'll see yer buildin' before we see any oil."

"Who knows?" replied the clergyman. "From what I heard before dinner, you managed to get your springpole up today. With that kind of determination and hard work, you could see your dream come true tomorrow."

"Not likely tomorrow," replied Jonah. "No one, includin' me, can drill without a drill bit."

As was often the case this time of day, Jonah could feel the outdoors beckon. Bidding the others "Good night," he departed for the barn only to find himself unable and unwilling to retire. Instead, as he lowered himself onto the bench beside the barn, he found himself returning to his earlier optimism that he was on the verge of striking oil.

Weariness, however, soon propelled him back on his feet and, after entering the barn, he stretched out on his makeshift bed, happy and hopeful.

CHAPTER 9

Before drifting off to sleep, Jonah decided to head into town after breakfast to see if the bit was ready. Then he would visit Barnes to see if the old farmer would drive into town to pick it up. With these decisions made, he fell into deep and restful slumber.

Jonah revealed his plans at breakfast, and Reverend Small responded by suggesting that they walk to town together.

"Even though I've passed by several times, I've never really looked closely at what's left of the old church," he explained. "If we are going to rebuild, I better get some idea of what's still there in terms of size and shape."

Jonah welcomed the company, and Betsy quickly assigned Seth some extra chores before he could ask to join the two men.

For the most part, they engaged in idle chat on the way to town. Though he tried twice to explore Jonah's interests beyond oil, Reverend Small turned to other topics when his queries were largely ignored.

As buildings of the town came into view, the minister asked Jonah to join him in his inspection of the church grounds. "Two heads are better than one," he kidded, "especially when one knows almost nothing about construction."

"Can't offer much help about church buildin's," said Jonah, much more seriously, "but it's no trouble to take a look if ya want."

Leaving the road, they soon came upon the church's stone foundation. Although one wall had toppled in a few places, the foundation remained in good shape. Even to an untrained eye, it had clearly supported a large, rectangular building.

"It must have been much bigger than I guessed," Reverend Small confided. "I'd be happy if we could just restore what was once here. How big a job do you think that would be, Jonah?"

"As long as there's enough men and timber, the frame could go up pretty quick," the dowser replied.

"What about the foundation?" probed the minister. "Will that have to be rebuilt?"

"Not likely," he was told. "A good stone mason could fix that one wall in a day or two. For the most part, it looks pretty good."

When there were no further questions, Jonah suggested that the minister continue to look about the site. "Gotta be gettin' to the blacksmith," he said, "but there'll be time to stop on my way back."

"I'd be much obliged," answered Reverend Small, drawing on the vernacular he had heard so often since he had arrived in this rural community. Though heartfelt, he found that the expression lingered in his mind. Although it seemed especially appropriate at that moment, he concluded that such phrases should not be used lightly. Embracing vernacular was one thing, he realized; being glib was quite another.

Jonah hardly seemed to notice. He simply turned, headed toward the road, and was soon out of sight.

The smith was nowhere to be found when Jonah arrived so the dowser made his way toward the forge and, finding it banked, scanned the inside of the shack in search of his bit. That effort quickly proved futile so Jonah headed outdoors and the road home. He had barely reached the road when he heard a voice behind him.

"Your bit is here by the house," announced the blacksmith as he emerged from the front door. His left arm was in a makeshift sling. As he moved toward the bit, which was lying on the ground beside the steps, he grimaced and swore softly.

"Can't help but notice," Jonah began. "Did ya break it?"

"Burned it bad," sighed the smith, revealing a hand that was neatly bandaged.

Jonah looked more closely. Partly hidden by the sling were five bandaged fingers wrapped in a glove of gauze.

"Looks pretty mean," sympathized Jonah. "How'd ya burn it."

"Finishing up your bit," the blacksmith answered without a hint of self pity or blame.

"Blast it!" cried Jonah as his mind raced once again toward the same persistent conclusion that drilling here was jinxed.

What's gonna happen next? he asked himself in silence.

Sensing Jonah's feelings of guilt, the smith was quick to assume fault. "Don't let it bother you none. I got a might careless. A man my age shoulda known better than to do what I did, especially after getting burned the same way a few years back."

The words whizzed past Jonah without effect.

Bad things come in threes, he brooded. *Tryin' to strike oil here is producin' nothing but trouble. First, it was the preacher, then it was Drake, and now it's the blacksmith. It's time to get outta here.*

"Sorry ya got hurt on my account," he finally muttered.

"Better take a look at the bit," the blacksmith advised. "Make sure it's right. It's way too heavy to carry all the way back to the farm. If you don't mind waiting a day or two, I can probably get someone to drop it off at your place."

All Jonah wanted to do was leave.

Having triggered one series of heartaches, he reasoned, *it's stupid to risk another. It's time to get away from this jinx!*

Ignoring the blacksmith, Jonah momentarily closed his eyes, took a deep breath, thrust his hands into his pants pockets, and turned toward the road.

As he watched Jonah depart, the blacksmith repeated his offer to deliver the bit to the farm. Baffled by the dowser's behavior, the smith hurried to Jonah's side, placed his good hand on the dowser's shoulder, and demanded an explanation.

"I've done you no harm," he shouted. "What's wrong?"

Jonah stopped. "Sorry," he apologized. "Drillin' ain't worth gettin' folks hurt. The farm's most likely got enough water."

"Well, maybe you haven't noticed," argued the smith, "but apart from a few sprinkles on Sunday, we haven't had a real good rain in quite a spell. At least a couple wells I know about have all but dried up. If you do hit an artesian, Miss Betsy can help folks that do run out of water.

"Besides," he added, "It's like I told you. I got careless. I'm to blame, not you."

Jonah was beginning to feel trapped. How could he abandon what now seemed like a growing emergency even though it was oil, not water, that fired his ambition and his labor.

"Know it's been hot and dry," admitted Jonah, "but no one told me wells were dryin' up. Chances of hittin' an artesian are pretty slim, but ya make a strong case to keep tryin'. Just get the bit out to the farm when ya can."

"Good enough," agreed the blacksmith.

Jonah bid farewell but instead of turning back toward the farm, he turned toward town. The contradiction of his public and secret objectives had now come to haunt him, and the road to town offered a way out of the valley that had welcomed and beset him.

Passing through the little village unnoticed proved to be a bigger hurdle than he anticipated. Women hanging clothes, men chatting outside Blake's, and youngsters fishing in the creek all seemed to recognize the dowser, and many waved a greeting. He simply waved back and soon found himself beyond the town on a road he had not yet traveled. One way or another, he concluded, it had to lead west.

Within minutes, however, he spied a buggy racing toward the town he had just left. "Just my luck," he groaned. "If it was goin' my way, it coulda been a ride outta here."

Neither he nor the driver recognized one another as the buggy passed Jonah, but the driver suddenly pulled the reins hard, took the buggy into an open field, and turned back toward the dowser.

"Jonah," shouted the driver. "What are you doing out here?"

Uniting the voice and the figure, Jonah realized it was Lucas, the man he had been instructed to avoid.

"You're a long way from home," observed Lucas as he pulled alongside the dowser.

"That's the trouble with small towns," retorted Jonah in uncharacteristic exasperation. "Ya can't do nothin' without the whole blasted town knowin' or tryin' to know yer business."

"Whoa, my friend," replied Lucas. "I don't really care what you're about. I was just trying to be friendly. You're a good ways from town, and I was going to offer you a lift."

Despite Betsy's disapproval of Lucas, Jonah found it hard not to like the amiable lender. Whatever faults Betsy had found, she had never shared it with him. While Lucas's offer to set him up in business was clearly self-serving, he reflected, the offer was generous.

"Ain't nothin' like a long walk to learn more about a place and enjoy Mother Nature at the same time," the dowser fibbed.

"Hop aboard," responded Lucas, "and tell me where you want to go."

There's just no escape, thought Jonah as he climbed into the buggy. "Well, my legs are beginnin' to complain a little," he fibbed again, "so it's best to head back into town."

"Good," said Lucas. "Where do you want me to drop you off?"

Jonah pondered his options for a moment or two. "If it's no bother," he answered, "the old church grounds will be fine."

The reply jolted Lucas though he failed to show it. "That's what I like about you, Jonah, you're full of surprises. Why in heaven's name do you want to go there? Except for the old stone foundation, there's nothing there but the cemetery."

"Probably gone by now, but the preacher could be waitin' for me there," Jonah explained.

"Well, it's none too soon to start thinking about rebuilding," proclaimed Lucas. "Before you know it, we'll be seeing snow. Folks have got to have someplace to go besides the old school grounds. Think you'll be done drilling in time to help build the new church?"

"Only the good earth and the good Lord know that," laughed the dowser.

Like the blacksmith, Lucas had become aware that some wells had failed. Even when the rains returned, there was bound to be a need for additional, reliable sources of fresh water.

"Neither Mother Nature nor the good Lord seem to be helping much with rain these days," Lucas countered. "Some folks are telling me that their wells are so low they're only drawing water once a day. You can make a fortune just drilling for the biggest farms, Jonah. What's holding you back?"

"Puttin' down roots," the dowser responded. "Startin' up a business means settlin' down, and that don't appeal to me. Before ya know it, it'll be time to start headin' west again."

Almost as soon as he said it, he regretted it. Although he had no reason to assume that Lucas would repeat his remarks widely, Jonah realized that his revelation could get back to Betsy, Seth, and others who would be disappointed, if not hurt, by such plans.

The news of failing wells, however, began to register with Jonah in yet another way. Given the growing need for water, it no longer seemed to matter what he struck drilling. Betsy and Seth would clearly benefit from oil or water. And that realization brought a fresh degree of happiness.

The two rolled through town without stopping until they got to the church grounds. Reverend Small was nowhere to be seen so Lucas volunteered to drive Jonah out to the farm.

"Better yet," the dowser said, "if ya really wanta help, ya can take me by the blacksmith to pick up my new drill bit."

"My pleasure," declared Lucas, clearly delighted that he would get a firsthand look at one of Jonah's tools of the trade.

They found the blacksmith puttering about in his shed, his arm raised and limp in the sling. His greeting took both men by surprise.

Looking squarely at Jonah, he demanded, "What are you doing with this character?"

Stunned by the hostility toward Lucas, Jonah tended to answer defensively. "Just takin' up his offer of a lift and savin' ya the trouble of gettin' my bit out to the farm."

"Do as you wish," said the smith, ending further discussion.

Jonah picked up the bit and, finding its weight well-suited for the task ahead, took time to admire the craftsmanship. "Reckon this'll do fine," he announced as he carefully eased it onto the back of the buggy.

Lucas gave his horse a light tap with his whip, and they set off at a fast but pleasant gait.

"What's he got against ya?" Jonah inquired.

"Wish I knew," lied Lucas, who was well aware of the rumors and accusations against him. "It's probably because I've never given him any loans."

That explanation seemed to satisfy Jonah, although neither man encouraged further conversation. Instead, they drifted off into their own private worlds until they arrived at the farm where, once again, Lucas's presence was unwelcome.

Betsy, hearing the buggy, came to the door only long enough to advise Jonah to wash up for dinner.

Jonah jumped to the ground, picked up the bit from the rear of the buggy, and thanked Lucas for the ride. "Ain't likely to ever settle down around here," he added, "but ya never know. Yer offer is temptin' enough to stick in the back of my mind."

"That's all I can ask," said Lucas as he turned toward town.

After carrying the bit to the barn, Jonah started to examine it much more carefully. He began by sitting on the bench, rolling the bit across his thighs and then holding it by the large eye at the top. Not only was it well balanced, it was well shaped for the task ahead. The smith was clearly a highly skilled craftsman. Jonah was pleased.

His fascination with the bit was brief since Betsy was back at the kitchen door calling him to dinner. Inside, he found everyone, including Reverend Small, at the table. The two men exchanged nods, but no one spoke until the meal had been blessed.

"Sorry it took so long to get back," Jonah apologized.

"No apology needed," replied the minister with a broad smile. "Once I had seen the foundation and the cemetery and walked around the grounds, I saw no reason to stay. In fact, I left long before I planned."

Betsy, growing visibly impatient, interrupted to ask Jonah about his encounter with Lucas. "You know I told you to stay away from that man," she said sternly.

"That ya did, ma'am, but ya never did say why," Jonah answered. "Can't see where takin' up his offer of a ride was wrong."

Realizing that she had not shared the same information with Jonah that she had shared with Reverend Small, Betsy softened her voice and her expression. "There are things you need to know," she acknowledged, "but for now, tell us about your day."

There was a long pause as Jonah looked down at his plate, wondering how to respond. "Truth be told," he began, "it seemed like a good time to start headin' west again. Coulda made it too if Lucas hadn't come along and ruined everything."

The disclosure stunned and dismayed everyone at the table. Tears began to well up in Seth's eyes. Remembering what he had done to Drake, he cried, "It's my fault, isn't it?"

"It's no one thing," said Jonah, "it's a bunch of things."

"Did I say or do anything at the church yard?" asked the minister, trying desperately to recall their time there together.

Struggling to be as honest as he could, Jonah replied, "Ain't got nothin' to do with the church yard. It's more about yer nitpickin' about drillin' for oil."

Reverend Small started to protest but decided against it.

"Fact is," Jonah continued, "trouble always comes in threes. If ya count yer nitpickin' as the first one, and ya count Drake as the second, ya start wonderin' what's gonna hit ya next."

"Is that why you decided to leave?" asked Betsy.

"No, ma'am," said Jonah. "It was the blacksmith. He got burned real bad makin' my bit."

"Jonah," interrupted the clergyman, "it would seem to me that the blacksmith was only doing what he does day in and day out. He's probably had more accidents than he remembers. You can't hold yourself responsible for what happened."

"Well, that's what he said too," Jonah admitted. "But once it got in the back of my mind, it seemed like the only right thing to do was to get outta here before somethin' else happened."

"What made you change your mind?" probed Betsy gently.

"And," queried Reverend Small, "how does Lucas figure into all of this?"

"That's the crazy part," smiled Jonah. "He comes along and starts talkin' about wells gettin' low and some even runnin' dry and what a great opportunity there was to start up a business locatin' water. About that time it occurs to me that it don't much matter whether we hit oil or water. Either way, Miss Betsy, yer bound to come out ahead."

"We're mighty glad you changed your mind," said Betsy, ignoring his reasoning.

Reverend Small was quick to express his delight too, and as he reached out to shake Jonah's hand, he chose to extend the conversation further. "Tell me, Jonah, did it ever occur to you that the hand of God might be at work in all this?"

"Can't say that it did," Jonah replied.

"Well, next time," suggested the minister with a broad smile, "instead of asking yourself whether it's a jinx or a curse of some kind or other, maybe you should ask yourself if the good Lord is trying to tell you something."

Jonah looked over at Betsy, who was also smiling. Trying hard to appear annoyed, Jonah titled his head toward the clergyman and remarked, "He never gives up, does he?"

Betsy smiled, nodded in agreement, and rose to clear the table. Jonah rose too, picking up his own dishes and, after depositing them in the sink, waited there as Betsy approached.

"What have folks got against Lucas?" he finally demanded.

Betsy added her dishes to the sink, exhaled slowly, ordered Seth off to bed, and returned to her chair at the table.

"He's cheated many people," she began in a hushed voice, concerned that her son might still be within earshot. "He even tried to take advantage of me after my husband was killed in the war."

As she watched her remarks sink in, she added. "And a lot of folks around here think he had something to do with the church catching fire."

Jonah listened carefully as Betsy related the same details she had shared earlier with Reverend Small. As she explained his offer of small loans at high interest, Jonah shook his head from side to side, trying to reconcile what he perceived as contradictions.

"It's all true, Jonah," added Betsy defensively.

"Don't doubt ya at all," said the dowser, still shaking his head. "Just wish ya had told me this sooner. He's been tryin' to get me to take his money to set up a business."

Then, over the next few moments, Jonah described each of the encounters he had had with Lucas and the repeated offers of money. Smiling somewhat sheepishly, he added, "Good thing he never showed me any of that money."

"Hurrah for that," affirmed Betsy.

Looking squarely at Reverend Small, Jonah mused aloud half seriously, "Who knows, maybe the good Lord kept his money outta sight."

After the three had a good laugh, Jonah headed for the barn. Instead of retiring, however, he found his way to the bench outside after picking up the drill bit. As his eyes adjusted to the moonlight, he found himself once again admiring the smith's craftsmanship. Confident that it would pierce its way through the ground swiftly, he appealed to the bit, "Be it oil or water, ya better get to it quick!"

So engrossed was Jonah that he neither heard the footsteps nor saw the shadowy figure that took cover just out of sight.

Though happy to be back at the farm despite his earlier decision to leave it, Jonah suddenly felt very tired, weary from all the stress and strain of the conflicting events of the day. He smiled admiringly once more at the drill bit and then laid it on the ground beside the bench. Within minutes after retiring to his makeshift bed, he was fast asleep.

It was Seth banging his milk pail against the barn wall, not the rooster, that awakened Jonah. Whatever his embarrassment at not being up first, it went unnoticed. Once on his feet, he quickly headed to the pump to wash–up.

Back in the barn, he exchanged greetings with Seth, who was still busy milking. "Before the day's out, we'll find out whether or not ya can kick down a well," declared the dowser. Then, before Seth could respond in any way, Jonah challenged, "Think ya can do it?"

"Can't be that hard," said the boy confidently.

As soon as Seth finished milking, they began walking toward the house for breakfast. This time, as he passed the bench, Jonah stared at the ground, looking for the bit he had left there only hours before. It was nowhere in sight.

"Did ya notice the drill bit when ya came down to the barn?" demanded Jonah as his eyes swept back and forth over the same terrain again and again, searching unsuccessfully for the missing tool. "It was by the bench."

"Last I saw it was when you took it off Lucas's buggy," Seth answered.

"It's gotta be around here somewhere," growled Jonah as he grew increasingly irritated. "Tain't likely it walked off by itself."

Without being told, Seth started walking toward the furthest corner of the barn, kicking at occasional clumps of grass as if they might be hiding the bit. Jonah headed in the opposite direction. And, as he reached the closer corner, he heard Seth shout, "Jonah, it's here."

Jonah's long strides took him to Seth's side in short order. Clearly visible at the boy's feet was the iron bit, reflecting some of the early morning rays of the sun.

"Looks like someone tried to make off with it," surmised Jonah, reaching down to pick it up. "Good thing it's heavy." Once he had it in his hands, he strode back to the bench, dropped it beside his favorite seat, and commanded, "Stay there, blast it!"

"Who do you think took it?" Seth wondered aloud.

"Probably never know," said the dowser, unwilling to share his suspicions. "Besides, it don't much matter. Ya found it. That's what really counts."

The disappearance and recovery of the bit engendered lively discussion over breakfast. Like Jonah, neither Reverend Small nor Betsy shared their suspicions in Seth's presence. But once the lad had been sent back outside by his mother to collect eggs, the three adults reached an almost instant consensus.

"It had to be Lucas," proclaimed Betsy. Both men nodded.

"Still and all, it don't make sense," opined Jonah. "Ain't much good to anybody without a springpole, and ya can't hide somethin' that big."

"Even though it may have been Lucas," suggested Reverend Small after second thought, "we don't know it for certain. Until we have something more than our mutual suspicion, it's not really right to accuse him."

Jonah agreed, but Betsy immediately demurred. "He's as guilty as sin," she insisted. "Who needs proof. We're talking about Lucas!"

"Well," Jonah countered, "it never got off the farm, and that's what matters."

"So it is," remarked the minister, "So it is."

"And if it don't get put to use real soon," added Jonah, getting up from the table, "it won't be much good to anybody."

Swinging open the kitchen door, he was surprised to see three men approaching the house from the road. Jonah recognized them as farmers he had seen at church on Sunday.

"Mornin'," he said, as they met near the outdoor pump. "How you folks doin'?"

"Could be better," responded one of the men, clearly senior in age and in authority. "We're hoping you can help."

"Our wells are bone dry," explained one of the other men. "We've had dry spells before, and even though the wells got low, they never ran out."

"Till now, that is," volunteered the third man. "We expected them to recover after a few hours or overnight, but they're still dry, and they're staying that way. Our neighbors are helping us get by, but they're beginning to worry about their own wells."

"That why we're here," interrupted the eldest. "We learned from the blacksmith that you're planning to drill a new well for Miss Betsy. We're here to hire you to find water for us."

"Whoa," laughed Jonah, unaccustomed to such an appeal. "Gotta finish here first."

The elder farmer pulled away from the group. His path took him to the kitchen door where Betsy, who had been listening, came to meet him. "We need this feller to find water for us," he appealed, coming straight to the point, "and we are hoping you can spare him. You've still got water, Miss Betsy, and we don't. How about freeing him to find water for us?"

"It's certainly all right with me," smiled Betsy, "but he's the one you'll have to convince."

"Can't," said Jonah solemnly. "My divining rod is broke."

"Get another," urged one of the men. "With all the woods there are around here, that shouldn't be a problem."

"Ain't that easy," argued Jonah. But then, seeing the battle virtually lost, he offered a compromise. "Findin' a good divining rod can take days, sometimes weeks. Somethin' that looks good on a tree or shrub can amount to nothin'. But give me a few days. We'll hold off drillin' till we've made a few passes through the woods."

"I guess that's fair," said the leader.

"Maybe we should all pray that Jonah finds what he needs,"

suggested Reverend Small who had just joined Betsy on the porch. "Something as urgent as this surely needs prayer."

"Lead the way, Reverend," said the old farmer.

"Let's all bow our heads," instructed the clergyman.

"Heavenly Father," he began, "Thou knowest our needs even before we utter them in prayer. But by turning to Thee, we demonstrate our faith and trust in Thee to help us find our way through the wilderness.

"Before us, O Lord, are converging needs: on one hand, we have farms struggling without water and, on the other, we have a man who might help if he can find a replacement for the implement that lies broken and discarded.

"May Thy hand rest upon Jonah and guide him in his search and, if it be Thy will, may this urgent need be met. Amen."

"Amen," repeated the farmers and Betsy in unison.

"Anything we can do to help?" asked one of the farmers.

"Not much now," replied the dowser. "But ya better see what a springpole looks like. Seth, here, can take ya down to see the one we built. Look it over, and when ya get home, see if ya can find the trees like that on your own land."

Seth, swelling with pride, started walking slowly toward the springpole, pausing only once to be sure that all three farmers were following him. Betsy returned to the kitchen, leaving Jonah and Reverend Small alone in the yard.

"What was that ya called Drake?" asked Jonah.

"An implement," answered the minister. "I could hardly call it Drake in view of all the questions that might conjure up."

"Why didn't ya just call it a water witch or something else?" Jonah continued.

"Well, to be honest, Jonah, I found it a little hard to pray for something called a witch," said Reverend Small. "Isn't there some other name for it?"

"Most folks just call it a divining rod," the dowser replied, starting off toward the woods in search of a new rod well away from the springpole and Seth and the three farmers.

"I like that much better," the clergyman cried out with a smile. "In fact, it almost sounds biblical."

With the discussion ended, the clergyman ambled over to the bench by the barn and began to examine the drill bit. Like Jonah, he couldn't help but admire the craftsmanship of the blacksmith. Maybe, he thought, he should search the Scripture for a name that would be as synonymous with water as Drake was with oil.

CHAPTER 10

Once in the woods, Jonah began a methodical search. Although there were several varieties of trees and shrubs throughout the woods, the dowser limited his search to hazel, certain that its supple branches could detect water better than any other. Yet, hours later, he had found nothing that met his rigid demands for a perfect replacement. Tired and thirsty, he climbed to the top of a hillside he had been exploring and found a large elm, felled by lightning, that offered a place to sit.

Scanning the slope carefully from his new vantage point, he began to wonder if Drake could ever be truly replaced. His search had proved futile, and lengthening shadows suggested it was time to head back to the house. As he rose, he realized he could avoid the same ground he had already covered simply by walking along the other side of the ridge.

Walking through hemlocks and spruce, maples and elms, he caught sight of rabbits and squirrels and even a large buck. Despite his lack of success, Jonah perked up with each new sighting of wildlife, and he especially enjoyed the songbirds that seemed to sing just for him. What soon captured his undivided attention was a small sparrow that flitted from branch to branch in the trees and shrubs ahead of him.

Eventually he realized that he was unconsciously trying to keep up with the tiny bird. So he stopped to rest, and almost immediately, the bird alighted on the ground nearby. When Jonah resumed his journey, the bird took flight as well; when he deliberately slowed his pace, the sparrow responded in kind, choosing nearby branches on which to rest until Jonah caught up.

By now, the dowser was convinced that if he continued to follow this tiny creature, he would be led to a perfect branch from which he could fashion a new Drake. So convinced was he that he stopped looking at individual shrubs and trees and concentrated only on those that the sparrow chose.

Suddenly the bird flew to the top of the ridge, waited until Jonah came near and then flew to the opposite side of the hill that the dowser had combed so thoroughly earlier in the day. Jonah followed obediently, only to watch the sparrow disappear into a thicket of branches. Certain that his goal was somewhere in his midst, Jonah began an almost desperate search. Yet nothing even remotely resembled the replacement now etched in his mind.

He searched methodically, radiating out from the spot where he believed he had last seen the sparrow. Optimism, however, soon gave way to discouragement and frustration for allowing himself to become charmed by such a small, common bird. He even began to wonder if it had been one sparrow or several.

The nearby call of his name ended his melancholy. Though he recognized the voice as Seth's, he was unable to spot the lad. With his ears and eyes focused on the direction of the call, he moved forward parting the underbrush and leaves that obscured his view. The strategy worked so well he nearly collided with Seth as he pushed aside a large, low-hanging branch.

"Did you find a new divining rod?" the boy asked.

"'fraid not," replied Jonah.

The walk back to the house proved much shorter than Jonah anticipated, and before long, they arrived at the pump where each took turns pumping cool water so the other could drink and wash.

Turning toward the barn, Jonah spied a large bough resting against his bench. Closer inspection confirmed his suspicions. It was a beautifully formed, Y-shaped branch of hazel, nearly identical to Drake. It was rough-cut with the stub and each of the branches still long enough to be trimmed as needed.

Jonah seized a branch in each hand and positioned it as he would when dowsing. It was comfortable and, he knew instantly, perfectly suited for the work ahead.

Seth, who had remained at a distance while Jonah examined the bough, moved cautiously toward the dowser. "Will that work?" he asked hesitantly.

"It's got potential," proclaimed a grateful Jonah. "Could be as good as Drake and maybe even better. Any idea how it got here?"

"After I showed our neighbors the springpole, I hiked into the woods and started looking too. Something told me that since I was the one who broke Drake, I was the one who had to find the replacement. It took a while, but I think this branch is almost the same as Drake," Seth recounted. "I just hope it's as good."

"Seems likely," confirmed Jonah. "We'll put it to work in the mornin' after we trim it up a bit. Given that ya found it, it's yers to keep, providin' of course that ya want to learn to use it."

Seth was overjoyed. The fact that he, not Jonah, had found an acceptable, and perhaps superior, replacement for Drake was far more than he could have wished. Jonah's willingness to teach him the art of dowsing was icing on the cake.

"It's yours," insisted a happy but stubborn Seth, "and if it doesn't work as good as Drake, I'll keep looking until I find one that does."

Seth's determination to make amends for breaking Drake won Jonah's admiration. "Only one way to settle it," Jonah decided aloud. "We'll trim it up now instead of tomorrow. Get me a good knife from the kitchen, and carry it like ya were taught."

Seth ran for the house, despite a standing injunction from his mother not to run, and nearly tripped over a rock near the water pump. Seconds later, he was back outside with a knife that Jonah had recently sharpened with the family's wet stone.

"That'll do nicely," commended the dowser, and the two began to walk toward the salt spring. Holding the new divining rod almost reverently, Jonah carefully reexamined it, paying particular attention to the point at which it separated into two thinner, mirror-like branches. It bore all the visible characteristics that had made Drake so responsive to underground water.

As they neared the spring, the springpole commandeered their attention. There was a certain beauty in its simplicity as well as a perceived promise that it would produce a well, be it water or oil.

As they continued their walk, Jonah gripped and positioned the twin branches just as he would when dowsing. Once he found a comfortable, functional grip, he directed Seth to cut a notch on each branch just beyond each hand. Once they reached the springpole, Jonah took the knife and removed the excess wood. The dowser then started to test the new rod in earnest, beginning some distance from the point where Drake had been most decisive.

Almost immediately, Jonah could feel energy trickle through

his hands, even surging from time to time as his paths along random vectors approached the point beneath the springpole tip. Midway through the exercise, he instructed Seth to notch the rod once more, this time along the base of the Y-shaped limb. After cutting away that excess, Jonah resumed the trial.

He began walking figure eights with long loops, working in a clockwise movement. The rod moved dramatically at times, fully reminiscent of the way Drake had behaved. Smiling broadly, Jonah moved toward the point beneath the head of the springpole, gripping the rod tighter and tighter as its tip was pulled by a powerful yet invisible force. Once again, his hands stung from the struggle.

"No question, it's as good as Drake," proclaimed Jonah. "Now, let's get back before we miss dinner."

For Seth, it spelled redemption and the growing likelihood that his friend and mentor would remain on the farm. At supper, Jonah regaled Betsy and Reverend Small with the details of his failure and Seth's success. After he reached the climax of his story, the reaffirmation of the drill site, Seth asked Jonah to repeat the story about the sparrow.

There was a long pause, somewhat typical of Jonah when he needed to think something through before he spoke. "Guess that sparrow was just havin' fun," he finally observed. "Could be he and maybe a cousin or two were just steerin' me toward this young fella since there was no need to keep lookin'."

Amid the laughter and good spirits, Reverend Small found himself thinking about Drake and how the name evolved. Was there not a biblical name he could associate with water, one that was fitting for the new divining rod? There must be, he thought.

The question persisted long after he retired. Still awake a few hours later, he finally rose, lit the candle by his bedside, and took up his Bible.

Water, he thought, appears throughout the Scriptures, beginning in the very first chapter of Genesis with the creation of heaven and earth.

His thoughts raced through a succession of other references: *Noah and the flood, Moses and the parting of the sea, the baptism of Jesus in the river Jordan. But this is clearly different,* he concluded. *This involves water beneath the ground, unseen water critical for survival.*

He thumbed pages randomly, trying hard to find anything that might serve as relevant. Eventually he realized he was stumped, and in the absence of any promising clues, Reverend Small turned to the first chapter of Genesis and began to skim each verse, pausing briefly at the sixth and seventh verses to review God's division of water and land. He paused again at the third chapter to reflect on the disobedience of Adam and Eve, which he had come to know theologically as original sin.

The temptation to meditate on good and evil was powerful, but the clergyman forced himself to continue skimming page after page, hoping he would come across a name for the new wishbone-shaped rod that Seth had found.

Once he reached the sixth chapter and the story of Noah, he lingered over the passages that told of man's sin and wickedness.

Small wonder that God regretted creating man, thought Reverend Small, *and yet even as God considered destroying man, His anger was overcome by His love. Because Noah had pleased God, he and his family would be spared. Mankind would enjoy a second chance.*

The late hour and the flickering flame of the candle began to take their toll, and the clergyman found it harder and harder to

The Lure Of Oil, The Cry For Water

keep his eyes open. His fingers began to flip several pages at a time, breezing through chapter after chapter. When it dawned on him that he had flipped halfway through Genesis, he stopped to find he had reached the twenty-sixth chapter.

His weary eyes quickly recognized the story of Isaac and the wells of his father, Abraham. Filled in by the Philistines, they were restored by Isaac's servants and given names. As he read, he was refreshed. Perhaps the clue he was seeking was here. His reading pace quickened. Reaching the thirty-second verse, he was immediately struck by its content. And after completing the next verse, he went back and reread both more slowly.

"And it came to pass the same day, that Isaac's servants came, and told him concerning the well which they had digged, and said unto him, We have found water. And he called it Shebah: therefore the name of the city is Beersheba unto this day."

Reverend Small closed his Bible, blew out the candle, and went back to bed. He slept soundly, so soundly in fact that even the rooster failed to awaken him. What did rouse him was the unmistakable summons of Betsy. Breakfast was ready.

Rather than wash and shave, as was his custom, he dressed hurriedly and raced down the stairs to the kitchen. There he found everyone seated, and all eyes were focused on him. For much of the meal he was teased about oversleeping, a ribbing he took good-naturedly. The discussion soon turned toward Jonah's promise to help farmers find new sources of water, and, when that opportunity arose, he was quick to suggest that the new divining rod be named Shebah.

Neither Jonah nor Betsy reacted, but their quizzical expressions were all the clergyman needed to begin expounding on his post-midnight search through the Scriptures and ultimately his findings in Genesis. Even that, however, did little to generate interest. In the face of indifference, Reverend Small became somewhat defensive.

"Maybe it isn't as ingenious as Drake," he argued, "but Shebah does allude to success in finding a new well."

"Sounds more fittin' as a name for a queen than a name for our divining rod," Jonah finally observed. "Besides, it ain't even mine to name. It's Seth's. It's his to name—if it's any good findin' water."

"Time we found out," urged Seth.

All four rose from the table, ending further discussion. As Betsy reached the sink, she spotted the three farmers with the dry wells coming down the road. "Looks like our neighbors are still looking for help," she reported. "Why don't you men go out to meet them. They'll be here in a minute or two."

Jonah was the first through the door, holding it open only long enough for Seth who, in turn, held it briefly for Reverend Small. Outside they soon encountered the three farmers.

"Well," asked the eldest, "did ya find one?"

"Nope," replied Jonah, with an expression that belied the truth, "but this young fella did."

"Does that mean you'll help us find water?" demanded the old farmer, well known for his abrupt, matter-of-fact style.

"Can't promise nothin'," Jonah retorted, "but we'll try."

"Thank ya kindly," the old man replied, clearly relieved.

"And then some," added one of the others, reaching out his hand to shake Jonah's. "We don't know what we'd have done if you had turned us down."

"We drew straws," interrupted the old farmer, "and Jake here gets the first well. If you're ready, we can walk over to his place now. 'Course, if ya got other plans, we don't want to rush ya. We just want to get on with it, ya know."

"Fine by me," said Jonah as he sent Seth scurrying for the new divining rod.

With the old farmer in front, Jonah and the farmers started toward the road, closely followed by Seth and Reverend Small.

Less than half a mile down the road leading toward town, the farmers turned into a field occupied by a half dozen cows, all indifferent toward the approaching men. The men passed through the little herd silently and headed toward a narrow, rutted path. Like the pasture through which they strode, the lane wandered gently toward the top of a long hillside.

When they reached the top, they paused briefly to point out Jake's farm, no more than a quarter mile away. A neighboring house and barn, lying on the opposite side of a road that also led into town, was identified as that of the old farmer.

As they resumed their journey, Jake tried to persuade the old-timer to ignore the outcome of their straw vote.

"Emmet," he appealed, "let Jonah do your place first. You need a new well a whole lot more than any of us."

But the old farmer shook his head dismissively. The matter closed, Jake and the other farmer took the opportunity to assure Jonah that all three had found trees that could be used as spring-poles.

"We're kinda hopin' you can find water we can reach by diggin' instead of drillin'," said Jake. "Any chance you can tell how far down we'll need to go once you find water?"

"Sometimes, but it's pretty hard," replied Jonah. "Drillin' usually makes better sense 'cause ya can always dig afterwards. Diggin' can leave ya with a pretty big pile of dirt if ya don't hit water where ya expect."

"It really doesn't matter that much," said Emmet. "Whether we dig or drill, we've agreed to help each other, even if it means waiting our turn."

Impressed by their commitment to mutual assistance, Jonah decided he would do all he could to make digging a viable option. But from past experience, he knew that predicting depth was far more difficult than divining the location of water.

Satisfied that his new divining rod was almost as good as Drake, Jonah was confident that even if it couldn't determine depth it could certainly pinpoint where to drill.

Their pace increased slightly as they descended the hillside toward Jake's farm. In a matter of minutes, Jonah's reputation would be truly tested, not only by the three farmers but by Betsy and Seth, Reverend Small, and everyone else in the valley.

"That's the old well," shouted Jake, pointing toward a hand pump beside his unpainted barn. "First time it's ever failed."

"Like to start close to the house and barn," revealed Jonah, "so ya won't have far to go."

All four men turned their eyes toward Jonah, waiting for the dowser to withdraw the divining rod from the gap between his belt and the back of his pants and begin his search. None of the men had seen a dowser at work before, and even though they were hopeful, there was still a degree of skepticism, if not disbelief, among them. For Reverend Small, still largely ignorant of rural life, there was a combination of fascination and doubt. And even though he had watched Jonah before, Seth too was filled with wonder.

Jonah stopped about fifty feet in front of the house, well away from the well that had gone dry. "Still pretty close to the old well," he remarked, "but it could be there's still more water around here, only deeper. How deep's the old well, Jake?"

"Probably eight feet or so," the farmer replied.

"Sure ya wanta dig deeper than that?" probed the dowser.

"Well, not a heck of a lot more," said Jake. "I guess it depends on what you find. We'll do as you say."

By now Jonah had begun to position the divining rod in his two hands, ready to search for water. Even without being told, the others moved away, giving him a wide berth. For Jonah, the ritual he had practiced so many times before was about to begin anew. This time, however, he approached the task with greater urgency, given the genuine plight of his companions. Gripping the twin branches with a determination he could barely contain, he began to traverse the ground beneath him.

His audience grew as Jake's wife peered from one of the windows. The men in particular watched for the telltale sign of movement by the rod. Though it seldom moved, it drew frequent murmurs when the men perceived real or imagined movement. Except for Reverend Small, none of the observers noticed Jonah's change in behavior, now bordering on an almost mystic state.

The dowser seemed oblivious to everything but his chosen path, back and forth across no more than a half acre of land. When the tip of the rod finally sprung toward the ground energetically, Jonah kept moving without a hint of emotion. Later, when his path brought him back to the same area and the rod again dipped aggressively, he paused but then resumed his walk, still seemingly detached from his surroundings. Only when the rod displayed its energetic behavior in the same area a third time did Jonah stop. Turning ninety degrees, he resumed his search, traveling back and forth across the promising site.

"Ya can drill here!" he proclaimed at last.

"As you say," cried Jake, running forward with a large stone he had dislodged from the field. The farmer carefully positioned the stone directly over the spot that Jonah indicated, and then he began to question the dowser.

"You figure it's too deep to dig?" he asked.

"Too hard to say," Jonah replied. "But drillin' should be a whole lot faster after ya get the springpole up. Once ya strike water ya can decide if it's worth diggin'."

"Either way, we're mighty grateful," declared Jake. "We've already got the trees picked out for the springpole, and I've got plenty of good heavy rope to get us started. About the only thing we don't have is a bit."

"Ya can use mine," volunteered Jonah, "provided ya let the others use it too."

Overtaken by the dowser's generosity, Jake nodded in agreement with a huge smile and then exclaimed, "You're a good man, Jonah!"

"That's a fact," uttered Emmet.

"Time to get to yer place," responded the dowser, carefully placing his divining rod back under his belt. "And ya better hold yer cheers til' ya see and taste new water."

"Let's go," grinned Emmet.

The old farmer bid Jake a hasty farewell and started walking. Summoning Jonah and the others with a resolute "Com' on," the old timer surged ahead.

Jake also joined the march to Emmet's nearby farm, partly out of curiosity but knowing too that his friends would return to his farm to erect the springpole once Jonah had surveyed all three farms. "If you need to drill," he assured Emmet, "we'll move my springpole over to your place. That'll save you the trouble of building a new one."

Moments later, the entourage rounded a bend in the road and, looking ahead, saw the familiar scene of a small frame house and a slightly larger barn. The view also included a hand pump that rose up between two large slabs of flagstone.

"That well's been a lifesaver over the years," Emmet remarked as he struggled to keep pace with Jonah. The old farmer had begun to limp, a condition that came and went—most often when he hurried or when it was about to rain. "It's not all that deep," he added.

Jonah acknowledged the comments with a nod and began scanning the landscape for alternative sites. Nothing looked particularly promising, but he said nothing, determined not to discourage the old man.

"What's better for ya," Jonah inquired, "a well close to the house or the barn?"

"The barn," responded Emmet. "Our stock drinks a whole lot more than we do."

Divining rod in hand, Jonah marched forth after finally spying what looked like a good place to start. Once more, he positioned the rod at an angle dictated by experience and gut reaction.

Reverend Small and the three farmers soon engaged in conversation, somewhat ignoring Jonah and his silent, repetitive march across the patch of land he had chosen.

"As you might suspect," the minister observed, "I still don't know everyone yet but, try as I might, I can't recall seeing any of you gentlemen at Sunday worship."

All three farmers appeared momentarily embarrassed until Jake chose to respond. "We don't get to church as much as we'd like," he explained. "No matter how hard we try, we never get caught up with all our chores. If we don't work Sundays, we just keep falling further behind, especially in summer."

"Any idea how the other farmers manage?" asked Reverend Small somewhat sympathetically.

As Jake and the others struggled for an answer, there was a loud cry from Jonah. "Ya can start diggin' here."

Only too happy to abandon the conversation, Emmet and his neighbors started running toward the dowser. Seth and Reverend Small chose to stay back after watching Emmet's pace drop off because of his nagging limp.

"Ya should find good water here," Jonah declared, "and if this new rod is true, ya won't hafta go down more than eight to ten feet. 'Course, if ya rather, ya can drill first. It depends on whether ya want to wait till Jake is finished with my drill bit."

"Your call is good enough for me," replied the old farmer, "but as long as the three of us promised to work together, I'll hold off on that decision till we get water at Jake's place."

"Guess we're ready for the next farm," announced Reverend Small, who along with Seth had been largely excluded from the camaraderie. "At this rate, we should be able to get back to Jake's place before lunch."

"Well, let's not jinx the last one," demanded Emmet, still somewhat uneasy in the presence of the clergyman. "Nothing personal, Reverend, but we've been doing so well we'd hate to see anything ruin this streak of good luck."

"Ah," cajoled the minister, "maybe you should put aside some of your chores and come to church on Sunday. There's much more to life than luck."

"There's no need for all of us to head over to my place," interrupted the third farmer, a man the others called Ned. "Jonah and I can go alone, and the rest of you can go back to Jake's place and start work on his springpole.

"The sooner we see water flowing, the better. Besides, Emmet's leg is acting up again, and, even though he won't admit it, he needs a rest. We'll join you back at Jake's once Jonah locates water on my place."

Emmet registered some weak opposition, but the majority quickly agreed. As the party began to split up, Seth announced that he would accompany Jonah and Ned.

Less than a mile away, Ned's farm was the largest and most picturesque of the three. Located on a large plateau, it featured well-defined fields, pasture and woods. Stone fences added to the beauty of the farm as did a small natural pond not far from the barn. The pond's muddy rim offered convincing evidence that it too was slowly drying up, a fact that Ned broached as he talked with Jonah.

"I've always counted on the pond for the livestock," he explained. "Although it's lower than it's ever been, there seems to be enough for now. However, if we don't get some relief soon, I'll have to start hauling water from the creek, and that's a couple of miles there and back."

Although he offered his familiar nod to acknowledge Ned's remarks, Jonah did nothing more to encourage conversation. Instead he set about his task, scanning the landscape more closely, looking for features that might signal an underground aquifer or spring. Try as he might, however, he saw nothing he regarded as particularly promising.

"This may take some time," he finally muttered, seemingly angry that his earlier good fortune was waning. "Don't see much promise anywhere near the house or barn, but it's worth a try just to be sure."

And, for the third time that day, Jonah grasped the twin

branches on his divining rod and began walking back and forth along an arc that skirted the two major buildings. An hour later, he conceded failure.

Heading next toward a line of trees that defined the edge of Ned's woods, Jonah noticed a slight depression that wove its way across the small pasture he had just entered. Ordinarily he would not have looked twice at such changes in terrain, but if nothing else, it offered a fresh place to start.

Ned and Seth followed Jonah across the pasture until he began his now familiar ritual. Keeping a safe distance away, they stopped and watched. Each time the divining rod began to oscillate up and down, they experienced a tinge of hope. And each time the activity faded as rapidly as it started, they moved further away to hide their growing disappointment.

But Jonah continued to sweep back and forth across the depression, hoping that his experience and intuition were wrong. After another hour of fruitless search had passed, even the dowser was beginning to lose the little optimism that drove him on.

Tired and thirsty, he started looking desperately for new ground. Seeing Jonah begin to falter, Ned and Seth headed toward him. "What do you make of it, Jonah?" asked the farmer.

"Water's here somewhere," replied Jonah. "It's just takin' longer to find."

"Let's head back to the house," Ned suggested. "Things are bound to look better after we've had something to eat and drink."

Their path took them to the rear of the house, presenting Jonah with a view that had previously escaped him. There just a few feet behind the building stood a small circular structure of stone and wood with a rope and bucket dangling beneath its roof. Annoyed that he hadn't asked to see the well earlier, Jonah shot a stream of questions at his host.

"How deep is that well?"

"Less than eight feet," replied Ned. "I dug it myself. The water's always been as good as any you could find. Nice and clear, and nice and cold."

"What happened to it?"

"It just got real low and stayed low," Ned explained. "For the past couple weeks, it been barely deep enough to reach the top of the bucket that we drop down."

"Ever thought about diggin' it deeper?" the dowser continued.

"Too risky," said Ned defensively.

"Well," smiled Jonah, "yer probably standin' pretty close to yer new well. Can't be sure till the new rod says yea or nay, but it does seem likely."

With that, Jonah retrieved his still unnamed divining rod, grasped it with new enthusiasm and, almost immediately, felt a surge that significantly surpassed all those he had experienced since his arrival on the farm. With the old well as his starting point, he began pacing back and forth in a large, rectangular grid. Each time he passed near one particular spot, he could see and feel spirals of energy. Then, less than twenty feet from the well, the rod swung down with force.

"Diggin' here ought to do it," he declared with confidence, "but be prepared to dig deeper than before. Maybe even twice as deep. Sooner or later, though, ya should hit water."

The certainty with which he spoke surprised even Jonah as he waited for Ned to bring a stone to mark the site. Never before had he given voice to such optimism, and he was at a loss to explain why he did so now. But, in the absence of any compelling doubt, he decided not to temper his assessment.

Ned was ecstatic. "I'll start digging as soon as we all get a bit to eat," he declared. "I know I promised Jake and Emmet I'd help them, but they're probably ready to quit for the day. I can join them first thing tomorrow."

Both Jonah and Seth welcomed the suggestion of food. Within minutes, Ned's wife Elizabeth had laden their kitchen table with bread, meat, greens, and a small cornucopia of fruit. She also brought a large porcelain pot of coffee to the table and, sensing Seth's obvious desire to emulate those around him, she returned to the cupboard to get a cup for him as well.

Jonah was quick to endorse her decision. "Drink up, Mister Fisherman," he commanded. "Ya earned every drop."

Once back outside, Ned removed the stone that marked the site and drove a stake into ground in its place. He then took a piece of rope about five feet long, tied a loop in one end and slipped the loop over the stake. Then, after tying a smaller stake to the other end of the rope, he dragged it across the topsoil to create a visible circle for the new well. Seemingly larger than it needed to be, it ensured that the well's earthen wall could be lined with stone. Ned and Jonah then took up shovels and began to dig. By day's end, they had dug down nearly three feet.

"I'm really obliged to you, Jonah," Ned remarked as the dowser and his young sidekick voiced their goodbyes. "One way or another, I'll do my best to make it up to you."

"Helpin' Jake and Emmet bring in new wells is about all ya need do," replied the dowser. "Ain't lookin' for nothin' for myself."

On the way home, Jonah made it a point to assure Seth that the new divining rod seemed a worthy successor to Drake. "This new rod's got a mighty good feel," he proclaimed. And, as Seth beamed in delight, Jonah added, "Might even be good for oil."

CHAPTER 11

Reverend Small rose early on Sunday morning, early enough to watch the sun rise over nearby hills strewn with spruce and pine, hemlocks and maples, birch and beech, and a variety of other trees and shrubs. Each contributed its own unique shade of color to the mosaic before him, a vista he had come to appreciate and enjoy throughout the day but especially at dawn.

Although confident when he retired that he was fully prepared for the worship service, which was only a few hours away, he awoke restless and disturbed.

Will my sermon really help ensure reconstruction of the church? Might this all come to nought? Am I ready to leave the outcome to the Blakes and ultimately to God?

Drawn once more to the beauty of the vista before him, he was almost instantly reminded of one of his favorite verses from Psalms: "I will lift up mine eyes unto the hills, from whence cometh my help. My help cometh from the Lord, which made heaven and earth." And, for the first time that morning, he smiled.

His happiness and optimism were short-lived, however, as lingering doubts about the Blakes' strategy recaptured his thoughts.

What if my ministry is found lacking? What if a movement develops against the reconstruction? What if no one steps forward to lead? What if harvests and the desperate need for new wells become paramount?

But wait, he reasoned, *shouldn't I as a minister be ready to leave such outcomes to God's purpose and will? Isn't this what I preach with genuine conviction? Could this be a test of my own personal faith? Where is that still, small voice that always seems to arise when I am assailed by uncertainty and doubt?*

The crack of the screen door slamming shut interrupted his spiritual struggle and, shifting his gaze from the distant hills to the yard directly below, he found himself watching with amusement as Seth raced toward the barn, milk pail in hand.

Seth, oblivious to the figure in the upstairs window, almost tripped when he heard the minister's familiar voice calling to him.

"Running a little late this morning?" teased the preacher. Seth looked up in the direction of the sound but chose to ignore the jest and soon disappeared inside the barn.

Moments later Reverend Small's smile returned and his cares seemed to drift away as he recalled a passage from the seventeenth chapter of Luke. Having used it often in his sermons, he marveled at its relevance to the thoughts that continued to trouble him.

The same promise that Jesus had made to his disciples was there for him as well: nothing is impossible—even for those with faith no bigger than that of a mustard seed.

Refreshed by that promise, he found his thoughts drifting once again, this time to the Lord's Prayer and its petition that "Thy will be done."

But what happens, he began asking himself, *when my wishes and desires conflict with God's will? The answer,* he decided, *is most likely in what I want, why I want it, when I want it, and for whom I want it.*

Aromas from the kitchen began to compete for his undivided attention and, before he knew it, he had started down the stairs to breakfast. Still trying to supplant worry with faith and trust, he resolved to nurture his personal faith, trusting that one day it might become as mighty as the symbolic mustard seed.

Less than an hour after breakfast, Reverend Small set off for the field that had become his outdoor cathedral. Accompanied by Betsy, Seth, and Jonah, he was quickly engaged in light-hearted give-and-take. By the time they reached the school grounds, he regretted that he had to leave them to prepare for the service.

Reverend Small spotted the Blakes almost immediately, and the three converged just outside the schoolhouse. "I hope you didn't eat a big breakfast," kidded Art. "Ruth has drummed up her best chicken dinner and, knowing her, she'll be real disappointed if you don't finish off the whole bird!"

"Maybe I should skip the service and head over there now," Reverend Small rejoined with a touch of laughter. "Care to take my place so I can go early?"

"Sounds a little risky if you want these folks to put up a new church," bantered Art.

"Well, then," replied the minister more seriously, "I'll stay and do my best because I'd love nothing more than see a new church rise up from the ashes of the old one."

"You've got plenty of company," said Esther, joining in the conversation for the first time. "Judging by the comments we've been hearing," she continued, "folks are not only happy that you're here, they're ready to contribute in any way they can."

"I'm guessing it'll be unanimous," added Art as he opened the schoolhouse to get the table that Reverend Small often used as a resting place for his Bible. "There's no telling what will actually happen, but we certainly have a good feeling about it."

"Whatever concerns I had are now behind me," confided the minister. "I'm pretty sure that most of the folks here share our dream for a new church." Then, looking at his watch and the large crowd already at rest on the field, he started the service.

"Can anyone doubt that this is a day the Lord hath made?" he began with a sweeping gesture toward the clear blue sky and its widely scattered puffs of white, cumulus clouds.

Reverend Small's voice grew deeper and louder as he spied an old woman with her head slightly tilted and a hand cupped beside one ear. "Can anyone doubt that Sunday is a day we all need to refresh our tired bodies and our troubled minds?

"I have seen you at work in your barns and your fields, your stores and your shops, and even your kitchens, and I know your work is never done. Having worked beside some of you, I also know how hard you work. God knows too. And just as he admires and respects constructive labor, he offers and provides Sunday as an opportunity for well-earned rest.

"Can anyone doubt that the God who created and declared the seventh day a day of rest is a caring, loving God?

"Have we not a longing, if not an obligation, to express our thanks to God for a love so great He sent His only son Christ Jesus to die on a cross so that we might one day join Him and His son and the Holy Spirit eternally?"

Here the minister suddenly paused, realizing that it was not the sermon he had prepared and committed to memory. Instead these were words that rose straight from the heart.

"And once we have accepted Christ Jesus as our savior and

friend," he resumed, "is not worship and praise a natural fulfillment of that longing?

"But what of those who deny there is a God, those who neither deny nor accept the fact that God exists, those who concede there is a God but choose to ignore Him? To each of them I submit the simple but eloquent tenth verse from the ninth chapter of Proverbs: 'The fear of the Lord is the beginning of knowledge.'"

"Praise the Lord," cried an old timer near the front of the crowd, a man who was known more for his absence than his attendance at Sunday services. It was Emmet.

"God welcomes, appreciates, and responds to our worship and praise," Reverend Small continued, smiling briefly in the direction of the voice.

"And that's why," he suggested, "we must carefully consider rebuilding your church. For it's much more than a refuge from the heat and the rain, the cold and snow. And it's much more than a sanctuary where we can worship and praise the Father, Son, and Holy Spirit. It is also a place where we study the Bible together and seek His will for our lives, yours and mine."

Art Blake rose, as if on cue. For a moment there was an awkward silence. The minister had unwittingly set the stage for Art, and even though he was not quite ready to surrender leadership, he promptly did so. "Here to lead that discussion," he gestured toward Art, "is everyone's favorite shopkeeper!"

"Well, maybe not everyone's," laughed Art, as he moved forward to join Reverend Small in front of the crowd. "If I was that popular, I wouldn't be a shopkeeper. I'd be a politician."

As the crowd responded with some laughs from the men and a few giggles from the women, Art turned a bit more serious and informed the gathering that he was about to direct the minister to "a more heavenly place, the kitchen of Ruth Black, where a fine Sunday dinner is waiting."

By now, Art was joined by his wife, Esther, who curtsied in front of Reverend Small, then took his hand and began to lead him through the crowd to Ruth's nearby home.

"I suspect that most folks are completely behind the idea of rebuilding the church," Art observed. "But we need to be sure we'll finish whatever we start. Let's have a little vote. Do we already have a consensus? Does everyone here want to put up a new church?"

Most of the men and women immediately raised their hands, and in those cases where wives did but husbands didn't, a stern look or a poke in the ribs made it a family decision. And once the parents expressed consensus, some youngsters waved both their hands. For Art, the task was not so much looking for those who approved but rather those who did not. And just as he had suspected, there were a few who appeared ambivalent or hesitant.

"Look around, good people, and see what I see," he suggested gleefully. "It looks nearly unanimous to me."

Genuinely concerned that those who seemed to be withholding their support might become outcasts in the eyes of the others, Art quickly added, "Nevertheless, there are bound to be folks who have perfectly legitimate questions or doubts. Some may be wondering whether this is the right time. Others may be hesitating because it will be difficult or impossible for them to contribute financially. Whatever your concerns, let's get them out in the open."

In the face of silence, Art continued with a lighthearted laugh, "Like they say at weddings, speak now, or forever hold your peace. Let's keep in mind that we all need to carefully consider the role we are ready to play. By agreeing to rebuild, we'll need to step forward and promise to contribute in whatever way we can. While we will certainly need money, we all know that money alone won't do it. We also need men who can handle saws and hammers.

"Who's ready to promise money and manpower?" he asked pointedly. Most of the same hands that were raised initially as well as a few new ones went up, another near unanimous response.

"And who will oversee construction?" appealed the shopkeeper. "Who's ready to take charge?"

That challenge went unanswered.

After scanning unsuccessfully from one side of the crowd to the other, Art chose another tact. "I've lived here long enough to know that you men have already raised some of the strongest, most beautiful barns in the state. It probably makes more sense if you just get together and pick someone you all respect."

As some of the men began to gather in small, separate groups, Emmet rose and stood silently until he had the attention of the entire crowd. "I'd volunteer if I was able," he began, "but since I can't do it, I'd like to propose someone who's got a real good head on his shoulders."

"Who'd that be?" asked Art.

"He's a newcomer to these parts," answered the old farmer, "a man named Jonah."

There was no real need to elaborate for a moment or two, and Emmet played his card masterfully. Almost everyone either knew Jonah or knew of him. Most knew he was a hard worker, and some knew that he was pretty clever with a divining rod. In an instant, most eyes fell on the dowser who, at that point, was sitting with Betsy and Seth. Jonah had just promised the boy that they'd go fishing after their dinner that afternoon.

"Most of you folks may not know it," Emmet resumed, "but if it wasn't for him some of us farmers would be pretty desperate about now. Not only has Jonah helped us find new wells, he's pitched in along side us. When he figured the water was pretty far down, he even showed us how to rig up a springpole so we can drill instead of dig. And on top of all that, he put off drillin' at Miss Betsy's place so we can use his drill bit."

Hearing his name not once but twice, Jonah looked up. Having missed most of what Emmet had said, he was a bit bewildered, a state that Emmet quickly exploited.

"I'm thinking you should head up the rebuilding," the old farmer suggested as he and Jonah made eye contact. "From what I hear, you're just passing through this part of the state. Seems you're bent on going west. So the way I see it, if we don't keep you busy, you'll up and leave. Ever built a church before?"

Jonah started to rise to his feet, thought better of it, sat back down and remained silent.

Betsy, who was sitting on the other side of Seth, reached out and rested her hand on Jonah's arm. "Don't let that old fox push you into something you don't want to do," she said, well aware of Emmet's reputation as a master of flattery. "He's already got you busy on three farms with dried up wells."

"Thanks for the kind words," the dowser finally replied, "but that's not my kinda work."

Most of the men were fully aware of troubled wells, but almost no one except those he had helped were aware of the work Jonah had done voluntarily. Emmet's revelation that there was a dowser in their midst sent several scurrying toward Jonah.

Finding himself surrounded by a small group of farmers and townspeople eager to know more, Jonah had little choice but to rise to his feet. As he did, he heard another familiar voice. It was Lucas, some distance away, standing on the perimeter of the crowd.

"Emmet's right, folks!" shouted Lucas. "We've got to keep Jonah here. If he can find water with that stick of his, I'm ready to bet he can find oil too!"

Lucas's words skipped across the crowd like a stone skipping across a still pond, sending out a myriad of ripples that offered hope and excitement. Everyone, including Jonah, looked toward Lucas in anticipation, eager for elaboration that was not to come. Lucas, having captured the imagination of the crowd, now withdrew to a crouched position. And once again all eyes shifted to Jonah.

The dowser remained seated and silent, ignoring the whirlwind of questions from those around him. Yet the secret that he and Betsy and Reverend Small had kept to themselves was suddenly public, in fact, very public.

How could Lucas know? agonized Jonah. *Did he simply guess or did he reach that conclusion some other way?*

It was Art who finally spoke next.

"Well, Jonah," he intoned slowly with a hint of amusement, "if we take Emmet's remarks as a nomination, we can treat Lucas's remarks as a second. Maybe I should close nominations now before someone else throws out another name."

"Start clapping," interrupted Emmet. "Let's show Jonah we mean it!"

As the crowd began to respond by clapping and chanting, Jonah stood up. Gesturing to the crowd with outstretched hands, he managed to quell its growing cry of "Jonah! Jonah!"

"It's one thing to find a well," he began. "It's another thing to build a church. There's lots of men here who have put up barns, and a good many that have put up their own houses. You've got more talent here than you can shake a stick at. Better pick somebody else."

Emmet, fully aware that he was risking Jonah's ire and possibly his wrath, persisted. "Looks like you gotta convince him, folks," he declared, smiling broadly for the first time. And the chant that Jonah had quelled began anew. "Jonah," they all cried. "Jonah!"

Hearing the crowd and seeing Emmet's smile proved too much for the dowser. Shaking his head in disbelief at the morning's turn of events, he broke into a huge grin. As the chanting became louder and louder, he motioned again for quiet.

Shoving his hands into his pockets, he repeated his refusal to guide the rebuilding. "What is possible," he countered, "is some help to anyone else who needs a new well, providin' they either put up some money or pitch in with the rebuildin'."

Women in the crowd began to clap and, as they were joined by men who shouted their approval, Art marched over to the outdoor school bell and rang it energetically. The commotion brought Reverend Small and Ruth running to the field.

"You'll get your church," Art shouted to the minister triumphantly as he continued to ring the bell with gusto. "Thanks to Jonah."

Try as he might, Jonah was unable to work his way out of the throng. His offer of help had doubled the number of men who had formed a ring not only around him but Betsy and Seth as well. It was Betsy who ultimately provided an escape. "Come by the farm this afternoon," she told the large cluster of men, "and you can talk to Jonah there."

The circle surrounding them opened almost magically, and the three captives eased their way toward the road, each wondering if the crowd would follow. Instead, the men turned toward Art, Reverend Small, and the dying tones of the bell.

"Now that we've got some help for our wells," shouted one of the men, "it's time we got someone to organize the rebuilding. It seems to me the best man around to handle the money and get the materials is that gentleman ringing the bell."

"Suits me," cried another. "Art's as honest as the day is long, and he and Esther know how to handle the money. They also know how to handle all the orderin' that's got to be done."

Esther, who had joined Art by the school bell, was smiling broadly. "Try to get out of this one," she teased.

"I'm not sure I want to," her husband replied with an equally big grin, just as the crowd began to chant, "Art! Art! Art!"

Stepping forward in front of Art and Esther, Reverend Small raised his hands to still his congregation. "Good people, this is a great day for us all," he proclaimed. "I'm deeply indebted to Jonah and Art and Esther, but we still need someone to manage the construction, someone who can read plans and work side-by-side all you men who volunteer."

Once again, the crowd watched as Emmet rose to his feet. "That would be Ned," he intoned with new seriousness. "Anyone who's seen his place knows that he's about as good a craftsman as they get." By then the crowd needed no further endorsements. "Ned!" shouted a few. "Ned!" echoed others. Though the well-known and widely respected farmer attended worship often, he was nowhere to be seen. Unknown to Emmet and the others, Ned had foregone the service to continue work on the new well he had started the night before.

"Guess I'm the one to tell him he's got a new job," shouted Emmet when he realized his neighbor was not in their midst.

Caught up by the energy and goodwill emanating from the crowd, Art rang the school bell once more to complement the cheers and applause that followed the selection of Ned.

"It really is a great day," he told Reverend Small, "and these are really great people."

"Speech," demanded the congregation. "Speech!"

Instead of trying to quiet the crowd, Art tried to shout above it. "Who's ready to come forward and contribute?" he challenged. "Who's going to step up and volunteer?"

Surprisingly, many of the men and women did accept his challenge, and many moved forward, encircling him as they had Jonah. Esther, who was generally prepared for most things, drew out a pad and pencil from her little handbag. As people pledged or contributed, she carefully recorded the names and their respective pledges and gifts.

Both Art and Reverend Small stood nearby to convey their thanks with a handshake, a simple pat on the back, or, in a few cases, a gentle hug. When the last family departed, Esther looked up at the two men beside her.

"We can tell the sawyer to start delivering the wood," she reported enthusiastically. Then, as she continued flipping through her notes, she suddenly added, "You'll never guess who made the biggest contribution."

"Probably not," agreed Art. "So why don't you end the suspense and tell us."

"It was Lucas," replied Esther somewhat matter-of-factly. "He gave me $30 and said that more would be coming when we needed it."

No one spoke until they reached the road and started to part. "Put Lucas's money aside," instructed Reverend Small, "until I know what to do with it." Arriving back at the farm, he was surprised to find Jonah and Betsy talking with several families from the morning service.

"These folks are really hurting for water," Betsy explained as the minister joined the gathering, "and everyone wants to be first. We're still trying to schedule Jonah's help fairly. It's not easy."

"Well, I may not have the wisdom of Solomon," volunteered Reverend Small, "but I'll be happy to help any way I can."

As Betsy was about to schedule visits to the last three families, one of the men offered to be last. "It seems like these folks need help sooner than we do," he told her. "We don't mind waiting provided Jonah can get around to us in a couple weeks or so."

"I can probably last a while too," said another man. "Put me down as next to last."

"That does it," smiled Betsy. "Thanks everyone. Jonah and Seth will be paying you a visit in the order you agreed. Now scoot so I can get Sunday dinner for these gentlemen."

Everyone laughed, and as Betsy and the two men started toward the kitchen door, the visitors lost little time heading toward their own homes. They were barely inside the house, however, when they heard a knock at the door and realized one of the men had returned.

"What is it?" asked Betsy.

"Just curious," answered the man outside. "What's all this business about oil?"

"Poppycock," roared Jonah. "Pure poppycock!"

"Just what I thought," replied the man as he withdrew.

—

Monday morning came quickly, and the cloudless sky at sun-up promised another hot, dry day. Arriving at Jake's farm, Jonah and Seth found all three farmers hard at work on the springpole. The hole for the upright that would support the pole was finished and, while Jake and Ned positioned the Y-shaped post, Emmet trimmed a few remaining branches from it.

"Well, look who's finally here," joked the old farmer, "now that all the hard work's done."

Then, more seriously, he added, "We weren't really expecting you, Jonah. After you promised to help all those other folks, we figured you'd be plenty busy with them."

Jake and Ned stopped working and joined Jonah, Seth, and Emmet just in time to hear the dowser report that Barnes had promised to hitch up his team and bring the drill bit over before noon. Once the springpole was in place, the bit attached and the drilling begun, Jonah continued, he fully intended to visit the other families.

"Good thing you came by," said Ned with a wink. "None of us have ever used a springpole before, and some of us might be too proud to ask how."

"Then let's get it up!" commanded Jonah, heading toward both the upright and the pole which was still lying on the ground near the drill site. "We can be finished in another hour or so if we don't hit any snags, and we can have some fun with ol' Barnes if we're just sittin' around doin' nothin' when he comes."

The men chuckled at the thought and quickly resumed work. With Jonah's strength and expertise at their disposal, the work went smoothly and quickly. While the other men anchored the upright, the dowser formed the stirrup in one of the two ropes that would hang from the springpole. And, as Jonah had predicted, they were finished before Barnes drove up in a small cloud of dust with Reverend Small sitting beside him.

"Been waiting all morning," teased Emmet as he rose to greet Barnes, a close friend.

"No point in hurrying," countered Barnes. "I plan to bill you by the hour."

As the farmers engaged in good-natured banter, Jonah carried the bit from the wagon to the second rope dangling from the end of the springpole. He then rested the drilling end on the ground where it would strike its first blow and carefully threaded the free end of the rope through the eye of the bit. He then pulled the loose end of the rope upwards until the bit was over two feet above ground. With the skill of a sailor, he quickly tied the bit at that height. He then wound the excess rope carefully in a tight spiral above the knot and secured it with yet another knot.

Fascinated by the speed and ease with which Jonah worked, the men fell silent, waiting to see what would happen next. They did not wait long.

Satisfied that the bit was mounted for maximum impact, Jonah raised his right foot into the stirrup. With his hands raised above his head, he grasped the rope and jumped up, allowing all his weight to fall on his right foot. The end of the springpole plunged downward, the bit struck the dry soil with an audible thump and, as the dowser released the rope and removed his foot, the springpole flew back up, lifting the bit from the ground. Unobstructed by hidden rock, it left a hole four inches deep.

"That's all there is to it," Jonah shouted as he repeated the cycle, this time using his left foot in the stirrup. There was another thud as the bit plunged deeper into the hole before the springpole pulled it free when Jonah removed his weight from the stirrup. With the rope still vibrating, he repeated the cycle once more.

"Let me try that," insisted Jake.

"Mind yer elders," argued Emmet, "I'm next!"

Amused by the old timer's feistiness, Jonah handed the rope to

Emmet. "Think yer heavy enough to sink the bit?" he asked with a big grin. "Ya look a little light to me."

"I'll bet he can't get it to hit the ground," laughed Jake. "He's gonna hafta go home and have the missus cook up a big dinner."

"That won't do us much good now," joked Ned. "What he needs to do first is load up his pockets with some big rocks."

Even Seth joined the fun, asking whether he should climb up on Emmet's shoulders.

While enjoying the camaraderie, Emmet found himself wrestling with the rope, trying to bring the stirrup down low enough to get his foot into it. Jonah, fully aware of the difference in their height, had anticipated the problem and, as inconspicuously as possible, helped pull the stirrup down. After managing to get his foot in the loop and his hands around the rope just below Jonah's grip, Emmet leaped up. Instead of plunging straight down, the bit swung from side to side, striking several inches from the edge of the hole.

"Can't say I didn't try," lamented Emmet, admitting defeat.

Jonah was quick to provide an excuse, easing the old man's embarrassment. "Wasn't yer fault," he declared. "I never let go of the rope."

Slightly taller and considerably heavier, Jake took the rope from Jonah. "It's my turn to come up short."

Contrary to that remark, Jake was entirely confident that he could easily duplicate the style and poise that Jonah had demonstrated. His first attempt, however, was not so smooth and, like Emmet, he swung the bit off center, and it crashed down outside the hole. Rather than risk entertaining his peers with failure, Jake repeated the cycle almost immediately. This time the bit hit its target with enough impact to deepen the hole.

"Nothin' to it, once ya get the hang of it," he told Ned as he handed him the rope.

There was a certain expectation among the men that if anyone could perform the routine with the same skill as Jonah, it would most likely be Ned. Although he had never seen, much less operated, a springpole before, Ned replicated Jonah's performance flawlessly.

Taking his cue from the dowser's example, Ned began repeating each cycle with only a brief pause. By his fifth or sixth cycle, he had developed a rhythm the others were forced to admire. When he finally stopped, nearly out of breath, the bit was barely visible before it reemerged from the hole. Yet everyone knew the drilling would only get slower and harder.

"Don't count me out," said Reverend Small, reaching for the rope. "The sooner we can get water for all those that need it, the better."

That said, he placed his foot into the stirrup and, much to everyone's delightful surprise, brought the bit down as neatly as Jonah and Ned. Before stopping, he too continued through several cycles.

The minister bowed to the cheers and applause that followed his turn at the springpole, and he bowed again when Emmet declared, "First preacher I ever met who could cut hay and drill a well!"

It was time for a break and, as luck would have it, Jake's wife appeared with bread and cheese and fresh milk. "We're trying to save water any way we can," she explained, and every one of the men nodded in agreement.

As they sat and ate, Jonah decided to prepare the men for the moment when the rope would have to be lengthened. "It won't be long now before the bit will be down as far as it can go," he told the farmers. "When that happens, ya need to add additional rope. Just keep the bit high enough so it'll hit hard and drill deep."

Ned was the first to fully comprehend the instructions. Confident that Ned would provide the leadership needed, Jonah invited Reverend Small to join him and Seth on their journey to the first farm on Betsy's list.

"Thanks for asking," replied the clergyman, "but I think I can do more good here."

So, with Seth at his side, Jonah set off for a place called Cooper's. "Anywhere near here?" he asked the boy.

"Good hour's walk," Seth replied. "It's the farthest away."

When Jonah failed to respond in any way, Seth resumed. "All the other farms are a whole lot closer. Think we can do more than one place this afternoon?"

"Could be," answered the dowser, "providin' it don't take this new rod forever."

Then, realizing that he had unintentionally reopened an old wound, Jonah added hastily, "It's been doin' real good so far, young fella. Ya picked good wood. One or two more wells and yer gonna hafta give it a name."

As the pained expression on Seth's face changed to a big smile, Jonah quickly decided to promote the whole idea further. "Got any ideas that way?"

"No," replied Seth thoughtfully. "How about you?"

"Not off hand," the dowser answered. "Let's cogitate on that for a day or two."

A long silence followed until they encountered a fork in the road, and Seth led them off to the right down a trail cut into the side of a hill. Looking ahead, they saw a man move from an adjacent stone wall to the road. Stopping, the man looked their way and waited.

At first, neither Jonah nor Seth recognized the man, but, as they drew closer, Jonah realized it was Lucas. Once face-to-face, it was Lucas who uttered the initial greeting.

"Headed for another farm?" he inquired.

"Yup," said Jonah guardedly. "Might even make a couple farms today."

"Why not stop, catch your breath, and chat a spell," Lucas urged, pointing toward the stonewall. "There's even a little shade over that wall."

"Don't mean to be unfriendly," the dowser said, "but me and the boy gotta keep goin'."

Ignoring Seth, Lucas pressed on. "I know you're not much inclined to do business with me, but, if you're willing, I've got a new proposition that's simple and worth your while."

"Can't stop," insisted Jonah, picking up his pace, "but won't turn ya away if ya wanta talk whilst we keep walkin'."

"Fair enough," responded Lucas. "Since you're not interested in making money hunting for water, why not use this tremendous power of yours to find oil?"

Jonah said nothing, hoping that Lucas would somehow reveal what led him to speculate about oil. Lucas, concerned that he might lose whatever interest Jonah might have in his proposition, hurried to present his pitch.

"You won't do anything but look for places to drill," he said enthusiastically. "I'll buy the bit, and I'll hire men to set up the springpoles. Tell me where to drill, and I'll buy the land or get the drilling rights. It'll cost you nothing, Jonah."

"What do I get out of it?" Jonah finally asked.

"That's the best part," said Lucas slowly, trying to gauge Jonah's real interest. When the dowser neither probed further nor changed his poker expression, Lucas made his offer. "Thirty percent after expenses!"

"That the best ya got to offer?" countered Jonah.

"Say yes now," argued Lucas, "and I'll go thirty–five percent."

"Tain't even worth discussin'," Jonah laughed. "What makes ya think lookin' for oil even appeals to me?"

"Because I suspect it does," challenged Lucas somewhat defiantly. "And what I'm offering you is a better deal than you'll ever get on your own. Just remember that you don't need to put up a cent. The risk is all mine."

Prolonged silence followed. When it finally got unbearable, Lucas demanded, "What's wrong with it?"

"Already said tain't worth discussin'," retorted Jonah.

"Well," replied Lucas, "I'll give you my final offer. You get fifty percent on the first well that comes in and forty percent on every well that comes in after that."

"That's probably worth sleepin' on," the dowser grumbled. "Just don't go orderin' that bit or anything else for the time bein'."

Satisfied now that Jonah might weaken, Lucas tried to persuade Jonah to agree to the partnership then and there.

"Don't be a fool, Jonah," he insisted. "You could get very rich, very quickly. All you have to do is tell that stick of yours to find oil. I'll do all the rest."

"That includes keepin' the books, don't it?" asked Jonah wearily.

"Of course," Lucas shot back indignantly, recognizing the suspicion behind the question. "It's all a matter of trust, Jonah. If I can trust you to find the oil, you can certainly trust me to put up all the money and honestly account for every penny we earn and spend."

"It ain't so much about every penny earned," Jonah retorted, revealing more and more of his New England temperament and skepticism. "It's more about every penny spent."

"Maybe you're going to have to sleep on that too," answered Lucas heatedly.

"And maybe it's time ya started pesterin' someone else," said the dowser more calmly. "Come on, young fella, time we got to Cooper's."

Though defeated, at least for the moment, Lucas displayed neither discouragement nor disappointment. Turning in the direction from which he had come, he offered a small smile, a half-hearted wave, and a final word. "Good luck finding water."

Seth could sense Jonah's annoyance long after Lucas had left and, for that reason, he decided to say nothing. However, when they finally came to a crossroad, the youngster pointed to his left and reported, "Cooper's down that road."

Jonah barely nodded. Seth tried picking up small stones and throwing them at trees along the way, hoping that his friend and mentor might do so too. Even that failed to pull the dowser from his preoccupation. When the Cooper farm finally came into view, Seth chose to say nothing, and it worked.

"That the place?" asked Jonah. Seth nodded in much the same way Jonah had earlier.

Jonah seemed puzzled for a moment and then, recognizing the likely cause of the boy's behavior, broke into a big smile and a hearty laugh.

"Sorry, young fella," he apologized, "Just tryin' to figure out how Lucas knows my primary aim is oil. Must be he's been sneakin' around your place and heard somethin'."

Once again, Seth responded only with a nod.

"Guess we'll hafta go fishin' after we get done here," suggested the dowser in the hope of helping Seth find his tongue.

CHAPTER 12

The Coopers had seen the pair coming down the road long before they arrived, and the whole family was waiting beside the road. Both the couple and their two teenage boys waved a welcome as the gap closed. "Sure glad to see ya!" thundered Cooper.

The greeting was quickly followed by a handshake and, with the formalities over, everyone headed toward the family's well. While the adults discussed the urgency to bring in a new well, the two teenagers began asking Seth about Jonah's divining rod. For Seth, the attention and respect of his peers was a new and pleasant experience.

Once the small talk was over, Jonah lost little time selecting his field of search and soon began pacing across it while the family stood by, ready and eager to help in any way it could.

Less than an hour later, Jonah stopped, put the rod behind his back, slipped it under his belt and surveyed the property for more promising ground. Cooper, clearly concerned with Jonah's initial failure, tried to hide his disappointment. "Don't worry if ya can't find water close to the house or barn," he shouted. "We'll carry it as far as we need to."

Soon after Jonah shifted his attention to another area, farther from the house and barn but still within easy walking distance, the rod began to display life almost immediately. Within a half hour, the dowser called for a stone marker.

"Ya can get out yer shovels, and put those boys to work," Jonah told Cooper with a grin. "If ya stick with it, ya oughta have water by the end of the week."

Cooper and his wife made several earnest attempts to persuade Jonah and Seth to join the family for an early supper, but each time the dowser begged off.

"Promised this young fisherman we'd go fishin' when we finished here," he explained.

"How high's the water in that creek of yours?" asked Cooper.

"It's lower and muddier," said Jonah, "but it's still flowin'."

"Guess we never really appreciate water 'til we run out," ventured Cooper, fully mindful of his own indifference in the past. "It's just so doggone easy to take for granted."

Jonah nodded in quiet agreement, and he and Seth took their leave. It was a long walk back, and although the dowser once again praised the feel and performance of the new divining rod, he spoke only of its potential for discovering water.

By the time they got home, Betsy had dinner waiting.

"Wash up and come inside," she shouted through the window by kitchen sink. "Food's already on the table."

"Guess fishin' will hafta wait," said Jonah.

Both Betsy and Reverend Small were engaged in casual conversation when Jonah and Seth swung the kitchen door open and took their places at the kitchen table.

"Did you get to Cooper's?" asked Betsy.

"Yup," answered Jonah.

"Found water too," volunteered Seth, well before Jonah chose to elaborate.

"Wonderful!" exclaimed Betsy. "Is it near the house?"

"No, but it's not all that far away," Seth replied as he reached for bread.

The three adults exchanged eye contact, each smiling at the boy's enthusiasm.

"Anything else happen today?" his mother probed, indulging in further curiosity.

"Saw Lucas," Seth answered.

"Oh!" exclaimed Betsy, shifting her eyes toward Jonah. "Where was that?"

"On the road to Coopers," Seth explained. "Going down that last hill to their place."

"And just what did he want?" asked Betsy, looking specifically for a reply from Jonah.

"He wants Jonah to look for oil," said Seth.

"True enough," added Jonah. "Still don't know how he come to find out but, fact is, he made me a pretty good offer."

"How can you even consider it, knowing all that I've told you?" challenged Betsy.

"Well, the man's ready to take all the risk and still give me roughly half the profits," the dowser replied. "Strikes me as a pretty good deal."

"Have you already agreed?" pressed Betsy.

"No, ma'am," answered Jonah. "Just promised to sleep on it."

"Jonah, I'm ashamed of you!" exclaimed Betsy. "That man's a scoundrel, and you know it. No matter what he says, he'll cheat you just like he's cheated everybody else."

"Won't much matter if we hit oil here on yer place," said the dowser defensively.

Though sorely tempted to join the conversation, Reverend Small refrained. Having spoken out so emphatically in the past, he was sure any comment he might make would prove counterproductive. Besides, Betsy seemed to be doing pretty well without help from him.

With a stalemate at hand, the three adults focused on supper instead. When Betsy finally pushed her chair back and began clearing the table, Jonah looked over at the minister, hoping he would reopen the discussion.

But Reverend Small remained silent so Jonah smiled and tried coaxing. "Ain't it about time we heard from yer corner of the table?" he cajoled.

"I'd like to think you'll make the right decision," said the minister simply.

"And what's that?" countered Jonah.

"Jonah, you not only have a great gift, you also have a very generous spirit. It's water, not oil, that folks need. Finish what you've started. You still have a long list of families to help. After that, you can start drilling here. Lucas can surely wait," replied Reverend Small, careful to avoid mentioning any future role in rebuilding the church.

"He's right, Jonah," interjected Betsy.

"Blast it!" cried Jonah. "Yer both just makin' it harder." Then, rather than apologize for his outburst, he added, "Never did say how much sleep it'd take." With that, he reached the door, bid them all good night, and headed for the barn. Midway between the house and barn, he stopped short, wheeled around, and returned to the house.

"Come on, young fella," he commanded. "There's still time for a little fishin.'"

An hour later, they reappeared with a half dozen bullheads and a large perch. Despite the darkness, Jonah insisted on cleaning their catch, and as he dressed each bullhead, he showed Seth how to skin the bullheads without getting hurt by their sharp thorn–like fins.

Jonah dropped the small fillets in a bucket of salted water, covered it with a damp cloth and, after bidding Seth good night, he left their catch in the sink for lunch or dinner the next day.

On his way to the barn, Jonah found himself gazing at the evening sky and, somewhat inevitably, was drawn to the bench that always seemed to offer him a special respite, night or day.

Almost immediately, his thoughts drifted from the stars to the offer from Lucas. Even if he couldn't completely trust the man, it seemed like a golden opportunity to determine whether his dowsing skills could lead him to oil and the riches it promised. What made it so tempting, he concluded, was Lucas's promise to cover all the costs, even in the event of a few early failures.

On the other hand, he mused, Betsy had allowed him to erect a springpole on her land so he could search for oil there. If he did strike oil, he would be in a better position to demand an even sweeter deal from Lucas. That thought clearly appealed to him and, rather than consider the possibility that he might not strike oil on Betsy's land, Jonah decided to avoid the commitment Lucas sought. Tired but content, he headed inside the barn and was soon asleep.

By suppertime on Saturday, he had winnowed his list down to three. On his way home from the farm family he had helped that afternoon, he had swung by Jake's place but, instead of finding a new well, he found Jake and his neighbors still taking turns on the springpole.

Whatever their disappointment, they kept it well hidden. More than happy to take a break from the monotonous cycle of drilling, Jake and his neighbors greeted Jonah and Seth with smiles, handshakes, and wit midway between the springpole and the road.

"Bet the only reason ya came by was to have the honor of hittin' water," kidded Emmet. "Well, make no mistake, that honor's gonna be mine."

"Could be if you ever set foot in the stirrup," teased Jake.

The conversation soon turned serious, however, and the men reported that they had hit underground rock so large they had to start over again. Rather than reposition the springpole, they explained, they simple moved the rope closer to its fulcrum in hopes of missing the rock. It was still too early, added Emmet, to tell whether their strategy had worked. It was slower and more tiring, they all noted, because moving the rope farther away from the tip of the springpole decreased the distance that the bit dropped. And that reduced its impact.

"Even if it's harder," agreed Jonah, "it makes good sense."

With the onset of afternoon chores, Emmet and Ned departed with Jonah and Seth. Jake resumed drilling alone.

Reverend Small, meanwhile, had spent much of his week meeting daily with Art Blake, pouring over drawings from Ruth Black. Although rough in nature, they provided sketches of both the exterior and interior of the old church. Developed years earlier by Ruth's late husband, they also offered valuable dimensions and, in some cases, clues to the woods used in construction.

The drawings, Ruth had explained, went back to a time when farmers in a neighboring township wanted to build a church modeled after theirs. Since no one knew what had happened to the original architectural plans, her husband collected critical dimensions and sketched basic layouts to facilitate the proposed sister church. Nothing came of it, she added, so she stashed all his notes and drawings away in a drawer and soon forgot them.

For Art and Reverend Small, they were a blessing. While Art compiled a list of lumber for the building's framework, the minister developed a list of changes, mostly to the interior, that he hoped would appeal to his parishioners.

As the collaboration between Art Blake and Reverend Small grew so too did their excitement. Along with new donations and pledges both from members and non-members, the idea of rebuilding quickly progressed from possibility to probability, from wishful thinking to near certainty. By the end of the week, Art was ready to visit the local sawyer to order the timbers and beams, joists and rafters that would soon rise up from the reconditioned foundation.

While preparing the latest tally of gifts and pledges, Esther was suddenly reminded of the contribution from Lucas, which Reverend Small had instructed her to put aside.

"If he joins us for worship tomorrow," declared the minister, "I'll have a talk with him. In lieu of all the things I've heard, I'm very uneasy about accepting that money."

"It's a tidy sum," countered Art, "and there could be more where that came from."

"I know," answered Reverend Small thoughtfully, "and that makes it even more difficult."

Only then did Esther join the conversation. "Do you really think a leopard can change its spots?" she asked her husband pointedly. "I'm not all that comfortable with it either. I know we need the money, but we don't need it that bad."

"Well, we've got a pretty powerful preacher here," teased Art. "Maybe Lucas has finally seen the light."

"I live in hope," said Reverend Small. " I like to believe that a man is innocent until proven guilty. Just the same, in view of some of the things I've heard recently about Lucas, I'm afraid that even if that money was not acquired illegally, it's not necessarily clean either."

"In any event," he continued, "I think a talk with Lucas is very much in order, and it should go without saying that this discussion should never leave this room."

"You can take that for granted," replied Esther.

Art immediately affirmed his wife's assurance of confidentiality and then added, "Lucas is a funny duck. I don't doubt that he's cheated a few people along the way, but I find it hard to believe the rumors that he deliberately set fire to the old church."

"That's interesting," responded the minister. "How do you think the fire started?"

"Well, there's always been plenty of speculation," Art said. "But my favorite is the story about a couple that went into the church to escape the rain. Seems ashes spilled from his pipe and started the fire long after they left."

"Nonsense," interrupted Esther.

"Has Lucas always lived here?" asked Reverend Small, trying to learn a bit more.

"No more than ten years or so," answered Art. "He came looking for a job at the bank and got it. Whenever folks asked, he told them he hailed from Philadelphia. That was about it. He never had much to say about any family."

"That could be a good way to start my conversation," mused the minister. "Who knows, maybe he and I know some of the same people in Philadelphia."

With that, Reverend Small took his leave, reminding Art and

Esther that he still had a sermon to prepare. "It's a pity that Lucas has aroused suspicion and distrust in so many people," he added as he headed for the door. "Keep us both in your prayers. Talking to Lucas will surely require help from the good Lord."

—

Sunday morning seemed like a carbon copy of so many recent days that month. Like the others, it began sunny and warm with hardly a cloud in the sky. By the time the clergyman reached the school grounds, it was hot and uncomfortable. His suit, which he regarded as a small but important symbol of his vocation, was wet from perspiration and dusty from his long walk. The temptation to remove his coat or at least unbutton it was, however, something he quickly and flatly rejected.

What appealed instead was the idea of positioning everyone, including himself, in the shade and the occasional breeze that awaited beneath the trees near the road. Once uttered, the suggestion won the instant approval of the crowd. In minutes, Reverend Small was surrounded by a smiling, happy throng.

Convinced earlier by Art that it was time to introduce hymns into the service, even though there was no piano, he deferred to the shopkeeper with a sweeping wave of his right hand. "If you like what you hear, join in!" shouted Art. He then began to sing "The Old Rugged Cross" with a rich, baritone voice often heard at worship services in the past. By the time he reached the end of the first verse, everyone was on their feet, adding their voices without hesitation. It was a very special moment as pleasing and stirring for the clergyman as it was for everyone there.

"I have never heard that hymn sung more beautifully," observed Reverend Small.

"Any need for a piano next Sunday?" asked Art aloud.

"No!" thundered the men, women and children in unison.

"No!" echoed Reverend Small with a smile as broad as the planet.

"Were it not for a sermon that I believe is important and timely in relation to the work we've begun, I would gladly see this service spent in music and song," he continued. "You can be sure, however, that with or without a piano, hymns will always be part of our future worship."

"Amen," responded a lone voice that sounded very much like that of Emmet.

The minister's huge smile reappeared as he searched his congregation for that voice. Try as he might, he failed to find Emmet. And for good reason. Emmet had eased down close to the ground, disappearing behind his friend and neighbor, Jake. What Reverend Small did see was Lucas, a lonely figure on the outermost edge of the crowd, far removed from everyone else. *Hope he stays to the end of the service,* thought the clergyman.

"Without even closing my eyes," he began aloud, "I can see a new building that will soon emerge where your former church once stood. In many ways, they will surely be alike. Dedicated to God the Father, God the Son, and God the Holy Spirit, both churches reflect the hopes, dreams, and prayers of the builders that God will dwell with us and we with Him. But there will also be at least one important difference. The old church was erected by your forebears whereas the new church will be built entirely by you.

"Each of you will have a personal stake in the new church, some by gifts, some by labor, and some by both. No contribution escapes God's notice. Many of you have made personal sacrifices to contribute money for materials. You can be sure that such sacrifices have special favor in God's sight. So too does He look with favor on those who will raise the new church with their heads and hands. For those of you who have so freely pledged, take pride in what you are about to accomplish.

"I fear, however, there may be some who have given in the belief that they can buy their way to Heaven. Any of you who have done so have failed to hear or understand the true nature of God's greatest gift, the promise of eternal life. Can any of us buy our way into Heaven? Of course not! Can any of us buy God's boundless love? Of course not. It's not for sale! Can any of us live our daily lives without sin? Of course not. Not even me!"

As Reverend Small offered and rejected each premise, his voice rose. And then he paused. His self-imposed silence was brief. When he resumed, he posed still another question. "If we can not buy it or live lives free of sin, how can we ever be certain of salvation?

"We must always remember that His promise of life eternal is a gift. And all He asks in return is that we acknowledge our sinful nature and seek forgiveness of our sins through His son, Christ Jesus. Yet as simple as this seems, it is probably one of the hardest steps we must take.

"While many of us are quick to accept the idea of a supreme being, we falter when it comes time to accept the salvation God offers each of us. This, my friends, is where we must make the critical leap from reason to faith. And unless we have the faith of a child, we will stumble and fail."

Pausing once more, the clergyman raised his Bible high above his shoulder.

"Disbelief is nothing new," he declared. "We all remember the story of doubting Thomas, found in the twentieth chapter of John, beginning with the twenty-fifth verse. Only when Thomas had beheld the wounds in Jesus' hands and side, did he believe. But the story does not end there. On the contrary. The following verses hold a special message for us all. 'Jesus said unto him, "Thomas, because thou hast seen me, thou hast believed: blessed are they that have not seen, and yet have believed."'

Reverend Small continued, encouraging his flock to understand that faith and trust are the keys to eternal life—never good deeds alone.

As he neared the end of his sermon he spotted Lucas once again, still sitting alone under the searing sun. After offering a closing prayer and benediction, Reverend Small tried to make his way toward the man that many of the farmers and townspeople regarded with suspicion and distrust.

Families eager to engage him unwittingly blocked his way, and he could only look in dismay as Lucas rose to his feet and started to leave the grounds.

Seeing Seth nearby, Reverend Small called to the boy and, as discreetly as possible, instructed him to run after Lucas to ask him to wait. Although it took longer than the clergyman had hoped, he eventually found himself face to face with Lucas.

"It's good to see you here this morning," Reverend Small began. "I hope you found my words worth further reflection."

Lucas ignored the remark and, with rising irritation in his voice and expression, demanded, "Why did you ask me to wait?"

"Well, to get straight to the point," the clergyman began, "I'd like to talk to you about your contribution to the new church. It's the largest we've received, and I understand from Art Blake that you've promised more in the future."

"That I did," confirmed Lucas.

"I'm certainly not eager to turn away your gifts," continued Reverend Small, "but it's important to me to know that they were derived honestly. Quite frankly, some folks say that you have resorted to usury, exacting high interest from those least able to pay."

"How I make my money is my business," growled Lucas. "If you don't want it, just give it back. I have plenty of other ways to spend it."

"There's no need to get unpleasant," responded the clergyman. "I could have rejected your donation outright, but I chose instead to discuss my concerns with you. It's only fair that I hear your side of this matter too."

"Making personal loans to people who the bank rejects is good business," said Lucas defensively. "I'm doing them a big favor. Along the way, I'm doing okay too. There's nothing wrong with that. Besides, it's really none of your business!"

Confronted with Lucas' take it–or–leave it attitude, the minister began to choose his words even more carefully. But just as he was about to tell the banker to retrieve his gift from the Blakes, he suddenly recalled their first encounter.

"Lucas," he asked softly, "do you remember the first words you ever spoke to me?"

"Can't say that I do," answered the lender, momentarily stumped.

"You walked up to me at the Blakes' store," said Reverend Small, "and without ever telling me your name, you said, 'Meet another sinner, damned like all the rest of these people.'"

"Sure you didn't just make that up?" retorted Lucas.

"Can't say that I did," replied the minister with a grin. "Those words were yours!"

Challenged with an indifferent "So what?" Reverend Small quickened the pace of the conversation. "Well, Lucas, I don't think you would have spoken to me that way unless you wanted my attention and goodwill. Where we go from here, however, is up to you. Just remember that while we're all sinners, not all of us are still damned."

Lucas, after first nodding in apparent agreement, declared, "Where we go from here is also up to you. You can turn down my donation, or you can accept it without reservation."

Rather than respond directly to Lucas's unyielding reply, the minister tried once more to break down the wall that Lucas had erected. "Why are you reluctant to openly discuss the way you obtain your wealth? Are you ashamed in some way?"

"Think what you will!" shouted Lucas in anger.

"Then reclaim your gift from Art Blake," responded Reverend Small, "but remember that you are always welcome at our worship."

"Don't hold your breath," snarled the lender.

Frustrated but undeterred, the minister moved alongside Lucas, put his hand on the man's shoulder, and offered a final word. "I'm beginning to suspect that your conscience isn't giving you much rest these days. Listen to it carefully, Lucas."

Surprisingly, Lucas stopped but said nothing. Instead, he looked deeply into the eyes of the clergyman, wondering why he was so persistent and uncompromising.

"Let me leave you with two stories," continued Reverend Small. "Both are from Luke, and both deal with earthly riches.

"The first is from the twelfth chapter where we learn about a rich man who decided to tear down his barns and build bigger ones for his growing harvests just so he could eat, drink and be merry.

"By storing up riches for his own pleasure, he angered God. The twentieth verse tells us that "God said unto him, 'Thou fool, this night thy soul shall be required of thee.'

"The second is from the very beginning of the nineteenth chapter. It tells us about a rich man named Zacchaeus who accumulated his wealth as a tax collector. He was curious about Jesus and, because he was small, he had to climb into a tree to see our Lord as he passed by—"

"I've heard that story," interrupted Lucas.

"But do you remember that after Jesus saw Zacchaeus, He called him down and then entered the tax collector's house as a guest? What makes the story special is that Zacchaeus was so grateful and happy that he promised to give back half his wealth to the poor and, to any man he had cheated, four times the amount."

When it was clear that Lucas had no intention of responding in any way, Reverend Small removed his hand and added simply, "Which man will you be, Lucas?"

Again, there was no response, only silence. Once more the minister tried to penetrate the wall Lucas had erected. "That choice is yours alone. I can only hope and pray that you will one day reject the folly of your present course and choose a path that's in the best interest of everyone, especially yourself. Until then, your gift is unwelcome. Take it back."

By then Lucas had turned his back to the clergyman and had started to walk away.

Reverend Small turned away too. Heading toward the road, he was surprised to see a small group still present on the field. Closer inspection revealed it was composed entirely of the farmers who had begun digging or drilling for new sources of water and the man who had used his skills as a dowser to help them.

"Not one of us has hit water," complained Emmet in a voice

loud enough for the approaching clergyman to hear, "even though we been digging and drilling way past the depths you said there was water."

"Predictin' where the water is ain't easy," conceded Jonah, "and predictin' how deep ya have to go is a whole lot trickier. It's easy to get it wrong."

"Could be wrong about ignoring prayer too," interrupted Reverend Small. "Maybe the good Lord is trying to tell us something."

"Can't say I didn't pray," retorted Emmet in his customary, impatient way. "Maybe it was just a little prayer but it sure came from the heart." Jake said nothing, fidgeting instead as the conversation shifted to prayer.

"What are you suggesting, Reverend?" asked Ned.

"Let's all try prayer," smiled the clergyman, "and not just for yourselves but for your neighbors too. Today is the day the Lord set aside for rest and prayer and praise. Use the rest of today that way. Tomorrow, we can all gather at Emmet's and pray together before you resume digging."

"Can't hurt," acknowledged Jonah.

"Sounds like we need an expert," suggested Ned, looking directly at Reverend Small. "I'm certainly not an expert on prayer, and I doubt my neighbors are any better. Join us if you can, Reverend. We need all the help we can get!"

"I'll be happy to join you," replied the minister. "Just remember that I can't guarantee success any more than Jonah can. What we need to recognize, however, is that our Heavenly Father does hear our prayers."

"Get your chores done early," instructed Emmet as he and his neighbors began to break away and return to their farms.

Jonah was the first to speak as he and Reverend Small ambled along the road home. "They shoulda hit water by now," he mused aloud. "That new rod is as good as Drake, maybe even a touch better. There's no mistakin' that!"

"Well, let's not forget that God sometimes works in mysterious ways," the minister responded with the often-heard expression. "I have no doubt that in His own time and in His own way, God will answer our prayers... provided that we trust in Him."

"Better count me out," proclaimed Jonah. "My faith's in my skills and my divining rod."

"Jonah," grinned Reverend Small, "you're already halfway there. You may not be ready to admit it yet, but you're probably closer to our Creator today than you've ever been."

"Maybe," conceded the dowser, "but what really counts is the gift I was born with."

Reverend Small was amazed and delighted with the dialogue. Never before had he and Jonah spoken so openly and freely. Before he knew it, he was challenging the dowser to probe more deeply. "Ever ask yourself why were you born with that gift or who gave it to you?"

As Jonah fumbled with the question, neither man spotted an approaching buggy until it was nearly upon them. By then the driver had seen the men, and he slowed his horse to avoid drowning them in dust. "What brings ya back out here in a buggy?" inquired Jonah, relieved that he could now ignore Reverend Small's question.

"Just wanted the good reverend to know that Lucas came by and demanded his money back," explained Art. "If you gentlemen jump aboard, I'll give you a lift to your place. On the way, you can tell me what happened."

Confronted with a narrow seat, Jonah ordered the clergyman

to sit while he chose to crouch sideways, grasping the back of the seat and the dashboard of the buggy.

"I tried to talk with Lucas after the service," Reverend Small began. "He was as ornery as ever. I got absolutely nowhere. I finally gave up and told him to take his money back."

"Well, it wasn't exactly unexpected," said Art, "but it was no small amount. Esther and I have been trying to figure out how we can replace it. It could delay ordering some materials we'll soon need."

"How much was it?" asked Jonah.

"Thirty dollars," answered Art, "with the likelihood of more to come."

"Now that I think about it," interrupted Reverend Small, "it's almost as bad as the thirty pieces of silver Judas was paid to betray Jesus. One way or another we'll get along without it. Any idea how to make it up?"

"Not yet," replied Art as they reached Betsy's farmhouse.

Betsy, who had seen them coming, was waiting on the porch. When the men kept on talking and failed to alight from the buggy, she walked over to join the conversation and almost immediately began to tease the shopkeeper. "This is a nice surprise, Mr. Blake, but how come you didn't offer my son and me a ride home?"

"Because I didn't know then what I know now," Art answered in all seriousness.

"Lucas took his money back after he and I had a little talk," explained the minister, "and now we're trying to figure out some way of making it up."

Jonah, speaking up for the first time, asked if they had ever tried a box social.

"What's that?" inquired Reverend Small.

"It's a wonderful idea!" exclaimed Betsy. "Why didn't we think of it before?"

Rather than leave the minister bewildered, Art quickly explained that rural communities sometimes raised money by encouraging their women to prepare their favorite dinners, package them in boxes, and put the boxes up for auction to the highest bidder.

"No one is supposed to know who made the boxes," added Betsy, "but single gals usually find a way to let their beaus know which box is theirs."

"That's when the fun starts," laughed Art. "Once a man starts bidding up the price for a certain box, all the other men figure out who made it. They can make it pretty expensive for the husband or beau, but it's all in good fun. Everyone has a good time."

"An auction?" inquired Reverend Small, looking perplexed. "A game of chance?"

"Not much different than buyin' cows or horses at an auction," said Jonah, trying hard to dispel the perception of gambling. "Just a bunch of menfolk competin' for a good meal and a good cause."

"Better be careful," admonished Betsy with a twinkle in her eyes. "Anyone comparing my cooking with cows or horses is looking for trouble."

Even Reverend Small laughed at Betsy's faux indignation, and the more he thought about it the more he realized his concern was unwarranted. "I suppose it's not really gambling," he surmised aloud. "Since folks bid instead of bet, no one loses money if they fail to win."

"Looks like you've got the job of pulling it all together if you'll take it," pronounced Art, reaching down to shake Betsy's hand. "And you can count on plenty of help from Esther."

"It will be fun," confirmed Betsy. "Tell Esther I'll be in to see her tomorrow."

Then, as Jonah and Reverend Small jumped down from the buggy, she grabbed each by an arm and started marching them toward the house. "Dinner's getting cold," she complained with a smile.

"Say no more," acknowledged Art, tugging lightly on the reins as he steered his horse and buggy back toward town.

CHAPTER 13

Jonah arose early, well before dawn. Once again, he had been restless during the night, still troubled by the fact that the first three sites he had plotted had failed to produce fresh water. Getting water from Miss Betsy's well took a few extra strokes than usual, but once it began running, it was cold and refreshing. After washing in the semi-darkness he retired to the bench outside the barn to struggle with the question of what he should do next.

As he grappled for the first time with the possibility of multiple failures, his eyes closed and he drifted off into unconsciousness. He was awakened by Seth, who, seeing his friend and mentor asleep, rapped his empty milk pail against the bench as he passed by. Jonah rose with a start, much to the amusement and laughter of the young boy. With a great yawn and an even greater stretch, the dowser headed toward the house for breakfast.

Betsy, knowing that he and Reverend Small were anxious to get to Emmet's farm as early as possible, had already begun the morning meal. Jonah had barely entered the kitchen when he and Betsy were joined by Reverend Small. There was a brief discussion among the three of them whether Seth should accompany the men. Although

Betsy wanted Seth to stay home to weed the garden, she relented just as the lad came in with the morning's milk.

The meal was eaten in haste, and the three left for Emmet's.

As they approached, they spotted the old farmer standing beside a gaping hole and a large mound of dirt and stone where Jonah had promised water. Once there they learned that Jake and Ned had insisted on bringing in the new well for Emmet before finishing wells for themselves.

"Got company," Emmet shouted to his neighbors. Jake and Ned stopped digging after taking a minute to refill the two buckets they used to remove dirt to the surface. With buckets in hand, they climbed out of the empty well on a crude ladder they had made from tall, slender saplings.

The greetings they shared were quick and perfunctory. Jonah complimented the men on the almost perfect circle and smooth walls they had dug thus far. Seeing a large pile of flat stone that had been brought to the site, he expressed hope they would soon see water seeping into the well so they could begin lining its wall with the stone.

"Amen," murmured Emmet.

"I guess that's a clue for me," said the clergyman, "but before we engage in prayer together, I can't help but remind everyone just how awesome and miraculous is this thing we call water.

"We all know water is critical to our daily lives. It gives and sustains life. Like the air we breathe, we can't get along without it. It was put here by God not only to quench our thirst but to wash and cook. It satisfies the needs of our poultry and cattle and our gardens and fields. It provides creeks and streams, lakes and ponds, for swimming in summer, ice in winter, and fishing year round. And let's not forget that it is the means of proclaiming our faith through baptism.

"Friends, when we rely entirely on ourselves, we ignore the greatest resource of all, the resource of prayer. In the seventh chapter of Matthew, Jesus said: 'Ask, and it shall be given you; seek, and ye shall find; knock, and it shall be opened unto you.' So let's humble ourselves before God, acknowledging His love and His power and imploring His help through prayer."

Each of the three farmers seemed lost in their private worlds, and even Jonah and Seth failed to respond in any way to Reverend Small's sweeping glance.

"Let's bow our heads," he continued. "Heavenly Father, you know our needs even before we ask for help. Though our faith and trust may be much smaller than a mustard seed, we come before you confident that in your own time and in your own way, you will answer our prayers.

"Oh Lord, you know how urgently Jake and Emmet and Ned need new sources of water and how unselfishly Jonah has provided his skills in their search. Help us to help ourselves, oh Lord. Help us to bring forth new springs, literally and spiritually, and help us to grow into more meaningful relationships with you and with your Son, our Lord, Christ Jesus. Amen."

"Amen," repeated Emmet.

There was a brief silence as everyone waited for someone else to speak. Jonah broke the impasse by raising his divining rod. "Back to work," he instructed the others. "Unless this rod says otherwise, this is where the water's gotta be."

Stepping away, with Seth at his side, he began retracing the paths he had trod before predicting that the men would find water where they were now digging. Each time his footsteps took him to the edge of the dry well, the rod responded more visibly there than anywhere else. Again and again, the rod behaved in the same dramatic way, reassuring everyone.

Although the men had re-entered the well and had resumed digging, they looked up every time they sensed Jonah's approach. Seeing the down-turned rod, they repeated the dowser's pledge, "This is where the water's gotta be."

Once he had satisfied himself that he had chosen the site wisely, Jonah joined the others, alternately digging, filling, lifting, and emptying the two buckets of ground and rock. Even Reverend Small joined the brigade, postponing his plans to join the Blakes to accelerate their efforts to rebuild the church.

By late morning the mound of excavated dirt had grown considerably, and the well was almost ten feet deep. Much of their early optimism had disappeared. With the sun nearing its peak, Emmet, who was emptying the bucket that the others had filled up, suggested that they break for their midday meal.

Jonah, who was digging alongside Reverend Small at the time, invited the minister to head up the ladder first. Then, with the pent up energy of frustration, he swung his pick into the hard surface of the well floor with such force that it was clearly embedded.

What began as simple annoyance at the elusiveness of water had unmistakably turned to anger. Jonah kicked the handle so hard it vibrated like a tuning fork, and the pick remained as immobile as the sword Excalibur. The pain that shot through his foot left little doubt it was time for him to exit the well.

Emmet's wife was ready long before Emmet announced the break for lunch. Known among neighbors as a wizard in the kitchen, she delighted everyone with her dishes and drinks, especially those unfamiliar with her culinary talents. A large sugar maple offered shade for the tired and disappointed men, but beyond the shade and good food there was little to promote conversation. Long after the dishes were bare, the men continued to sit in silence. No one wanted to ask the question on everyone's minds. "Is it time to stop digging?"

"No more than a couple feet," Jonah finally declared. "It's there, or it ain't."

With nearly an hour's rest and a stated end, the men rose to their feet, seemingly impatient to get back to work. Jake was the first to reach the ladder and the bottom of the well. Unaware that the pick was so firmly anchored, he nearly sprained his arm trying to free it. "Good Lord," he exclaimed. "Who sunk this pick so deep?"

Jonah, who was looking down from the edge of the well, reluctantly admitted his guilt with a simple "Must'a bin me."

"I'll get a sledge to free it," volunteered Emmet, heading toward his barn. Minutes later he returned with a sledgehammer almost too heavy to swing. Given its weight, Emmet carried it down the ladder rather than drop it into the well.

Jake examined the pick carefully, concerned that a misplaced blow might damage or even break it. Even after deciding where to hit it, he landed a heavy blow only to find that the pick remained frozen. Adding muscle to the next blow, he heard a loud metallic ring as the sledge struck the pick. The pick was as immobile as it was when Jonah left it.

Jake quickly changed the site of each blow from the sledgehammer and, in time, he began to feel and see the pick move slightly after each hit. "'Bout time ya gave it a good hit, ain't it?" teased Jonah, clearly amused that the pick was so unyielding.

Despite two more solid blows, the pick remained solidly in

place. Frustrated by the good-natured ribbing, first from Jonah and then his friends, he paused and looked up at Jonah. "You're the one who buried this thing, guess you're the only one who can get it out."

"Happy to do it!" laughed Jonah, heading for the ladder. He waited briefly for Jake and Emmet to climb out of the well and then headed down, two rungs at a time. When he reached the bottom, he gave the pick a kick just to determine how fixed it remained.

Confident that it was loose enough to pull free, he reached down with his right hand, grasped the wood handle next to the head of the pick and, looking as carefree as possible, pulled with all his strength. The extra effort proved unnecessary. The pick pulled free so easily that Jonah nearly lost his balance. The men looking down immediately roared in admiration.

"Nothin' to it," he declared with a big grin.

Jonah was about to lean the pick against the well wall when he noticed something quiver. Looking more closely at the small hole left by the blade of the pick, he realized it was almost completely filled with water. Dropping to his knees for a better look, he discovered that the water was about to overflow the hole and seep onto the floor of the well.

Yet even before he could announce his discovery, there was a sense of victory among those looking down from the rim of the well. While the lower reaches of the well caught little of the brilliant daylight above ground, there was more than enough light to capture Jonah on his knees where the pick had once been imbedded.

Nonetheless, no one dared to speak. Every eye was on the dowser, and every ear was primed for his next words.

"We hit water!" he finally shouted. "Start bringin' down some stone. We need to start layin' the wall before it gets ahead of us."

"At last!" cried Emmet.

"We did it!" uttered Ned, shaking his head in relief.

"I can hardly believe it," admitted Jake, who had all but given up.

Then, as the farmers scrambled to gather the largest stones to lower into the well, Jonah hastened to give the men credit. "It's yer patience and hard work that's been rewarded!" he added solemnly.

"And all your prayers," said Reverend Small softly.

The comment was just enough to get Emmet thinking. "Let's stop and thank the Lord," he told the others. "And then let's thank Jonah."

Reverend Small was quick to seize the opportunity. "Both Jonah and Emmet are right," he observed. "Your hard work has been rewarded and so has the long hours Jonah spent searching for the most promising places to dig. As we celebrate, however, let's not forget our Creator and our supplications for his guidance and direction—"

"Amen," interrupted Emmet.

As the clergyman bowed his head, the others followed, and he began to pray. "Heavenly Father, you know from the joy in our hearts the very depth of our gratitude, not only to Thee but to each other. Hear our thanksgiving, O Lord. Help us, we pray, to seek only those things we truly need. Help us, we pray, to trust always in Thee. For this we pray with humble and contrite hearts. Amen."

Silence prevailed for a moment or two, and then Jake spoke out. "I hate to admit it, but if there is any doubting Thomas around here, it's me. Truth is, I never put much stock in dowsing or the people that promise they can find water. What's worse, I've never really believed in God. It could be that God was waiting for me to come around before He let that water loose."

Jake paused, waited for a reaction and when there was none, he added, "If it's my fault that it took so long, I'm sorry."

"God does indeed work in ways that are mysterious to us, but whatever His reasons," insisted Reverend Small, "I'm pretty sure your doubts were not one of them. To be honest, I'm no more certain than you are that dowsing is a foolproof way to find water. What I do know is that Jonah embraces it as a special gift, and he has shared it freely with those of you in need. This is a time for thanksgiving and celebration, not guilt."

"Then lets get crackin'," said Jonah with a twinkle in his eye. "There's already water on the floor of our first new well."

By the time Emmet and Ned had to leave for their afternoon chores, the men had built a stone wall more than halfway up the inside of the well. And, in the meantime, the level of water had risen nearly three feet.

As they prepared to stop for the day, Emmet disappeared into the house. When he returned he held six small glasses, three in each hand. He handed them to Ned, who was still on the ladder laying stone, instructing the farmer–turned–mason to fill each with water from below. After fulfilling Emmet's command, Ned set the glasses near the edge of the well where the setting sun revealed water still lightly discolored by sediment.

"As soon as that dirt settles," announced Emmet, "we'll drink a toast to all concerned." Impatience prevailed, however, and without waiting any further, Seth and the five men raised their glasses to an enthusiastic toast by Emmet, "To water and to all who delivered it."

"That," declared Ned, "is good, fresh water."

The celebration resumed again later that afternoon when Jonah, Reverend Small, and Seth shared their story with Betsy. From deep inside a cupboard, she produced a freshly made berry pie and, when their evening meal was over, cut it into three pieces. Seth and Reverend Small each got a quarter. The remaining half went to Jonah, who, she said, was "clearly the most deserving." When the dowser tried to share it with Betsy, she declined, admitting that she had nibbled on a smaller pie made from leftovers.

Instead, she begged for more and more details, laughing harder and harder as the men told and retold the story of the immovable pick. As the story reached its climax, the men deferred to Seth to give his version of the excitement when Jonah freed the pick from the earth's viselike grip, and water broke the surface.

The next morning, Ned rejoined Emmet to finish lining the well with stone. Jonah, Reverend Small, and Seth left for Jake's farm soon after breakfast to help him resume drilling. As they approached the farm, they could see the springpole, snapping up and down.

Jonah quickened his pace and reached Jake well ahead of Reverend Small and Seth. By the time the clergyman and the boy got to the springpole, Jake had stepped out of the rope stirrup, eager to let Jonah calculate the depth the drill bit had reached. Discouragingly, they found it was time for the dowser to put his divining rod back to work.

Grasping the rod in the manner now familiar to each of them, Jonah lost little time in retracing the same ground he had covered nearly two weeks earlier.

"No different than before," he muttered after more than an hour's labor in the hot, dry unshaded terrain. "But givin' up ain't the answer. Let's keep drillin' 'til sundown tomorrow. If we don't hit water by then, we'll try lookin' elsewhere on yer property."

Jake, who was clearly unhappy at the prospect of moving the springpole and starting all over again, agreed. And he moved aside promptly when Reverend Small stepped forward to take over the drilling.

It took the clergyman nearly a quarter hour to redevelop a smooth, uniform motion. With the encouragement and an occasional admonition from Jonah, he soon mastered the art of jumping up and letting his weight pull the tip of the springpole down, freeing the drill bit to plunge into the cavity below.

While the rhythm he developed pleased and satisfied Jonah, it was especially satisfying to the clergyman himself. This was hardly the stuff of theological training, he thought, yet it seemed now more than ever an important dimension of his ministry. Not only was he there to share the gospel message, he was there to share their burdens.

When finally Jonah noticed a wobble or two in Reverend Small's rhythmic motions, he stepped forward, motioning the clergyman to stop.

"Time to add some rope to the drill bit," he explained, even though it was not particularly urgent.

The three men took turns throughout the day, driving the drill bit further and further into a stubborn landscape that refused to yield whatever water might lay beneath it. Although certain that the bit was down more than double the depth of Emmet's new well, Jonah tried his best to keep up Jake's spirit. "Bound to hit it soon," he repeated from time to time.

Eventually, as the shadows from the setting sun grew longer and longer, he found they had little choice but to quit for the day. Seth, who had spent most of the day just watching, summed up their disappointment and frustration. "Maybe the rod only works some of the time," he lamented. While the remark drew a quick rebuttal from Jonah, it also generated some laughter from Jake and Reverend Small.

With that, the young lad and his two mentors headed for the road and the long walk home. Jake's farm was barely out of sight when Seth noticed three men several hundred yards ahead. Seconds later, Jonah and Reverend Small also spotted the approaching trio.

"Whoever they are, they ain't in much of a hurry," observed the dowser.

"Looks like they're too busy talking," added Reverend Small.

"Maybe that's because one of them is Lucas," said Seth, squinting slightly to confirm his initial sighting. "The one in the middle looks like someone I know, but I can't remember his name. The other one's a stranger."

"Let's hope you're wrong about Lucas," murmured Reverend Small. "After working that springpole all day, I can do without another encounter with him."

"That guy's like cow manure," chuckled Jonah. "He's all over the place."

Although Reverend Small managed to suppress an inclination to laugh at the comment, he was far less successful in suppressing a huge grin. "That may be," he replied slowly with an irrepressible smile, "but let's not corrupt this young fellow with such images."

Just as Jonah was about to defend his remark, Seth recalled more about the man he had recognized. "That's one of the farmers who live on the road to the pond," he exclaimed. "I can't remember his name, but I know he's on our list of folks that want help finding water."

Neither man responded to Seth's revelation, and, as the distance between the two groups continued to close, it became obvious that Lucas and his companions were enjoying their conversation.

"They look too happy to be bothering with us," suggested Jonah.

"Well, we'll know soon enough," replied Reverend Small. "They're pretty close." With closure now imminent, he found his spirit refreshed, and it was he who waved and voiced the first greeting.

But Lucas chose to ignore the minister and instead called out to Jonah, beckoning him closer. "Glad we ran into you," he said gleefully. "I've got a couple of friends here that I'd really like you to meet."

Jonah moved within an arm's length of the three men, raised his hands to his hips and offered a barely visible nod in greeting.

"You might remember this gentleman," continued Lucas, placing his hand on the man's shoulder. "He was one of the farmers waiting for you to come by. You can drop him from your list because this other gentleman has already shown him where to dig a new well."

While Jonah mulled over the remark, the stranger thrust out his hand toward Jonah. "Good to meet a fellow dowser," he said cheerfully.

Jonah took the man's hand, shook it twice and uttered a simple "Likewise."

"My name's Brady," the man continued. "Hope you don't mind a little competition. From what Lucas tells me, though, there's more than enough work for the two of us. It might even be fun to see who brings in the most wells, especially after we shift from water to oil."

Both Jonah and Reverend Small managed to conceal their mutual surprise but, in that instant, they knew that a genie of dubious character was now loose. Faced with a muted response, Lucas decided to needle them further. "We've already signed up four farms," he revealed, "first to find water and then the oil."

"Sounds like a lot hinges on findin' water first," said Jonah.

"Not when I've got an expert like Brady," responded Lucas contemptuously. "Farmers like my offer. I charge nothing for finding water. If we find oil when we return in the future, they get a nice share of the profit."

Jonah felt a surge of anger. Whatever hopes he had had to achieve personal wealth locally were now dashed, largely because of his earlier failure to team up with Lucas. "More power to ya," he replied softly, depriving Lucas of any pleasure he hoped to enjoy from the conversation or Jonah's outward expressions.

Reverend Small waited until he was sure Jonah and Lucas were through engaging one another. Then, confident that Lucas would remember the biblical stories he had shared during their last encounter, he remarked, "It looks like you've reaffirmed your choice."

"See you in church," laughed Lucas as he and his companions resumed their journey.

Both Jonah and Reverend Small lapsed into private thought and, for much of the way home, no one spoke. Even Seth seemed to grapple with what he had heard and, somewhere along the way, his mind shifted to boyhood curiosity. "Why can't we just take our drill bit back and start drilling for oil on our place?" he asked innocently.

"It's a matter of priorities," answered the clergyman after Jonah ignored the question. "We can get along without the oil, but Jake can not get along without water."

From the moment they opened the door and marched into her kitchen, Betsy knew she would be facing two very glum men at dinner. "Just turn around and go back outside and clean up," she commanded. "You included, Reverend. I don't need all that dirt in the house."

Hopeful that she had pierced the cloud the men were under, she began setting the table as fast as she could, correctly assuming that the day had gone by without striking water. Betsy carefully avoided the subject when her trio re-entered the kitchen, and she soon sensed that the events of the day held something ominous. Even Seth was unusually quiet. Faced with a trio who had retreated into themselves, she grew impatient and frustrated.

"Whatever it is, it can't be that bad!" said Betsy.

"Sorry," replied Reverend Small, "but it's not good."

"Let me decide that," responded Betsy crisply. "You two can't ignore me and expect me to leave you alone."

"It's Lucas," the clergyman began. "He's found someone who claims to be a dowser, and the two of them have been going around getting rights to explore for oil in return for finding water. Four farmers have already signed up, including at least one on Jonah's list."

It was hardly what Betsy expected. As she tried to understand the implications, she soon recognized Jonah's dilemma. If he chose to actively compete with Lucas, he would in all likelihood alienate not only Reverend Small but some in the church, perhaps even her. By choosing not to compete, he would ruin his chances of realizing his dream.

"Reverend," she finally joked, "can't you call down a thunderbolt to deal with Lucas?"

The clergyman laughed, allowing that such prayers might be welcome by some on earth but not in heaven. As for Jonah, Betsy settled for a small smile.

"Did it ever occur to either of you to ask me what I did today?"

she continued, buoyed by their responses. "Would it interest you to know that I saw the Blakes and Ruth Black, and we have decided to hold the box social two weeks from Saturday?"

"They love the idea of getting everyone out for some fun," she continued triumphantly, "but what carried the day was the whole idea of showing Lucas we don't need his money."

"And there's one more thing," said Betsy, blushing slightly. "I have no intention of letting any of you see the basket I put up for auction, but one of you better outbid everyone else for my supper, or you'll all go hungry for at least three days!"

Looking at Jonah through the corner of her eye, she caught a hint of interest but nothing more. Reverend Small, on the other hand, was clearly amused.

"Better get your hands on some extra money," she smiled. "It's all for a great cause!"

Jonah remained subdued, however, so Betsy tried once more, addressing him directly. "Jonah," she declared sternly, "no one is allowed to sulk in my house. If you want to sulk, go outside."

Her rebuke took everyone by surprise, especially Jonah. "Sorry, ma'am," he mumbled, shaken by the sharp edge of her voice. "Don't mean no harm."

"You can fight back by doing what you have been doing," she responded more kindly. "Most people here will always hold you in higher regard because you've never asked for anything in return. Some may fall for that scoundrel, but sooner or later he's bound to fail."

"Miss Betsy is absolutely right," intervened Reverend Small. "The more I think about it, the more I realize I need to address this on Sunday. People need to understand that if there is oil, it will certainly bring its share of scoundrels and opportunists. Our farmlands will be destroyed, and our woods will be ravaged for derricks and barrels and saloons and dance halls. At the very least, they need to look ahead.

"The easy wealth that Lucas offers is an enormous temptation to farmers, especially those who are really struggling. I suspect that for every farmer who rejects him one or more will leap at his offer. This has all the makings of a potential tragedy."

Jonah rose from the table. Though no longer looking downcast, he was clearly troubled. "Pretty much my fault, ain't it?" he asked.

"You may have raised the prospect of oil," conceded Reverend Small, "but it's Lucas who is trying to exploit it. Never once did you mention locking up a host of farms so you could enrich yourself as he is trying to do. And when all is said and done I wonder how much cash these farmers might actually see after Lucas deducts expenses."

"No need to blame yourself, Jonah," added Betsy. "We still don't know how Lucas came up with the notion that there might be oil in these parts, but something tells me it was from being sneaky."

"The important thing is for you to keep helping folks find water," said Reverend Small. "Everyone in this valley probably knows by now that you found water for Emmet. No one knows for sure if Brady is half as good as he and Lucas claim."

"Guess my only option is to whittle down my list 'til there's none left," said Jonah. Then, after a long pause, he added, "Can't say what'll happen after that."

Touched by his integrity, Betsy rested her hand on his arm. "That's fair enough. We won't ask for anything more."

Weary from all the physical, mental, and emotional strains of the day, the two men were quick to agree when Betsy suggested it was time for them to leave the kitchen and catch some sleep. Seth remained to help clear the table, but as soon as he got the dishes to the sink, she sent him off to bed as well. As she dried the last cup, she silently shook her head in disbelief at all she had heard. "What a day!" she sighed aloud.

Over breakfast, the three adults decided that it was more important than ever for Jonah to spent the next few days visiting as many farms on his list as possible. Reverend Small would alternate with Jake on the springpole, and Seth would accompany Jonah.

It took almost an hour to reach the next farm on Jonah's list. Once there, he and Seth received a warm welcome from the farmer, a man named Frank. Also on hand to greet them were a well-trained dog and a large sow that roamed freely between the house and barn. "Can't keep that hog penned up no matter how hard we try," lamented the wife, Mabel.

While Seth was distracted by the animals, Jonah and Frank wandered about the farm, stopping at various points of interest to the dowser. Then, without fanfare, Jonah retrieved his divining rod from beneath his belt, found a comfortable grip on each branch, and began his search for fresh water.

Mabel retired to the house soon after Jonah's arrival but, from time to time, she could be seen pulling back curtains in different rooms to keep abreast of the search. Seth, who had already found a suitable rock to mark the site, watched patiently as Jonah swept back and forth across the land. Frank, in the meantime, disappeared into the barn.

Seth noticed the rod move from time to time but never with the emphatic motion that seemed to satisfy his friend and fishing companion. Throughout the morning, Jonah stopped several times to reexamine certain spots that seemed promising but, in each case, he rejected them and moved on. By midday, he found himself a good walk from the house and barn. And just as he started to look for a place to sit and lunch, he felt an especially welcome tug on the divining rod.

Jonah immediately gave up his inclination to eat, despite a complaint or two from his stomach, and instead began the ritual of confirming the potential of the site. Within minutes, he was certain he had found water. Moreover, he was confident it was not far below the surface, probably no more than eight to ten feet. And even though it remained to be proven, Jonah experienced a moment of deep satisfaction. Maybe, he thought, this was his real purpose in life.

The dowser looked toward the barn, expecting to see Frank. No one, however, apart from Seth who was nearby, was in sight. He summoned the youngster with a wave and then pointed down at his feet. There he remained until the Seth dropped his stone to mark the spot.

Rather than search for the missing farmer, Jonah decided to lunch on the small meal that Betsy had prepared. He and the young fisherman devoured their meals quickly and then set off toward the house and barn. Of all the wells he had located thus far, this was the most distant from the buildings where the water was most needed.

As they approached the barn, the family dog barked a greeting that brought Frank and Mabel from the house.

"We were just about to call you for a bite to eat," said the farmer.

"Thanks anyway," replied Jonah. "Seth's ma fixed us a lunch."

"Looks like you got pretty far from the house by the time you stopped," observed Frank. "Any luck finding us water?"

"It's out there," answered Jonah confidently. "Wish it was closer, but at least it's there for the diggin'. It's pretty close to the surface."

There was a long silence. Frank neither hailed his good fortune nor offered thanks for all the labor Jonah had invested in the search.

"Afraid I've got a little confession to make," he finally announced. "Lucas was out here yesterday with a friend of his who found water right over there by the side of the barn. I was just about to start digging this morning when you and the boy came by. Maybe I should have told you, but I figured it was better to see what you came up with."

"Woulda been better if ya had told me," replied Jonah, feeling a tinge of anger.

"Well, let me ask you," challenged the farmer, unapologetically, "Where would you dig? Here by the barn or way out there where you ended up?"

Jonah, who had not only passed over the area by the barn but had actually gone back over it to reassess some light tugs he had experienced there, was convinced beyond doubt that the only water within the range he had swept was under the spot marked by Seth.

"Did they tell ya how far down ya hafta go?" queried the dowser.

"No more than ten feet," declared Frank.

"What did it cost ya?" continued Jonah.

"Nothing," smiled the farmer. "In fact, they promised to come back and search my place for oil. And it doesn't much matter whether they find any or not. They pay for everything, and if they do get lucky and strike oil, we still get nearly half the profit."

"Might as well go back and pick up our marker," said Jonah. "Guess ya don't need it."

"That's up to you," conceded the farmer, "but you might just want to leave it there in case Lucas and his friend are wrong."

Without another word, Jonah started walking back toward

the stone marker. As his anger increased so did his stride. Seth was forced to walk and run to keep up. Frank, sensing the dowser's mood, remained behind.

When they reached the stone, Jonah paused. "Leave it or heave it?" he asked himself aloud, forgetting that Seth was close at hand.

"Leave it," declared the boy without hesitation.

"Why's that?" asked Jonah.

"'Cause you're right," the lad answered.

"Well, Mister Fisherman," replied an amused Jonah, "yer forgettin' that right or wrong, Lucas can come back and look for oil. Why let 'em benefit?"

"'Cause they're probably no better at finding oil than they are at finding water," replied Seth with a degree of wisdom well beyond his years. "It won't take the folks around here long to figure that out."

"Yer gonna grow up to be a real smart fella," laughed the dowser. "We'll leave it!"

At the next farm, an extra warm greeting awaited them, but this time Jonah knew enough to ask if Lucas and his friend had been there first. The question seemed to baffle the farmer, a man whom his friends called "Digger" because he was always digging rocks and roots out of his fields to expand and improve them.

"There's been no one here before you," he assured Jonah. "Why do you ask?"

Jonah responded slowly, revealing not only the unpleasant discoveries of the morning but those of his earlier encounter with Lucas himself and his dowser, Brady.

"That man's got quite a reputation," replied Digger, "and that sounds like the way he goes around trying to cheat people. If he had come by here, he'd have been turned away long before he got to say why he came."

Though his expression never changed, Jonah experienced a sense of relief and, with it, the realization for the first time that he had become uncharacteristically agitated and tense.

"Enough of this jawin'," the dowser declared, returning to his more natural, easygoing nature, "Ya better show me around."

Digger quickly took Jonah and Seth over to his well. It was rectangular in shape, and the stone that lined its walls rose up above the ground more than three feet. A small hip roof, supported by two sturdy poles that sank into the ground alongside the stone, protected a rope, pulley, and a bone–dry, wooden bucket that Digger used to pull up water from the well.

"My well is spring–fed. That's why it's here," he explained. Then, pointing to a small cluster of darker, moistened stones inside the well, he asked, "See those damp stones down near the bottom; we've always had water several feet above. At least until a few weeks ago."

Jonah had already pulled his divining rod from his belt and without a word began moving around the well toward the side with the moist stones. As he neared the site, he felt a slight twitch or two from the rod even though it did not visibly move. Moving back and forth over that ground, he tried to determine the underground path to the spring. The effort, however, soon became tedious and seemed to be leading nowhere.

"Ever see any other signs of that spring?" he inquired.

"Never did find the source," replied the farmer. "And believe me, I sure tried."

Even though the spring was no longer keeping the well full, it is keeping the stones wet, Jonah observed, and that should be enough to lead him to the source. Why then was his rod unable to pick up the telltale signs he sought?

Unable to explain the phenomena, he was suddenly overcome with the thoughts of failure. The fact that only one well had come in, the rivalry created by Lucas, the difficulties he experienced recently on other farms—all began to take their toll.

For the first time in his memory, Jonah began to question not the rod but his skills as a dowser. Was this truly a gift? Did he really possess an extraordinary skill or was he a charlatan who had managed to fool even himself? The sudden, overwhelming nature of self-doubt found expression. "Blast it!" he cried, tossing the divining rod to the ground.

Digger, clearly startled by Jonah's behavior, began to sense the dowser's frustrations but said nothing. Recovering from his outburst, Jonah reached down and carefully picked up the divining rod. It was unbroken and sound, none the worse for the abuse it had just undergone.

"Never did give this new rod a proper name," said the dowser calmly and thoughtfully. "That's probably why it ain't workin' like it should. Either of ya got a name fir it?"

"It took me three weeks to name my dog," replied Digger with a big grin. "Hope you're not in much of a hurry."

"Nah," cajoled Jonah. "How about three minutes, give or take a minute?"

"When I think about water, I think about our pump and the little dipper we use whenever we want a drink," volunteered Seth. "Why don't you call it Little Dipper?"

"Not bad, young fella, not bad," answered Jonah.

However, after mulling it over for a few seconds, he hesitated.

"Seems like that name's only good for water. What if I ever want to hunt for oil?"

"Well," said Digger, "the Little Dipper reminds me of the one in the night sky. How about the other one, the Big Dipper? You should be able to do more with a Big Dipper."

"Why not!" shouted Jonah. "Big Dipper it is!"

"Take us to the spring," he bellowed in mock seriousness as he grasped Big Dipper's two branches and pointed the rod toward what he hoped was the path to the elusive underground stream. Then, crisscrossing the same familiar landscape, he felt a light throb and then another. "Like followin' a bird dog," he explained excitedly to Seth and Digger. "It's gonna take us to the spring."

But it did not. After he and his companions moved forward several feet, whatever impulses he had sensed vanished as suddenly as they had started.

"Might be here," speculated Jonah, pointing at his feet, "but it don't seem likely."

Instead, he decided, it was time to forget about looking for the spring, and he shifted his search to other possible locations. As he had done elsewhere, he took a few minutes to scan the entire landscape. With renewed confidence, he set out for a field that Digger was using for pasture.

Once out of earshot, he gave the Big Dipper a dual command. "Find water and find it fast!"

Jonah's brisk pace across the field caught Seth's attention immediately. Fueled by renewed confidence and purpose, he offered his newly named divining rod little time to respond to whatever natural phenomenon it desired. But respond it did.

Less than a quarter hour after the new search had begun, the rod dove decisively. Jonah paused momentarily. He then began walking in an ever-widening spiral until he decided to reverse the spiral. Moments later, he discovered a spot that matched all his instincts as a dowser.

Both Seth and Digger had become enchanted by the zeal Jonah displayed. As the search reached its conclusion, the youngster darted toward the dowser with a large stone, which he dropped where Jonah and the Big Dipper pointed.

"Can't tell exactly how far down it is," apologized Jonah. "But as sure as there's little green apples in yer orchard, there's water down below that rock."

"I'm mighty grateful," stammered Digger, reeling somewhat from the dowser's initial frustration and subsequent invigorated recovery. "I'll get my pick and shovel and maybe dig a little tonight after I finish chores."

"Still more farms to get to or we'd stay and help." said Jonah, admiring Big Dipper and the nearly perfect performance he had demanded. "Let me know when ya strike water."

Jonah scanned the afternoon sky carefully as he and Seth reached the road. "Two in one day is enough," he announced. "Besides it's time to be gettin' home, Mister Fisherman, and, if ya don't dilly-dally, there might be time to work in a little fishin' before dinner."

Arriving back home, they learned that dinner was at least an hour away. So, with his fishing pole in one hand and his little packet of hooks in the other, Seth set off for the creek, looking back only once to be sure Jonah was close behind.

What he saw caused him to pause. Back at the pump, Jonah was actively engaged in a casual conversation with Reverend Small. Convinced that the dowser would not linger any more than necessary, Seth resumed his journey toward his favorite fishing hole.

"It about floored me," Jonah confided to the minister after summarizing the experience that morning at the first farm. "Just sorry we didn't pick up our marker so that Frank won't have a place to go after he gives up diggin' by the barn."

"Seth was right," Reverend Small insisted. "If, as you think, Frank fails to find water where Lucas and his friend told him to dig, Lucas will wind up embarrassed if not disgraced. If Frank does find water where you told him to dig, it may help end Lucas's scheme."

"Maybe," conceded Jonah, "but Lucas probably had half the county sewed up by noon. Even if Brady can't find water in a cup, Lucas has the rights to all those farms to drill for oil."

"Still dreaming of great riches for yourself?" asked the clergyman sympathetically.

"Not so much as before," answered the dowser. "But it ain't much fun watchin' Lucas gettin' farmers to give away their rights. All he's gotta do is hit oil once."

"I understand," replied Reverend Small shaking his head in agreement. "But it could be fun to watch Lucas get his comeuppance if Brady turns out to be completely incompetent."

As both men laughed at the thought, Jonah suddenly realized he had forgotten Seth.

"Gotta get down to the creek," he explained. "How about comin' along. Who knows, maybe we can make a fisherman outta you too someday."

Tired and still sore from working the springpole on Jake's farm, the clergyman was about to decline when he realized it was Jonah's way of treating him as a true friend and as an equal. Moreover, it was an opportunity to talk about Jake's latest refusal to drill deeper.

"As long as I can sit on the bank and rest up a bit," agreed Reverend Small. "Truth is my legs and back are pretty unhappy right now. I was hoping to nap before dinner. "

Jonah had noticed earlier that the minister was favoring his right leg, the leg he tended to use when he was working the springpole. Jonah himself often fell into the same habit even though he knew it was best to alternate, using one leg and then the other to kick down a well. But even then, pain in the legs, arms, and shoulders seemed inescapable.

Rather than commiserate, Jonah simply acknowledged the minister's pain with a knowing nod and chose instead to prolong their conversation without the presence of Betsy.

"Don't know exactly how to put it," he began slowly, "but somehow ya gotta help me get outta that social that's comin' up. First of all, it don't interest me much. Second of all, it's gonna take money to bid on them boxes."

The issue took Reverend Small by surprise. If anyone deserved to have some fun, it was surely Jonah. Not only had he spent week after week helping Betsy work her farm, he had given freely of his skills and energy to neighboring farmers.

"That's a fine kettle of fish," the clergyman replied, recalling Jake's use of the phrase during a fit of frustration. "Maybe this box social isn't such a good idea after all. I haven't shared my own concerns with anyone, but I'm worried that Lucas will show up."

"Ya can count on it," said Jonah. "And ya can't stop him from biddin' once he's there."

"That's bad enough," said Reverend Small, "but he's wily enough to figure out which box is Miss Betsy's. He knows she dislikes him, and he could outbid everyone else just for spite. If that should happen, it could get unpleasant!"

The image of Betsy refusing to eat with Lucas or, better yet, watching her dump the contents of her dinner into Lucas's lap, started Jonah laughing. "Maybe ya could charge extra for the fireworks," he suggested as he came to a halt and laughed even harder. And his laugh was contagious. Even Reverend Small enjoyed the humor, and he too started laughing freely.

The diversion was brief, however, and their discussion quickly turned serious. "Trouble is, there ain't no easy way outta this except maybe takin' charity," lamented the dowser. "And ya know my conscience ain't gonna let that happen. And before ya know it, Miss Betsy's gonna be mad at me."

"No doubt about that," agreed Reverend Small. "Unfortunately, I don't have any ready answer, but I'll sure try my best to help you find one."

"What do ya think about tryin' to borrow a few dollars from ol' Barnes or the Blakes?" asked Jonah. "It'd be pretty easy to lose to somebody else every time. As long as Miss Betsy saw me lose, she might not get mad, and all the money could be returned the next day."

"Perhaps," surmised the clergyman, "but I think most folks would see right through it."

Both men fell silent. After giving it more thought, Reverend Small added, "I suspect a lot of men would quit bidding just to make sure you wound up with a good looking box. And even if the men didn't do it on their own, their wives most likely would see to it!"

The two men had been ambling along toward Seth's favorite fishing hole, unconsciously ignoring the youngster. As they neared the site, still distracted by their conversation, they were largely unprepared for the sounds and sights of Seth suddenly engaged in lively struggle with a long, energetic, and unhappy fish.

Despite the somewhat muddy nature of the narrow stream, the fish was briefly visible just beneath the surface. "It's another good–

sized pickerel," declared Jonah as he watched Seth run along the bank of the creek. After first racing into a bed of weeds, the fish reversed its path and headed toward the widest and deepest part of the creek.

Once again, Seth proved to be an able fisherman, alternately walking and running, pulling and relaxing the pole in an effort to tire his quarry without breaking his line or tearing away his hook. His skill quickly won the cheers of both adults. Then, with victory seemingly at hand, the men watched in disbelief as the line went slack.

Seth froze, fearful that his prize had gotten away. Unwilling to quit, he raised the tip of his pole slowly and deliberately until the slack disappeared. Hopeful and ready for a new burst of resistance, he was nearly overwhelmed when it came. The back of the pickerel emerged from the water just enough to reveal the beauty of its size and color and, for an instant, to flash its defiance. It then plunged back to the depths of the creek, nearly ripping the pole from Seth's hands.

Seth clung stubbornly to his handmade pole, playing the line as it darted from one direction to another. Suddenly the line turned directly toward him. He raced backward and, with an impulsive jerk on the pole, landed the pickerel so close to the edge of the bank that it nearly slipped back into the slow-moving creek.

Jonah and Reverend Small roared their approval, and Seth quickly stepped on the line near the mouth of the flopping fish. Dropping the pole, he reached down and seized the pickerel with one hand and removed the hook with the other. In a sign of defeat and submission, it stopped its gyrations. It was long and slender, shiny and still. Seth held it high, momentarily examining the corner of its mouth where the hook had been lodged.

Then, while the three were admiring the catch, it suddenly sprang back to life, broke free from his grasp, and with only a flop or two, plunged back into the safety of the creek. "Blast it!" cried Seth, repeating the oath he heard Jonah utter in the past.

Reverend Small, sharing the lad's surprise and frustration, said nothing. Jonah, however, was quick to comment. "No need to fret about it, Mister Fisherman," he declared. "Fish like that are only good for fightin'. They're fun to catch but ain't much good for eatin'."

Seth found the statement small consolation and, realizing there was little else he could do, began to wind the fishing line around top of his pole.

As they neared the house, Betsy emerged from the kitchen and summoned them to supper. Her voice was clear and mellow, yet there was no mistaking the urgency she attached to her summons. Subconsciously, the three males picked up their pace.

CHAPTER 14

The dinner topic that night was largely devoted to the fish that got away, but before everyone had a chance to leave the table, Betsy began to inquire about the well-drilling at Jake's place.

"It's slowed down badly," reported Reverend Small. "Jake has become so pessimistic that he doesn't seem to care any more. When it's his turn on the springpole, he simply goes through the motions. I doubt that the drill bit is going anywhere."

"Any idea how far down ya got?" asked Jonah.

"It's hard to tell," answered the clergyman, "but the last time we added rope, Jake estimated we were down at least twenty feet."

"That ain't so deep," said the dowser, exasperated. "Water's there, but he ain't never gonna hit it if he keeps givin' up."

"Are you really sure?" Betsy asked, sparing Reverend Small the same question.

"His place is the only one where the water seemed too deep to dig," said Jonah. "Tried a couple times to get an idea how deep he'd hafta go but couldn't. Chances are it ain't much deeper, but he's got to keep at it."

"I did all I could to encourage him," said the clergyman. "But when we quit this afternoon, Jake said he was finished. In fact, he told me not to bother coming back tomorrow."

"Maybe he'll change his mind if ya ask him for my drill bit," Jonah speculated. "Seems like he's got three choices: he can keep drillin'; he can give up and start beggin' for water from his neighbors, or he can do what Frank did—let Lucas tell him where to find water."

"No, no, no," countered Betsy. "You get out there tomorrow morning and reassure Jake, and if you must stay to help drill, you better do it. Whatever Jake lacks in ambition, he makes up for in other ways. He's always there to help Emmet."

In addition to Betsy's vocal insistence, the twinkle in her eyes and her radiant smile left Jonah without recourse. "If ya say so, ma'am," relented Jonah, skillfully hiding his annoyance at Jake's lack of confidence in him and his divining rod.

"Who knows," said Reverend Small. "If we all put our hearts and minds and prayers to it, maybe we'll bring in that well tomorrow."

"Best we sleep on it," replied Jonah, rising from the table and heading for the barn.

Betsy awoke early, roused Seth, and sent him off to the barn half-awake to do the milking and his other chores. As he started to pass the stall where Jonah was still asleep, he paused for a moment, grabbed a handful of hay and threw it at Jonah's head. As he expected, it triggered a series of sneezes. Jonah bolted to his feet, still sneezing. Seth laughed.

Reverend Small was already shaving when he heard Betsy's call for breakfast.

The meal was simple but filling and, in no time at all, the table was cleared, the dishes were washed, and all four of them were off for Jake's farm. As they walked, Betsy and Reverend Small peppered Jonah with questions, unintentionally challenging his assurances that water was waiting somewhere beneath the springpole.

Jonah took their questions patiently, answering them thoughtfully and good-naturedly. So engrossed were they in their conversation that they failed to see or hear a buggy approaching behind them. It was Lucas and his dowser, Brady. By the time Betsy and the others became aware, they instinctively moved toward the ditch to let him pass. As he drew alongside, however, Lucas pulled his horse to a stop.

"Good morning!" shouted Lucas over the whinny of his all-black mare.

"Mornin'," replied Jonah on behalf of his companions.

"Could it be that you're all headed over to Jake's?" asked the lender.

"Matter of fact, we are," responded Reverend Small. "Why do you ask?"

"Just guessing," replied Lucas. "We're on our way there too. I got word from Jake last night that he wanted some help finding water. It seems he's giving up on Jonah."

"Suppose you and Brady can save him the trouble of drillin' deeper," challenged Jonah, clearly irritated but not yet angered by what he was hearing.

"That's what we're here for," said Brady proudly.

"Well, it's time for us to be getting along," declared Lucas. "I'd offer you folks a ride, but my buggy just isn't big enough."

"We prefer walking," replied Reverend Small quickly, hoping to prevent Betsy and Jonah from responding in any unpleasant way.

Lucas flipped his reins just enough to start the mare but, a moment later, slapped the animal with his whip and began racing toward Jake's farm.

"Not much point in goin' on," said Jonah, somewhat dejected. "Except maybe to see who's got the gift and who don't."

"Sounds like you're giving up, Jonah," cried Betsy. "But we're not going to let you!"

"Miss Betsy is right," added Reverend Small. "Thanks to you, Emmet now has water. We all know it took a lot of work. It didn't come easy. Nothing really good ever does. And let's not forget that the water was found exactly where you said it would be."

"Amen," laughed Seth, mimicking Emmet's characteristic optimism and enthusiasm.

All three adults tried to stifle laughs with only limited success.

"That's the answer," roared the clergyman. "Seth, run ahead and ask Emmet to meet us at Jake's farm. We all need his help and inspiration."

Without even waiting for his mother's consent, Seth began to run.

"Maybe we should all run," said Betsy somewhat seriously. "Who knows what Lucas will demand if we don't get there soon. Jake may not know it, but he really needs our help now."

Betsy tried to quicken their pace but quickly realized she and Reverend Small were only holding Jonah back. "You better not wait for us," she soon told the dowser. "Try to keep Jake from doing anything foolish. Remind him that you found water for Emmet, and Brady hasn't yet proven he has skills as good as yours."

Although reluctant, Jonah agreed and, with his long strides, was soon out of sight.

By the time Betsy and Reverend Small reached the farm, they found Jonah and Lucas both vying for Jake's attention and confidence. Seth and Emmet were within sight, and Brady was traipsing about with his divining rod searching for water.

"It's time for a fresh start," they overheard Lucas tell Jake. "You've wasted enough time and energy on useless drilling. If there was water there, you'd have hit it by now. Why go to bed exhausted every night when we can help you find water and maybe oil too."

"Do as ya might," Jonah retorted, "but there ain't much sense in wasting all the work ya did so far. Besides, both me and the reverend gave ya some help. No need to be wastin' that too. We'll stick with ya till ya hit water, but ya gotta work as hard at it as we do."

"If you want to drill all the way to China," snorted Lucas, "just keep on drilling."

The words were barely out of his mouth when Brady yelled out, "It's here. It's right here under my feet. And there's plenty of water down there. You can probably reach it in a few days of hard digging." As he spoke, he headed directly toward Jake, eager to press his case.

"Hold on, Jake," interrupted Betsy. "Just in case you didn't notice, Brady didn't even mark the spot where he claims there's water. And there's a good reason for that. His divining rod didn't move an inch. I was watching closely. It never even twitched."

"It's what I feel, not what you see!" stormed Brady defensively.

"He'll go back and mark the spot after you sign with us," Lucas told Jake. "Why should we give it away. By now you should know what free advice is worth."

"It's worth plenty," promised a familiar voice.

Drawing their attention was Emmet, limping slightly from the brisk pace that Seth had set for much of their walk. "Best advice I ever got."

Stymied by Emmet's arrival, Lucas and Brady held their tongues.

But Emmet did not. "Jake," he continued, "don't make the mistake that Frank did. He was lookin' for an easy way out too. All he's got to show for all his diggin' is a sore back and an empty hole."

"Frank will hit water a whole lot sooner with us than he will with Jonah," argued Brady.

"Time you sent these two packin'," suggested Emmet.

"Why don't you all leave," frowned Jake. "All your arguing has just made things worse. I don't know who to believe or what to do next. Maybe some peace and quiet will help."

"Our offer won't last forever," protested Lucas as he and Brady headed for their buggy.

"Let me take a look at the springpole and the drill bit before we leave," petitioned Jonah. "Maybe there's somethin' I missed."

Jake nodded his consent but said nothing. As everyone except Jonah headed for the road, Jake turned toward the house. Wrestling with a myriad of competing thoughts, he paused and lashed out at Jonah. "Don't bother!" he cried. "If you knew what you were doing, I'd have water by now. You and Brady are both phonies."

The words stung Jonah like an attack by angry bees. For a moment, he did nothing. Then, with Betsy, Seth, Reverend Small, and Emmet waiting on the road for him, Jonah turned his back to the springpole, shoved his hands deep into his back pockets and ambled toward the road.

"Guess you can't please everybody," observed Reverend Small rather seriously.

"Give him time," counseled Emmet. "Jake may not work as hard as the rest of us, but he usually does a pretty good job sorting things out. Before today is over, he'll come to his senses and beg you to come back to help."

"Leave it to Lucas to get everyone stirred up," observed Betsy in an effort to reduce the tension. "I'm sure he had a lot to do with Jake caving in that way."

Jonah ignored her comments. What troubled and tormented him most was Jake's readiness to work with Lucas and Brady. Both Jonah and Reverend Small had invested large amounts of personal time and effort into Jake's well. Being dismissed as though none of that mattered rankled the dowser deeply, so deeply that he suddenly wheeled back toward the farm.

"Goin' back for my drill bit," he announced matter-of-factly. And off he went.

Betsy started to follow, but Reverend Small reached out, took her arm and simply shook his head to discourage her, "Let them deal with this privately," he suggested.

Jonah's long strides and angry pace got him back to the farm quickly. At first, there was no sight of Jake, but as Jonah headed toward the springpole, he spotted the farmer squatting beside the heavy rope that hung from the pole.

"Came back after my bit," muttered Jonah as Jake looked up. "Other folks can use it while ya think about it."

"Take it then," replied Jake. "And good riddance."

Jake's indifference served to annoy Jonah even more. The dowser bent down, grabbed the rope just above the point where it entered the ground and began to pull. At first, the bit rose easily inside the hole it had bored. But its weight and girth, combined with loose debris that broke free from the sides of the hole, quickly impeded its progress. Jonah soon found himself lowering the bit and then jerking it upward. It was slow, repetitive work that would have quickly exhausted most other men.

Watching the rope collect in a coil as the drill bit came closer and closer to the surface, Jake reluctantly concluded that his best prospects of finding water was with Jonah. He rose and moved alongside the perspiring dowser. "Guess I'm about as dumb as they come," he began, resting his hand on the dowser's shoulder in a show of penitence.

"And just about as lazy too," replied Jonah, unable to hide his anger.

"Not really," said Jake defensively. "Maybe I could have put a little more heart and soul into it, but I've been at it every day. Neither you nor Reverend Small can say that. Guess I was hoping it would be a whole lot easier."

"Me too," agreed Jonah. "Me and the boy can come back later on if ya wanta start drillin' again."

"I'd appreciate that," said Jake, extending his hand. "Sorry I let you down. Let's go back at it after lunch."

After a brief handshake, Jonah released the rope he had continued to hold in his other hand, letting the bit drop all the way down until it hung just above the bottom of the hole it had created. He then headed back to the others.

Less than a half mile down the road he rounded a gentle bend and came upon Betsy, Seth, and Reverend Small. Emmet had stayed with them briefly but had left. After deciding to wait until Jonah rejoined them, the three had scrambled to a stone wall beside the road and sat and talked.

"Looks like you decided to leave the bit," observed the clergyman as Jonah approached empty-handed. "Were you and Jake able to resolve things?"

"Said he was sorry," Jonah reported. "And unless he changes his mind again, we'll both get back to the springpole this afternoon. Couldn't help but promise to lend a hand."

"We're really proud of you," exclaimed Betsy. "We know that wasn't easy."

"It's true, Jonah," added Reverend Small. "You had every right to retrieve your bit and let Jake risk his future with Lucas. The fact that you were willing to forgive and forget is really commendable. I'm sure the good Lord is looking down and smiling too."

As the conversation turned to Lucas and Brady, a consensus soon emerged that it was important for Jonah to do what he could to help both Jake and Ned bring in wells. Only then, they agreed, would other farmers think twice before sharing their rights with Lucas to whatever there might be beneath their land.

Unknown was the current situation at Ned's farm. With Jonah committed to Jake, there was no one to support Ned except Reverend Small, who was also anxious to see reconstruction of the church get underway.

"Looks like the church will have to wait a little longer," said the clergyman. "I may not be much help to Ned, but I'll certainly try."

"Let's head there now," urged Betsy. "We need to know where Ned's at with his well."

"If ya want," agreed Jonah somewhat indifferently.

It took nearly a half hour to get to Ned's farm and, by then, neither the adults nor Seth were finding much to talk about. The broiling sun, dusty road, and growing thirst had brought their conversations to a virtual halt. Silence prevailed until Seth spotted Ned outside his barn.

"I wonder if Ned's given up too," speculated the youngster, pointing to the lone figure in the distance. "He's nowhere near the new well."

"Could be he's hit water, and the well is full," countered Jonah.

"Any water in that well," said Reverend Small, "is an answer to prayer."

"Prayer with an *S!*" interjected Betsy. "You're not the only one praying!"

"Not to mention skill and a good divining rod," laughed Jonah for the first time since the day had begun. "Let's not forget our young fisherman and the branch he found."

Seeing them approach, Ned waved a greeting and headed toward the road to greet them. His welcoming smile and enthusiastic "Good Morning" drew an equally enthusiastic reaction from Betsy and her companions.

"Hope I'm not in trouble," he joked. "It's not every day that I get a visit from such a distinguished group. But, if you're wondering why I haven't started helping at church, it's because I'm still trying to bring in the new well."

"Actually," interjected Reverend Small, "we're not here about the church. We're here about the well. We were hoping you had hit water."

"It's funny," replied Ned. "This morning, the bottom of the well was a little muddy, but there wasn't any water to speak of. And as soon as I shoveled away the mud, I was right back to hard, dry ground. Any idea what that means, Jonah?"

"Not off hand," said the dowser. "How deep have ya gone?"

"About as deep as Emmet," replied Ned. Smiling more broadly than ever, he added, "Before I quit every day, I drive my pick into the floor of the well trying to do what you did. Guess I lack the knack. It still hasn't worked."

All five meandered over to the well where, to everyone's amazement, they saw what appeared to be dampness around the bottom of the well. Jonah immediately descended Ned's ladder and slowly examined the entire well floor. Yet try as he might, he was unable to pinpoint moisture. He then inspected the well wall but again to no avail.

The others remained above near the edge of the well, peering down and, from time to time, pelting Jonah with questions. Although he responded to each new query, he was clearly bewildered and frustrated by the mystery.

"Don't know what to make of it," he declared when he finally rejoined the others.

"Guess I just keep digging," said Ned without his earlier exuberance.

"We brought some help," volunteered Betsy. "Reverend Small has offered to stay and dig with you. It's important to all of us that you hit water soon. Lucas has been popping up all over the place, getting people to give him rights to drill their land for oil after he promises to tell them where to dig for water."

"I know," replied Ned. "He and someone named Brady have been here too. They just laughed and called me a 'sucker' when I told them to get off my property."

"Well, I'm ready to get to work if you are," said Reverend Small.

"There's a pick and shovel still down in the well," replied Ned with a laugh. "I've already done my share of digging for now; they're all yours."

"What did I get myself into?" muttered the clergyman with a make-believe frown.

Betsy and Jonah joined in the repartee as Reverend Small headed for the ladder and then descended below the rim of the well. "Guess I'll just have to show you folks how it's done," he kidded in a final exchange as he seized the pick.

At that point, Ned moved over to the edge of the well and called down. "I hope you know how much I really appreciate this, Reverend. I'll make it up to you as soon as the well is finished."

"This is not exactly the best time for a sermon," shouted Reverend Small, "but let me remind you of the eighth chapter of Romans, verse twenty-eight. 'We know that all things work together for good to them that love God, to them who are the called according to His purpose.'"

Betsy, Jonah, and Ned nodded in agreement without uttering a word. Then Jonah broke their silence. "This ain't exactly the best time to leave either, but if we don't bring in some more wells soon we'll be singing hymns in the snow this winter."

"Jonah's right," added Betsy. "Seth, go back to Jake's place with Jonah. I need to go home from here and get my own chores done."

As they began to separate, there was a shout from the well.

"I think I've hit water," cried Reverend Small.

The others raced to the well almost simultaneously and, looking down, saw what was unmistakably a trickle of water inside a small cavity in the floor of the well. Barely the width and half the depth of the shovel that created it, the hole was becoming a tiny pool.

"Dig that hole bigger," ordered Jonah. "See if you can't get that water to run faster."

The clergyman started digging with fresh energy and enthusiasm, removing shovelful after shovelful of dirt from the hole. But instead of increasing the flow, he seemed to restrict it. And what little water there was quickly turned to mud. Bewildered, Reverend Small stopped digging.

Ned quickly motioned Jonah to descend the ladder ahead of him and, within seconds, both men alighted at the foot of the ladder. Like Reverend Small, their eyes were fixed on the manmade basin that had showed so much promise.

"What happened?" demanded Betsy from above. "One minute there's water, the next minute there's nothing. Did digging just plug it up?"

"Either that or Mother Nature's playing a mean trick on us," answered Ned.

With his patience growing weary, Jonah reached for the shovel and began digging in a slow, methodical manner, carefully removing dirt from the edge of the hole without deepening it. When that failed, he began to increase the depth of the hole. That too failed, and in no time at all, the hole was bone dry.

"Maybe it's time to give it a rest," suggested Ned. "Let's see if water starts collecting again, either there or somewhere else."

"That's as good an idea as any," said Jonah, tossing the shovel toward the wall of the well in frustration. Seconds later he emerged from the well.

"If Jake don't see me comin' down the road soon, he'll probably call Lucas and Brady back," Jonah declared, only partly in jest. "One problem's enough. You folks can deal with this one. It's time for me to get back to Jake's place."

Ned raised his hand in a half-hearted gesture of thanks while trying to hide his disappointment.

Seth, who had been sitting on the edge of the well, sprung to his feet and joined Jonah. Neither said a word. They simply began their walk toward Jake's.

"Well," challenged Betsy, looking hopefully at Ned and Reverend Small, "it looks like it's up to you gentlemen to either hit water or at least figure out why it's disappearing."

"I'm ready to go back down the well as soon as we agree it's rested long enough," replied the clergyman enthusiastically. "Trouble is I don't have any idea how long we should wait. What do you folks think?"

"About as long as it took to spot that trickle while you were digging the first time around," guessed Ned after a moment of reflection. "It could be you just hit a little pocket of water that's been trapped there for years and, if that's the case, there's not much sense waiting."

One by one, Betsy, Ned, and Reverend Small looked down from the edge of the well hopefully and, seeing nothing but dirt and stone, stepped back.

"This is no time to give up," declared the clergyman after observing the disappointment in the faces of Betsy and Ned. "That water is just waiting for us to reach it. What we need is a little more optimism and sheer persistence!"

"Amen," laughed Betsy. "Now I can go home."

"Okay, Reverend," said Ned, breaking into a smile. "Call me when you want a break."

With their spirits refreshed, Betsy headed home, Ned headed for the barn and Reverend Small descended the ladder to resume digging.

"Why couldn't you find where that water came from?" Seth finally asked Jonah as they came within sight of Jake's farm.

"Never seen anything like that before," said Jonah a little defensively. "But water can really be strange sometimes. Even when ya find it, it ain't always good enough to drink. It can look bad and smell even worse. That don't happen often, but water's full of mystery."

Jonah was just about to tell Seth about a case of bad water that came to mind when they spotted a horse and buggy kicking up a cloud of dust less than a quarter mile ahead.

"That's gotta be Lucas," surmised the dowser. "No one else pushes a horse like that."

He and Seth moved toward the ditch and stopped, hoping the driver would begin to slow down so that they wouldn't be enveloped in all the dust and dirt left in the buggy's wake.

"Looks like you're right," said Seth as the buggy got closer without slowing down.

When Lucas finally did pull up on the reins, he had misjudged badly and the horse came to a stop well beyond Jonah and Seth. Like the buggy, the dense dust swept past them and left both man and boy lightly covered.

"This dirt belongs on the road, not on us," protested Jonah, just loud enough to be heard by the men in the buggy. "Guess ya didn't realize what a storm ya were kickin' up," he added in a tone that failed to hide his displeasure.

"Got some great news!" shouted Lucas, ignoring the unpleasant environment he had created. "We just hit water at the Walker place, thanks to Brady here. The water came up so fast, old George didn't even have time to lay up a wall inside the well."

"Yeah, he's gonna get his feet wet laying up that wall," chuckled Brady, "but he's as happy as a pig in a wallow. First thing he did was dance a jig; then he says, 'Now that you got me water, get out there and get me some oil.'"

Lucas's big grin disappeared with the reference to oil. "Not anything we can do soon," he insisted, cutting off Brady. "We've got too many other farmers to help find water. How are you coming along, Jonah? Hit any new wells beside Emmet's?"

"Still workin' at it," replied the dowser.

"Guess that makes us one for one," said Brady. "Want me to show you how it's done?"

Jonah thrust his hands deep into his pants pockets, overriding a strong urge to respond physically. "Maybe someday," he answered.

"Just let me know," teased Brady, knowing he had struck a nerve. "Always glad to help an amateur."

Though clearly amused, Lucas interrupted the exchange, explaining that he and Brady had other farms to visit. Then, with another grin, a small wave and a crack of his whip, he and Brady were off.

"Them two ain't nothin' but trouble," muttered Jonah, and Seth nodded in agreement.

As they resumed their journey towards Jake's farm, Jonah found himself preoccupied with a contest he had never imagined. With Brady's success in finding water and the certainty that he and Lucas would soon begin searching for oil, Jonah was confronted once again with the question of whether to stay or move on.

Why face an opportunist like Lucas when there's an outside chance he and Brady could show me up? Seems like there's a lot hangin' on the wells we started at Jake and Ned's farms.

"Are you really certain that Big Dipper can find water?" Seth asked, breaking Jonah's concentration. "Wouldn't Drake have done a better job?"

From time to time even Jonah had wrestled with that question, but knowing how troubled Seth had been after accidentally breaking Drake, he hastened to reassure the boy that the new divining rod was definitely as good if not better.

"Thought we were done with that, Mister Fisherman!" roared the dowser, "Of course yer branch can find water. And more than likely, it'll find oil too!"

Seth smiled weakly, still unconvinced. "Guess we'll never know 'til you try the new rod out at our place," he continued. "I'll feel a whole lot better if my branch points to the same spot that Drake did. Can we do that when we get back home?"

Funny, thought Jonah. The idea hadn't crossed his mind, and the more he thought about it, the more he found himself resolving to do so.

"If ya won't stop pesterin' me about Big Dipper," answered Jonah, "guess we'll hafta."

Jonah's thoughts lingered on Drake and the question of whether it had found oil rather than water. *Will the new divining rod lead me to the same spot? If it does, will it reveal whether it's water or oil or will it simply confirm that it could be either?*

The cascade of questions finally stopped as they approached the springpole at Jake's. Could it be, pondered Jonah, that it was oil, not water, where they were now drilling? Since oil was almost certain to be deeper, could that explain why water continued to elude them?

"Glad you're back!" shouted Jake as he left the house and started walking toward Jonah and Seth. "About a half hour ago, the drill bit seemed to drop a ways without hitting anything. I couldn't make up my mind whether to add some new rope or pull out the drill bit so I took some time off to have a bite."

"Let's do both," replied Jonah. "It's time we pulled that bit outta there but, before we do, let's add some rope and see how far the bit drops till it hits somethin' solid."

Though he didn't make a point of it, Jonah had another reason for wanting to pull the drill bit back up. It was the only way he could tell how far it had driven its way down from the surface. There was always the risk that it would snag on its way up but, to

Jonah, the risk now seemed worth it. If they were lucky, it would be wet or muddy.

Jake had already brought some additional rope from the barn. As he uncoiled it, Jonah started pulling the bit up until several feet of the rope had collected beside the hole. Once he was satisfied he had amassed enough rope, he stepped on it, preventing it from dropping back into the ground. Jonah then searched for the knot that tied it to the shorter, original length that hung from the springpole.

Jonah's large hands proved deft as he untied the knot and spliced a few feet of new rope to the old. He then removed his foot from the rope and watched as the weight of the drill bit drew it to a new depth well below the point it had been. When it stopped of its own accord, Jonah wrapped an old rag around the rope where it entered the ground and tied it tightly. With the marker in place, he started to pull the bit up to the surface.

It was a slow and arduous task. Whenever he felt the bit begin to snag, he would release it just enough to fall back a foot or two. Like a fisherman gently playing a big one, he eventually brought the bit out into the bright, midday sun.

"Hardly wore," he mused. "The smith sure did a fine job."

Like Jonah, Jake and Seth admired the condition of the bit as Jonah rotated it slowly, again and again, looking first for signs of water and then for signs of wear or imperfections. Apart from a scratch or two, it seemed almost new. But what Jonah had really hoped to see was absent. Nowhere was it wet or muddy, a fact that Jonah kept to himself.

With the inspection complete, the dowser began to carry the bit away from the drill site, unraveling the rope that had collected in a pile. When Jonah finally stopped, Jake let loose a long, high-pitched whistle. The bit had pounded its way to a depth of nearly thirty feet.

"Well," declared Jake, taking immediate credit, "no one can say I laid down on the job. That's mostly my work."

"Sure enough," agreed Jonah somewhat amused.

"Trouble is," Jake continued, "this is a lot deeper than I expected. If this means we have to keep on drilling here, I'd rather give Lucas and his friend a try."

"Can't blame ya," said Jonah. "About ready to quit myself."

After staring briefly at the extended rope, Jonah reached down and picked up the bit from the dry, dusty ground where he had let it drop. Once again, he found himself examining the bit, first the rounded, blunt head that had pounded its way so deeply and then the rough, slightly dirty circumference. He also looked closely at the eye of the bit and the rope that was threaded through it. Neither seemed damaged in any way but, as he turned the bit to see the other side of its eye, he spotted a dab of mud inside the eye between the iron and the rope.

Despite its weight, Jonah lifted the bit to eye level to inspect it more closely. "Could be mistaken," he finally drawled, "but looks like there's a speck of mud in there."

Jake moved closer to join Jonah in the inspection. Earlier, when the bit first emerged from the hole, he too had seen what looked like mud but had kept it to himself, deciding to wait for Jonah to confirm his suspicion.

"If that's not mud, we both need specs," agreed Jake.

By now, Jonah had begun to feel the rope near the eye of the bit, testing it for moisture. Try as he might, he could not detect moisture with any certainty. He extended the bit and rope toward Jake, explaining what he had tried to do. "See if it feels wet to ya," commanded Jonah. Both Jake and Seth tried, and both shook their heads in failure.

"Got anything in the house or barn we can drop down on a rope?" the dowser asked. "Somethin' that'll hold a little sample if there's any water down there."

"Can't think of anything off hand," replied Jake. "Let me look."

Once again, Jonah found himself pondering the developments that seemed so unique, if not bizarre, at this site.

How can there be mud inside the eye of the drill bit without more evidence of water on the rope? Have we hit a shallow, underground pool or an empty, underground cavity? Is there any point in drillin' further?

"I didn't turn up much," apologized Jake as he approached from the house, "and we better not break what I did come up with." What he displayed was a glass pitcher, considerably smaller than most.

"This should be small enough to slip down the hole but big enough to bring back water. Just be ready to head for the hills if it's broken. It's my wife's."

To Jonah, it looked like an ordinary pitcher except for size. It also looked pretty fragile. "Sure ya wanta take a chance with it?" asked the dowser hesitantly.

"As long as you think there might be water down there," Jake replied.

Jonah took the pitcher and positioned it over the hole. Although it appeared small enough, the chances of it getting down to the bottom and back up undamaged seemed much too risky. "Better give it back to your missus," he ordered softly, handing it back to Jake.

As Jake headed back to the house, Jonah retrieved his pocketknife and sliced the rope just above the eye of the drill bit. He then began to unbraid and unravel the cut end until it was as bushy as the end of a cow's tail. Satisfied that it would fulfill its intended purpose, he began to lower the rope's frayed end into the hole.

From time to time he jiggled the rope to keep it from catching on the wall of the hole. When almost all of the rope had disappeared, it suddenly stopped its descent and coiled around the surface of the hole. Jonah was about to swear but caught himself.

"It's hung up," he muttered, trying desperately to jiggle it free. "Can't be more than a foot or two from the bottom."

All his efforts seemed to no avail. The more he jiggled the rope, the more it seemed to inch back toward the surface.

"Instead of jerking it up and down," suggested Seth, "why not try twisting it?"

It took a moment for Jonah to comprehend what the lad was suggesting but, as soon as he understood, he relaxed and began to spin the rope in his hands, first clockwise and then counter–clockwise.

After several rotations it began to descend once again. Clearly delighted by Seth's solution, he chuckled. Not only did the rope resume its downward path, it soon inched past the point of blockage. Jonah continued rotating the rope and letting it fall freely until it was taut. He then paused, almost afraid to begin pulling it back up.

"Proud of ya, Mister Fisherman," he exclaimed. "That was a mighty good idea!"

By the time Jake rejoined them, Jonah was nearly finished drawing the frayed end of the rope back to the surface. "What have you been up to?" asked Jake earnestly.

"You'll see in a minute," roared Jonah with renewed confidence. And when the bushy end of the rope emerged from the hole, there was no need to touch it. It was wet enough for all to see. Inside the loose strands of hemp were multiple drops of water. Much less obvious was the point on the rest of the tightly wound rope where the wetness ended. As a result, they were unable to determine the depth of the water.

"Hallelujah," cried Jake, running back toward the house to summon his wife.

"Amen," added Jonah in a deep and sincere act of gratitude.

Jake's wife, Emma, had been watching from a window. After seeing him race toward the house, she met him at the door, and the two laughed happily as they headed toward Jonah and the well.

"God bless you," she cried as they reached the dowser.

"Let's not get too excited," Jonah cautioned. "Still don't know how much water is down there. Before ya run off to buy pipe and a new pump, we better be sure there's enough water to make it worthwhile."

Although Jake quickly agreed, Jonah's caution did little to end the farmer's exuberance.

"Been thinkin'," Jonah resumed, "we can lower a board down that hole, leave it set for a spell and try to bring it up before the water mark dries out."

"There's bound to be something in the barn we can use," Jake replied, setting off almost immediately for the barn. He soon returned with a six-foot board that was too wide for the hole. After dropping it near the drill site, he again set off for the barn. Several minutes later, he reappeared, struggling with a pair of sawhorses and a saw.

"How long a board do you need?" he queried.

"No harm in usin' the full length," answered Jonah.

So Jake began by ripping the board lengthways, producing a strip about three inches wide.

By the time they drilled small holes through each end of the board, tied a thinner rope to one end and a weight to the other, and then lowered the board down the hole until it had reached the very bottom, it was late afternoon.

"Let it sit overnight," counseled Jonah. With that, he bid farewell and headed home with Seth, who had been unusually quiet all afternoon.

CHAPTER 15

During the long walk home, Jonah tried to engage the boy with talk about fishing, but Seth rejected the topic, arguing that most of the creeks, including his favorite, were becoming too low and muddy for decent fishing. Instead, the lad steered the floundering conversation toward the upcoming box social, now just a couple days away.

"If I tell you what my mother's box is going to look like, will you bid on it?" Seth asked.

"Keep that to yerself," said Jonah, still concerned over his insolvency. "It's more fun when ya don't know such things. What yer supposed to do is bid on the best lookin' boxes and baskets with the best lookin' dinners, not the women that cooked 'em."

Rebuffed, Seth wondered how he might persuade Jonah to reconsider, but he soon decided against any further attempts. "Guess I'll have to buy it myself," he announced with an air of obvious disappointment. "I sure don't want Lucas or Brady winning it."

Jonah wanted to reassure Seth that he wouldn't let that happen, but the idea of trying to outbid someone with Lucas's wealth was too forbidding. No longer preoccupied with the likelihood that he had finally struck a second well, Jonah found himself annoyed by his personal poverty. How sweet it would have been, he dreamed, if he had struck oil instead.

Jonah's reverie was short-lived, however, as Seth reversed himself and tried once again to ensure that his mentor and friend would recognize and buy his mother's entry.

"Maybe I should tell Lucas," reflected the lad, hoping to goad the dowser into agreeing with his adolescent scheme. "At least that way, it should get some real good bids."

"Maybe so," agreed Jonah, resigned to the reality before him.

Neither spoke again until they sat down at the dinner table and Betsy asked somewhat hesitantly if there had been progress. Seth beamed and proudly announced that they had in fact struck water. But before she or Reverend Small had a chance to express their joy, Jonah dampened their reactions by minimizing the discovery.

"No need to get excited," he cautioned. "Won't know 'til tomorrow what we hit. Could be nothin' more than a tiny pool."

Jonah's reluctance to declare that he and Jake had struck a dependable supply of water did little, however, to restrain the interest and hope of his peers.

"You can't stop there," insisted Betsy. "What happened?"

"Jake told us that the rope on the springpole dropped more than usual without hitting anything," explained Seth. "So Jonah pulled the drill bit out and then ran the loose rope back down. When he brought it back up the end of the rope was wet."

"What makes you so cautious, Jonah?" probed Reverend Small. "It sure sounds like you brought in a good well."

"It's a long way down," replied the dowser, unsmilingly. "Can't risk havin' Jake buyin' all that pipe and then findin' there ain't enough water to make it worthwhile."

"How will you know?" demanded Betsy impatiently.

"We dropped a wood board all way to the bottom for a water mark," answered her son when Jonah hesitated. "When we pull it up tomorrow, we'll have a better idea how deep the water is."

"We should be celebrating, not begging for details," lamented Betsy, deeply frustrated by Jonah's hesitancy. "Finding water, no matter how little, confirms your skills and your new divining rod. Jake should be as happy as a lark."

"He's pretty happy," allowed Jonah. "Trouble is, he and everybody else wants that well so bad they don't want to wait 'til we know for sure that it's a good one. Just 'cause ya don't see me stompin' up and down is beside the point. It don't stop me from hopin' and prayin' too."

At that point, Jonah pushed his chair back from the dinner table, excused himself, and started toward the kitchen door. Betsy, headed toward the table with dishes of food in each hand, dashed in front of the dowser, blocking his way.

"I'm sorry, Jonah," she began, motioning him back to the table. "I'm so anxious to see you show up Lucas and his lackey that I couldn't stand your misgivings. Down deep I know you're right. It would be horrible if you said the well was good and it wasn't."

"That's all right, ma'am," said the dowser, waiting for Betsy to step aside. "Guess there's too much on my mind to be hungry."

"Seth," shouted his mother, "come take these dishes." As soon as the boy did so, Betsy seized Jonah's shoulder, pulled it down as if to whisper in his ear, and kissed his cheek. "You are going to eat," she insisted with a huge smile. "You'll need plenty of nourishment tomorrow if that board does come up dry. Besides, you had no lunch today."

Jonah responded with a small, fleeting smile but remained immobile. "Reverend Small," summoned Betsy, "I need your help."

As the clergyman scrambled to his feet, Seth did too. Together with Betsy, they encircled Jonah, laughing as she declared, "There's only one way to go, Jonah, and that's back to the table. Everyone's dinner is getting cold."

Outnumbered and cheered by their expression of heartfelt camaraderie, the dowser relented, feigned surrender with upraised arms and was promptly escorted back to his chair. Both Betsy and Reverend Small continued to give vent to their natural curiosity about Jake's well but did so with more sensitivity. Jonah answered between bites after announcing good-naturedly that, much to his surprise, he was indeed hungry after all.

With Jonah responding more vigorously, there were fewer opportunities for Seth. He seized those opportunities whenever they appeared, however, and to everyone's delight added a fact or two that Jonah had failed to mention.

In time, it was the dowser's turn. "Anything good happen at Ned's?" he finally asked.

"We're still digging, but it's getting much harder," said the clergyman. "Ned says we've hit a deep vein of shale. We're spending more time with picks than with shovels. He's about ready to give up, and even though I hate to admit it, I am too."

"Sounds hasty but reasonable," acknowledged Jonah. "See any more signs of water?"

"Every now and again," replied Reverend Small, choosing a phase he had heard Ned often use. "But when we get down for a close look, there's hardly anything there. Sometimes there's a cupful or so; nothing more. I've never believed in mirages, but I'm beginning to now."

"Tomorrow's another day," suggested Betsy, ending the discussion, "and so is the day after. Let me remind you both: that's when we have our box social, and from what I've been hearing, there could be more women than men. You gentlemen better be ready to buy at least one dinner if not more. And that includes you, Jonah!"

Jonah, anxious to escape the subject, smiled weakly and headed for the kitchen door. Having made her point, Betsy retired to the sink with a few dishes. Reverend Small remained briefly to learn the latest that Betsy was ready to share about the social and then left in search of Jonah. Once outside, he scanned the area around the barn, including the outdoor bench that the dowser often occupied after dinner. The bench was empty and upon further inspection, so was the stall that Jonah used to bed down at night. On a hunch, the clergyman started walking toward the drill site where Jonah had erected his now dormant springpole. His hunch paid off. Even when he was some distance away, he could see Jonah leaning against the upright pole.

The two men simply exchanged nods. As the dowser turned and began to look away, Reverend Small reached into his pocket and withdrew fifteen dollars in bills and coins. "Got something here that should make your life a little easier," he announced.

Without even looking at Reverend Small's outstretched hand, Jonah replied almost immediately, "Don't want it. Just put it back in yer pocket."

"It's from Ned," continued the clergyman. "He wants you to have it for all you've done. In fact, once you've struck water, he wants to pay you any amount you feel is fair."

"Already told him and everyone else, there's no charge," said Jonah adamantly.

"I realize you don't want to go back on your word," began

Reverend Small, "but you have been helping folks in an indispensable way. Without new, reliable sources of water, these people are truly desperate. Just helping them find the most promising places to dig or drill offers them genuine hope. Most of them want to do something more than say 'thank you.' Don't reject their gratitude so quickly. Don't deprive them of that."

Reverend Small stopped and, looking Jonah squarely in the eyes, watched as the dowser began mulling over the clergyman's appeal. But minutes passed, and Jonah remained silent.

Unwilling to drop the matter, Reverend Small finally resumed. "When I look at both you and Lucas," he said softly, "I am very much reminded of a verse in Proverbs: 'Wealth gotten by vanity shall be diminished: but he that gathereth by labour shall increase.'

"You have done much more than choose places to find water," the clergyman continued. "You have put your skills and your very reputation at stake. Even more, you have poured your personal time and backbreaking labor into it. As a laborer worthy of his hire, you are certainly entitled to recompense. Don't hesitate to take what is rightfully yours."

Whatever his thoughts, Jonah kept them well hidden. Neither his continued silence nor his lack of expression offered Reverend Small even the slightest hint that he might accept the money from Ned. After patiently waiting for some response, the clergyman resorted reluctantly to the only proposition he had left.

"If you can't accept it as compensation," he pleaded, "then at least accept it as a loan."

"Maybe half of it," Jonah finally responded. "Ya can give the rest of it back."

"If that's your wish," replied Reverend Small, counting out seven dollars and fifty cents. "Take this and I'll give the rest back to Ned in the morning. From here on out, however, any further discussion about wages and loans are strictly between you and him."

For the first time since he left the kitchen, Jonah seemed relieved, if not completely happy. "Havin' some money helps," he confided, "but it ain't a real answer. Still gotta figure out how to keep losin' to everyone else once the biddin' starts."

Reverend Small began to laugh. "You're on your own, my friend," he chuckled. "I'm sure the ladies will figure out your scheme very quickly. But one thing is certain: If we don't bid, we're both in trouble. You heard Miss Betsy. I can't get out of this anymore than you can."

"Thanks, Reverend," said Jonah, shaking his head gently in amusement.

When Jonah arrived alone at Jake's farm the following morning, he was not amused. There beside Jake under the head of the springpole were Lucas and Brady. The long board that Jonah had hoped would confirm a plentiful supply of water below had been pulled back to the surface, and the three men were examining it closely. When Jake eventually looked up and saw Jonah approaching, he threw the board down in apparent disgust.

"Just like I figured," he told the dowser. "There's not enough there to fill a teapot."

Although prepared for a setback, Jonah still found himself somewhat stunned. He bent over, picked up the board, and quickly discovered that there was no clear watermark. What had appeared so promising was now bitter disappointment. Jonah let the board slip from his grip, waiting for whatever comment Jake was inclined to add. Instead, there was only derision from Lucas and Brady.

"Think you could find water if someone handed you a glassful?" teased Brady.

"Maybe you should try a crystal ball," sneered Lucas.

"Or a full moon," scoffed Jake.

It was bad enough that he had to tolerate the remarks of Lucas and Brady but, after all he had tried to do for Jake, he found the farmer's mocking intolerable. Somehow he managed to wish Jake good luck and, at the same time, promise to return for his drill bit.

"Why not leave it with someone who knows how to use it?" demanded Lucas in obvious seriousness. "After deceiving Jake with a lot of false promises, it's the least you can do."

For an instant, Jonah seriously considered the challenge and, just as quickly, dismissed it, realizing that they probably did not have a bit of their own. "Don't see why ya need a drill bit," he replied carefully. "If yer as good as ya say ya are, just tell Jake where to dig. Seems like ya should be able to find water without havin' to drill."

"Take it whenever you want," interjected the farmer.

Jonah left without further word and began his trek towards Ned's farm. During the walk, he found himself troubled by the sudden realization that although there was no obvious watermark on the board, he had sensed the presence of moisture before he dropped the board to the ground. And then it struck him, the reason there was no watermark was because the entire board had probably been waterlogged. Either someone had dried off the outside of the board or the board had been out of the well long enough to begin drying. He was virtually certain, however, that the pores of the wood had been damp from overnight submersion.

As his destination came into view, he could see two figures standing idle near the well. Why, he wondered, wasn't one of them digging? Concerned that they had lost hope and had decided to cease digging, Jonah quickened his pace. His fears, however, proved unfounded. It wasn't long before Ned spied Jonah in the distance, and he waved an enthusiastic greeting. Satisfied that nothing was wrong, the dowser returned to a normal gait. The whole episode at Jake's farm had left its mark; he was drained physically, mentally, and emotionally.

As soon as he was within earshot, Jonah shouted a serious query, "Why ya loafin'?"

"Just resting up before we start filling in this hole," answered Reverend Small with a peculiar grin, mirrored in large measure by Ned.

The dowser shook his head sadly and, once again, quickened his pace. Upon reaching the manmade crater, he had only to look down. Shimmering across the floor of the well were several small, shallow pools of a dark, tar–like fluid. Jonah was speechless.

"Are ya really serious about coverin' it all up?" he finally asked incredulously.

"That pretty much hinges on just one question," replied Ned, whose expression had now turned serious. "Is there any chance of hitting good water if we keep on digging?"

Jonah took a long time answering. At first, he was inclined to climb down to inspect the pools more closely. But the more he hesitated and the more he considered Ned's question, the more he realized they would have to try for water somewhere else.

"Not likely but ya could," the dowser eventually responded. "Even so it'd probably be a mistake."

When no one asked why, Jonah took a deep breath and continued, "Ain't never actually seen crude, but that's gotta be crude seepin' up through seams in the shale. The water that come up before was probably trapped in there too. Once ya removed all this ground, the crude must'a forced the water out ahead of it. Could be there's more water below, but even if there is, ya don't want to risk foulin' it up with crude."

"That's good enough for me," said Ned. "Let's get this dirt back into the well."

"Whoa!" cried Jonah. "With a little more time, that might just become a huge pool of crude oil."

Ned had grasped his long-handled shovel with both hands up near the top of the handle. His chin rested on his right hand, and he peered up at Jonah.

"It's water I need, not oil," he began slowly. "I can't drink this stuff, and neither can my stock. I don't think I need any more reason than that, but I do have another. I don't want to be the one to start a rush for oil. Just because I want to cover it up now doesn't mean I can't come back and uncover it in the future."

Jonah couldn't help but empathize with Ned's rationale but decided to challenge it anyway. "Once they see this hole filled up, Lucas and Brady will have all they need to make a fool outta me and sign up all the farmers that still are sittin' on the fence," he argued.

"I've been thinking about that too," replied the farmer, looking first at Jonah and then at Reverend Small. "All I've got to say is that we did hit water but it wasn't enough to meet my need. That may not be the whole truth, but it's not exactly a lie either."

Whatever Ned's purpose in trying to involve the clergyman, he was quickly disappointed. Reverend Small did not comment nor did he offer any expression of support.

"Can I still count on you to help me find water?" asked Ned as his eyes caught Jonah's.

"Yeah," sighed the dowser, reaching for a spare shovel.

In minutes, the bottom of the well was covered with dirt and stone. What little evidence there had been of oil was now gone. For

Jonah, each shovelful was a painful reminder of how close he had been to a dream that would not go away.

The three men shoveled throughout much of the day and, by the time they finished, there was a only small mound of dirt over the site that had been a deep, wide hole.

As Jonah and Reverend Small prepared to leave, Jonah suddenly remembered the money that Ned had sent. "Mighty obliged for the seven–fifty," said the dowser, addressing Ned. "Hope the reverend told ya yer gonna get it all back."

"He did," confirmed the farmer, "but the subject's not yet closed."

"If ya can wait til' tomorrow," said Jonah, ignoring Ned's obvious intention to compensate him, "I'll start looking for a new place to dig or drill in the mornin'."

"Good," replied Ned. "And as far as the oil is concerned, we've got to keep it a secret. Can we shake on it?"

"That shouldn't be necessary," said Reverend Small. "If that's your wish, Jonah and I will honor it. We know that an oil boom is just what Lucas wants. Your argument for putting off that disclosure strikes me as reasonable and self–sacrificing. To be absolutely honest, I admire your integrity. I'm sure the temptation to exploit this potential is hard to resist."

"Agreed, at least for now," affirmed the dowser. "Can't see any big need to tell folks about it today or tomorrow. But the day is gonna come when it's gonna get out, and before that time comes, we better know what we're all gonna say."

Instinctively, he thrust his hand out toward Ned. "No harm in shakin' on it," he added. With that, each of the men shook the hands of the other two, resigned to their compromise.

Betsy was outside, sitting on the porch steps with her eyes

closed, catching both the last rays of a declining sun and the warbling of a pair of nearby songbirds, when she heard the voices of Jonah and Reverend Small. She rose slowly, showing signs of her own weariness, brushed off her dress and, with a disarming, captivating twinkle in her eyes, welcomed her two boarders home.

"Wash up," she instructed. "Dinner's been ready for the past hour."

Seth, who had been down at the creek fishing after helping his mother with her daily chores, had seen the men return and had started his trek back to the house, proudly bearing a good-sized bullhead he had caught only minutes before. At first, he was tempted to throw it back. Knowing that all three adults would tease him if he did so, he decided to bring the evidence with him.

Neither he nor his mother were keen on cleaning and skinning bullheads because of their sharp, horn-like spines and the pain they can inflict. A few, however, could provide a tasty meal, and Seth resolved to return to the creek after dinner to see if he could add to his catch.

Once everyone was sitting at the table and Reverend Small had offered a blessing, Betsy lost little time in pursuing her insatiable quest for details of the day. It was not until she began to pepper Jonah with her questions that he and Reverend Small realized that they had never discussed the day's events at Jake's farm. They had been so occupied with the discovery of oil at Ned's place and the subsequent decision to keep it secret that the earlier developments had never come up.

Now, as Jonah began revealing what had happened, a gloom settled over the kitchen.

Before sharing his suspicions that he had struck a major reservoir of water, he shared his bewilderment at Lucas's success in persuading Jake to reject him, not just once but twice. It was especially galling in view of the personal time and energy that Jonah had devoted to the search and subsequent drilling. That was labor that could have benefited others whose needs were as great if not greater than those of Jake, Jonah lamented.

Downcast but supportive, Betsy and Reverend Small shook their heads in agreement.

After a long, deep breath, Jonah resumed his story, revealing his growing certainty that there was plenty of water at the bottom of that shaft and that Jake and Lucas had deliberately concealed it by drying off the board.

"Pretty stupid when ya think about it," Jonah continued. "Whole idea of leavin' the board down there all night was to let it soak up any water we had hit. Jake knew that. Wipin' off that board wasn't gonna stop what was inside from sweatin' out.

"Guess they reckoned that since there was no watermark as such, and the outer surface of the board was pretty dry, they had no cause to worry."

"Well, if you're right," challenged Reverend Small, "how can they draw water from your well without us all discovering it?"

"That's not so hard," reasoned the dowser. "All they hafta do is move the springpole a little bit and claim it was Lucas and Brady that struck water not me. Chances are that reservoir is big enough to hit even if they move the springpole a few feet away."

"But Jake needs that water now," persisted the clergyman. "Why would he give up a bird in the hand for one in the bush?"

"Haven't figured that out yet," Jonah replied.

"Where's your drill bit?" asked Betsy perceptively.

"Still over there," responded Jonah. "All three of 'em were after me to leave it. Told 'em no, but the sooner it's outta there the better. Kinda hopin' ol' Barnes will lend me his team. The bit's far too heavy to carry any distance by myself."

"The more I hear about these shenanigans," interrupted Betsy, "the more I think you better help Ned. Seth and I will ask Barnes to help us pick up your drill bit. The question is, do you want us to bring it back here, or do you want us to drop it off at Ned's place?"

"Ned's," replied Jonah without the slightest hesitation.

"What are Lucas and Brady most likely to do after Miss Betsy picks up your drill bit?" asked Reverend Small, trying to help Jonah anticipate their next moves. "Aren't things pretty much at a standstill unless they can get a bit of their own?"

"Don't really know," confessed Jonah, "but most likely they'll tell Jake to start diggin' somewhere else on his property."

"Maybe it's not such a good idea to go running over there first thing in the morning," mused Betsy after listening to the exchange between the two men. "Maybe I should give them a little time to start doing whatever they plan to do. That could be interesting."

Clearly amused by Betsy's suggestion, both men found it hard to keep from laughing.

"There's no need to hurry on my account," shrugged Jonah. "Bit's not much use to me 'til there's a new place to drill or dig, and that might take a day or more. Just be sure to get the bit outta there by tomorrow afternoon."

"I really need to get into town to see the Blakes and, after that, spend some time working on my next sermon," observed Reverend Small, catching Jonah's eye. "But if you think Miss Betsy and Barnes need my help, I'll put everything else aside."

"No reason why ya can't tend to yer own affairs," answered Jonah. "Ain't expectin' trouble but, come what may, we'll handle it."

"Lucas and Brady would love to draw you into a fight," Betsy told the dowser. Then, resting her hand on Reverend Small's arm, she added, "Maybe it's better if you do go with us. They may try to annoy me, but I don't think they will try to provoke you."

"Of course, I'll go," said the clergyman. "And if they're unwilling to lift the bit onto the wagon, I'll be there for that too."

"Sure nice gettin' to know folks like you," declared Jonah, getting up from the table. "Ya always seem to know just what to say or do, 'specially when things ain't quite right."

Jonah retired shortly after leaving the kitchen and drifted off into a peaceful sleep almost immediately. He awoke early, well before dawn, and soon found himself distressed by the almost certain discovery of water at Jake's and the almost certain discovery of oil at Ned's. What made it so painful was the secrecy that surrounded both discoveries.

Yet in the midst of his torment came the realization that he actually had more reasons to be happy than unhappy. He had proven his prowess as a dowser, and even in the absence of public recognition of his success, he still had won widespread respect and admiration throughout the community. Moreover, for the first time in many years, he had won the love and affection of the people closest to him. What also struck him now was his growing readiness to believe in the God he had learned about as a child.

Despite the warmth of such feelings, however, Jonah's mind soon turned to the nagging conviction that Lucas and Brady were about to seize his well and claim it as their own.

Eventually, Jonah chose to push it all aside and dwell instead on the forthcoming box social. Confronted with Seth's obvious willingness to identify the box his mother would bring, he reconsidered his plan to end up hungry and return the seven–fifty to Ned.

As nice as it might be accommodate Seth, he mused, it might

be more fun to bid at random, letting chance be the final arbiter. His thoughts then shifted to some of the unmarried women he had seen at various places, among them Blakes' store, Sunday worship, and farms he had visited. *Looks as though there's a little devil in me yet,* he concluded as he plotted to avoid several old maids he had met. And that made him smile.

Jonah's daydreaming was soon shattered by Seth, who deliberately slammed his milk pail against the barn door. "Sun's up," he hollered.

After breakfast, there was a brief review of everyone's plans, and Jonah and Reverend Small left the kitchen together. As the dowser headed toward the barn for his divining rod, the clergyman headed toward the road. "Godspeed," he whispered as he and Jonah separated.

Ned was nowhere to be seen when Jonah arrived on the farm, a fact that pleased the dowser. Rather than begin searching immediately for a new site, he strode directly to the old one, grasped his divining rod in classic fashion, and began moving in concentric circles closer and closer to the center of the mound that hid the once-empty well. When he got within ten or twelve feet of that point, he began to feel gentle but unmistakable tugs on the rod.

Although he continued working toward the center, there was no change in the strength or frequency of such tugs. Nor did they appear on any single vector. By the time he reached the center, he was perplexed and dispirited. What happened to the distinct surges that originally led him to that site, assuring him that water lay below? So absorbed was he with that mystery, he was nearly startled by Ned, now just a few feet away.

"Good to see you back so early," greeted the farmer. "Looks like you've already started, but why here?"

At first, Jonah was inclined to ignore the question. His usual candor prevailed, however, and he explained unhappily, "Just tryin' to see if oil draws the rod any different than water."

"That sounds smart to me," Ned replied.

"Problem is it ain't workin'," lamented Jonah. "Even lost the feel that was here before, and it's the same rod. Be a whole lot easier to figure out if Drake had found the site before it got broke. Gotta be the new rod or me."

Though sympathetic, Ned had nothing to offer, and he remained still.

"Guess it's time to walk around and look some more," volunteered the dowser. "Can't find nothin' standin' around here."

Looking toward the road, he wandered off, leaving Ned uncertain whether to follow. When he finally realized he had left Ned behind, he turned, gave a big c'mon wave, and ambled on toward the spot he had chosen. While still a hundred feet or more from the spot, he pulled the divining rod from his belt and began dowsing.

Almost immediately, there were tremors in the rod. Hiding his excitement, Jonah created an imaginary square with one hundred foot sides and began searching enthusiastically within it. Within minutes the rod quivered dramatically. Ned who was now nearby watched the quivering rod with admiration and undisguised glee.

Time and again, Ned assumed from the rod's behavior that Jonah had located the best possible site to dig or drill, but each time the dowser would move on, often losing the visible signs of energy. Jonah continued to move back and forth across the grid, seemingly indifferent to the wild dips of the rod. As Ned began to appreciate Jonah's thoroughness, he also began to wonder what it would take to satisfy Jonah's quest.

Eventually, Jonah stopped and summoned Ned. "Bring a stone."

The farmer scrambled to the site like a child racing toward a new toy, armed with a large rock he had already chosen as a marker.

"Do we dig or drill?" he asked excitedly.

"Now that the drill bit's available, it's best to drill," answered Jonah with a huge grin. "No point in diggin' like we did. Water could still be a long way down."

"What do we do next?" probed Ned, anxious to accelerate their new momentum.

"Best head for the woods and get the trees we need for the springpole," replied Jonah, trying hard to suppress his own eagerness to bring in new water for Ned's escalating needs. "No sense just standin' around waitin' for ol' Barnes' wagon."

Ned immediately headed off to the barn in search of axes and saws for the work ahead. Minutes later, he emerged with a two-man saw and a couple of axes. Jonah, meanwhile, had ambled over to a small apple tree where he had carefully deposited his divining rod over a low hanging branch for safekeeping.

As Jonah reached for the saw, he was taken by the shiny edges of the teeth, a sign they had been sharpened recently. So too, he observed, were the blades of the axes. "Sharpen 'em yerself?" he asked.

"Almost always right after I finish using them," Ned replied. "I like to keep them clean and sharp. They're not much good if they're dull or broke. I treat all my tools like friends."

Of all the farmers and townspeople Jonah had come to know, Ned was the one he had come to respect most for his work ethic, his sound judgment on numerous fronts, and his standing in the community.

Walking toward the woods, Jonah spotted a couple trees in the distance that looked suitable, and he headed in their direction, pointing them out to Ned. The farmer nodded in agreement and, when they reached the first tree, they discovered it was a fine choice. Jonah was tempted to spell out all its particular features but immediately realized it was unnecessary. Thought silent, Ned had clearly observed the same attributes. It was a well-formed hemlock, straight as an arrow, somewhere between thirty-five and forty feet tall.

While Jonah watched, the farmer circled the tree, looking for a clearing where it could fall without damage to itself or other trees.

"How about dropping it there?" he asked, pointing in the direction of choice. After Jonah affirmed the choice, Ned notched it with experience and skill. When he finished, Jonah offered one of the handles of the saw.

"Let's drop our springpole," murmured the dowser with a faint but unmistakable smile. The two men carefully positioned the blade of the saw on the opposite side of the notch and began sawing with a rhythm they clearly enjoyed. The tree fell quickly.

The task of felling the second tree also went smoothly and, once it was down, the two men separated so that each could trim independently. Ned remained with the second of the two, a hickory they both favored, while Jonah returned to the huge hemlock.

As they finished, they were surprised by the appearance of Ned's wife Elizabeth and the lunch she carried. It was a welcome break which they cut short because of all the work that remained. Less than an hour later, they harnessed Ned's only horse and skidded the two trees to the drill site.

Ned immediately began cutting the long, slender hickory into two equal lengths while Jonah began digging a narrow but deep rectangular hole. When the men finished their respective tasks, they slid the largest end of each log into the hole. Jonah then positioned the logs in an upright position, and Ned tied them together as high as he could above ground. After creating a fulcrum for the springpole in the shape of a large X, they anchored it in the ground by returning the dirt and stone Jonah had dug out.

The hemlock they planned to use as the springpole was noticeably larger than either of the two previously put up by Jonah, a fact that Ned eventually questioned.

"Should give us a bigger arc and faster drillin'," replied the dowser. Sweating profusely, he showed little interest in prolonged conversation. But neither did Ned. It was hotter than it had been in days, and he was entirely satisfied with the abbreviated explanation.

It was then that they saw Betsy, Reverend Small, and Seth approaching on foot. "No buggy, no bit," predicted Jonah unhappily as he and Ned awaited the trio.

It was Betsy who was first to speak. "They're as crooked as the day is long," she began, trying hard to maintained her composure. "As soon as we got there, Jake headed for the house so he wouldn't have to face us, and Lucas and Brady claimed they accidentally lost your bit."

"How'd they do that?" asked Jonah expressionless.

"They said they lost it while trying to drill deeper at your site before choosing a new site of their own," interjected Reverend Small. "Brady claims that after he spliced in a new length of rope, the bit snagged while he was lowering it down the hole. According to him, when they tried to pull it back up, the rope broke."

"Sounds like your bit is lost for good," lamented Ned.

"Suppose so," confirmed Jonah, "if that's what really happened."

"Whether it's true or not," said Betsy, "they have managed to keep you from drilling a new well here at Ned's."

"Or anywhere else," added Ned.

"I know it sounds hard to believe," said the clergyman, "but I guess I'm inclined to give them the benefit of doubt. When I asked who was going to pay for a replacement, Brady insisted Jake would. He claims Jake will come by the farm tomorrow with the money."

"That's bound to be Lucas's money," snapped Jonah. "Besides, no amount's gonna make up for that bit."

"We can deal with their offer later," declared Ned. "What's more important is getting a new bit. Even if we have to start digging instead of drilling, you're going to need a replacement sooner or later. If I put up the money right now, how soon can you get a new bit?"

"Don't know," confessed Jonah. "Depends on how busy the smith is and whether or not he's recovered enough and got the iron to make it."

Reminded that the bit had been made by the local blacksmith, Ned was almost jubilant. "Looks like you folks get a ride back home," proclaimed the farmer. "As soon as I can get my horse hitched up to the wagon, we'll head over to the smith."

"Can I help?" asked Seth, somewhat tired of being seen but not heard.

"You sure can," said Ned, turning toward his barn.

Whatever their individual thoughts, neither Jonah nor his companions seized the opportunity to reveal them. There seemed little doubt, however, that Lucas and Brady had won that day's rivalry.

Betsy joined Ned on the wagon's only seat when he and Seth

reappeared. The others simply jumped in back and sat on the rig's floor, bracing themselves for a welcome but bumpy ride.

Only then did Jonah announce a decision he had reached shortly after he had first seen his companions approaching on foot. "Everything now kinda hinges on the smith. Come Monday, we'll either start diggin' or we'll finish up the springpole and start waitin' for the drill bit."

The smith was at his forge, pumping a small but effective bellows at dying embers in the middle of his fire. Though there was no sight of the sling, his injured hand remained bandaged.

It was not everyday that a wagonload of four adults and a young boy pulled into his yard. Amused and curious, he set aside his work and ambled over to his visitors.

"Which is it?" he joked. "Did I do somethin' wrong or somethin' right?"

"We'll all know soon enough," laughed Ned. "It depends on what you tell Jonah."

"Need a new drill bit," said the dowser as he climbed down from the wagon. "Just like the one ya made before."

"How'd you break the first one?" teased the blacksmith, with a wink toward Betsy.

"With my bare hands," roared Jonah, seizing the opportunity for some light-hearted banter.

"Musta been cheap iron," shot back the blacksmith, leaning back with a snicker. "But even if it wasn't, I can't be wastin' my time makin' bits for you to go around breakin'."

Given the defeat, frustration, and suppressed anger from the events of the day, the repartee was a respite not just for Jonah but for the others as well.

"Even if he pays you well?" probed Ned with mock seriousness.

"Well, maybe, since he's my favorite dowser," said the smith. "But he's not gonna get off cheap."

"Truth is," began Jonah, "my bit's come up missin'. Fella workin' with Lucas claims the rope broke and it dropped down the well hole at Jake's place. For now, that's all spilt milk. We need a new bit for a springpole for Ned."

The blacksmith started to ask how Lucas and Brady got possession of the bit but, recognizing the need to move on, assured Jonah that he could forge a replacement. "Same size and shape?" he inquired.

"Maybe a little longer and heavier," replied the dowser.

"That'll add a dollar or two more," said the blacksmith earnestly.

Breaking her silence for the first time, Betsy heightened the urgency. "The springpole's almost finished. How soon can you deliver the new bit?"

"Gimme four days and eleven dollars," answered the smith. After a momentary pause to reconsider, he added, "That's providin' I don't run outta iron. Come to think of it, ya better make it five days. Sunday's the day after tomorrow, and I don't work the Lord's day."

The remark took Reverend Small somewhat by surprise. Though he had come to know of the blacksmith through Jonah, he could not recall seeing him at any worship. Concerned that Ned or Jonah might encourage him to make an exception, he intervened to commend the blacksmith. "It's good you rest on the seventh day," he remarked.

"Been meanin' to hear one of yer sermons," responded the smith appreciatively.

"Well," laughed the clergyman, "like you said, Sunday's the day after tomorrow."

The conversation turned completely serious once more as Ned withdrew five silver dollars from his pocket and handed them to the blacksmith. "We'll give you the rest as soon as you come by with the new bit, and we'll add another dollar if you deliver on time."

The customary handshake followed. With business now complete, Ned and the others reboarded the wagon and began the trip to Betsy's farm. Despite the promise of a new drill bit in a few days, it was still a somber journey. None of them seemed able or willing to discuss the decision by Jake to reject Jonah and embrace Lucas. Nor could they easily accept Brady's glib explanation for the disappearance of Jonah's bit. Adding to their gloominess were the telltale signs of the drought, field after field of parched land and straw-colored grass.

"See ya in the mornin'," promised Jonah as he jumped down from the wagon when they arrived at Betsy's farm. While Seth and Reverend Small disembarked, Jonah moved within easy reach of Betsy and, once she slipped her feet over the edge of the wagon, he grasped her by the waist and gently lowered her to the ground. Surprised and pleased, she blushed as she praised his chivalry and curtsied.

CHAPTER 16

True to his word, Jonah arrived at Ned's farm shortly before the farmer finished his morning chores. Buoyed by the blacksmith's promise to forge the new drill bit quickly, the two men resumed work on the springpole.

Of all the men with whom Jonah worked, he most enjoyed laboring side by side with Ned. Each seemed to anticipate the expectations of the other and, without indulging in long discussions or lengthy breaks, simply moved from one obvious task to the next.

By midday, they had wrestled the long, trimmed hemlock into the crotch of the hickory uprights. Two stout lengths of rope dangled from a point near the tip, one ready for the drill bit being forged by the blacksmith and the other ready for the stirrup.

The only remaining task was to bury the trunk end of the hemlock in an elongated hole they had excavated together. After that final step, they carefully examined the towering device and declared it fit for the critical, urgent task ahead.

Moments later, they were summoned to the house by Elizabeth, eager to reward their labor with a belated lunch.

During the meal, both Ned and his wife seized the opportunity to tease Jonah about his single status and even suggested an eligible maid or two. It was all in good fun, and it left Jonah with the same warm feeling he had experienced with Betsy and Reverend Small.

The box social was now just a few hours away, and it was time to clean up and dress up.

Betsy spotted Jonah from her kitchen window while he was still on the road. She summoned Seth and gave him a number of instructions to pass along to the dowser, beginning with a decree that he wear the new shirt she had placed in the barn.

By late afternoon, Betsy had wrapped a colorful cloth around the outside of her dinner box, embellishing it with ribbons and bows and then concealing the entire box under an old tablecloth.

And just before joining Barnes and his wife Bessie for the trip into town in their wagon, she called her son and her two boarders to the porch where each was carefully inspected and told to be on time. Then, with a radiant smile reserved for each of them, she departed.

Once she was out-of-sight, Reverend Small, Jonah, and Seth commenced the trip into town on foot. Despite earlier misgivings about the event, the clergyman was clearly upbeat but, at the same time, somewhat circumspect.

"Tell me, Jonah, how should I bid? Should I start with the very first basket, or should I wait until something catches my eye?"

"It don't seem right to bid on the first one," replied the dowser earnestly. "On the other hand, ya better not wait too long either. When ya do bid, make sure someone else has already started the biddin'. Then stay with it for a few bids. Ya don't wanta disappoint the ladies, either by winnin' or by droppin' outta the biddin' too soon."

"That sounds like a pretty good strategy," laughed Reverend

Small. After reflecting further on Jonah's suggestions, he soon added, "Maybe we could make it interesting if I just follow your bid and bid against you."

"Trouble with that," warned Jonah quite seriously, "if there's no one else biddin' either you or me is gonna wind up winnin' whatever basket that happens to be." The reply gave the clergyman pause, and neither man spoke for some time.

"It doesn't matter if it's my mother's basket," challenged Seth after prolonged silence.

Rather than address the point, Jonah simply looked down at Seth and declared, "Time to let this young fella show what he's made of!"

As Seth and Reverend Small waited for Jonah to elaborate, the dowser scratched the back of his head, pondering a variety of options. "Could let him tell us when to bid, or maybe let him do the biddin' for us," he suggested. "Not likely he'll do any worse than we'd do; could be he'll do a whole lot better."

"And what do you say, young man?" asked Reverend Small, delighted that Jonah had involved the youngster.

"What happens if I pick some old maid's basket, and one of you win it?" probed the lad somewhat apprehensively.

Both men laughed aloud, amused by Seth's foresight.

"Well, we could let you be the one to eat with her," roared Jonah.

"And what happens if I pick my mother's basket?" continued Seth.

Choosing to ignore the question, Jonah broached a subject he was still unable to reconcile—the behavior of men like Lucas. "Why does he do it?" demanded the dowser.

"The simple answer is sin," answered Reverend Small, weighing his words carefully. "It's the very nature of man. We're all guilty in countless ways. Whether it's greed or arrogance or envy or theft or any number of other sins, we all fall short every day. It all started with Adam and Eve when they disobeyed God."

"How come God keeps lettin' Lucas get away with it?" demanded Jonah.

"There will always be a reckoning," assured the clergyman.

"Even for good folks?" asked Jonah skeptically.

"Even us," replied Reverend Small. "No one can and no one will escape judgment in the life hereafter."

"Guess that's somethin' to think about," replied the dowser.

Turning their attention back to the youngster, the two men resumed kidding the lad, ultimately winning his promise to tell them when to bid. By then, they had reached the school grounds and were pleasantly surprised to find a large, early turnout.

A large canvas tarp had been set up over a few poles to provide shade for all the picnic dinners the women had brought. Both the table used at Sunday services and a few others had been set up for the auction that would soon begin. Two smiling Brunnehildes stood guard at the tent–like structure, each holding a rolling pin. Intended to keep the men from inspecting the boxes too closely, their smiles and overall demeanor betrayed their seriousness and, in no time at all, they were besieged by some of the most fun–loving males.

In the faux melee that followed, one of the men was accidentally hit on the head by a rolling pin aimed at someone else, and the blow was enough to send him to his knees. The crowd roared in delight until it realized the man was truly dazed. One of the women quickly prepared a cold, wet compress and gave it to the man's wife to apply. After several minutes, the crowd erupted once more as the man struggled to his feet, recovered but embarrassed.

Esther Blake appeared behind the table closest to the crowd. Grasping a large cowbell she had brought from the store, she began ringing it with gusto. Satisfied that she had everyone's attention, she relaxed, put the bell down on the table's gingham cloth, and summoned her husband and Reverend Small to her side.

"You all know why we're here," she began. "We're here for some fun, some good food, and a very worthy cause. We're going to rebuild our church, and whatever we make tonight is going to help pay for the lumber and all the other materials we need to get started. Now let me turn this over to Art for a little progress report. Then it's Reverend Small's turn. After that, the fun begins!"

As she stepped aside for Art, she could be heard by nearly everyone informing him, "If you want to go home with me, darlin', you better pick the right basket and pay lots of good money for it!"

Art had to wait for the crowd's howling approval to subside. Amid the residual whistles and shouts, he feigned an appeal. "Sounds like I might have to do a little negotiating if I win the wrong dinner!"

The storekeeper then held up a large piece of paper for all to see and, in a more serious vein, began enumerating various quantities of the most urgently needed materials like stone, wood, and nails.

Folks at local quarries and the owners of two nearby sawmills had promised stone and lumber at cost, he announced, noting that he and Esther would also provide at cost any other items they ordered through their store. He invited the donors to stand, and after a long round of applause, he alerted volunteers that they would soon be in demand.

With a sweeping wave of his arm and a cheerful injunction that

"It's all yours," he retreated, leaving Reverend Small in the limelight.

Deeply moved, the clergyman was unable and unwilling to hide his emotion.

"Good people," he began, "this is indeed a special moment in our lives. Rebuilding our church is only a part of what we are about; less obvious but no less important is the opportunity to nourish and strengthen our spiritual lives. By giving so freely of our goods and ourselves, we are not only offering our God and Father a temple of wood and stone but also a spiritual temple within us in which He can dwell. Please join with me, in your hearts and minds, in a collective prayer of thanksgiving:

"Heavenly Father, we rejoice in your promise to enter our midst whenever two or three are gathered in your name. We rejoice in your unbounded love, we rejoice in your promise of salvation to those who accept your son, Christ Jesus, as their Redeemer and Lord. We rejoice in the fellowship and goodwill that has brought us together to rebuild what was lost, both spiritual and temporal, and we rejoice in this opportunity to renew and expand our relationships with Thee and with one another, all to Your honor and glory. Amen."

"Amen," cried Emmet.

"Amen," shouted the crowd with somewhat less divine inspiration.

As Art and Reverend Small moved away from the table, Esther was joined by Ruth Black, who was carrying a large, gaily decorated box. It had high sides wrapped with a bright, colored cloth. There was a cluster of contrasting handmade, multi-colored bows in the front, and the top was covered with a piece of the same cloth, hiding its contents.

"Well, I'll be darned," laughed Esther. "I can't even see what's inside, but the box sure looks good enough to eat! Who's ready to take a chance—even though he could go home hungry!"

"Fifty cents if I get to keep it," called out a man surrounded by friends. "And fifty cents more if there's a good meal inside."

"Now there's a brave soul," countered Esther, as her eyes swept the huge gathering. "Who'll give me five dollars?"

Almost immediately, a hand shot up. The man was sitting with two others and was so far back that Esther had no idea who they were.

"That must be the husband," she joked. "Who'll make it ten?"

"Six dollars," shouted a farmer known to be struggling to make ends meet.

"Six fifty," cried someone in the distance.

"Seven," shouted the farmer, raising his right arm to be seen.

"Come on, folks, we're here to make sure we can pay for all the materials we need," challenged Esther. "I'm still looking for at least ten dollars. With a box as pretty as this, there's bound to be a great feast inside."

"Nine dollars," bid a fellow from town.

"Nine fifty," shouted the hapless farmer to the cheers of his wife and small daughter. Displaying what appeared to be the extent of his funds, he added, "It's all I've got."

A full minute passed without another bid.

"We're not there yet," cried Esther. "Ten dollars for this fancy box is a real bargain."

"Ten and fifty cents more," bid a man standing near Jonah.

"Going once, going twice!" yelled a gleeful Esther, confident there would be no further bids. "It's all yours, Ned."

Before moving forward to claim his dinner, Ned looked over

toward the farmer who had helped keep the bidding alive, and he watched in genuine admiration as the farmer and his wife embraced, kissed, and quietly parted.

Ruth had already provided Esther with a new dinner box by the time Ned reached an adjacent table where money was to be collected and the winning bidder awarded his prize. There he encountered the wife of the poor but proud farmer.

"There are lots of tasty dishes inside," she assured him. "My husband insisted on it."

"Will he join us if we ask?" replied Ned.

"Now that my dinner basket has been bought, he wants to buy someone else's," she answered. "He's so anxious to see the church rebuilt that he brought every cent we have. He was determined to drive up the bidding on my dinner basket to at least ten dollars, and he was ready to buy it himself if he failed."

"It's a shame you folks have fallen on hard times," sympathized Ned. "If my wife and I can help, let us know."

"You already have," she murmured as they reached a spot near Jonah, Reverend Small, and Seth. There she opened the cloth on top of the basket, spread it on the ground, and began distracting everyone nearby with a mouth-watering array of simple but appealing dishes. Only then did she remind Ned they should wait until everyone was ready to eat.

"Ya sure ya don't need help with all that food?" teased Jonah.

"Better not wait all night to bid," suggested Ned while ignoring the kidding. "Esther's already auctioned off two more boxes since this one."

"Just waitin' for this young fella to tell me when," replied the dowser.

Having failed to identify his mother's dinner box before she left the farm, Seth waited until he saw Ruth set down a new, large, unadorned basket in front of Esther. "Now," he cried. "No one's going to offer ten fifty for that."

Jonah sized up the situation quickly and agreed. As soon as Esther called for an opening bid of at least two dollars and fifty cents, Jonah raised his hand enthusiastically. "Two fifty," he roared without giving Reverend Small an equal chance.

"Four dollars," challenged a bidder well behind them.

"Four fifty," cried Jonah, picking up the gauntlet.

"Five dollars," said Reverend Small, just loud enough to be heard by Esther.

"Well now," laughed Esther, "are we going to let the reverend get this fine dinner for only five dollars? Let's not be afraid to outbid him. Remember this box social is for our new church. Who will give me five fifty?"

Just when it appeared that none of the men would raise the bid, Seth tapped Jonah on the arm and insisted, "Don't stop now!"

The dowser hesitated, momentarily unwilling to go beyond five dollars since he still regarded the money in his pocket as a loan. But just as Esther was about to close the bidding, Jonah raised his hand and his bid. "Five and a quarter," he declared firmly.

Esther was delighted and began cajoling the other men. "Are we going to let these two gentlemen decide which one of them is going to get this great meal? I can tell you this box contains some fine samples of a wonderful cook. Don't go by the outside of the box. Remember, you can't judge a book by its cover."

Another long pause. Then one of the men from town thundered, "I'll make it five fifty."

"Come on, gentlemen," coaxed Esther. "If you don't start

bidding faster than this, you'll be eating these great dinners for breakfast."

"Five seventy–five," bid Jonah after deciding it would be his final bid.

"Six dollars," answered Reverend Small, putting his hand on Jonah's shoulder in a gesture of friendly competition.

"They're gonna hafta do better than that," shouted Emmet. "Six fifty."

"Do I hear seven?" challenged Esther. After waiting less than a minute, she began the closing litany of a more experience auctioneer. "Six fifty once, six fifty twice, sold to Emmet for six fifty!" Widely popular among townspeople and farmers alike, Emmet received a long and loud round of applause while everyone waited to see who had put together the plain, simple box. And when Emmet's wife rose to claim it from Ruth, the crowd roared even louder.

As the evening wore on, the bidding proved extra spirited at times and less enthusiastic at others. What pleased everyone, however, was the fact that several of the winning bids exceeded Ned's initial benchmark of ten dollars and fifty cents. Then, when Ruth started putting one box after another on the table without interruption, the crowd suddenly realized that there were only five left to be auctioned.

At that point Jonah and Reverend Small began to take note of their situation. Although each had bid on several dinners and had come close several times, they had in every instance been voluntarily outbid. Now they faced the very real prospect of going home hungry to an unhappy landlady.

"This is when it starts getting real exciting," Esther told the crowd, most of which was anxious to start dining. "It shouldn't take you long to figure out who prepared these delicious meals, and it should it take you even less time to figure out who needs to bid a little more bravely."

"You must mean the preacher!" shouted one man, well known as a bachelor who had also failed to bid successfully and may have wished to divert attention away from himself. And to some extent it worked because the crowd murmured in amusement.

"Looks like Jonah needs a little more courage too," chimed in another male in the crowd.

"Now don't go picking on such outstanding citizens," ruled Esther. "There's plenty more out there besides Jonah and Reverend Small, and, just in case you're too busy talking to figure out who cooked up these remaining dinners, let me make it easy for you. First of all, there's me, and you all know what a great cook I am. Then there's Ned's wife and Jake's wife; after that there's Ruth, and, last but not least, there's Betsy. Every one of us can cook and bake like angels, and that pretty much guarantees some heavenly meals for you procrastinators."

By now, many had begun wondering where Esther was leading them.

Seized by the sudden impulse to create a last-minute mystery, she gleefully explained. "We're now going to auction off all five boxes *before* you get to know which of us goes with which dinner."

"How's that for a little added suspense?" coaxed Ruth.

As anxious as everyone else to sit down to eat, Ruth quickly held up an attractively adorned basket with lots of ribbons. She lifted one corner of the cloth and announced teasingly, "With aromas like this, I'd go at least ten dollars myself!"

"Ten it is!" roared the bachelor.

"Looks like we waited too long," lamented Jonah to Reverend Small.

Yet despite the fact that there were still several men without dinner partners, no one seemed interested in out-bidding the man. As this became more and more obvious, Esther finally announced the inevitable, "Going, going, gone!"

"Maybe there's still hope," suggested Reverend Small optimistically.

The next box held up by Ruth was somewhat unusual in that it had been completely camouflaged with old newspaper.

"Well," began Esther, "if you don't want to talk with whoever produced this fine dinner, you can always read the news. On the other hand, if you don't win this one, you'll be missing out on gingerbread that's good enough to win a blue ribbon at the county fair."

The mere mention of gingerbread only deepened the mystery since most of the women in the crowd couldn't recall anyone who excelled with this particular dessert. Men, who had hoped to identify the baker, found little help in the dialogue they managed to overhear.

Yet as intriguing as she had made it, her remark failed to trigger a single bid.

"Now," suggested Seth, tapping Reverend Small on the arm.

"Ten dollars," shouted the clergyman somewhat desperately, after quickly concluding that a lower bid might diminish his standing among some of the men and women.

"Far be it from me to deprive our good parson from a divine meal," cajoled Esther, more in jest than seriousness, "but isn't there someone out there willing to go a little higher?" Then, a moment later, without really wanting or waiting for another bid, she declared, "Sold to the gentleman who is waiting to bless all these wonderful meals."

Ruth, meanwhile, raised one of the remaining baskets and slowly turned it completely around so that everyone could see it from all sides. Yet apart from fresh buttercups and daisies that helped hide the basket's remaining contents, there was little to distinguish it. But that was enough for Esther and her marketing skills.

"It's been a long time since I've seen posies as beautiful as these," she began. "And whoever is this gifted in the garden is bound to be even more gifted in the kitchen. I'll bet this basket's got as many great vittles from her pantry as blossoms from her flowerbed. It's bound to go for a whole lot more, but I'll take six dollars just to open the bidding."

Seth, who was deliberately kept in the dark by his mother, knew there were buttercups and daisies on most farms, including his own. As he grew more and more convinced that this must be Betsy's basket, he urged Jonah to begin bidding.

The dowser raised his arm for all to see. "Six dollars," he proclaimed proudly.

For a moment, there was silence. Then, from the back of the field, a man seemingly alone on the edge of the crowd, raised the bid to six fifty.

"Seven," roared Jonah confidently.

"Seven fifty," cried his challenger, whose face was largely hidden under a wide-brimmed straw hat that seemed intentionally tipped forward.

Briefly forgetting that he had only seven fifty, Jonah raised his bid to eight dollars.

"Eight fifty," persisted his rival, whose face remained largely obscured by his straw hat.

"Nine," stammered Jonah somewhat desperately. The bid had

barely slipped from his tongue when he heard the unwelcome retort, "Nine fifty."

Ned, realizing that Jonah was bidding well beyond his means, moved as quickly and as inconspicuously as possible to Jonah's side. Once there, he pressed the seven fifty Reverend Small had returned into Jonah's left hand. "We can talk about this later," he whispered as he moved away as quickly as he had appeared.

"Nine fifty," repeated Esther in the absence of a counter bid.

"Fifteen dollars," contended Jonah, rising to his feet.

"Twenty dollars," railed the man, choosing to remain seated.

Only those closest to the seated figure recognized him. While those farther away began to speculate, his identity began to dawn on Esther and Ruth. The mystery bidder beneath the hat was Brady, who now rose to his feet waving money in his hand.

The sudden escalation of the bids, the identity of Jonah's rival bidder, and the apparent absence of Lucas quickly derailed the auction.

As the crowd grappled with each new unfolding surprise, Esther and Ruth exchanged glances, not only between themselves but with Betsy and the wives of Ned and Jake. Whatever their individual thoughts, no one spoke. With the possible exception of Jake's wife, Emma, they all concluded independently that Brady was bidding in behalf of Lucas.

"I trust you're bidding for yourself and not for anyone else," tested Esther with a smile.

"What difference does it make?" snapped Brady.

"It's something called fairness," replied Esther patiently. "We'd all like to think that everyone is representing themselves and not someone else."

"It's my bid and my money," argued Brady, "but if I want to give my box to someone else that's up to me."

As Brady spoke, Esther looked pleadingly at Art and then at Reverend Small. Each man responded with a grimace, but neither offered any means of solving the potential impasse.

"As you wish," ruled Esther. "Sold to the gentleman named Brady."

Almost immediately, Ruth raised the next basket in the row of the remaining dinners. By all appearances, it was the largest and least attractive of any displayed. There was no cover of any kind. Its high sides hid its contents, and its simplicity generated a rather unique mystery of its own.

Challenged once again to arouse interest, Esther seized that simplicity. "I'll bet you men are ready to ignore this one," she began. "You can if you like, but I've looked inside. I can't tell you what's there, but if you like smoked ham and cheese and apple pie and ..."

"Seven–fifty," shouted Jonah without any encouragement from Seth.

Esther waited eagerly for the next bid, but there was none. There was not a sound from the crowd. Although pleased by what she suspected was a silent consensus favoring Jonah, she pressed on, hoping that her instinct was right.

"Need I say more," she teased. "If it's not the best dinner I've seen today, it sure is the best runner–up. I'll have no sympathy for anyone who complains that it went for seven–fifty."

Then, in her next breath, "Going, going, gone to Jonah."

The crowd responded almost instantly in obvious approval with shouts and whistles and conventional applause. Happily, she called for the last remaining box.

"Well, here it is," she proclaimed. "This is the one you've been waiting for!"

Ruth held it high. It was a plain, shallow box with thin wooden walls. Even at a distance, most folks could see the colorful bowls and glasses, tablecloth and napkins that loomed above its sides.

Many began to wonder why Ruth had held this particular box until last.

"Chances are some of you have seen this box before," revealed Esther. "Until very recently, it was in our store, loaded with crackers. So the question is, is it my cooking inside, or is it someone else's?"

"Could be mine," interrupted Ruth with a big smile.

"Or mine," laughed Betsy, standing well behind Ruth with the wives of Ned and Jake.

"Now I know you all want to get this over so you can start eating," declared Esther, "but this is the last chance to top off our coffers with money for the new church. We don't want to see it go for anything less than ten dollars. Now, who's going to start the bidding?"

There was momentary silence, and then someone nearby called out, "Ten dollars."

Try as she might, Esther could not make out the bidder and turned toward Ruth with a quizzical expression. "It's ol' Ben," Ruth whispered. "You know, the widower."

"Thanks to Ben, we're off to a great start," Esther declared with a friendly wave to the old farmer.

"So... who will make it twelve fifty?"

The hand of another unfamiliar bidder shot up.

"Twelve fifty," roared Esther, without trying to identify the source. "Let me hear fifteen."

Almost simultaneously Ben and someone on the periphery

of the crowd lifted their hands just enough to be seen. The crowd began to chap, delighted that the bidding for the last basket had begun to accelerate.

Esther quickly acknowledged the multiple bids and then challenged, "Which one of you gentlemen will make it seventeen fifty?"

"Fifteen fifty," Ben called out.

"Seventeen fifty," shouted his rival.

"If there are no other bidders," said Esther somewhat hoarsely, "it's going, going, gone for seventeen fifty to the gentleman by the rail fence."

And once again the crowd burst into applause.

After summoning Ruth and the three other homemakers to her side with a roundhouse wave, Esther called the winning bidders forward. As the five men advanced, she and the rest of the crowd discovered that the final victor was Lucas.

"Okay, gentlemen," she continued, "you've won these fine dinners but you'll have to wait a little longer to see which of us goes with which box or basket. First, you've got to pay up!"

Ruth collected the outstanding amounts while the four other women began to shuffle from one position to another, perpetuating the mystery. Once the last five payments were safely stored in a little strong box, Ruth joined the others.

"Now," cried Esther, and by prearrangement the women turned their backs to the crowd, stood motionless for a moment and then, one by one, shuffled the remaining boxes and baskets on the table.

The first to step forward with her entry was Esther, who with a wink to her husband Art, moved from behind the table, curtsied in front of Brady and grasped his arm. For an instant, Brady appeared annoyed but then laughed and led Esther to an opening the crowd had already created for the homemakers and their dinner companions.

Only those closest heard him mutter, "Shucks," and those who did hear him completely ignored it. Except Esther. Looking back at Betsy, she quickly surmised that Brady had hoped to win dinner with the young widow. But, she wondered, had he been trying for himself or Lucas?

Esther had barely taken Brady's arm when Jake's wife Emma moved forward and, in an playful gesture, walked behind the four remaining men, forcing them to turn around toward the crowd. Then, moving up and down the line like a commanding general inspecting his troops, Emma briefly prolonged the mystery, much to the amusement of spectators, until at last she seized her basket and took the arm of Jonah.

Ned's wife Elizabeth, unwilling to be outdone, threw her head back as if in a huff and began to walk away from the three remaining men. As her friends and neighbors and Ned began to whistle and cheer in good fun, she stopped and looked back. Milking the moment for all she could, she raised her right hand to her chin to ponder her next step.

The cheers and laughter grew louder. Changing her look to one of admiration and approval, she raced back to the table, picked out her dinner for all to see, and extended her right hand to Reverend Small. As the crowd roared its approval, the two joined Jonah and Emma.

Despite her advancing years, Ruth, with girlish glee, reached out, took Betsy's arm and raised it as a referee often does with the winner. The two then bowed with a flourish, pushed their baskets to the front of the table and with a sweep of their arms, invited the men to pick up a basket without knowing who had prepared it.

Lucas and the bachelor, a man named Matthew, seemed bewildered for a moment but then bowed to one another as the women had done. Lucas then placed his hand on Matthew's shoulder and in a magnanimous gesture, gave Matthew first choice.

The two women turned toward each other once more, bowed and moved in opposite directions, each rounding a different end of the table. Advancing toward the men as they did, it appeared that Betsy was about to take the arm of Lucas. The presumption proved false as she and Ruth passed the man closest to them.

"Thank you for winning my entry," smiled Ruth to an unsmiling Lucas as Betsy joined Matthew.

Reverend Small, who had been kneeling on a bright, multi-colored cloth that Elizabeth had spread across a vacant spot on the ground, quickly rose and asked everyone to stand and bow their heads.

"Heavenly Father," he began, "it's been a wonderful afternoon, filled with fun and good spirit, filled with acts of kindness and goodwill, filled with generosity and great charity. Who can doubt that You are in our midst. Bless those who have prepared these wonderful meals as well as those who have given freely to partake of them. With these gifts may we erect a church that will be acceptable and pleasing in Your sight. For we pray in the name of Your son, Christ Jesus. Amen."

"Amen," repeated many in the crowd, including Emmet, who was the most audible of all.

"Let's eat," cried Esther, holding up a huge chicken drumstick.

The weather that evening was mild and pleasant, a far cry from the soaring heat that had prevailed for several consecutive days. A light breeze swept across the field, rustling the leaves of trees that had offered late afternoon shade to those who sought it. Even songbirds chipped away happily in anticipation of the feast that would be left behind on the ground.

With the auction over and the leisurely dining now underway, the sounds from the crowd were subdued, except for an occasional outbreak of laughter or the give and take of friendly contests.

Lucas, who had deliberately steered Ruth to a place near Betsy and Matthew, began speaking loudly almost as soon as they had settled to the ground. Ruth tried to encourage him to speak more softly by doing so herself. But it soon became clear that he was determined to claim the attention of those close by, especially Betsy.

Seth, who had joined his mother with Matthew's immediate consent, had hoped for an invitation from Emma and Jonah. When that failed to materialize, the youngster just picked at his food, having taken an unwarranted but expressionless dislike to the bachelor.

"Did you hear we found water on Jake's farm?" boasted Lucas aloud. "And that's just the beginning. Once Brady's finished showing folks where to find water, he'll show them where there's oil."

"What makes you think that's such a good thing?" asked Ruth in a carefully chosen, measured response. "It seems to me that the most important thing in the world to us right now is water. We can't drink oil, and neither can the cattle or the crops."

As Betsy became more and more convinced that Lucas was trying to impress rather than annoy her, she took increasing delight in Ruth's subtle, public rebukes.

Even Jonah and Emma, who were farther away but still within earshot, couldn't help but overhear the exchange between Lucas and Ruth.

The conviction that he—rather than Brady—had found the water at Jake's farm began to grate on Jonah once more. The thought of intervening vocally if not physically was a huge temptation, but deep down he knew that any such action on his part would only serve to embolden his nemesis.

Jonah's discomfort and his suppressed anger did not go unnoticed by Emma. She tried in several ways to engage the dowser, expressing her gratitude for the countless hours he had devoted to the search for water for her and her husband, Jake. When Jonah did nothing more than acknowledge her thanks with a nod, she tried as tactfully as she could to offer an apology for the shabby way Jake had treated him. And when that too failed, Emma decided to focus on food rather than conversation.

Lucas, meanwhile, had taken up Ruth's reply, arguing that the drought would soon pass, and water would be abundant once more.

"It could come tonight or tomorrow or some day next week," Lucas argued, "but you can be sure that it will rain and the creeks will rise and the wells will recover. The wells we bring in now will simply become reserves for future dry spells."

"Not if they become contaminated with oil," argued Ruth, whose reputation as a formidable debater had apparently escaped Lucas.

Others, in fact, tended to avoid Ruth for that reason, and over time her skills slipped in the absence of opponents. Lucas's remarks rekindled her spirit and her taste for a good argument. Like a tiger attracted to a calf who had wandered away from the herd, she began to look on Lucas as easy prey for her wit and her tongue.

Her eagerness for a verbal scrap was soon tested, however, as Lucas, who quickly sensed the level and caliber of her repartee, decided to avoid a public contest and chose instead to shift his remarks to her superb cooking. "This ham is the best I've ever tasted," he declared between mouthfuls of smoked ham, baked beans, and scalloped potatoes.

"I never turn down a compliment," purred Ruth, "but I never walk away from a chance for some good, old-fashioned give-and-take either, especially if it's a debate worth having."

"May I defer 'til we've finished this great meal?" replied Lucas, rising to Ruth's bait.

"Why can't we enjoy both at the same time?" she challenged with a huge disarming grin.

"What exactly do you wish to debate?" quizzed the lender.

"Let's keep it simple," said Ruth as she reached for a small jug of tea. "Why do you think oil is more important than water?"

Although Lucas had lowered his voice, their exchange had caught the attention of those around them. Conscious of the growing interest in their conversation, Ruth pushed on, raising the bar.

"It's not just about the water that we all need to live. It's about the water that all the plants and animals need too. And, now that I think about it, maybe it's time for you to try a meal where everything has been washed and cooked in your precious oil."

"Don't be silly," countered Lucas. "We all know that water is critical, but there is no reason why we shouldn't seek both. Suppose there was oil under your land; wouldn't you like the money that the oil would bring? Just think about all the things you could buy."

"I'm grateful for what I've already have," said Ruth, realizing that Lucas's argument was likely to appeal to others. "I guess it boils down to what's enough. What does it take to make us happy?"

"Why settle for little pleasures?" replied Lucas. "Why be content with a cotton frock when oil could pay for one made of silk? Look at that sunset! It's beautiful. But once it goes down, it's nothing more than a memory. With the money that oil can bring, you can enjoy the fragrance of an expensive perfume or admire the beauty of a gold bracelet any time you please."

"True," admitted Ruth. "But when all is said and done, you can't take them with you."

"No," agreed the banker, "but you can leave them to someone or some good cause like the church to do more good."

As the debate seemed to swing more and more in Lucas's favor, those within earshot began to take sides in their own minds. While everyone agreed that water was paramount, very few apart from Ruth and Reverend Small saw any objection to the subsequent search for oil. Even Betsy found herself straddling the fence, almost ready to side with Lucas.

It was then that Reverend Small entered the fray, seizing the initiative before Ruth could think through her next reply.

"If you simply wish to become rich so you can buy the things you don't really need," he interrupted, "you may be pleasing yourself but you are certainly not pleasing God. Moreover, you may be condemning yourself to an eternal life of pain and suffering.

"Just think about the words in Scripture," he urged. "The nineteenth chapter of Matthew, beginning I believe with the twenty-third verse, is pretty explicit. It goes like this: 'Then said Jesus unto his disciples, Verily I say unto you, That a rich man shall hardly enter into the kingdom of heaven. And again I say unto you, It is easier for a camel to go through the eye of a needle, than for a rich man to enter into the kingdom of heaven.'"

Ruth, relieved by the clergyman's intervention, smiled broadly in his direction. To the others, including Lucas, it precipitated a pause. Finally, unable to find a suitable reply, Lucas deferred to Reverend Small who was clearly waiting for a response.

"Far be it from me to argue with the Bible," conceded Lucas.

Emma, who had squirmed about like a child to catch every word of the exchange between Ruth and Lucas, soon realized that his arguments were the same ones he had used to woo her and her husband away from their relationship with Jonah. The lender had skillfully used the likelihood of oil and the lure of wealth to persuade them not only to abandon Jonah but to deny that Jonah had discovered the water that Brady and Lucas now claimed.

At the time she and her husband had only their consciences to overrule. Now, in the light of the remarks by Ruth and the Scripture recited by Reverend Small, Emma began to wish that she and Jake had never entered into their pact with Lucas and Brady.

Although Jonah held Jake solely responsible for the alliance with Lucas and Brady, he had found it nearly impossible to be anything more than civil to Emma. Having rejected his skills, his labor, and his friendship, neither she nor her husband warranted more. And yet, as the meal progressed, he found such distance unkind. Trying to be more pleasant, he looked directly at Emma and shared his own assessment of all they had overheard. "Contrary to what the Good Book says," he smiled, "seems like God is on Lucas's side these days."

Emma smiled back weakly, then turned to hide the tear she could not hold back.

Sensing her growing discomfort, Jonah tried once again to exhibit friendship. "Can't really blame you folks for givin' Lucas and Brady a chance," he added. "Just wish they hadn't lost my bit. That's kinda set back my helpin' other folks that need to drill instead of dig."

"Excuse me, Jonah," replied Emma as she rose quickly to her feet. She soon spotted Jake some distance away even though his back was toward her. Stepping carefully around the people that separated her from her husband, she found herself inching past Reverend Small. She paused for only a second, then forcing as big a smile as she could, she looked at Elizabeth and asked softly, "Can I steal the parson for a minute?" Elizabeth, observing the moist eyes behind the smile, nodded energetically as Reverend Small invited Emma to join them.

"I just had a great idea for the new church," Emma replied. "Since you might not like it, maybe it's best if I tell you about it privately."

Intuitively, Reverend Small rose, drawing his napkin to the corner of his mouth and then dropping it near his unfinished plate. "I'll bet it's a great idea," he responded enthusiastically. "Let's head for that little spot just beyond Art Blake, and you can tell me all about it."

Like the occasional movement of others, their move drew little attention. But, as they took seats on the ground, Emma ensured that her back was toward the crowd. The tears she had largely held back now flowed freely. "I hate lies," she sobbed quietly, "and ever since Lucas started coming around that's all I see and hear."

The revelation caught Reverend Small somewhat off guard, and he hesitated to respond. He simply nodded, slowly and patiently.

"They have Jake on a string," she continued. "Once he signed a paper letting them look for oil on our place, they got him to throw Jonah out and claim the water that Jonah had found. Then Brady took away Jonah's bit so he couldn't use it on other farms. When my husband said he was going to tell Jonah the truth, they said they would tell everyone that he contrived the whole scheme because he liked their offer."

Throughout her anguished admission, her gaze was locked on her clasped hands, pressed hard against her lap. After revealing the lies and the guilt that tormented her, Emma began to look up until she saw Reverend Small's familiar but expressionless face. Then, as they made eye contact, he smiled and, once again, simply nodded.

"They have no shame," she added contritely, "but we do."

The clergyman took a deep breath, nodded once more and waited, uncertain whether Emma was simply revealing the dilemma she and Jake found themselves in or whether she was desperately searching for forgiveness and spiritual counsel.

Her tears subsided and her voice grew angry. "What in heaven's name do we do now?"

"Do you believe in God?" asked Reverend Small.

"Yes," she replied, again looking down in distress and shame.

"Then let's ask Him to help," the clergyman continued. "We don't have to attract attention by closing our eyes or bowing our heads, but down deep in your heart you can ask His help. Once you and Jake get back home, you can ask God's forgiveness together. Then you can repeat your prayer for help."

"Can't you pray for us?" pleaded Emma.

"Of course I will," answered Reverend Small. "But sin is something that we must also confess privately to God. Not only that, we must have complete faith in His promise to forgive and in His assurance that we are forgiven."

"But how do we set things right?" persisted Emma.

"God will show the way," he replied. "Remember the promise in Saint Matthew: 'Ask, and it shall be given you; seek, and ye shall find; knock, and it shall be opened unto you.'"

"How will we know God's answer?" asked the weary but earnest parishioner.

"God's answer to those things we ask in prayer is often found in Scripture," suggested the minister. "What's important is the fact that you and Jake are anxious to repent and discover God's will for your lives. I'm sure you'll recognize and understand His answer."

"We'll try," promised Emma, rising slowly to her feet. The thought of rejoining Jonah, however, created a new crisis. Rising until she could kneel on one knee, she looked pleadingly at Reverend Small. "I can't face Jonah again," she whispered. "If I tell him you want to see him, will you tell him what we've done and how sorry we are?"

The clergyman got to his feet, reached for Emma's hand and, as he helped her stand, replied gently, "This is something that you and Jake need to do yourselves, Emma. Although Jonah was hurt by all you've done, you also have the power to help heal those wounds. Telling him what you've told me will mean much more to him than anything I can say for you."

Emma shook her head in dissent. "We're too ashamed," she sighed. And before Reverend Small could reply, she headed back toward Jonah.

"Sorry for mentionin' my bit," Jonah apologized after Emma rejoined him.

"That wasn't the reason I rushed off," Emma fibbed. "I just had an idea for the church that I thought the parson might like. But I'm afraid it wasn't a very good idea. I'm the one who should apologize. It was rude of me to leave you like that."

"Afraid there ain't much left," confessed Jonah. "Yer cookin' was pretty hard to resist."

For a moment, Emma was tempted to share with Jonah all that she had just shared with Reverend Small. But the reality of the surrounding crowd and the risk of an outburst by Jonah proved terrifying, and Emma held her tongue. Instead, she assured the dowser that she had had quite enough between the portions she had eaten and the samples she had tried while preparing the basket.

Their mutual struggle at conversation was short-lived. Some folks in the crowd began humming a hymn and, in short order, others began singing the words. The spontaneous nature of the hymn-sing also prompted a host of smiles. Before long the entire crowd was engulfed in song. As each hymn reached its end, someone would begin singing the first stanza or the chorus of another old favorite, and it soon became obvious that no one wanted to repeat a hymn that had already been sung. Pauses between hymns became longer but laughter always filled the gap that would otherwise have been silence.

For Reverend Small, it was another facet of the culture and lifestyle he was still getting to know. The product of an urban childhood and urban schools, he had known little of rural life. Once in its midst, he found it easy to appreciate its hills and vales, its crops and its animals and, above all, its people. He admired their stoicism and resourcefulness in the face of the drought and the growing threat of costly crop failures. He especially valued their outreach to one another whenever there were fields to be hayed, wells to be dug, and buildings to be raised. Looking across the crowd, he felt a special sense of happiness and privilege.

CHAPTER 17

Worship was well attended the next morning. Many who had lingered long after finishing dessert were clearly delighted that Sunday was a day of rest. And just as suddenly it was Monday.

Without a drill bit, there was little reason for Jonah to return to Ned's. The question remaining was whether to check on the blacksmith's progress or to resume his visits to some of the other farmers who were growing increasingly desperate for new wells.

As Jonah washed up at the pump, Seth wandered by en route to the barn. "Hope you don't blame me for pushing Emma's box," he probed, thinking Jonah might be angry at the outcome of the bidding.

"Not at all, Mister Fisherman," declared Jonah. "That dinner was just fine."

With the encouragement of Betsy and Reverend Small, Jonah headed off to visit some of the remaining farms on Betsy's list. Several, he discovered, had not yet been approached by Lucas and Brady.

The combination of warm welcomes and the convincing performance of the new divining rod refreshed and renewed Jonah's spirits. After several long, tiring days and a series of promising discoveries, he awoke to find it was already Thursday.

Seth, assuming Jonah was asleep, seized several opportunities to bang his milk pail against anything that would make a clamor. But Jonah had been awake for some time. After deciding it was time to visit the smith, he soon found himself trying to reconcile his feelings toward Jake and Emma. Even though he saw Lucas and Brady as the real villains, he remained angered by the fact that the farmer and his wife seemed to be willing partners. *Still*, he wondered, *does it really matter? Isn't it all best forgotten?*

As Jonah ambled toward the house for breakfast, Seth raced by with the morning's milk. "Plannin' to head into town to see the blacksmith," volunteered the dowser. "Care to come along?"

"Mother wants me to weed and water the garden," Seth shouted back while trying hard not to spill the milk. After coming to a halt, he added, "If you help me with the garden, we can go when we finish. I sure would like to see the new bit if it's ready."

Weeding the garden was not exactly what Jonah had in mind when he invited Seth to go with him, but as breakfast progressed the dowser volunteered to help Seth with his garden chores as long as Betsy had no objection to their going into town together. Once they secured Betsy's permission, the two headed straight to the garden.

They quickly discovered that it was watering, not weeding, that was urgent. At Jonah's suggestion, they got three pails, one of which had a spout well–suited for the task. The other two were best for transporting the water from the well to the garden, a job that Jonah chose for himself. Together, they salvaged as many plants as possible.

In the course of pumping water for the garden, Jonah noticed sediment in the last pailful he pumped. The drought was about to add Betsy's farm to its toll.

Rather than alarm anyone, the dowser suggested that he and Seth wander across the road to inspect the small spring that had seized Reverend Small's foot while haying. Although he knew the field well, Seth was unable find it easily. Once in the vicinity, it took him several minutes to find the dry, hard remains of the once–marshy spot.

"Guess we better take a look at the salt spring too," said Jonah, hoping they could use that water for the garden. While much easier to find, given the nearby springpole, the outcome was just as discouraging. What had been a small, running stream was now nothing more than moist soil. The prospect of Betsy and her household becoming dependent on water from others was beginning to loom large.

"Best we get into town," said Jonah.

Despite his youth, Seth too recognized the significance of the dried up streams. Though unaware of the sediment Jonah had pumped from the well, he was anxious to hear Jonah's assessment of what they had seen.

"I've never seen that salt spring dry before," he prodded. "That's a pretty bad sign, isn't it?"

"Too early to tell," replied the dowser.

The reply was hardly satisfying, but Seth knew that until his friend was ready to reveal his thoughts, it was folly to press him further. So he tried instead to determine what Jonah planned to do after their visit to the smith. But that too achieved nothing.

As they rounded the front of the house, heading toward the road, they were hailed by Reverend Small who had just emerged from the kitchen. "Mind if I join you?" he asked, aware of Jonah's plan to visit the blacksmith. "Now that the box social is behind us, I want to see how soon Art plans to have material and volunteers at the church yard."

"No need to ask," answered Jonah. "Yer always welcome; you know that."

"Remember the marsh where you got your foot stuck when we were haying?" asked Seth, looking up at the clergyman. "It's as dry as a bone. And so is the stream from the salt spring out by the springpole. Jonah's not very worried, but I am."

Reverend Small shot a questioning glance toward Jonah, raising his eyebrows in the process. "Is this as serious as it sounds, Jonah?" he demanded.

"Well, it could be better," drawled the dowser. "Way things look, we'd best start drillin' at our place as soon as we finish up at Ned's. Question is, where to drill or dig. Could be water or oil under the springpole. Been thinkin' oil all along, but Drake coulda been pinpointin' water."

"Maybe you should go around with Big Dipper," suggested Seth. "That way we'll know if there's other places that might be good."

Reverend Small quickly endorsed the idea. "That certainly sounds smart."

"Been thinkin' the same way," said Jonah. "Makes little sense to drill for water out by the salt spring just 'cause the springpole is already set up out there. Could be better spots closer to the house. Might even be water close to the surface. Ya never know without lookin'."

"Does that mean you might be able to bring in a new well without having to wait for the new drill bit?" asked Reverend Small.

"All things considered," answered Jonah, "it makes sense to take another look after we get back from town. Had been thinkin' about tryin' to help another farmer this afternoon, but that can wait. Sooner we search with the new divinin' rod, the sooner we'll know what our options are."

"With so many men digging wells, with or without your help, it could be that Art can't find any volunteers for the work on the church," said Reverend Small, adding a question that had been nagging him for some time. "But if he has lined up a few men who are ready to start, can you find time to get them going? It seems pretty unlikely that Ned can do so now."

"Guess we'll hafta work out somethin'," promised the dowser.

It was an awkward moment for the clergyman. Throughout the past few days, he had wrestled with Emma's confession. Should he share it with Jonah as Emma had asked, or should he continue to hope and pray that Emma and Jake would soon find the moral and spiritual strength to do so themselves. With renewed hope, he chose the latter.

Rather than go directly to the Blakes', Reverend Small decided to accompany Jonah and Seth to the blacksmith. As they approached his house and shed, they spotted the smith at his forge, fanning the white–hot coals with his bellows even as daytime temperatures soared.

"Figured you might be by sometime today," he said without looking up from the fiery bed of charcoal and the large mass of iron in its midst.

"Not meanin' to pester ya," Jonah replied. "Just tryin' to see if the new bit might be ready early. Seems like everything is goin' from bad to worse. Soon as we finish up at Ned's place, we're gonna hafta start at Miss Betsy's."

"See this clump of iron?" asked the smith. "It's got just about every sliver of metal I could find. It'll be a trifle smaller than you asked, but it should do the job just as good. I know you're anxious, so I started on it right after you and Ned left. Lord willin', it'll be ready for you tomorrow morning."

"Sure wish there was somethin' more we could do to make up fer all yer doin'," Jonah replied. "How's your own well holdin' up?"

"A bit low but holding its own," said the blacksmith.

"Just come runnin' if it gets worrisome," instructed Jonah.

The blacksmith gave the coals another blast of air from the bellows beside the forge, much to the discomfort of his visitors. He then turned the clump of iron slightly to inspect it more carefully and, in so doing, disturbed the coals enough to produce a momentary shower of spectacular sparks.

"I don't know how you can stand it, especially on days like this," said Reverend Small in genuine admiration. "I sure hope it'll be a little cooler on Sunday," he added as he, Jonah, and Seth moved away from the forge and turned toward the road.

"Tell Ned to come by and pick it up in the morning," commanded the smith.

"Any chance you can go with me to see Art Blake?" Reverend Small asked the dowser as they reached the junction where a decision was inescapable. "With all the work that lies ahead, you can probably do with a little diversion. Tomorrow will be here soon enough."

"Long as it don't take forever," yielded a reluctant Jonah, anxious to get back to the farm to begin searching for alternative sites.

The trio was greeted warmly by Esther and Art. "Everyone is still talking about how much they enjoyed the social," announced Esther, confirming what they all assumed. "And we made almost two hundred dollars, thanks to some of those nice big bids."

"Along with some other donations that have come in," interjected Art, "we have enough money to start the framework and the roof. There's probably even enough left to cover the bell tower and the main doors."

"You two deserve a lot of credit," proclaimed Reverend Small.

"Ya sure do," added Jonah.

"The problem is we're ready to go, and we don't see how we can ask Ned to take charge," revealed Art. "I sent some men out to touch up the foundation, and they tell me we can start putting up the frame anytime we want. The question is, if I can get the timbers and some men over there next week, who can we get to replace Ned?"

Both men looked directly at Jonah as Art pleaded, "Can you fill in for him until he's brought in a new well?"

"Can't go every day but should be able to get 'em started," allowed Jonah.

"I'll have the men and the wood there first thing Monday morning," promised Art. "They all have a pretty good idea of what to do and how to do it. We need you to pull them together as a team. Once you do that, you should be able to go back to helping Ned."

"Make sure they bring their own tools," counseled Jonah. "Always better to have more than we need."

"It won't be easy for Jonah," interjected Reverend Small. "Not only is he still needed at Ned's, we're now facing the possibility that the well at Miss Betsy's place is running dry."

"That's why we need to be gettin' back," added Jonah. "With a little luck and the help of the good Lord, Seth and me are hopin' to find a place to dig instead of drill at Miss Betsy's. It's be a whole lot better than waitin.'"

"We understand," said Esther softly. "There's no need to dally here. The sooner you can find more water for Betsy the better. Just remember that you're always welcome here whenever you have the time to sit a spell and chew the fat."

After laughing at the choice of words, Reverend Small quickly explained it was a phrase he hadn't heard before.

"Time to take our leave," he declared. "We'll see you folks bright and early at church on Sunday."

On their way home, Reverend Small expressed concern over the mounting burden he had helped create for Jonah. "I'm sorry I can't do more," he apologized. "Unless you can make a carpenter out of me by Monday, I doubt that there's much I can do."

"Been thinkin' about that too," said Jonah. "If ya can learn how to read Art's plans as quick as ya learned to mow with a scythe, it could spare me some. Every mornin' we'll figure out what needs to be done that day, and then it'll be yer job to make sure it gets done."

"Men with more experience aren't about to listen to me," argued Reverend Small.

"Don't sell yerself short," rebutted Jonah. "Yer the preacher. They'll listen to ya so long as ya don't get too bossy. If ya can show yer worth with a hammer and a saw they'll be downright pleased to work with ya."

"And just when are you going to teach me all that?" asked the astounded clergyman.

"Once we discover a place to dig for Miss Betsy's new well, it shouldn't take long," Jonah assured him. "Trouble is, finding the site could take up the rest of the day."

As soon as they reached the farm, Jonah strode directly to the barn and, minutes later, emerged with his divining rod. Before he could explore a site he once considered promising, Betsy called them all to lunch. At first, Jonah declined. But Betsy persisted, and the dowser eventually relented. At lunch, Seth disclosed the dry marsh and the dry streambed that he and Jonah had found earlier that day.

Still reluctant to mention the sediment he had seen in the water pail, Jonah said nothing.

At that point, Reverend Small, bewildered by the dowser's silence, chose to inform Betsy of the plan that had emerged. "Rather than risk letting your well go dry before he finishes drilling at Ned's place, Jonah has decided to do another search with his divining rod to see if he can find water close enough to the surface to dig instead of drill."

"Let's hope you find a good place to dig," said Betsy, looking squarely at Jonah. "If it's water we're after, your springpole isn't going to do much good where it is now. Remember, you chose that spot because there might be oil there." After pausing only a second, she added, "On the other hand, if you manage to find water, I'll be happy wherever it is."

Jonah quickly found his voice. "There's a fair chance that it was water—not oil—that made Drake behave the way it did. No way of tellin' what's really there till we actually drill. If we don't find another promisin' spot, it's probably best we drill where the springpole's already set up."

The discussion was bittersweet. While she was keenly aware that her own well could go dry, Betsy had tried to ignore the reality. Now, forced to accept what she could no longer avoid, she shifted her thoughts toward a shrinking list of neighbors who were still in a position to help if her well failed. *Thank God for Jonah*, she thought.

"Time to be gettin' to it," said Jonah, rising from his chair.

Reunited with Big Dipper, he started his search fairly close to the house, moving slowly but deliberately toward his goal, a site once considered promising.

As time wore on, however, he not only reached the spot but continued beyond it, getting farther and farther from the house and barn. Troubled by the fact that the rod had showed little reaction to the landscape beneath it, Jonah began to wonder if he should retrace his footsteps.

Seth, who had walked alongside Jonah throughout his search, sensed the dowser's frustration. "Has the Big Dipper lost its power?" he inquired woefully.

"'Course not," said the dowser, trying hard to reassure his young friend even though he too had started to wonder about the rod's effectiveness. "It's bound to find another good well or two around here."

Only once in the next two hours did the divining rod offer any sign of hope and that lasted so briefly that Jonah dismissed it as a false reading. With almost no landscape left in the vicinity of the house and barn, he summoned Seth from the comfort of a shade tree where he had finally taken refuge.

"Shoulda done this ages ago," he announced as the lad approached. "Since ya found this rod, it's time for ya to take it up yerself. Ya found it on yer land, and ya need to find water on yer land. It's probably just waitin' to show ya where the water is."

Within minutes he had helped Seth position the rod correctly and had coached the lad in the subtle changes he needed to recognize. "Go wherever ya please," counseled Jonah.

Seth took up the challenge with enthusiasm and maturity. He scoured the landscape as his mentor had done and, saying nothing, walked off in the direction of the springpole. When he was midway between Jonah and the drill site, he stopped, repositioned the rod in his hands and, having successfully duplicated Jonah's grip and style, resumed his search. While Jonah's path had been largely parallel to the house, Seth's set off on a perpendicular grid.

Jonah watched with admiration and delight. Seth was conscientious, focused, and obviously proud of the confidence Jonah had demonstrated in him. His manner and bearing were as professional as any Jonah had seen in other dowsers. Yet despite his diligence and care, Seth was no more successful than Jonah. The one thing they both noticed, however, was the fact that the closer he got to the springpole, the more active the rod became.

Though ready and willing to continue, fatigue began to take over the youngster and, at that point, Jonah intervened again, this time taking a path that would lead to the opposite side of the house. The divining rod quivered slightly on a few occasions but never with the power and authority that Jonah had expected from his years of experience. Eventually, he concluded that nothing offered the same degree of promise as the springpole site.

Though he seldom displayed disappointment visibly, Jonah was unable to conceal it at the dinner table. "Don't know what to make of it," he confided when Betsy and Reverend Small took turns carefully and discretely questioning the outcome of his latest search. "Times like this make me wonder if it's skill or luck," Jonah added.

"Lotsa folks think it's just hocus-pocus," he continued, "and sometimes that makes me wonder too. But how do ya account for all the wells that do come in? And what do ya make of the rod when it bends up and down like a sapling in a wind storm?"

"Don't be so hard on yourself," insisted Betsy. "We know you'll find water if there's any out there. No one's blaming you if you can't find water next to the house."

Reverend Small, who from time to time experienced his own

bewilderment about dowsing, said nothing but also reflected on Jonah's doubt.

No one could deny that Jonah has had some successes but, as Jonah himself has asked, was it skill or just plain luck? On the other hand, might it not be a combination of the two? It is, he concluded, *a good, old-fashioned conundrum that might best be left that way.*

What is more pressing, Reverend Small realized, *is my Sunday sermon and the urgent need to focus on forgiveness: Why is it necessary? Why is it a critical dimension of spiritual growth? Who benefits most?*

These and a number of other questions as well as scriptural answers and insights cascaded through his mind along with occasional glimpses of the people he hoped most to reach.

"Have you nothing to say?" asked Betsy, as she poured coffee for the clergyman.

"As much as I'd like to think that the wells are due to Jonah's skills," he answered diplomatically and truthfully, "I can't help but believe that his successes may also be answers to our prayers."

Both Betsy and Jonah smiled broadly, then laughed. "Could be!" murmured Betsy.

As soon as he retired to his room, the clergyman seized paper and pen as he began jotting down an outline for the sermon, recalling as many Scriptural passages as he could from the torrent that had overwhelmed his thoughts.

The homily he had already prepared bore little resemblance to what he now wished to say, and it was set aside for another day.

As he worked, he turned to his Bible frequently to refresh his memory and to flag the passages he considered the most germane. By the time he turned out his lamp, the night was half-gone.

Friday was buoyed by expectation and hope. Since Jonah had

chosen to wait to inform Ned that the bit would be ready that morning, he politely declined Betsy's offer of a second cup of coffee. With Seth, who was already on his feet, he set off for Ned's farm.

The exchange with Ned was brief, and the three were soon on their way into town. The wagon bounced noisily as the normally patient farmer drove his horses faster than usual. During their journey, Jonah revealed he had promised to fill in for Ned during the early stages of rebuilding the church.

"Yer the one they really need and want," insisted the dowser. "But they all know ya got yer hands full."

"Guess it's time to start calling you Saint Jonah," declared Ned in genuine appreciation. "Somehow I'll find a way to make it up."

For Seth, sitting on the wagon floor, the ride grew increasingly uncomfortable. By the time the blacksmith's house and shed had come into sight, the youngster was on his feet, clinging to the backrest of the seat occupied by Jonah and Ned.

Even though his hand remained bandaged, the smith hoisted the new bit as if it was weightless. Jonah took possession as if it was bullion, and began to rotate it slowly so that both he and Ned could appreciate the smith's craftsmanship. Once Jonah pronounced it fit for its particular task, Ned completed the transaction quickly.

By mid-morning, the bit was plunging its way through the hard, dry soil. Eager to make up for lost time, the men took shorter turns in the stirrup and, by resting more often, quickly exhausted the maximum depth of the rope. When they finally agreed to stop for the day, they had extended the tough, rugged cord three times.

The following day they drilled at a more relaxed pace, engaging in longer but less vigorous turns. The new bit proved superb, a realization that helped Ned and Jonah maintain high spirits even when they finished up that afternoon without hitting a new source of fresh water.

Sunday morning revealed a refreshed and chipper Reverend Small, who arose from the breakfast table long before the others and promptly set off for the school grounds.

On his arrival there, some of the men and boys who had already gathered for the morning service helped fetch the table from inside the schoolhouse. After setting up his outdoor pulpit, they returned to their families. Reverend Small remained inside to pray and revisit his notes.

From time to time, he looked out, enjoying the growing number of families and individuals taking their places on the withered lawn. Before he knew it, he was enjoying the hymns that the congregation had begun singing with the help of the Blakes. He emerged during the last stanza of the fourth hymn and, as the crowd sang "Amen", he applauded vigorously to the delight of all.

By now, almost everyone except the youngest children knew the various parts of liturgy that he had introduced during his very first Sunday service. This day, however, he surprised them by leading them through the Lord's Prayer before—rather than after—the sermon. With their curiosity thus raised, he began to preach.

"The prayer that Jesus taught us seems as easy and as simple to fulfill as it is to learn. As we repeat it, we acknowledge and praise God; we call for God's kingdom and urge that His will be done here on earth as it is in heaven; we ask for our daily bread and then we ask Him to forgive our sins as we forgive those who sin against us.

"In the twenty–fifth and twenty–sixth verses of the eleventh chapter of Mark, we're told that we must learn to forgive as God forgives. Listen to what Jesus taught his disciples, 'And when ye stand praying, forgive if ye have ought against any: that your Father also which is in heaven may forgive your trespasses. But if ye do not forgive, neither will your Father which is in heaven forgive your trespasses.'

"Suddenly, it's not so easy or so simple, is it?" Reverend Small continued. "And yet, as we grow spiritually by reading His word, by engaging in prayer, and by joining others in worship as we have today, we begin to realize that the more we strive to be like Jesus the more we truly need and want to forgive as God forgives.

"It is, of course, easiest to forgive someone who has hurt or offended you when they appeal for your forgiveness. Who can easily turn away someone who is genuinely contrite? The greater difficulty is when you have been wronged and those responsible seem to enjoy your discomfort, your shame or, in the extreme, your loss or injury.

"Yet what better example do we need than that found in Luke? In the thirty-fourth verse of the twenty-third chapter, we learn that after being betrayed, scorned, and nailed to the cross, our Savior still cried out, 'Father, forgive them...'

"Nor can we simply forgive once and for all and presume we have fulfilled this imperative. Remember how Jesus answered Peter in the eighteenth chapter of Matthew when Peter asked, 'Lord, how oft shall my brother sin against me, and I forgive him? till seven times?'

"As many of you will recall," declared Reverend Small, "Jesus told Peter, 'I say not unto thee, Until seven times: but Until seventy times seven.' With examples like these, we hardly need more," he continued. "And yet if we look at the third chapter of Colossians, the thirteenth verse, we are told by Paul to be 'forbearing one another, and forgiving one another, if any man have a quarrel against any: even as Christ forgave you, so also do ye.'"

Although pleased to see Jonah and both Emma and Jake in the crowd, Reverend Small carefully avoided extended eye contact with them as individuals. Having earnestly prayed for reconciliation between Jake and Jonah, he was therefore keenly disappointed as he watched Jake and Emma leave almost immediately after the service. Jonah, on the other hand, waited with Betsy and Seth until they were joined by the clergyman.

On the long walk back to the farm no one mentioned his sermon. Having had several compliments from other parishioners, he was mystified by the silence of Betsy and Jonah. They were almost within sight of the house when his curiosity peaked, and he could no longer resist appealing for their reactions. It was Betsy who replied first.

"I often wonder what I would do if I met the man who killed my husband. I know he was a soldier just like my husband, and I know my husband must have killed too," she began. "But I often wonder whether he was driven by fear or duty or hatred. Did he himself become just another casualty of the war? Could I find it in my heart to forgive as you say I must?"

Both Jonah and Reverend Small were awed and saddened by the deep and suppressed grief that Betsy revealed. It was a particularly awkward moment for Reverend Small since his purpose had been to promote healing and restore goodwill between Jake and Jonah. Betsy's heartfelt struggle was clearly an unexpected outcome. Resisting platitudes, the clergyman said simply, "Sometimes all we can do is strive to forgive as best we can."

The focus on Betsy's pain was shattered a moment later when Seth announced that he could see people at the house. "It looks like Jake and Emma."

"Seen enough of them already," growled Jonah. Growing more and more irritated by their presence, he added, "Them two are about as welcome as the drought."

And even though Reverend Small realized the unannounced visit was most likely an answer to prayer, he would clearly have wished for a less inconvenient moment.

"Who knows," interrupted Betsy, emerging from her personal contemplation, "maybe they've come to apologize for the way they treated you, Jonah. Maybe they want to make some kind of amends. Maybe they were touched by Reverend Small's sermon too."

Grateful for Betsy's foresight and alacrity, the clergyman picked up quickly where Betsy had left off. "If they are penitent, Jonah, we are all counting on you to show how gracious and forgiving you can be."

Jonah's only response was to drop back, allowing Reverend Small and Betsy to move a few steps ahead of him.

Hoping for the best, Betsy waved and shouted a warm welcome. "Hope you haven't been waiting long. We'd have been home ages ago if I hadn't gone on and on about all the fun we had at the box social last Saturday."

Emma stepped forward to meet them, smiling and trying hard to be sociable, while Jake remained on the porch looking extremely uncomfortable. "We were hoping we could spend a few minutes alone with Jonah before we head home," explained Emma.

"I don't see why not," replied Betsy in a voice both reassuring to Emma and somewhat compelling upon Jonah. "And, if you can spare the time, you and Jake are more than welcome to stay for a bite to eat. It's nothing fancy, but there'll be plenty for everyone."

"We don't mean to impose," said Jake. "If you don't mind, we'll just talk with Jonah a spell and be on our way."

"Feel free to change your minds," answered Betsy, snatching Seth by the arm while starting toward the kitchen door. Looking back, she tilted her head first toward Reverend Small and then slowly toward the door, bidding him inside.

"Hope you'll stay for dinner," said the clergyman before joining Betsy and Seth.

By now Jonah had a pretty good idea of their intentions, and he motioned them toward the barn and the bench he occupied so often. "No sense standin'," he suggested.

"Surprised you didn't run us off," declared Jake, "after all we did to you."

"Good thing ya didn't bring them other two with ya," replied Jonah solemnly.

"We're really and truly sorry for what we did," intervened Emma. "We don't know what got into us. We should have realized a long time ago that Lucas will stop at nothing just to get richer."

"We might fib every now and then," confessed Jake, "but we don't go around lying the way we did to you. That's not right. It took Emma here to make me see how far away we got from the truth. They weren't fibs anymore; they were downright lies."

Jake and Jonah sat at opposite ends of the old bench, and Emma was in the middle, close to Jake. As Jonah listened, he leaned forward, with his elbow on his knee and his chin on his hand. His only response was a nod or two and an occasional glance at Jake or Emma.

"We don't expect you to forgive and forget overnight," said Emma. "But we want you to know that we have told Lucas to get off our land. He's madder than you are, and he's making a bunch of nasty threats. The point is we listened to him twice; we'll never listen to him again."

"And just so you know," added Jake, "we have your bit. It was never lost down the well. Lucas and Brady were hiding it so you couldn't use it. They even talked about using it themselves to drill for oil later on. We'll bring it here or anywhere else whenever you like."

Jonah looked up directly at Jake, broke into a huge smile, sighed audibly, and reached out to shake the farmer's hand. "No need to apologize," declared the dowser. "Yer not the first folks to be charmed by that character. And what ya did is past. Somehow we all gotta try harder to live by the Good Book."

"Guess we all agree on that," replied Jake as he grasped Jonah's hand and shook it as vigorously as if it was a pump handle.

After releasing his grip, Jonah added, "Can't tell ya what it means to get my bit back."

Emma too extended her hand, anxious to reciprocate in some way to Jonah's goodwill. The dowser hesitated for a moment, unaccustomed to shaking the hand of a woman, but did so as gently as possible. Then, turning back toward Jake, he remarked, "Sure hope there's no chance of Lucas gettin' his hands on that bit again."

"It's safe enough," assured Jake. "We moved it into the barn and hid it in the haymow. We're the only ones who know where it is."

"Mind if we come by in the mornin' to fetch it back?" asked Jonah. "There's a chance the well here might dry up. The springpole is already up. Just need to hook up the bit. We'd kinda like to get started as soon as we finish helping Ned."

"We'll bring it over ourselves, either this afternoon or right after chores in the morning," insisted Emma. "It all depends on when we can borrow Emmet's buggy."

Betsy, busy at the kitchen sink preparing Sunday dinner, happened to look out at the barn when Jonah extended his hand to Jake as a sign of renewed friendship. She too smiled and murmured softly to herself, "God surely moves in mysterious ways, His wonders to perform."

Reverend Small, who had earlier disappeared to his room, reemerged in the kitchen after Betsy summoned him to dinner. After summarizing what she had seen, she proposed that he join the trio outside and repeat her invitation to Emma and Jake. This time they agreed, and Emma left the men to help Betsy set the table.

As they sat down, Emma took a seat beside Reverend Small, caught his attention and by expression and by word whispered her thanks. The clergyman acknowledged her gratitude with a smile and then offered a brief but heartfelt grace. Obviously delighted by what had transpired, he continued his remarks, telling Jonah and their guests, "Each of you have my greatest admiration and esteem."

They were still in the midst of the meal when they heard the sounds of an approaching team and the rumble of wagon wheels. Betsy rose and, after peering out through the screen door, announced that it was Lucas and Brady. "They're headed here."

After registering initial disbelief, the three men at the table coalesced with unspoken suspicion: Lucas and Brady were once again up to no good.

Rather than risk a free-for-all, Reverend Small rose to his feet and asked Jonah and Jake to remain in their seats. "Who knows, they may be here to apologize and make amends," he speculated unconvincingly. "Let me be the one to find out."

Satisfied that his caution would prevail, the clergyman moved swiftly, reaching the yard just as Lucas pulled the team to a halt. "Good day, gentlemen," he began. "I missed you at worship this morning. And you missed a good sermon! What brings you here?"

"It depends on who else is here," snapped Lucas. "If Jake and Emma are here, I've got a message for them. We found what they hid."

"That sounds intimidating," replied Reverend Small. "Isn't it about time you men changed your ways? Acknowledge the sin in your lives; accept the forgiveness and salvation that Jesus promises and start living fuller, more meaningful lives."

"Save that for your flock," roared the infamous lender, pulling the reins to turn the team back toward the road. "We don't need your God." And as suddenly as they had appeared, the two men were gone.

Back inside, the clergyman found Emma in tears and Jake and Jonah deeply agitated. "Came pretty near forgettin' myself," said Jonah, "especially after he said they found my drill bit. Woulda been out there in a flash if ya hadn't made me promise to stay inside."

"We're so sorry," cried Emma. "We're really trying to do what's right."

As Betsy tried to console Emma, Reverend Small rested his hand on Jake's shoulder. "Whatever you do, don't lose sight of the fact that you folks took an enormous step forward today. Everything will work out; you'll see."

"Time someone dealt with them two," said Jonah, unwilling to harness his anger.

"No, Jonah," argued the clergyman. "Revenge is something God saves for Himself. As much as we'd like to take matters into our own hands, we're told in Romans twelve not to do so. The fourteenth verse declares 'Bless them which persecute you: bless, and curse not.' And the seventeenth verse tells us to 'Recompense to no man evil for evil.' The strongest admonition is in the nineteenth verse: '... avenge not yourselves, but rather give place unto wrath: for it is written, Vengeance is mine; I will repay, saith the Lord.'"

"Easier said than done," lamented the dowser.

"One thing's sure," laughed Betsy, trying to dispel the lingering anger, "our preacher really knows the Good Book. He not only knows what verses to use, he quotes them by heart. I can't even remember how many books there are in the Bible. Is it sixty-five or sixty-six?"

Betsy's effort was rewarded with laughter and, in the lighter atmosphere, Reverend Small encouraged everyone to resume eating. Although everyone tried, most just nibbled half-heartedly at the food that remained on their plates.

"I guess we're all wondering what we should do now," the clergyman finally observed. "This is certainly a setback."

"Somethin' ain't right," mused Jonah. "If them two found the bit, they woulda had more fun waitin' around and watchin' for Jake and Emma to find out it was gone. Most likely, they tried to get it this mornin' while everybody was in church. When they couldn't find it, they musta waited for Jake and Emma. When they didn't come home right after church, Lucas probably figured they were here. Could be they were tryin' to get Jake to run home to check."

"What do you think they'd have done to Jake if that's true?" asked Betsy.

"Can't say for sure," answered Jonah, "but it ain't very likely they'll do anything if me and Jake go over there together."

"If your suspicions are correct," said Reverend Small, "I'd better go too."

"We'll all go," declared Betsy, "as soon as these dishes are cleaned up!"

CHAPTER 18

Once underway, they found themselves besieged by speculation and strategy. If the bit had not actually been found as Lucas and Brady claimed, wasn't it likely that they would try in some way to learn where it was concealed? And, if that was the case, wasn't it best to preserve the secret by staying away until they had the means to get the bit back to Betsy's farm?

Ultimately, they concluded that, one way or another, Lucas was bound to find the drill bit if it remained in Jake's barn. Given that likelihood, they decided that Jake and Betsy would go into the house, Emma and Reverend Small would wander over to the barn, and Jonah and Seth would head toward the small patch of dense trees and shrubs beyond the barn that would most likely be used by Lucas and Brady as a hiding spot to spy.

After allowing Jonah and Seth ample time to reach and stroll about the woods, everyone would converge at the well that Jonah had brought in. And, if Emma confirmed that the bit was where they had hidden it, Jake and Reverend Small would go for Emmet's wagon. What no one seemed ready or willing to a discuss was the possibility that it had been found and stolen.

Like battle-hardened soldiers, they split apart silently when they reached the farm. Each team commenced its mission just as they had agreed. Those in the house and barn completed their inspections quickly and then waited until they saw Jonah and Seth approach. At the well, before a single word was spoken, the men knew from Emma's smile that the bit was still there.

Emma, the first to speak, confirmed what the others had surmised but, in the next breath, reported that the barn had been searched while she and Jake were away. "They must have been within a whisker of finding it," she revealed angrily. "They pitched half the hay from one side of the mow to the other. If Jake hadn't buried it as deep as he did, they'd have found it."

"They were in the house too," reported Jake. "We could tell they had been in the wood box by the stove because they left it open."

"Somebody's spent time in that patch of woods," added Jonah. "Saw lotsa broken underbrush, kicked up leaves, and dislodged rocks. Seth even found a couple of fresh footprints."

"The sooner that bit's back in your hands the better," declared Jake. "I'm going after the wagon. I sure hope Emmet's not out gallivanting."

With Jake's departure, Emma urged everyone inside to escape the afternoon sun and the unrelenting heat. It was then that Jonah noticed a white, enameled cup sitting beside the newly installed pump at the well. "Gotta taste this water," he announced as he worked the pump and watched the torrent that spilled from its spout. "Never did have a chance to sample it back when the bit broke through."

Eager to witness his reaction, the others all paused as he drank from the cup. "Water this good and this cold makes it all worthwhile," he declared. Jonah refilled it with a short stroke of the pump handle, and at Betsy's urging handed it to her. To the surprise and amusement of the others, she took several gulps and then tipped her head forward and emptied the remaining water over the back of her neck, laughing like a child.

"Try it," she suggested, handing the empty cup to Reverend Small. After duplicating the short stroke with the same ease that Jonah had used, the clergyman raised the cup before his companions and offered a simple prayer, "Thanks be to God." Holding the cup with reverence, he drank slowly, swallowing each mouthful with obvious pleasure until there was nothing left.

"My apologies," said Reverend Small when he realized he had failed to offer Emma the cup before drinking himself. She quickly dismissed his gesture as welcome but unnecessary and, once she and Seth had enjoyed their turns, they all set off for the house, refreshed by their drinks, physically and emotionally. By the time they finished the cake left from Emma's box social baking, they heard the unmistakable whinny of Emmet's mare.

Almost everyone raced for the door despite Emma's suggestion that they linger a little longer in the comfort of the house. "Let Jake get the drill bit down by himself," she said, "since he's so anxious to set things right." By then, however, the kitchen was nearly vacant.

With Jonah in the lead, the group descended on the barn. As he followed Jake up to the haymow, the others waited impatiently by the barn doors, ready to guard the bit during its initial journey to Betsy's farm. There were smiles and a collective sigh of relief when they heard the dowser tell Jake, "Sure is good to see it again. There's plenty of work left for it."

Jake laid it gently in the back of the wagon and then returned to the wagon seat, motioning Betsy to join him there. After giving Emma a big hug, she did so. Reverend Small followed Seth and Jonah aboard, and all three waved their gratitude to Emma who chose to remain at home. Just as they reached the road, however, Jonah called to Jake and suggested that they first go to Ned's, explaining to no one in particular, "Maybe we better let him know what's happened."

As they neared Ned's drilling site, they could see that the rope between the springpole and the ground was taut. But Jonah jumped from the wagon and headed toward the house, intent on warning Ned that leaving that bit unprotected could be a big mistake. After sharing events of the day and expressing his concerns, Jonah promised to reappear Tuesday morning. Ned voiced some hasty thanks, and Jonah jumped back on the wagon to resume the trip to Betsy's farm.

Despite Betsy's plea to store the bit in the house until he was ready to attach it to the springpole, Jonah declined, saying only that it was probably safest with him. He took it into the barn alone. When he did not emerge as quickly as expected, Jake and the others peered inside but remained by the door while Betsy called to Jonah. "Everything all right?"

Emerging with a grin, he replied, "Hope it ain't hid too good."

Relieved, Jake shook Jonah's outstretched hand, jumped

up onto the wagon and with an enthusiastic wave left to return Emmet's horse and wagon.

At supper, Reverend Small reminded Jonah of his earlier agreement to spend some time with volunteers the following morning. "I know you're eager to begin drilling now that you have your drill bit back," the clergyman continued, "so if you want to stay here and drill, I understand. I'm sure I can keep everyone busy till you can join us."

"Can't stay much beyond the mornin'," replied the dowser, "but a promise is a promise."

"Once you get everyone started and tell me how to keep them on track," answered a relieved Reverend Small, "I'll be delighted to chase you away."

The two men arrived at the site early that Monday morning, and both were immediately impressed by all the materials that had been delivered. Jonah was even more pleased by the number of volunteers, armed with toolboxes, who were already on hand. And hard to miss were saws, drawknives, drills with big wooden handles, adz, and a variety of other tools.

While waiting for Art and the building plans, Jonah began examining the restored stone foundation that would bear the new building. The repair, he discovered, had been done well. As he worked his way toward the men gathered around Reverend Small, he was attracted to a stone, larger than all the others, that was located at the right front corner of the foundation.

Closer inspection revealed it was a new cornerstone. There was a flagstone cover, cut to the same length and width, which simply laid on top, not yet mortared. Lifting the cover, he found the cornerstone hollow and empty. Oddly, it bore no date.

By now, there were at least twenty men ready to commence work. Art had arrived and was deep in conversation with Reverend Small. Jonah slid the cover over the cornerstone and joined the shopkeeper and the clergyman. "We're really glad you're here," said Art, "especially after all that happened yesterday. Sounds like Lucas has stooped to a new low."

"Tryin' to put all that behind us," answered Jonah. "Rather get these men workin' than waste time talkin' about Lucas. What are ya plannin' to put in that empty cornerstone?"

"We missed a chance to dedicate it after worship yesterday," Art replied, "but that needn't stop us. What we plan to do now is put a few items inside, have Reverend Small offer a few words and then mortar it shut. When the church is finished, we'll get a stone cutter to engrave it with this year and the year the original church was built."

"There wasn't much in the old cornerstone," Art continued, "just a Bible, a copy of the title to the land, and a list of the families that started the church. Unless someone objects, we'll put them all into the new cornerstone along with a little history about the church between the time it was built and the time of the fire."

Following the arrival of Esther, Art summoned everyone to the cornerstone where he removed the flagstone cover, exposing the cavity inside. He reminded the men that the cause of the fire remained a mystery and that the original cornerstone had been brought to the store by several members of the church. It had been opened without fanfare and, even though there was nothing of monetary value, he and Esther had kept the contents of the cornerstone in their store safe.

Preserving the items in the new cornerstone, interjected

Reverend Small, seemed to be the most appropriate option of all.

Esther then handed the Bible, the title, and the list of original members to the men closest to her, encouraging them to examine, enjoy, and appreciate the history each item represented. Both the title and the list of members circulated through the gathering rather quickly. The Bible, however, got stalled in the hands of ol' Barnes who, despite his age, was determined to work alongside the other men as long as his hands, arms, and bad leg would allow. "I know a thing or two about shaping wood and barn building," he insisted after men who were younger and more fit started teasing him good-naturedly to stand aside and let them do the work.

Neither Art nor Reverend Small could hear the old man because of his soft voice, but as they got closer, they realized he was pointing to something near the front of the open Bible. "If you're going to read something from the Good Book," said Art jokingly, "you're going to have to read a lot louder. We can't hear you back here!"

Barnes stopped pointing, looked toward Art, and then moved toward the storeowner. "Didn't anyone go through this old Bible after they took it from the cornerstone?" he demanded. "It's not just any old Bible."

"Most of the folks who brought it in looked it over pretty carefully," said Art defensively. "I did too, and I didn't see anything terribly special about it."

"Well," began Barnes, "you must have seen that it's a family Bible and that family was named Light. That should have meant something to somebody beside me, especially anyone who took the time to look at the list of members."

"Suppose so," agreed Art diplomatically, "but nothing registers yet."

"Let me see that list again," said Barnes, looking over at Esther. Once in his hands, he ran his finger down through the families. "See here. Ezra and Mary Light and their three daughters, Mabel, Priscilla, and Florence."

"Get on with it," encouraged Art, "those names mean nothing to me or Esther."

"All right," responded Barnes, who had managed to keep everyone in suspense. "The oldest daughter was Florence. She married a man named Henry Mason, and before you knew it, they had a boy."

"Mason, Mason," mused Art. "That name rings a bell. It seems to me there was a Mason who farmed some land out past Ned's place years ago. But he's been gone longer than I care to recollect."

"That's right," confirmed Barnes. "Henry didn't do too well. And one night they just picked up and left." The old farmer then paused, thinking someone might know where that thread led. But no one did so he resumed. "Henry and his family moved from one place to another and, after getting into some kind of trouble, Henry changed their name to Bennett." As his audience began to make the connection, Barnes added, "That boy of their's was none other than Lucas."

While the Blakes were clearly surprised, Reverend Small was clearly stunned. "Are you absolutely sure?" asked the clergyman. "How do you know all this?"

"Could be my wife and I are the only ones around here who know," explained Barnes somewhat hesitantly. "Mary Light would oftentimes tell my mother-in-law about letters she got from Florence. Even though Henry was a bit of a ne'er-do-well, Florence always stood by him, and that was good enough for Mary and Ezra.

"After Lucas grew up," Barnes continued, "he got a good job in Philadelphia. Every now and again, he'd help out his folks and Mary and Ezra with a little money. But Ezra was too proud to take it, and he always made Mary send it back."

When Reverend Small started to raise a question, Barnes interrupted, saying, "I don't mean to be talking about Lucas behind his back; it all just started coming out when I saw the name of his kin in the front of this Bible."

Jonah, although interested in his adversary, was even more interested in getting back to the farm to begin drilling. "Best we be gettin' on with buildin' the church," he suggested.

Nodding in agreement, ol' Barnes closed the Bible and passed it on to Esther along with the faded list of church members. She, in turn, handed them to Art who promptly put them in the new cornerstone along with a new Bible.

"Wait," cried out Reverend Small, raising his hand to reinforce his plea. "In view of all that we learned this morning, I think we have an obligation to offer the old Bible back to the one descendent that still remains here."

"You mean Lucas?" asked one of the volunteers incredulously.

"That is exactly who I mean," responded the clergyman without hesitation. "We now know that he is a descendent of a truly devout family and, if not for him, then let us do it for the Lights.

Whether Lucas accepts or rejects this sacred heirloom is entirely up to him. To that end, of course, we can all pray that he will."

"That mean we hafta stop buildin' while we wait for an answer?" demanded Jonah with undisguised annoyance.

"Not at all," insisted Reverend Small. "When the time comes to mortar the cornerstone closed, we will do so. If need be, we can always find an appropriate place inside the new church to display this Bible as a sacred link with our past."

"That's an excellent idea," declared Esther.

Confident that all was well, Reverend Small began to read aloud the history Esther had written, praising those who had brought the church through the past in good times and bad. He then asked everyone to bow their heads as he prayed. "Oh Lord, let us never forget the role each of us must play to keep your Word alive, not only for our own generation but, as these folks did, for generations to come."

After completing the prayer with a barely audible "Amen," he turned to the Blakes and the rest of the group and proclaimed, "Fire may have destroyed the building, but the flame of the Holy Spirit continues to burn in the hearts of each of you. With all your gifts and your labor we will soon gather inside a new building, a new temple, dedicated to the same Almighty God of our parents and our parents' parents." Then, with a broad sweep of his hand toward Jonah, he added simply, "Let's get started!"

Jonah was immediately surrounded and, based on Art's plans and the men's skills, he began to divide the men into groups, one for each of the four sides of the building. Each group was instructed to pick its own leader, and those who were chosen joined Jonah to inspect and study the plans.

With Reverend Small at his side, Jonah answered the questions raised until one by one they wandered off. Within minutes some of the huge timbers that would be used to frame the church began to disappear from the stacks that had been delivered. Tools of all shapes and sizes emerged all over the site, and the sounds of construction quickly broke the morning calm.

With the work now underway, Reverend Small took possession of the plans, and Jonah hastened back to the farm.

Seth, who had stayed behind with his mother, spotted Jonah approaching and set off to meet him. As he and Jonah reached the house, Betsy ventured outside to inquire, "How was the turnout?"

"Lotsa men out there this mornin'," reported Jonah. "Just hope they all keep comin' like that 'til the walls are up and the roof is on."

"If they were there today, they'll be there as long as you need them," assured Betsy.

Jonah cut the conversation short, explaining that he was going to the barn for the drill bit. Emerging with the bit cradled in his arms, he rolled it slowly looking for nicks or gouges that might affect its performance. Throughout the inspection he continued toward the springpole that he had hoped would vindicate both his skills and the divining rod he had called Drake. Still ambivalent, Jonah could only trust that drilling would bring in one or the other: oil or water.

Betsy and Seth joined the dowser but remained silent. Their presence forced Jonah to refocus. "Did ya ever see what they found in the cornerstone of the old church?" he asked Betsy, realizing that she would be intrigued more than most folks by Stephen Barnes discovery.

"No," replied Betsy. "Esther said there wasn't much. All I can remember was an old Bible and a list of early members."

"Ever hear of folks named Light or Mason?" continued Jonah.

"I don't believe so," Betsy answered warily. "Why?"

By then they had reached the springpole, and Jonah set the drill bit on the ground next to the ropes dangling from its slender tip.

"Seems they're kinfolk of Lucas," he continued slowly—deliberately trying to string out each revelation to accelerate Betsy's curiosity.

"If you're trying to intrigue me, you have!" declared Betsy. "What else have you learned about this contemptible creature?"

"Well," explained an amused Jonah, "the Bible they found in the old cornerstone was from the Lights, a real God–fearin' family who had a daughter by the name of Florence who married a fella by the name of Mason."

After a brief pause that failed to generate any kind of response, Jonah continued. "Seems they pulled up stakes and moved about from one place to another—even took on another name, according to ol' Barnes. They only had one child, and it was Lucas."

Betsy shook her head in disbelief and then finally muttered, "Guess he never learned anything from his grandpa or grandma."

Jonah went on to tell how Reverend Small decided not to put the Bible in the new cornerstone but planned to put it in a prominent place in the new church unless Lucas took a personal interest in it.

"Not likely," said Betsy. "Unless there's a dollar to be made."

"Can't be chitchatin' all day," declared Jonah, reaching for the rope that would bear the bit. "There's drillin' to be done."

For a moment Betsy said nothing, uncertain whether to mention her discovery after Jonah and Reverend Small had left for the church that morning. "My well's getting down," she finally blurted out. "When I drew water for the wash this morning, it came up dirty."

"Let's hope we hit water," was all Jonah could manage to say.

Working quickly but carefully, he slipped the rope through the eye of the bit, found the optimum point at which to secure it and then tied it with a series of knots he had learned from a sea captain back in New England. Once his foot was in the stirrup, he began a series of slow but accelerating jumps to let the bit begin its course through soil and stone.

With each plunge of the drill bit, Jonah felt increasingly confident that it was an ideal site. Nevertheless, what awaited below remained a genuine mystery—was it the oil he had craved or the water Betsy desperately needed? Eventually, the rhythm of his movements offered an escape for his mind.

Betsy soon retreated toward the house, promising to return with his favorite bread and jam as well as drinking water from the spring she used to refrigerate milk and butter

Once his mother departed, Seth eased himself to the ground, close enough to hear and be heard whenever Jonah was in a mood to talk. Nearly an hour passed, however, before the first words were spoken. "Sure could do with some of that water your ma promised," said Jonah after stopping to rest. "How about gettin' me a drink, Mister Fisherman?" Eager to end the boredom, Seth rose immediately and raced toward the house.

Progress had been far more rapid than Jonah had anticipated and, rather than resume the repetitive, robotic demands of drilling, he decided to continue resting until Seth returned with the water. Even then, he concluded, he would put off further drilling until the rope between the tip of the springpole and the drill bit could be extended.

The break also gave Jonah time to dream about the moment when the bit might break into a subterranean reservoir. One issue overwhelmed all his other thoughts: *What do I really want most: oil or water?* And as Jonah began to question his motives, hopes, and dreams, he began to realize that few things were as clear-cut as they once were.

In the midst of his soul-searching, he suddenly found relief in the sight of Betsy and Seth approaching with the meal and the water she had promised. The three found a shady place to sit, and although she had brought nothing for herself, Betsy had brought extra bread and jam for Seth. In the course of their small talk, Jonah reported that he had drilled deeper than he expected in the few hours he had been at work, but he also cautioned against undue optimism.

Surprisingly, Betsy withheld all her questions about Lucas and the Lights and the Masons, having decided to wait until supper so she could indulge in her curiosity with both Jonah and Reverend Small.

She remained, however, to watch as Jonah and Seth inserted a new length of rope between the springpole and the drill bit. After joining the new and old ends with simple but effective knots,

Jonah instructed Seth to release the bit which had been raised to the surface.

The sheer weight of the drill bit drew the lengthened rope into the ground so quickly it quivered like a bowstring. Betsy showed her approval with childlike applause and then ambled back to the house.

Jonah resumed his labor, jumping with new vigor and determination. He could almost feel the bit boring its way through the earth below as gravity multiplied its freefall. The rhythm he had developed earlier returned as naturally and as effectively as ever.

At supper, Reverend Small repeated the story that Barnes had shared with everyone that morning, satisfying Betsy's questions as best he could but, in the end, adding nothing new to Jonah's earlier account.

Turning to Jonah's interest, the clergyman reported major progress on framing the church. "It's been great fun to watch," he said enthusiastically. "The men really know what they're doing, and the leaders they chose seem to be keeping everyone busy and happy."

"There was very little for me to do today," he confided, "except to stand around holding the plans and confirming what the men already seemed to know."

By the time the meal ended, Jonah and Reverend Small had agreed the dowser would return to the site the next morning. On the one hand, Jonah was anxious to see for himself what the men had accomplished on their first day and, on the other, the clergyman was looking for Jonah's assurance that the work was satisfactory. They also agreed that inasmuch as no one had heard from Ned that day, Jonah would return home by way of Ned's farm.

Fatigue dictated the balance of the evening. Shortly after dinner both men retired and, less than an hour later, so did Betsy and Seth. At breakfast the next morning, Betsy announced she would accompany the men so that she too could inspect the construction.

Even before they reached the church, they could hear the sounds of men at work. And from the moment they set eyes on the site, they were both delighted and amazed by the teamwork and all that it had achieved. It was immediately apparent to Jonah that at the current rate of progress, the skeleton framework for the walls and roof would be rising within days.

The dowser moved about the site with undisguised glee, stopping to visit not only with the leaders of the four crews but with individual volunteers. And, while he praised the work, he also encouraged the men to avoid undue haste and carelessness. "Can't stand crooked walls," he joked, "'specially on a church."

After circumnavigating the site, Jonah realized he had spent far more time there than he had planned. Rather than depart without further conversation with Reverend Small, he walked over to the clergyman and commended his leadership as well. "Looks like ya managed to keep everyone happy," he remarked with a smile. "Didn't hear a single complaint that ya interfered!"

For Reverend Small it was more than a compliment; it was evidence of acceptance, not just by Jonah but by all the men, including some who had not yet found their way to worship. With Ned's farm his next objective, the dowser took to the road, hoping to make up some of the extra minutes he had not planned to spend at the church. Betsy and Seth, meanwhile, had slipped away to visit the Blakes.

With Jonah now gone, Reverend Small began reviewing the roughly drawn plans, hoping to identify potential issues that might delay or even halt the work. Nothing in particular caught his attention and, as he looked up momentarily, he was unprepared for the man bearing down on him. It was Lucas and, judged by his grim expression, he was extremely unhappy.

"What's all this business about a Bible?" he demanded.

"It was in the cornerstone of the old church," replied Reverend Small, trying hard to be neither defensive nor intimidated. "It's a family Bible that bears the name of Light. Some folks seem to think it may have belonged to forebears of yours on your mother's side."

"Impossible," said Lucas dismissively. "That's a rumor you better put down fast."

"It will be much better if you refute it yourself," replied the clergyman. "In fact, you can do so after our worship service on Sunday, if you wish."

"You started this nonsense," argued Lucas. "You stop it."

"Even if it's not kinfolk of yours," said Reverend Small in slow measured terms, "maybe you can take a minute to look at the Bible and help us figure out who the family might be. You know far more people around here than most of us."

Lucas did not immediately reject the idea. And, in the absence of refusal, Reverend Small assumed that some interest had been aroused. "It's right here in this small satchel with my own Bible," added the clergyman as he hurried to preserve the lender's interest.

After locating the Bible and handing it to Lucas, Reverend Small noted that if there were no longer any interested local heirs to the Bible, he planned to display it in a prominent place inside the new church. "Locking it away in the new cornerstone just doesn't seem right," he continued.

For a moment, Lucas seemed reluctant to take the Bible. When he finally did, he tried to diminish any possible importance to his doing so. "There's not much chance of my knowing anybody tied to this book, dead or alive," he insisted. Nevertheless, he thumbed through it from front to back, skimming the pages with seeming indifference.

Reaching the New Testament, he suddenly stopped, worked back to Proverbs and began to hunt page by page for something in the margins that had caught his eye. What he sought and found was an exclamation point that had been entered long ago beside the seventh verse of the third chapter.

Though long forgotten, he knew that verse by heart, "Be not wise in thine own eyes: fear the Lord, and depart from evil." With those words came a rush of memories, those of childhood when his grandfather would read aloud his favorite Bible verses after dinner.

Amid those memories were the words of the two preceding verses, "Trust in the Lord with all thine heart; and lean not unto thine own understanding. In all thy ways, acknowledge him, and he shall direct thy paths."

When uttered by his grandfather years ago, the words had been a joy to hear; now they stung sharply, forcing Lucas to look away.

Even though he had no idea what the lender had searched for and found, Reverend Small could tell by the man's behavior that the Scripture was hardly foreign.

Lucas quickly resumed thumbing through the Bible, concentrating on the first few pages until he found the names of its owners, Ezra and Mary Light, handwritten with great care on a page dedicated for that purpose. Seeing those names brought a smile that came and went. If others knew his grandparents, they surely knew his father. As much as he wanted to disown the Bible, the more impossible it became.

Faced with curiosity he could no longer deny, Lucas finally acquiesced. "I doubt that I can help, but I guess there's no harm in looking it over more carefully. One way or another, I'll get it back to you by Sunday."

"I appreciate your willingness to try," emphasized the clergyman.

Lucas started to walk away with the Bible in hand when he suddenly turned around and asked, "By the way, who seemed to think it belonged to my family?"

"I believe it was Stephen Barnes," answered Reverend Small almost involuntarily.

"Just curious," said Lucas. "I can't imagine why he spouted off that way. Any idea what made him think it was kin of mine?"

"Barnes is a good man," replied the clergyman. "I'm sure there's an explanation, but I'm afraid I can't give you much help. Why not pay him a visit?"

"Maybe," agreed Lucas, resuming his departure.

On his way to Ned's farm, Jonah wrestled with the question of efficiency. Was it wise for the two men to work their springpoles independently? Wouldn't it make more sense to join forces so they could spell each other and, by the end of the day, achieve more? Neither farm would be ignored for more than a day if they worked one day at Ned's, the next at Betsy's, and then back to Ned's. It had to be less tiring for both men and ultimately more productive at both sites.

As he approached Ned and his springpole, Jonah couldn't help but grin when he found the farmer taking a break from the demanding routine of kicking down his well. After uttering nothing more than a "good mornin'," the dowser went straight to the rope, ran his foot into the dangling stirrup, and began to work.

"I was just about to start drilling again," claimed Ned with a laugh that betrayed his little white lie. "It's the first break I've taken all morning."

"Been thinkin'," said Jonah, driving the stirrup down with such force that the drill bit hit with a distinctly audible thud despite its distance well below ground. "If we double up, we should drill both wells a whole lot faster."

Ned recognized Jonah's reasoning immediately but, just to be sure, he pressed for more details. "What have you got in mind?" he asked.

"Pretty simple," said the dowser. "Yer place today, Miss Betsy's place tomorrow. Then back to yer place and so on."

"It sounds good to me," agreed Ned. "In fact, it's darn near brilliant."

"Can't deny that," cracked Jonah with his characteristic wit.

While continuing to kick down the well, Jonah allowed Ned to do most of the talking, first in relation to the approximate depth of the drill bit and then with respect to Jonah's plan. "By my calculation, I'm down somewhere between six and seven feet," said Ned. "Since you just started on Miss Betsy's well, maybe we should give that priority today."

When there was no immediate response from Jonah, Ned reiterated his suggestion. "Let's quit drilling here and head to your place," he said in a slightly louder voice.

"Nah," answered the dowser between jumps. "Today's half gone. Rather get a full day outta ya tomorrow. Ya can start right in as soon as ya get there. No need to wait till I get back from the church. Seems fair enough, don't ya think?"

Ned could see the big grin on Jonah's face and, deeply grateful for the dowser's selfless acts, he consented with an equally big smile. He then ordered Jonah to take a break.

The only time the springpole was idle that day was when the men paused for lunch or when the rope had to be lengthened as the bit bored deeper and deeper. Jonah and Ned kept up the accelerated pace throughout the afternoon, stopping long after the time Ned would have normally begun his late day chores.

"No harm done if ya bring in Miss Betsy's well before my turn comes around," kidded the dowser as he headed home.

"I'd hate to deprive you of that honor," laughed Ned, "but I probably will anyway."

That night at dinner, Jonah explained his absence at his own springpole that day and expressed hope that he and Ned would prove more productive by rotating between the two drilling sites. "Seems like we got a whole lot deeper than Ned would have alone," he reckoned, "but we'll hafta see what happens here tomorrow."

For Betsy, Seth, and Reverend Small, it was a promising strategy that neither required nor got further attention. No one probed beyond the few salient details Jonah offered.

Reverend Small, on the other hand, not only commandeered everyone's sustained attention but drew a flurry of questions as well as when he began telling them about his encounter with Lucas.

"It came about so quickly," he reported. "One minute I was looking at the plans, and the next I was looking at a man who was belligerent at first and then seemingly temperate."

"With all that Barnes knows," asked Betsy, "do you think Lucas would even try to deny that the Lights are his kinfolk?"

"Can't see where it makes much difference one way or the other," interjected Jonah.

"It will be interesting to see if he takes my suggestion and goes to see Barnes," said Reverend Small. "I've even been thinking about going over to see Stephen after dinner just to let him know he might be getting a visitor."

"If Lucas was going to do that," said Betsy, "he's already done it."

"How can you be so sure?" asked the clergyman, intrigued by her certainty.

"Well," began Betsy a little less emphatically, "he came by here, and Barnes's place is only a skip and a jump from here." Although both men registered surprise, neither prodded her to elaborate as she had hoped.

"It couldn't have been more than an hour or so after I got home," she reported. "I figured you were probably back from the church by then, and so I told Seth to fetch you some water. The next thing I know Seth's back in the kitchen telling me that Lucas is pussyfooting around the springpole, trying to jiggle the rope."

"I hope you didn't challenge him," said Reverend Small.

"Of course I did!" declared Betsy. "I asked him what he was doing, and he said he had come to see Jonah. I wasn't so sure about that so I asked him why he was playing with the rope on the springpole. Instead of answering, he just took off in a huff."

"Sounds like he was tryin' to steal my drill bit again," speculated Jonah.

"That's what I think too," said Betsy. "And since he didn't have Brady with him, he probably couldn't get it up by himself."

"I think it's time to go see Barnes," announced the clergyman.

Despite suggestions by Jonah and Betsy that he wait until morning, the clergyman set off for the neighboring farm, confident that the moon and stars offered all the light he needed.

He walked briskly, enjoying the evening's cooler temperatures as well as the opportunity to satisfy his own curiosity. As he neared the house, he was pleasantly surprised to see Stephen and Bessie sitting outside enjoying a few moments of leisure.

"Evening, Reverend," welcomed the old farmer. "We've half expected you tonight or tomorrow. And, just like you suspect, Lucas has been here."

The clergyman smiled, not so much because his suspicion was confirmed so quickly but because of the wit and wisdom of Barnes. "Why is it you're always a step or two ahead of me?" he joked. "Do you do that with everyone or just people like me that grew up in a big city?"

"It wasn't all that hard," answered Barnes. "After all, it was you who told Lucas to come to see me, wasn't it?"

"Well, now that you've told me what I wanted to know, I guess I can turn around and go back," joked Reverend Small. After noticing that Mrs. Barnes had pulled up another chair, he added hastily, "On the other hand, it'd be nice to sit and chat a spell."

"He didn't stay long," said Barnes. "I pretty much told him what I'd already told others. He seemed genuinely surprised. Before he went, he wanted to know how much we remembered about old Ezra and Mary. About all we could say was that we knew they were real fine folks, and that it was Bessie's mother who knew them best."

"How about letting the preacher get a word in edgewise," interrupted Bessie.

"He's doing just fine," responded Reverend Small. "Unless he really goes astray, I'll just sit and listen … and listen … and listen!"

They all laughed together, but as soon as the laughter subsided, Barnes resumed his monologue. "As far as his folks were concerned, I told him we knew his ma Florence and her sisters pretty well and liked them all, especially his ma. His pa was another matter. He wasn't from here so we didn't know him as well. I also told him that lots of folks fell on hard times the same time his pa did, and we were sorry he didn't stay like the others did."

"What time did he come by?" asked Reverend Small.

"Probably an hour or so before our midday meal," said Bessie. "I was going to invite him to stay but he seemed bent on leaving."

After deciding not to mention Betsy's encounter with Lucas, Reverend Small sighed, "I wish I knew how to reach him. If he would only change his ways, he could become an invaluable member of the community and the church."

"One thing's clear," said Barnes. "He sure hated being poor."

"I suppose that could be a clue," replied the clergyman as he rose to go. "I hate to leave, but those stars are my clue it's time to get home and get some sleep. Next time, I'll try to stay a little longer so we can talk about something besides Lucas."

At that point, Barnes too rose from his chair. He put his hand on Reverend Small's shoulder and offered some parting words of praise. "I hear you're doing a great job at church. There's aren't many preachers who could or would do all that you're doing."

"From what we hear," added Bessie, "you've managed to get the respect of all the men and all the women too. We're all mighty glad you've come."

Flattered and flustered by the degree of their approval, Reverend Small was momentarily tongue-tied, managing little more than an expression of thanks and a promise to try to live up to their expectations. Leaving on that high note, he made his way to the road and before long saw the outlines of the house and barn on Miss Betsy's farm.

CHAPTER 19

"Looks like Ned plans to get an early start," announced Betsy as she looked out the window by the kitchen sink. Both Jonah and Reverend Small gulped down whatever coffee they had left and headed for the door, forgetting to slide their chairs back into place at the table. When Seth started to follow in their wake, Betsy stepped into his path.

"Everyone's forgetting their manners," she stormed in mock indignation. "Before you take another step, young man, do what you were taught."

"Sorry, ma'am," said Jonah and Reverend Small in unison. "Do ours too, will you Seth?" appealed the clergyman, looking back at the chairs they had abandoned haphazardly.

"I woke up with a good feeling about the day," said Ned. "So I got my chores out of the way early to get a head start drilling." Then, with a giant grin, he added, "No matter what you think, it has nothing to do with bringing in the well before you get back from church."

"Not much danger of that," laughed Jonah, "'cause the reverend here can handle the church by himself today."

The remark caught all three men by surprise, including Jonah, who had uttered it more in jest than seriousness. But the more he thought about it, the more he realized that there was no compelling need to accompany Reverend Small.

The clergyman immediately agreed. "Once I tell the men that the need for the new well is getting more and more urgent, they'll understand. Besides that, I can take Seth with me, and if you're needed, he can come back for you."

"Good idea," agreed Jonah. "Just make sure this lad puts in a good day's work."

Seth beamed. Watching the construction was bound to be more interesting and exciting than sitting idle while others kicked down the well. And with luck, he might even get to help cut, drill, or chisel a timber or two.

Jonah and Ned set off for the springpole, forgetting that their plan for Seth needed Betsy's approval. Seth and Reverend Small forgot as well, and they were almost to the road when they heard Betsy cry out from the house, "Where's everybody going?"

Rather than shout a reply, the clergyman started back toward the house while Betsy made her way toward him. The plan for Seth to accompany Reverend Small to the building site won her immediate blessing, and the two set off without further discussion.

One of the first things Jonah did after arriving at the springpole was to tug at the rope to ensure that the bit had neither disappeared nor become stuck from Lucas's apparent attempt to make off with it. Fortunately, both concerns proved groundless.

"Guess I go first," proclaimed Ned, reaching for the rope.

"Go to it," agreed Jonah as he began to inspect other parts of the springpole, especially the yoke on which it rested. He was about to declare everything sound when the rope with the stirrup suddenly snapped, allowing the springpole to fly up unrestrained.

Ned, who had just started to relieve the springpole of his own weight, plunged to the ground, unable to maintain his balance. His right knee struck first, then his right hand and shoulder. His right foot, which was still deep inside the rope's stirrup, landed partly inside the hole created by the drill bit, putting him at further risk.

"Don't move," ordered Jonah, realizing that Ned had to be extricated from the rope.

"I'm all right," protested the farmer as he started to push himself up from the ground. "As far as I can tell, there's no broken bones."

"Gotta get yer foot outta that rope first," insisted Jonah, quickly kneeling beside Ned and interrupting his efforts to stand. "Just 'cause ya didn't break anything don't mean ya gotta spoil yer good luck. That hole's just waitin' to twist that leg of yer's."

Free of the rope, Ned pushed himself away from the hole, acknowledging the danger. Once on his feet, he uttered a simple but earnest "Thanks."

Jonah immediately started an intense examination of the rope, beginning with the piece attached to the stirrup and then the section dangling from the springpole. Ned neither said nor did anything but chose to wait for Jonah's assessment. It wasn't long in coming.

"Can't see where it was cut anywhere," he declared. "Looks like it just broke."

Although confident in Jonah's judgment, Ned looked carefully at the end hanging from the tip of the springpole and soon came to the same conclusion.

After the two ends were tied to Jonah's satisfaction, he began to examine the rope bearing the drill bit in search of any weakness that had previously gone undetected. Finding none, he stepped into the stirrup and began the cycle of jumping up and plummeting down in order to drive the drill bit. And Ned, who had lowered himself to the ground to rest, began to notice a dull ache in his right knee.

—

Reverend Small and Seth reached the church shortly after the first men began to arrive. Within an hour, construction was in full swing, and the foremen reported that some framing would most likely be erected that afternoon.

Returning to his simple but indispensable plans, Reverend Small tried to envision the completed church, realizing that most of the congregation would be returning to a replica of the one in which they had worshiped in the past. While continuity was important, he mused, the new building demanded something unique.

Reverend Small soon found himself engrossed with that challenge. Should it be outside or inside? A religious symbol or icon? A painting, a sculpture, a window of stained glass?

As he pondered these and other options, an old leather-bound Bible was suddenly thrust between him and the plans.

"Do with it as you like," declared Lucas, whose arrival had

been largely ignored by the workers and completely unnoticed by the clergyman. "It's of no value to me."

Reverend Small's initial reaction was to accept the Bible and express disappointment but something deep inside compelled him to resist. "I'm surprised, inasmuch as it belonged to your grandparents," he declared.

"Just take it," demanded Lucas.

As the minister did so, he resumed his almost involuntary persistence. "I don't know why you've chosen to disown this link with your past, Lucas, but there is a coincidence here that I find almost prophetic."

When Lucas made no effort to leave, Reverend Small added, "It's one thing to dismiss the fact that this Bible was found inside the cornerstone of the old church, but it's quite another to disregard the fact that it was put there by Ezra and Mary.

"Your rejection brings to mind the very words of Christ Jesus in the Gospel of Matthew, 'Did ye never read in the scriptures, The stone which the builders rejected, the same is become the head of the corner... .' Jesus can and should be the very cornerstone of the lives of all of us, including yours, Lucas. This discovery is the Lord's doing! Don't reject His outreach to you in such a personal way!"

Surprisingly, Lucas remained. "Please take this Bible back," pleaded Reverend Small. "If you wish to find the parable I've just quoted, look up the twenty–first chapter of Matthew, verses thirty–three through forty–four. Better yet, read the entire Book of Matthew and then go on to the other Gospels of Mark, Luke, and John."

"Well, if you're in no hurry to get it back, maybe I'll keep it for another day or two," Lucas replied, reaching for the now familiar tie to his past. But instead of leaving, he began to fidget slightly, shifting the Bible from one hand to the other without uttering a word. As his uneasiness became more and more apparent, Reverend Small chose the initiative, asking simply, "Do you remember anything about the Gospels?"

"No," answered Lucas matter-of-factly. "What I do remember was my grandfather Light reading from the Bible many times after dinner. After we moved away, my mother tried to read a verse or two every evening until my father made her stop. Even when she tried to read alone, he'd argue that 'the Bible isn't worth the paper it's printed on.'"

"That's a shame," said Reverend Small, speaking softly to avoid being overheard. "Any idea why he treated the Bible the way he did?"

"I was pretty young at the time," recalled Lucas. "But I remember how mad he would get when he did something that my mother would say was 'contrary' to the Bible. Most of the time though he was good."

"Sometimes the Bible does make people uncomfortable," acknowledged the clergyman. "But it's usually because of the lives they have chosen. It's something we call original sin, and it goes all the way back to Adam and Eve. They were the first to disobey God, and mankind has been disobeying God ever since."

"Can I show you something?" asked Lucas, lifting the Bible so he could thumb through it at chest height. "It's something I found last night."

"Of course," replied Reverend Small, eager to maintain the conversation.

But just as Lucas was about to reveal his discovery, one of the foremen called to the minister, summoning him to a nearby stack of lumber.

Lucas immediately drew back, slammed the Bible shut, and was soon out of sight.

Although crestfallen that the conversation had ended so abruptly, Reverend Small was encouraged by the very fact that it had occurred. Hopeful there would be more, he joined the foreman and was told the stack was leftover from the framing.

"It's an awful lot of waste," lamented the foreman with an undisguised frown.

"Are you certain these were intended for framing the walls?" asked Reverend Small. Referencing his plans and drawings, he provided his own answer seconds later. "These planks were never meant for the walls; they're rafters for the roof."

"Thanks for clearing that up," said the foreman with a mischievous grin. "And, just so you know, we'll be needing nails before long. No one's been able to find any."

"If you can tell me what size nails you'll need, I'll see that they're here when you need them," responded the clergyman with an all-knowing smile that he had just been tested.

Then, realizing he had proved himself able, he began to laugh. So too did the foreman, who then spelled out the size of spikes he and the others needed. Armed with specifics, Reverend Small quickly dispatched one of the men to Blakes to secure the nails.

With the second 'crisis' solved, he began to meander about the construction site and was delighted to see that one of the foremen had put Seth to work, cutting a small plank with a man-sized saw. As the blade cut cleanly through the wood and the waste fell away, the lad examined the finished board carefully and, with an air of satisfaction, dragged it over to the foreman. He too judged it satisfactory and soon found another task for the quiet but agreeable lad.

Back at the farm, Jonah and Ned had reached an optimum rotation that kept the drill bit hammering away at a pace that pleased them both. By the time they stopped for the midday meal, they had extended the rope twice, a measurable sign of progress.

Pleased by the headway that their teamwork produced, they tended to compete and cajole one another toward faster and longer stints in the stirrup. The arrival of lunch caught them both by surprise.

Betsy stayed with them only long enough to learn about their progress and their confidence that water was close at hand. After words of encouragement and the promise to return later with more water, she was gone, unaware that Jonah and Ned had challenged one another to greet her with water by bringing in the well before her next visit.

Reverend Small, meanwhile, had detached himself from the din of construction and had resumed his mental quest for something unique to distinguish the new church from the old. Hearing a cry from one of the foremen, he looked up just in time to see the framing for the front wall of the church being raised slowly and carefully into position.

Once upright and declared straight and true by the men with levels, a roar of pride and delight drowned out the hammers that began to lock the framing into place. One by one the remaining frames were erected, each dovetailing perfectly with its adjoining counterpart.

As the last of the nails were driven into the shell, the clergyman called for a moment of silence and prayer.

"O Lord," he declared, "hear our thanks for the hands and hearts, skills and talents, diligence and determination that have come together to achieve this milestone. May your hand rest upon each of these men, guiding them not only in the completion of a new, visible temple dedicated to Thee but to the growth and development of each of us as the temples You would have us become. Amen."

"Amen," repeated several of the men as they all reached for their tools to resume work.

At both the church and the springpole, the men labored under a scorching sun, resolute in their goals. For Reverend Small and the men at the church, there were multiple challenges but very little that was subject to uncertainty. For Jonah and Ned, there were far fewer challenges but a far greater degree of chance. What they shared in common, however, were the imperatives of cooperation, determination, persistence, and optimism.

With the setting sun, both groups could point proudly to major achievements. For the builders, it was the timbers that stood ready for the rafters and the roof; for Jonah and Ned, it was a drill bit that rested deeper inside the earth than either could have predicted.

Throughout the township that night, it was the achievements not the tasks ahead that dominated dinner hour discussion.

Much of the interest at Betsy's kitchen table was devoted to Reverend Small's account of how flawlessly the framework had been erected at the church. And although he reported on the prank that the men had tried to play on him as well as his good fortune in recognizing it, he made no mention of his encounter with Lucas.

Delighted by Reverend Small's progress report, Jonah decided that he could safely postpone his visit to the site for another day. But he was soon overwhelmed by curiosity, and by the time dinner was over, he realized he could not resume work on Ned's well without first visiting the construction site.

"Need yer help, young fella," said Jonah, resting his hand on Seth's shoulder. "Gonna be a trifle late gettin' to Ned's place tomorrow, and somebody's gotta let him know. Looks like yer the best man for the job. Afterwards, ya can head to church and work there."

Seth quickly agreed, excited by the prospect of learning carpentry from some of the best.

Everyone, including Betsy, again rose earlier than usual the next morning. By the time she had fixed breakfast, Jonah had spent a good half hour drilling at the salt spring and Reverend Small had used his extra time meditating and preparing for his Sunday sermon.

Even their morning meal was undertaken with dispatch. Jonah and Reverend Small were the first to rise from the table and, minutes later, were on their way toward town. Seth was next, leaving behind an unfinished glass of milk and half-a-slice of bread. Although Betsy had been tempted to join the men to inspect the milestone in construction, she chose instead to stay at home to do her own day-to-day chores.

The brisk pace that the two men maintained during the early stages of their walk began to diminish as they were joined by men converging from the small crossroads that joined the main road.

By the time they reached the church, the group had grown considerably.

What had been in his mind's eye was now a reality in full view. The wooden skeleton that rose up before Jonah was as striking as a work of art. And try as he might, he found nothing that he could question or challenge.

"Not bad for amateurs," Jonah kidded the foremen and other nearby volunteers. "Guess it's time to bring in the expert."

"Who'd that be?" demanded one of the men. "We've already got the preacher here, and if he's not the final word, we could be in real trouble."

"You'll just hafta wait and see," teased Jonah, enjoying the camaraderie as he departed.

Having spent so little time at the site, he was pleasantly surprised to encounter Seth on the outskirts of town. Ned was already at work when he arrived, the lad reported, and seemed undismayed by Jonah's decision. After their brief exchange, each resumed his journey.

Ned stopped working the springpole as soon as Jonah was close enough to carry on a conversation. Jonah's first person account of the teamwork and the progress drew praise and admiration, but as Jonah shifted to the subject of leadership, Ned was suddenly silent.

"Ya gotta get in there yerself," insisted Jonah. "The preacher and the foremen are doin' fine, but yer the boss they really want."

"Then let's quit jawin'," laughed Ned, handing the rope to Jonah.

The two men labored throughout the day and into the early evening, silently hopeful that each plunge of the drill bit would be the one that would strike fresh water. But as dusk turned to darkness, they surrendered to the reality that there would be no success that day.

"See you at your place in the morning," promised Ned as Jonah headed for the road.

The following day was Saturday, and Ned arrived early, shortly before Reverend Small and Seth were about to leave for the church.

"Jonah tells me you'll be joining us at church once you men bring in wells," the clergyman began as he shook hands with Ned. "We look forward to that. Now that the framing is up, we need both you men to avoid mistakes that could delay us."

"And we need your prayers to find the water soon," replied Ned earnestly.

"There's not a day that goes by that I don't begin and end the day without such prayer," Reverend Small assured him. "It's truly a matter of faith. Jesus tells us in Matthew twenty-one, verse twenty-two that... 'whatsoever ye shall ask in prayer, believing, ye shall receive.'"

"And if memory serves me correctly," Ned responded, "Mark tells us about a father who asked Jesus to heal his son. When Jesus told the man that 'all things are possible to him that believeth,' the man replied, 'Lord, I believe; help thou mine unbelief.'"

"That's a prayer that even I utter silently when everything seems hopeless," confessed the clergyman, concealing his surprise and admiration of Ned's command of the Scripture. "As impossible as it seems to achieve, perfect faith must always be our goal."

"Tell the men we'll have a look at the church after worship

tomorrow," interjected Jonah, hoping to cut the conversation short. "Meanwhile, we got some drillin' to do."

Reverend Small caught the not-so-subtle hint immediately and turned toward the road. Seth, who had been busy with last minute chores, appeared simultaneously, and the two began the trek to the church. There was a perfunctory exchange of greetings when they arrived and, after discovering there were no burning issues, Reverend Small dug into his back pocket for the sermon he had begun. Seth wandered off, searching for the men most likely to put him to work.

Unhappy with what he had written earlier, Reverend Small started to search the recesses of his mind for a more appealing topic. When that failed, he seized the drawings for the church and focused on details he had previously ignored. The distraction was fruitful; he soon found himself discovering ways to enhance the building inside and out.

In the midst of his musings, the clergyman was reminded of the suddenness with which his last meeting with Lucas had ended. With his memory refocused, he began to wonder what it was that Lucas had intended to show him.

Certain that there appeared to be some genuine interest in things spiritual, Reverend Small couldn't help but smile. No one was beyond redemption, he reminded himself. Not even Lucas.

Rather than join the men during their midday break as he often did, Reverend Small approached two of the foremen who had not yet started lunch. "Any need for me to stay?" he asked. "I could sure use the rest of the afternoon to finish my sermon for tomorrow."

"If you promise to keep it under an hour, we'll let you go," replied the older of the men, trying hard to appear serious.

"Well, if you want me to leave out the best parts," the minister joked in reply, "I'll do it. Just remember that when your wives want to know why I cut my sermon short, I'll have to tell them that you two made me do it."

"Better let him go without any conditions," counseled the other foreman with a laugh.

"If you don't, and I catch either of you falling asleep tomorrow, I'll call it to the attention of the entire congregation," grinned Reverend Small, enjoying the give-and-take.

"Be off!" declared the older foreman, again unable to hide his amusement.

Minutes later, Reverend Small was on the road home, accompanied by Seth, who continued to gain the respect of his elders as he accomplished more and more complex tasks. Both were silent. The clergyman was increasingly troubled by the fact that he still did not have a verse, chapter, or book on which to pin his sermon while the lad was swelling with pride as he reminisced about the skills he was beginning to master.

As they came within sight of the house, they spied a familiar wagon and its driver. It was Lucas. Hoping that he might renew the conversation that Lucas had abandoned, Reverend Small encouraged his young charge to run ahead. Seth raced off happily. By the time Lucas had closed the gap, Reverend Small was alone.

"Got time to climb aboard and talk?" he was asked.

"Absolutely," the clergyman replied, stepping up onto the wagon and lowering himself onto the seat with Lucas. By then, the former banker had tied the reins around a short upright in the front of the wagon. He then reached down beneath the seat. When his hand reemerged, it was holding the Light family Bible.

"There's something I want you to see," he began, thumbing through the pages several times in search of a particular page. And, when he finally found it, he handed the opened Bible to Reverend Small with a simple exclamation, "Look at that!"

The clergyman scanned the two visible pages quickly, looking for the object of Lucas's interest and wonder. Yet nothing caught his attention.

Unable to contain his impatience, Lucas pointed to a verse where, for the first time, Reverend Small noticed a small pencil mark beside the number. Only then did the clergyman isolate it. It was the sixth verse in Isaiah fifty-three, one of the verses he had used in his very first sermon. His voice trailed off as he began to read, "All we like sheep have gone astray ..."

"There's certainly no doubt about that," added Reverend Small.

"I've been through this Bible several times since you gave it to me," explained Lucas, somewhat excitedly, taking the Scriptures back into his own hands. "And do you know what? There are only two verses in this entire Bible that are marked like this."

Once again he started thumbing through page after page, quickly at first and then more slowly as he found the book he was searching for in the New Testament. He then shoved the Bible back toward Reverend Small, declaring, "Here's the other one."

Although the mark was only slightly more visible, the minister immediately recognized that verse too. It was the tenth verse in the fifteenth chapter of Luke, the preface to the Prodigal Son.

He read it aloud with fervor. "Likewise, I say unto you, there is joy in the presence of the angels of God over one sinner that repenteth."

"You know I'm not very religious," said Lucas with a hint of remorse. "What I can't get over is the way this Bible ended up in my hands after all these years. It's almost as if Grandpa Light put my name on it and had it delivered straight to me."

"If it wasn't your grandpa; it was certainly the Lord," suggested Reverend Small. "But more than likely, it was God working through your grandpa. They both want you to take these verses to heart."

"Is it too late to set things right?" asked Lucas.

"Not at all," the pastor replied. "It's never too late."

"What should I do?" continued Lucas.

"All you need to do is respond favorably to God," replied Reverend Small, "and He'll help you find your way. Together, we can delve into the subjects of repentance and salvation, but first, I'd like you to reread these passages, beginning with the verse that your grandpa marked in Isaiah. It's important that you understand that the person who bore our iniquities was Christ Jesus. Then read the verse your grandpa marked in Luke, and the parable of the Prodigal Son that follows. When you finish, I hope you'll stop and think long and hard about the last verse."

"Aren't you going to preach to me now?" asked Lucas in bewilderment.

"Not today, but definitely tomorrow," smiled the pastor. "I'll look for you at the service."

"So you can condemn me in front of all the others?" protested Lucas.

"On the contrary," replied Reverend Small. "It's so we can all look at ourselves."

With that the clergyman stood up and jumped back down to the ground, exuberant and anxious to return to the task of writing the sermon that had been so elusive.

"I'll be there," promised Lucas as he unwound the reins and flipped them lightly, just enough to set his horse in motion. "If I can't trust you, who can I trust?"

By the time Betsy was ready to call her household to dinner, she discovered that Jonah had not yet returned. With Seth busy examining his late father's toolbox and Reverend Small still in his room writing, she decided to wander outside to enjoy the occasional light breeze she had noticed earlier.

Leaning back against the trunk of her favorite shade tree, Betsy watched as her son cleaned and oiled several of the tools he had removed from the toolbox. Betsy smiled broadly in pride, confident that her late husband would be proud as well. Their son was fast becoming a thoughtful and resourceful youth.

Her preoccupation with Seth was broken by the sight of a figure in the distance. And even though it was dusk, she could tell it was Jonah, moving with familiar dispatch yet visibly weary. She welcomed him with both a big smile and a light-hearted admonition after sensing another unsuccessful day of drilling. "You're late."

During dinner, when Betsy turned to Reverend Small for an account of his activities, all she learned was his growing fascination with the building and some of the ways he hoped to make it more functional and more attractive. For the second time, he chose not to reveal his encounter with Lucas.

When the table talk turned to Seth, the lad provided a genuinely modest summary of his work at the church and his growing interest in tools. Although he had seen Lucas, the event conveniently slipped his mind.

Knowing intuitively that it was his turn, Jonah looked up from his nearly empty plate. "It was downright strange," he began. "We finally broke through into some kind of cavity. The drill bit dropped like a rock until the rope stopped it, but when we sank a wood pole, it came up dry."

"Sure it got all the way down?" asked Reverend Small.

"Pretty much," answered the dowser. "But there's no tellin' for sure even though we tried a few times. It was pretty late in the day. Guess it'll hafta wait till Monday."

Unwilling to let Jonah end on that note, his three tablemates peppered him with more questions, hoping to latch on to more encouraging details. Even Seth joined the interrogation with an astute query. "Why didn't you just drop an unbraided rope?"

Jonah laughed. "Coulda, and maybe shoulda."

"Looks like you and Ned need Seth more than the men at church," exclaimed Reverend Small with a hearty laugh of his own. "Makes me think water would be gushing out of that hole tonight if Seth had been there."

"No doubt about it!" added Betsy, reaching over to pat Seth's arm and shoulder.

When the laughter subsided, Reverend Small quickly excused himself from the table and left to complete his sermon, a task he now embraced enthusiastically.

Sunday morning began like every other day of the week with a wake-up call from the farm's unsympathetic rooster. Convinced that it was crowing earlier than usual, Jonah pictured it on a kitchen platter, featherless and golden brown.

For the first time in a long time, the dowser was unable to ignore sore muscles and a sore back. Both the monotony of kicking down a well and the longer and longer days doing so were taking their toll. Jonah was tired. Thank the Lord, he thought, for setting aside Sunday as a day of rest.

Yet despite his fatigue, he looked forward to his now weekly rendezvous with the men and women of the community and, he had to admit, the powerful and persuasive sermons that Reverend Small delivered. Nevertheless, the lure of a few more minutes of sleep was powerful enough to postpone getting up, and he lingered in a semi–conscious state until he heard the approach of a clanging milk pail.

Jonah scampered to his feet, pulled on his trousers and reached the barn door just as Seth entered. The dowser yawned a "mornin'" to the lad and then hurried to the pump to shave and wash up. Although often cloudy, the well seemed to make modest recoveries overnight. By breakfast, he felt refreshed but still conscious of a nagging ache in both legs. The walk to the school grounds helped some and, after taking a seat, he began to feel better.

Had he looked about before choosing a place to sit, Jonah would have noticed Ned and his wife as they took their place near the table that Reverend Small used each Sunday. Instead his eyes were drawn to a figure emerging from the road. It was Lucas, and he was alone.

Betsy and Seth meanwhile had ambled over to the Blakes,

who were already engrossed in conversation with ol' Barnes and Bessie.

Jonah, feeling a little lonely at the sight of these and other gatherings, was about to get up to find a friend or two when he realized he was being joined by Emmet, Jake, and Emma. As he started to get to his feet, the others restrained him, insisting that they were about to sit too. Less than a minute or two later, Reverend Small appeared at the schoolhouse door, shouted a hearty "good morning, everybody" and took his place behind the table.

With the help of Esther and Ruth, he led the growing crowd through two hymns before leading the assembly in prayer. In a voice well suited for his ministry, he began his sermon.

"Apart from the children, is there anyone here who does not know the story of the Prodigal Son? And, among all of you who do know the story, is there anyone here who has not felt sorry for the son who served his father faithfully but was never treated to a 'fatted calf'?

"Small wonder that the faithful son took his father to task. But before we totally embrace these images, let's all go back to the Scripture and read the story once again, remembering that it is one of the many parables of Jesus. It's in the fifteenth chapter of Luke, and it begins with the eleventh verse. 'And he (Jesus) said, A certain man had two sons.'

"How's that for a simple beginning to a profound spiritual lesson? 'And the younger of them said to his father, Father, give me the portion of goods that falleth to me. And he divided unto them his living.'

"'And not many days after the younger son gathered all

together, and took his journey into a far country, and there wasted his substance with riotous living.'"

Pausing to let these first few verses develop in the minds of his flock, Reverend Small became aware of an unusual silence that now enveloped the field. No one was stirring, not even the children. The breezes that sometimes swept gently through the hollow were missing, and even the birds which often sang in the background were strangely quiet. Man and nature, it seemed, were captivated by the words and the significance of their message.

"What happens if we envision ourselves as the father?" the minister resumed. "Can we ignore the notion that he loved both his sons very much? That deep within he hoped, perhaps even trusted, that both young men would use their inheritances wisely?

"But even more to the point, what happens when we envision the father as God, our heavenly father, and each of us as His sons and daughters? Haven't we often rebelled against the hopes and wishes of our own earthly parents, let alone the desires of our heavenly Father? And like the younger son, have we not also squandered many of the gifts and blessings that our heavenly Father has given so freely to us?"

Unconsciously, he lowered his voice. Though audible, it conveyed an inescapable hint of personal reflection. "Yet few, if any, of us are truly ready to see ourselves as this young man. Instead, most of us tend to see ourselves as the older brother, loyal and obedient, reliable and hardworking, fully devoted to the wishes and expectations of his father.

"Fortunately, the parable doesn't end there. It's time we got back to it. 'And when he had spent all, there arose a mighty famine in that land; and he began to be in want. And he went and joined himself to a citizen of that country; and he sent him into his fields to feed swine. And he would fain have filled his belly with the husks that the swine did eat: and no man gave unto him.'

"'And when he came to himself, he said, How many hired servants of my father's have bread enough and to spare, and I perish with hunger! I will arise and go to my father, and will say unto him, Father, I have sinned against heaven, and before thee, And am no more worthy to be called thy son: make me as one of thy hired servants.'"

Reverend Small stopped, smiled, and proclaimed unequivocally, "Out of hardship came wisdom, and out of wisdom came repentance."

A muffled but unmistakable "Amen" from Emmet was quickly followed by a murmured wave of agreement from the crowd. "Read on!" urged Emmet in a genuinely pious and eager fashion.

"'And he arose and came to his father,'" continued the clergyman. "'But when he was yet a great way off, his father saw him, and had compassion, and ran, and fell on his neck, and kissed him. And the son said unto him, Father, I have sinned against heaven, and in thy sight, and am no more worthy to be called thy son.'

"'But the father said to his servants, Bring forth the best robe, and put it on him; and put a ring on his hand, and shoes on his feet: And bring hither the fatted calf, and kill it, and let us eat, and be merry: For this my son was dead, and is alive again; he was lost, and is found. And they began to be merry.'"

Once again he paused, hoping that images of the somber,

repentant son and the loving, jubilant father would emerge vividly in the hearts and minds of his listeners.

"Make no mistake, my friends," he continued. "Jesus himself is assuring us that God is ready and anxious to embrace the repentant just as the father in this parable has done. What's more, He will do so with the same love and joy. What we must ask ourselves is how desperate must we become before we recognize our own sinful natures and truly repent."

"Amen," said Emmet softly, barely audible to even those closest to him.

"Those of us who have repented and found our way into God's loving care often emulate the older son," added Reverend Small. "Instead of rejoicing with the father, we too can become angry and aloof, unforgiving and resentful. Listen then to the words of the last two verses of the parable, 'And he said unto him, Son, thou art ever with me, and all that I have is thine. It was meet that we should make merry, and be glad: for this thy brother was dead, and is alive again; and was lost, and is found.'

"Good people," he declared, "whether you have repented in the past or do so now, whether you have come to experience God's unfathomable love or yearn to do so now, there is never a day that goes by in our lives that is unmarred by sinful thoughts, words, or deeds. May we never lose sight of our personal need for God's everlasting forgiveness, and may we always rejoice when those who were lost are found."

"Amen," he concluded—in unison with Emmet.

Almost immediately after the closing hymn, led by Ruth and Esther, and the traditional benediction, Reverend Small found himself surrounded by a number of individuals and families.

Several revealed a new appreciation for the parable in the light of his sermon. Others extended invitations to Sunday dinner. And even though he normally encouraged such opportunities, he graciously declined. Fatigue, he confessed, had finally caught up to him.

By the time he was able to break away, he discovered that Betsy and Seth had already started walking home. Jonah, however, remained. For several minutes, they simply walked side–by–side on the now deserted road. Neither spoke until Jonah called attention to the song of an unseen, but musically gifted, feathered friend. But even that led nowhere, and they were almost back to the farm when Jonah finally alluded to Reverend Small's sermon. "Been thinkin' a lot about yer preachin' this mornin'," he confided. "Suppose there's any hope for me?"

"Don't ever doubt that," exclaimed the clergyman. "God loves every one of us, saint and sinner alike. The real crux of the matter is how we respond to that love."

"Ya know I try to do good," replied the dowser, using the personal pronoun he normally avoided in all his conversations and comments.

"If the key to heaven was based entirely on good deeds," smiled Reverend Small, "I'm pretty sure yours would be gilded. But good work alone fails because it ignores God's desire that each of us develop a personal relationship with Him though His son Christ Jesus. Until we are ready and willing to accept Jesus as our Savior and Lord, we are actually rejecting God's love and grace. It's as simple as that."

Jonah's expression turned thoughtful, and he resumed his steps toward the barn. "Seems like it's all up to me," he concluded.

"That it is," replied Reverend Small, keeping pace alongside Jonah. "You can approach God alone in prayer or, if you wish, we can pray together. Whatever your wish, you can be sure that I will continue to include you in my daily prayers."

"Still kinda hard to compare myself with the prodigal son," said the dowser. "And it's even harder to think about forgivin' someone the likes of Lucas or his sidekick Brady."

"Don't try to deal with too much at once," counseled the minister. "The most important thing is simply recognizing that all of us, including you and me, are sinners in the sight of God. Once we do that we can accept the salvation that God offers through His son, Jesus."

By now the two men had reached the barn. "See ya at dinner," said Jonah, effectively bringing the conversation to a close.

When Betsy finally summoned everyone to dinner, Jonah was the last to appear and, when subjected to a few teasing probes by Betsy, sheepishly confessed to an uncharacteristic nap.

As laughter from Jonah's revelation subsided, the clergyman bowed his head and the others instinctively followed.

At Betsy's insistence, the responsibility of offering grace rotated around the table although there were times when they grasped each other's hands and voiced a common prayer. Sunday dinner, however, required a blessing by Reverend Small.

"Heavenly Father," he began. "Hear our thanksgiving for all your blessings and mercies, seen and unseen, recognized and unrecognized. Hear our thanksgiving for this food and drink, for clothing and shelter, for all the privileges we have enjoyed and all those we now enjoy.

"Hear our thanksgiving for the countless prayers you've

answered, and most of all hear our thanks for the greatest gift of all, the gift of salvation and its promise of life everlasting with Thee and the Holy Spirit and our Lord and Savior, Christ Jesus. For we give thanks in Jesus' name, Amen."

As soon as Reverend Small ended his prayer, Betsy rose from the table, certain she had heard something outside. After looking up and down the porch, the steps, and the path leading in from the road, she returned to the table, wondering if she was hearing things.

Although Reverend Small had hoped his sermon might launch some further discussion, it did not. The conversation was launched instead by Seth who asked whether it was Jonah's turn to help Ned or Ned's turn to help Jonah.

"Well, by rights, it's Ned's turn to come here tomorrow," answered the dowser. "But until we know what to make of that well of his, the burden's on me to get over there in the mornin'."

With that mystery still unresolved, the conversation quickly evolved into a spate of ideas and theories. Wasn't there at least a fifty-fifty chance that they had struck water? Didn't it make sense to send down a frayed rope instead of a board as experience and Seth suggested?

As Jonah was about to tackle this growing stream of questions, Betsy shot up from the table again, certain that what she had heard was much closer. By the time she reached the door, she was face-to-face with a nearly breathless Ned, who somehow managed to shout, "We did it! We hit water!"

CHAPTER 20

During the euphoria that followed, Ned explained that after returning home from worship, he assembled some pipe and a pump he had bought in anticipation of a new well. With his wife's help, he maneuvered the apparatus into the hole beneath the springpole. Once in place, he pumped furiously until his weary arms gave out. Resigned to failure, he was about to remove the pump and disassemble the pipe when his wife, Elizabeth, realized the pump was never primed.

At first Ned was reluctant to use the little water they still had. But as he and Elizabeth reviewed the risk, his waning optimism inexplicitly returned. Once the pump was primed, they watched transfixed as fresh water flowed in torrents with each stroke of the pump handle.

In the midst of sharing greater detail, Ned suddenly stopped and addressed Reverend Small. "I know it's Sunday, and I shouldn't have been out there working on the Sabbath, but when I saw all that water gushing out of the spout, I figured the good Lord wasn't all that mad."

"It's not a matter of the Lord being angry," responded the clergyman. "It's more a matter of His being disappointed. You could have waited until tomorrow to do what you did today. Still and all, the good Lord knows your heart. I'm sure He is just as delighted as we are that you struck water. Asking His forgiveness should put it right."

Jonah, noticeably silent while Ned recounted his triumph over the unyielding well, finally broke into a big grin and said simply, "Guess that means you'll be here first thing in the mornin'."

Amid the laughter that followed, the dowser was quick to add his admiration. "Yer idea was mighty smart," he added. "Even though it woulda meant extra work if ya came up dry."

"It sure was," exclaimed Betsy excitedly, inviting Ned to join them at the table.

Ned was quick to decline, however, explaining that he had eaten while installing the pump. "It wasn't our usual Sunday dinner," he roared. "But when I finally got to wash it down with water from the new well it was the best doggone feast I've ever had."

Promising to return by sunrise, Ned was off, anxious to return home.

With Ned's good news fueling further conversation, Betsy's midday dinner stretched into the late afternoon. When she finally rose to take her plate to the sink, she found herself drawn toward the kitchen door once more, certain she had again heard someone outside.

Reminded of her earlier experience, Betsy was unable to ignore the soft but persistent sound of footsteps. Looking out across the yard, she saw nothing. But when she moved outside to the porch, she was suddenly tempted to close her eyes. There beside the barn, trying to get comfortable on Jonah's bench, was Lucas.

Lucas, realizing he had been seen, responded by waving and then walking toward the house.

"How much excitement can we stand in one day?" muttered Betsy.

The words were hardly out of her mouth before she found Jonah, Reverend Small, and Seth at her side and Lucas just a few feet away in the yard.

"I don't mean to disturb you," he began, focusing on the plate Betsy was still holding. "But if it's all right I'd like to wait by the barn till we can talk for a few minutes."

"About what?" demanded Betsy impatiently.

"Well, I'd really like to talk with Reverend Small privately," replied Lucas, "and then with the rest of you after that."

"Give me a minute, and I'll join you by the bench," agreed the clergyman.

"Good enough," said Lucas, turning toward the barn without waiting for a response from the others. "I'll wait there."

After watching him depart, Betsy backed herself and the others into the kitchen, easing the screen door closed. "What nerve!" she fumed, turning toward Reverend Small. "He knows he's not welcome on this property even if he wants to speak to you."

"Don't be too harsh," countered the minister. "Maybe he's ready to change his ways."

"About the time hell freezes over," challenged Betsy, instantly regretting her choice of analogy. "I just hope they broke the mold after they created that ogre."

Betsy's fiery retort tickled Jonah so much that he started to snicker. And seconds later he broke out into an old-fashioned belly laugh. That proved contagious. Faced with laughter from both Jonah and Reverend Small, Betsy soon mellowed and began laughing too.

"I know I shouldn't feel that way," she protested defensively between her giggles. "But if there's such a thing as an old reprobate, he's it!"

Concerned that the laughter might undermine Lucas's visit, Reverend Small decided not to return to the table to finish his plate. "Guess I better get out there now," he said, "or, before you know it, you'll have me convinced too."

In his haste to get to Lucas, Reverend Small forgot Betsy's commandment about the screen door and, when it slammed shut behind him, he groaned involuntarily.

"It's good to see you, Lucas," he began. "What brings you out here?"

"It's taken me a while," answered the lender. "But I think I've finally figured out how those marks got into the family Bible."

"How so?" he was asked.

"Grandpa probably put them there unintentionally while pointing to the passages with a pencil, either to my mother or father," Lucas proposed. "In hindsight, I'm certain he thought my father was the closest thing to a prodigal he had ever seen."

"Interesting conjecture," replied Reverend Small thoughtfully. "But where does that leave you with respect to your own values and behavior?"

"Call it coincidence or whatever you wish," said Lucas, "but the discovery of that Bible with those marks meant nothing to anybody but me. I'm not much for signs, but I'd like to think that grandpa was trying to steer me onto the straight and narrow."

"Whether it's your grandpa or God or both, I'd like to hope and pray that it's working," said the minister respectfully. "How can I help?"

"You have helped a lot already," Lucas answered, "but there are a couple more things you can do: first, you can pray that there's still time for me to do some good for a change, and then you can pray that I won't backslide."

"You're already in my daily prayers," Reverend Small assured him. "But what about you? Have you begun to pray on your own?"

"I try," said Lucas hesitantly. "But I usually wind up just saying the Lord's prayer."

"That's a fine way to start," said the clergyman. "What's important is that you not only confess your sins and ask God's forgiveness, but that you acknowledge His son Jesus Christ as your Savior and Redeemer.

"For many people, that's the hardest part. They find it easy to believe in God. The idea that He sent only His son to bear our sins on the cross is a stumbling block for a lot of people. Is it for you?"

"Well, when I think about it," admitted Lucas, "I wind up asking why?"

"Lucas, that's the heart of the Gospel message," answered the minister. "It's because God truly loves each and every one of us."

"Why do we sin?" Lucas persisted in earnest.

"Because we are free to choose between right and wrong, good and evil," Reverend Small continued. "God knows what's in our hearts and minds. It's not just what we say and do. We may be thinking one thing but saying or doing something quite different.

Down deep, each of us knows, or at least senses, our defiant and rebellious ways.

"Originally, God gave us laws and commandments. When our sinful nature helped us find ways to duck and dodge and fudge our way around these laws, God provided another way to assure eternity with Him.

"And this is where faith comes into the picture. Scripture tells us that the wages of sin is death. It also tells us that Jesus bore our sins on the cross, that he died and rose again. Once we accept His son, God promises us that the Holy Spirit will begin to live within us and help us to resist sin. When we do sin, God promises forgiveness when we ask forgiveness in Jesus name. Whether we accept or reject God's grace is again a matter of choice. It's as simple or as difficult or as impossible as we choose to make it."

"I understand," said Lucas, "and I believe."

"Thanks be to God," praised Reverend Small. "Let me call Jonah and Betsy and Seth so that you can share the good news with them. I know it won't be easy, but the sooner we do it the better. Just remember: if they say or do things that hurt, it will be your turn to forgive."

"I'll do my best," promised Lucas.

The words were barely out of his mouth when Reverend Small started toward the house, tugging Lucas by the arm. Betsy, who had spent much of that time at the kitchen window, saw them approaching. With Jonah in tow, she and everyone else seemed to converge at the porch steps almost simultaneously.

Jonah could feel hostility welling up inside him yet he said nothing. When his eyes met those of Lucas, the two men focused on one another, virtually ignoring everyone else. It was a tense moment, one that demanded relief. And it was Lucas who seized it.

"I'm here to tell you I've changed," he began slowly. "I know I've hurt a lot of folks in the township and a good many elsewhere. And even though I can't undue all that I've done, I can try to make amends with your help and the help of my new friend, Reverend Small."

Sensing what could become too long a pause, the minister quickly acknowledged his new regard for Lucas and confidence in his change of heart. "No one can change completely overnight," Reverend Small declared, "but it's clear to me that Lucas is genuinely trying. What is so amazing is the way that this has all come about!"

"Seeing is believing," retorted Betsy, unable to restrain herself.

"We can get to that in a minute," answered Lucas without any hint of hurt or pain. "But I would like all of you to know that I'm trying to find my way with the help of Reverend Small and the family Bible that they found inside the cornerstone of the old church."

"The church that some folks think you burned down," challenged Betsy.

"Believe it or not, as God is my witness, I had nothing to do with that fire," insisted Lucas. "After the rumors began, accusing me of setting the fire in revenge, I tried to get to the bottom of it myself. All I can tell you is that I didn't do it."

Even though Betsy could feel her anger subsiding, she continued her verbal assault. "And what about all the people you cheated and all the lies you told about Jonah?"

"One way or another I will try to return ill-gotten gain and, when that's not possible, I'll try to use it in some positive way. As for Jonah, I'm here to apologize. I'm also here to tell you that I plan to rip up all the oil contracts and support Jonah in any way I can in his search for water."

"What happened to Brady?" asked Betsy somewhat meekly.

"We split up several days ago," Lucas explained. "Once he decided he could do without me, he set off on his own."

"Sure looks like yer turnin' a new leaf," interjected Jonah. "No need to apologize but with all the folks that still need water yer help will come in handy. Once we hit water here for Miss Betsy, there's loads of folks still waitin' for help."

With the tension now gone, Reverend Small took advantage of the chance to lighten things up further. "Let's not forget there's plenty to do at the church too."

Lucas smiled, nodded agreeably and then resumed his own agenda. "There is something else," he began. "While I was waiting for you folks to finish up your Sunday dinner, I went out to see your springpole. Something happened while I was fidgeting with it. I jumped up and down with my foot in the stirrup, and the next thing I knew the bit just sank until it used up all the free rope. I tried to pull the bit out to see if it was wet, but I couldn't."

Even before Lucas finished, Betsy unobtrusively pointed Seth toward the well. The lad set off immediately, although somewhat bewildered because he had no idea what to look for or what to do.

Once he reached the well, however, he decided to try working the springpole just as he had seen Jonah do. Almost instinctively, he raised one foot into the stirrup and grasped the rope well above his head. Jumping as high as he could, he let the weight of his small frame pull the tip of the springpole down rapidly. His fingers picked up vibrations of the plummeting drill bit. But there was no thud, no sudden impact of the bit striking solid earth. Instead there was an instant change in direction as the springpole began lifting him upwards, completing the cycle it was meant to perform. Exhilarated, he tried jumping even higher, hoping that he might in some way bring in the well himself.

Back at the house, Reverend Small considered reprimanding Lucas for putting the drill bit at risk but decided against it. Jonah extended his hand in friendship to Lucas, a gesture that Lucas promptly and enthusiastically accepted. Betsy, whose antipathy toward Lucas was overcome by his change in attitude and behavior, engaged in her typically irrepressible curiosity and sought more details about his experience at the well.

Her curiosity proved contagious and, at the suggestion of Jonah and Reverend Small, the four headed toward the drill site. Engrossed by all that had happened that day, they began to change their conversation from the past to future.

Suddenly Betsy spied Seth racing toward them, hollering at the top of his lungs but too far away to be heard. Trying hard to catch his cries, she cupped her ear with her hand, diverting everyone's attention to her approaching son. And at that instant, they all knew that another well had come in.

"Sure hope it's water," murmured Jonah, just loud enough for the others to hear.

"Amen," exclaimed Reverend Small.